Elam's chest grew so tigh[...] spent plenty of solitary nights, hiding from his bro[...] darkness. And it hadn't changed a thing. Annabel was still gone. Worse still, the memories of the time they'd spent to-gether were beginning to fuzz around the edges.

He couldn't seem to remember what she liked for breakfast or her favorite television shows—and was that threadbare cotton nightie she wore in the heat of summer pink or white? The trivial minutiae of their lives together were seeping through his hands like sand, and he found it harder and harder to pull the images back.

Suddenly, the grief he'd held at bay for so long flooded his body, filling him with an exhaustion that made breathing too much of an effort. Closing his eyes, he tried to remember what it felt like to have a woman's lips upon his own, the caress of velvety fingers. But for some reason, the image that came to mind wasn't of Annabel, but another woman.

Elam tried to push the thought away—tried to remember his wedding night and making love to his wife under the stars. But much like the song he'd just heard, he couldn't seem to find Annabel's spirit anymore. At least not enough to comfort him during the long, solitary hours.

And heaven help him, it felt like a betrayal to think of anyone else.

Desperado

LISA BINGHAM

BERKLEY SENSATION, NEW YORK

BERKLEY
SENSATION

Published by the Berkley Publishing Group
Published by the Penguin Group
An imprint of Penguin Random House
375 Hudson Street, New York, New York 10014

DESPERADO

A Berkley Sensation Book / published by arrangement with the author

ISBN: 978-0-425-27837-6

PUBLISHING HISTORY
Berkley Sensation mass-market edition / June 2015

PRINTED IN THE UNITED STATES OF AMERICA

10 9 8 7 6 5 4 3 2 1

Cover art by Danny O'Leary.
Cover design by Lesley Worrell.
Interior text design by Kelly Lipovich.

Penguin
Random
House

*Dedicated to all the gang at Browne and Miller,
and to Leis Pederson, my editor,
for embracing the Taggart men and their stories.*

ANNABEL

Soft and sweet like a lullaby,
She came to me 'neath a summer sky,
Filled my life with immeasurable grace,
With a gentle smile and a hint of lace.

Annabel, oh, Annabel. What I'd give for one more smile,
Or to sit and talk to you for a while.
Annabel, Annabel, where did you go?
Won't you come back home for the winter snow?

She taught me how to live and love,
Like an angel sent here from above,
For a time this girl was mine to hold,
'Til she went in search of a future bold.

Annabel, oh, Annabel. What I'd give for one more day,
With you by my side for a day of play.
Annabel, Annabel the joy you bring.
Won't you come back home for the flowers of spring?

I know she's in a happier place,
With constant sunlight on her face,
Someday she'll visit us, this I know,
Once she's spread her wings and learned to grow.

Annabel, oh, Annabel. Think of me where'er you are,
Whether close to home or miles afar.
Annabel, Annabel, you're etched on my heart,
You'll be there with me through this brand-new start.

ONE

———•◦•———

P.D. Raines had learned early in life that she couldn't give up, couldn't give in—even though it sometimes felt as if the world was out to get her. Take her name, for instance. The moment P.D. announced she was Prairie Dawn Raines, it was a foregone conclusion that strangers would assume she was a stripper or a fanatical, tree-hugging activist. Even worse, with such a fanciful name, they assumed she didn't have a brain in her head—and she wasn't being overly sensitive. Time and time again, she'd been told she would never amount to anything.

But P.D. refused to believe that she was predestined for failure because she'd been raised by a pair of drug-addicted, free-loving parents who drove from place to place, searching for Nirvana in a home-on-wheels fashioned from a refurbished school bus. Defying the odds—and the lack of a public school education—she'd sworn to herself that she would go to college, get a degree, and have a career. One that would pay for a house with a foundation dug solidly into the earth, honest-to-goodness electricity, and indoor plumbing.

Her determination hadn't always been so iron-clad. Even her parents had scoffed at her plans, telling P.D. that her dreams were the "milksop of a blind Western capitalist society" and, even worse, a denial of the freedom her parents had taught her to value. Nevertheless, as the years had piled one on top of the other, P.D. had grown increasingly dissatisfied with her parents' itinerant lifestyle. She wanted to live like the other families. Those with warm golden windows that flashed past her as they traveled down back road highways to the next "perfect spot." She wanted to know what it was like to sit at a table and eat casserole from a steamy dish or cuddle on overstuffed couches in front of a glowing television set. More than anything, she wanted to belong somewhere. To be . . .

Normal.

In the end, P.D. had refused to let her parents dent her enthusiasm—especially when it became more and more apparent that Summer and River Raines thought she was an inconvenience, a burden that detracted from their own need for oblivion, and worse yet, a voice of conscience when they really didn't want one. She'd ignored their lack of physical and emotional support as well as their callous regard of her dreams, and she'd begun to plot out her own future.

Unbeknownst to her parents, P.D. had taken what little home-schooling her mother had provided to keep Social Services at bay, and she'd read anything she could get her hands on: art, literature, philosophy, science. As soon as she'd turned eighteen, she'd struck out on her own, finding a community center that would help her to complete her GED, take the ACT, and win a plum, full-ride scholarship. Within another four years, she'd earned double degrees at Nebraska State University. And the minute she'd had that diploma in hand, she'd vowed to put the pain of her adolescence in her rearview mirror and forge a future for herself as a world-class physicist.

But life had a way of biting a person in the butt by giving them what they wanted most. After a failed relationship with a coworker, and a stint in a research lab that had been nothing short of torture, P.D. decided to follow her passion rather than a paycheck. She'd returned to the one spot on earth where she'd felt most at home during her childhood wanderings.

Bliss, Utah.

The name itself was inspiring.

But even with the courage born of such experiences, as P.D. pulled to a stop in front of Elam Taggart's half-built cabin and the dust settled around her rattle-trap truck, she knew she couldn't go through with this. She could not ask a man like Elam Taggart for help.

Not now.

Not ever.

"I'll talk to him first," Bodey Taggart said, gathering his crutches and opening the door. "Don't come out unless I give you the signal."

"Bodey, I—"

But just as she'd been about to beg Bodey to drop the whole thing, a figure rounded the corner of a half-finished upper deck at the rear of the house. In that instant, P.D.'s protests died before they could ever be formed.

Oh. My. God.

A man stood illuminated in the late-afternoon light. As if the moment had been staged for a special-effects shot for the Hallmark Channel, rays of gold slipped across the contours of his bare chest, the faint patch of dark hair at his breastbone, and down, down, to the low-slung jeans and dusty boots.

"That's your brother?" P.D. whispered. Although she was a regular at the Taggart home, she'd never had the chance to meet the illusive Elam Taggart. He seemed to spend most of his time at his cabin.

"Yeah, that's him."

Elam Taggart stood still for several long moments, one hand raised as he tried to discern who had interrupted his solitude. At the sight of wide shoulders, well-developed arms, and a set of abs that looked like they'd been carved with a chisel, warmth flooded P.D.'s body, settling low in her belly and causing her breath to hitch in reaction.

God bless America, she thought, echoing the code phrase that her best friend, Helen, used whenever a fine specimen of manhood crossed her path.

Bodey struggled to slide from the truck with his crutches, orthopedic boot, and cowboy hat intact, but P.D. hardly noticed.

Elam Taggart bent and grasped the edge of the deck with his hands, then swung down to the ground, the muscles of his arms, shoulders, and back rippling. He landed softly—making the "dismount" look as effortless as jumping from the curb.

He walked toward the pump a few feet away, his jeans slipping even farther to reveal the weight he'd lost and a set of killer obliques. As he moved, P.D.'s gaze followed the hard ridge of muscle separating his abdomen from his hips until her eyes came to a stop at the faint line of dark hair that disappeared beneath his fly. She'd always been a sucker for low-slung jeans on a well-built man—not that she'd seen anyone in Bliss who could qualify for being truly "gawk-worthy."

Until now.

Unaware of her prurient interest, Elam unlatched the pump handle and waited for the water to run cool. Now that he was closer, P.D. could see that his bare arms and chest gleamed with sweat and a fine layer of sawdust. Over six feet tall, Elam was built like a runner, all lean, sinewy strength. The work he'd done on his cabin had given him a tan that blended well with the coffee-colored hair that brushed his shoulders and a beard that darkened his jaw.

When he leaned over to duck his head beneath the running water, P.D. could not have yanked her gaze away if her shoes were on fire. Instead, she watched like an adolescent Peeping Tom as he thoroughly doused his head, then snapped back to attention, droplets of water flinging into the air around him. The movement could not have been choreographed better had he tried. Bits of liquid scattered jewel-like into the air while rivulets cascaded down his face and chest. Then he stood there, dripping, waiting for Bodey to approach.

Thunder Down Under, eat your heart out, P.D. thought. Because this wasn't a man who manipulated his sexuality. He was completely unaware of the powerful picture he presented—or the fact that he could probably bring any woman to her knees with a single glance.

Shifting in her seat, P.D. knew she should look away.

Dear sweet heaven, she should definitely look away.

But she didn't.

Not when she knew that, at any moment, Elam would realize he was being watched by someone other than his brother and reach for the shirt that lay a few feet away.

And wouldn't that be a shame.

Bodey had finally managed to traverse the uneven ground to his brother's side, but P.D. had grown so distracted, she didn't bother to listen to their conversation as they exchanged the internationally recognized male-to-male greeting ritual—an awkward hug with lots of back slapping, an exchange of insults, then a punch to the arm. But P.D. was probably the only one who realized that even though Elam went through the motions, the happiness that radiated from Bodey never even touched Elam's eyes.

In an instant, the whispers of gossip that P.D. had heard in town raced through her head.

. . . too young to be a widower . . .

. . . Navy EOD . . . injured in Afghanistan . . .

. . . tortured soul . . .

. . . PTSD . . .

P.D. had always dismissed the stories as being exaggerated and fanciful—and the nickname they'd given him, *Desperado*, had seemed ludicrous. But watching Elam now, in this unguarded moment with his brother, she began to believe that everything she'd heard was true—true and probably only the tip of the iceberg. It was obvious from the sharp, too-lean contours of his face and the raised scars that wrapped around one side of his waist, that Elam had been through hell and back—and he was pissed at the world. Even his posture—head slightly forward, shoulders tensed, hands held away from his body—relayed his wariness at what other obstacles Fate might throw his way.

He was the kind of man who could help P.D. with her current dilemma. Strong, determined, and stubborn—which was a moot point now. Because there was no way in hell that Elam Taggart would ever agree to her proposal. Even though, as was her prerogative as a woman, she had suddenly changed her mind again. She really, *really* wanted his help.

Geez. She was freakin' out of her mind for even considering it.

P.D. killed the engine and strained to hear over the ticking metal. Bodey was talking now, and despite the growth of beard on Elam's face, she could lip-read most of his end of the conversation.

What the hell happened to you?

He winced at Bodey's response.

Don't you know any better than to get out from under a horse before he rolls on you?

Then, he grew still, listening intently to what Bodey was saying.

P.D. froze, her fingers gripping the steering wheel, knowing that Bodey would now be presenting her case. Her gut tightened in apprehension and she was at once embarrassed and nervous.

Elam would probably say "no."

There was no way he'd say "yes."

But what if, miracle of miracles, he did agree? Did she really want to ally herself with someone so . . . *intense?* Could she withstand four days and nights of constant contact with a man like Elam without completely cracking from the strain? Or worse yet, begging him to—

P.D. brought her thoughts to a screeching halt, banishing the images of Elam Taggart wearing nothing but a smile. But the tingling that pooled low in her belly couldn't be so easily dismissed.

She was nuts. Absolutely nuts.

Or maybe, much like Helen had repeatedly warned her, it was time P.D. brought a halt to her self-imposed "dry spell" where men were concerned and let it rain. Granted, a man like this would never look to someone like her for a meaningful, long-lasting relationship. But that didn't mean she couldn't have some fun if it were offered.

"I am so going to hell for even thinking about Elam Taggart that way," P.D. whispered to herself. He was Bodey's brother, for heaven's sake. You didn't mess around with a friend's brother. It was an unspoken rule. Worse yet, it was asking for trouble.

But for the first time in her life, P.D. wasn't sure if the "friend code" really made a heck of a lot of sense.

* * *

"YOU want me to do what?" Elam grumbled, sure he hadn't heard his younger brother correctly.

Truth be told, Elam was used to his younger brother's harebrained schemes. There were four Taggart siblings, with Barry being the youngest. But since Barry hadn't come along until Elam was about to join the Navy, it was Elam, Jace, and Bodey who'd grown up together.

As kids, Elam had always been the cautious one, the planner, the plotter. Even as a boy, he didn't commit to anything until he'd studied it from every angle and formulated a plan of attack. Three years younger, Jace was the peacekeeper. Quiet, laid-back, he had a meticulous eye for detail and a talent for collecting strays. But Bodey . . .

Well, Bodey was a different animal. From birth, he'd been mercurial, impetuous, and mischievous, forever getting the three of them into trouble. He tended to jump first and think about the consequences later. And nothing had changed since then, Still in his twenties, Bodey was a master at raising hell. He lived for little more than the National Cattle Cutting Competition circuit, women, Single Action Shooting Society matches, women, the next adrenaline rush . . . and women. Hell, if anyone could draw the ladies like flies, it was Bodey. And somehow, his brother always managed to wriggle out of his broken relationships having gained a friend rather than a crazy ex. Even so, Bodey had always displayed a good grasp of reality.

Until now.

Bodey eased closer on his crutches, obviously worried that their conversation would carry as far as the truck. It wasn't until that moment that Elam realized his brother hadn't driven himself up the canyon. With the sun in his eyes, Elam could only guess who was inside.

"Please, Elam. I'm desperate. If you can't bail me out . . . well, I don't know what I'll do."

Sighing, Elam raked his fingers through his hair, then wiped the water from his face. "Start again. I still can't figure out what the hell you think *I* can do."

Bodey backtracked and began with, "It's about time for Wild West Days in town."

Elam nodded. As kids, they'd lived for the annual Wild West Days' celebration with its week-long festivities honoring the first settlers to enter the valley. There were water games with the volunteer fire department, a carnival in the park, and a parade down Factory Street. The Rotary Club served breakfast at the bowery near the town hall, and the police grilled hamburgers at night. In the evenings, there was a rodeo at the fairgrounds, where professional riders were integrated with mutton-busting kids and the high school roping team. And each night, fireworks would bloom in the sky over the mountains like Indian paintbrush, providing the perfect ambience for wooing the latest girl.

Dear heaven above, Elam thought with a pang of nostalgia that faded into a knot of pain in his chest. It seemed like only yesterday when he'd loaded his high school sweetheart, Annabel, into his truck and taken her up the old service road to the same spot where his cabin now stood. He'd been what . . . sixteen . . . seventeen? He'd spread out a blanket on the sweet, sweet grass, and they'd lain watching the streaks of color appearing above them. Then Annabel had taken his hand and placed it at the buttons of her shirt . . .

For a moment, Elam could hardly breathe. His hand rose to unconsciously rub at the pain that lodged in his chest like molten lead.

From somewhere far away, Bodey continued his narrative, ". . .*town's hundred and fiftieth anniversary . . . something new . . . Wild West Games.*" Elam barely heard him. His mind was flooded with images of Annabel, of the way she sighed with desire as he unfastened her blouse and cupped the delicate swell of her breast for the first time.

He'd been young and inexperienced, but then, so was Annabel. When she'd pulled him on top of her, he'd thought his heart and his body would explode. And, sweet heaven above, she'd felt the same. But as the image of her head flung back, eyes closed in passion, faded into the pale form of his wife's body lying posed in her casket, Elam jerked his attention back to Bodey, knowing that he couldn't allow his thoughts to plunge down that trail.

Because he didn't think he could handle one more drop of pain.

Bodey was looking at him expectantly—and for the life of him, Elam had no idea what response was required of him. So he finally scrambled to say, "What does any of that have to do with me?"

"I signed up for the Games in January. Me and P.D. Raines. First prize is ten thousand dollars! And we were a shoe-in for the winner's circle. The competition is nothing more than displaying the skills used by the original settlers—riding, shooting, driving a team." He bent to whack the black plastic and Velcro contraption that covered his foot and leg to the knee. "Then this happened . . . and I can't let P.D. down. I've already talked to the contest committee and substitutions can be made up to this Friday."

Finally, Elam understood the purpose for Bodey's trip up the mountain. Evidently, he was hoping that Elam would take his place.

"No." Elam turned away, intending to get back to work. Another few days and he should be able to finish up outside and start painting inside. And then . . .

Well, he didn't know what he'd do to fill his time and occupy his thoughts. He'd made a promise to Annabel on their wedding night that he'd build her a house on the hill in the same spot where they'd first made love. He'd begun the project hoping to feel closer to Annabel. Instead . . . he felt gutted. Lonely. Especially with the project so close to completion.

"Why can't you help me out?"

Why? Because the last thing Elam wanted was to throw himself back into Bliss's mainstream, back among people he'd known his whole life, where he would have to field sympathetic looks and well-meaning comments like: "How are you faring?" and "Time heals." Because he wasn't "faring" well at all and "time" hadn't done a damned thing. He was still angry at God and the world for taking away the only woman he'd ever loved.

"Get Jace to do it," Elam said, referring to the brother sandwiched between them in age. Striding away, Elam signaled to Bodey that he was done with the conversation.

But Bodey didn't take the hint. He merely dug the tips of his crutches into the dirt and swung along behind him. "I already asked. He's got mandatory pesticide certification that week."

Elam sighed, lifting his hands in an apologetic gesture. "Then you'll have to find someone else to do it."

He tried to move toward the cabin, but Bodey planted himself in Elam's way just like he used to do when Elam and his friends were going fishing and Bodey wanted to come along. "I can't," he said urgently. "I've already tried. Do you think I'd be here if I hadn't asked everyone I know?"

Briefly, Elam wondered if he should be insulted by that remark. Was he last on the list because Bodey thought he wasn't capable of doing the job? Or was it because his little brother knew, deep down, that Elam wouldn't help him even if he begged?

He felt a nudge of conscience. There'd been a time when the Taggart brothers had been thick as thieves. There was no exploit too risky, no demand too wild, that would keep them from banding together to help one another.

But then, everything Elam had thought he'd stood for— family, country, and honor—had begun to implode. First, he'd been sent overseas—the deployments coming one after another with only a few months in between to spend time with Annabel. Then, he'd received word that an automobile accident had claimed the lives of his mother, father, and baby sister, Emily, while Emily's twin, Barry, had suffered irrevocable brain damage. And then, worst of all, he'd received the call that Annabel had suffered a brain aneurism. Before he could even make his way home, Annabel was gone.

After that, life seemed to crumble around him. He was suddenly alone. Numb. As soon as he'd been able to rejoin his unit, he'd headed back overseas, not really caring what happened to him. It had only been a matter of months before he'd been injured. Then, he'd been sent back to the States for good.

Elam knew that since returning from Walter Reed, he'd been keeping his brothers at arm's length. At first, he hadn't wanted their pity—no, not pity. They'd never pitied him. But their concern had been just as stifling, reminding him of everything he'd lost. And knowing that he'd crack if he allowed himself to give in to anything other than anger, he'd purposely erected a wall between them—first literally, then figuratively. His gaze lifted to the sturdy logs and river rock of his new place. A home away from the "Big House" as it was known. It was the first time in generations that any of the Taggarts had chosen to live somewhere other than the ancestral property.

"Shit," he whispered under his breath. He'd been back in the States for more than a year now, but in all that time, his brothers hadn't asked him for a thing. Even though Elam was the eldest, Jace had calmly taken over the management of Taggart Enterprises, overseeing the business aspects of the prize-winning quarter horses they bred, trained, and sold; the herds of beef cattle kept on local and mountain pastures; and the three thousand acres of land they farmed to support the livestock. Even more, he'd stepped up to take care of Barry, ensuring their little brother got to his doctors and therapists, classes and social activities so that Barry could become the sweet kid that he was.

Bodey had worked just as hard. He not only oversaw the purchasing and breeding of the livestock, but he was their major source of advertising. As one of the top cow cutting competitors, he juggled a grueling rodeo schedule with the responsibilities of the family ranch.

Elam was fully aware that his brothers had deftly left Elam with little more to do than break the new colts upon his return to the States—a physically demanding job that helped him to forget how hellish his existence had become amid the exhaustion.

But they'd never asked more of him.

Until now.

With a rush of shame, Elam realized he was a bastard through and through. What kind of man said "no" to his family? Especially with the way they'd been carrying most of the responsibility for Taggart Enterprises for so many years?

"Look, if you know someone else I can ask, give me a name," Bodey was saying. "P.D.'s taken over that old restaurant in town—Vern's?—and needs half of the prize money to make some improvements in the kitchen. I can't let down a friend, Elam. And it's my own damned fault I got trapped under that horse. I felt him falling and should have kicked free sooner, but—"

"I'll do it," Elam said from between clenched jaws—regretting the words the moment they'd been uttered—even though he knew he had no other option.

Bodey couldn't disappoint a friend.

And Elam sure as hell couldn't add refusing to help a brother to his already long list of sins.

He looked up in time to see Bodey's face split with a grin that spread like sunshine over his features. "Really?"

"Yeah."

Bodey crowed in delight, pumping one fist into the air. Twisting, he threw a thumbs-up sign toward the truck. As if an all-clear signal had been given, the driver's door opened and P.D. Raines stepped out.

It wasn't until the shape stepped free of the truck and the orange of the setting sun streaked over each line and hollow that Elam realized that P.D. Raines was a woman.

P.D. knew the precise moment when Elam Taggart grasped the fact that she wasn't a man.

It wasn't the first time someone had assumed she was male. "P.D." was androgynous enough that such mistakes had happened before. But she would have given money to have a camera aimed in Elam's direction when the fierce wildness in his expression eased to one of pure and utter shock.

Just as quickly, the emotion disappeared, and his features became carefully blank. But the transformation wasn't entirely successful, because as she walked toward him, the muscles of his jaw flicked in a betraying manner.

"P.D., this is my older brother Elam."

She held out a hand for him to shake. "Nice to meet you. I've heard a lot about you."

His grip was firm and sure. "Probably all bad." The words were meant to be light, she was sure, but Elam's tone held a thread of something darker, as if he were aware of the rumors circulating around town.

P.D. promised herself that she'd keep things cool, professional. Friendly. But when his palm swallowed hers, she was toast. Some women were butt-aficionados; others were turned on by a man's chest. But P.D. had always been first attracted to a man by his hands.

Elam Taggart had sexy hands, with long slender fingers and bony knuckles. Faint scars and calluses attested to the fact that he was accustomed to hard work. They were broad hands, the perfect size to handle tools or a woman's breast—probably with equal finesse. A dusting of dark hair led up to sinewy forearms and shoulders with taut musculature.

P.D. could feel the heat rise in her cheeks and avoided staring at his bare chest, training her eyes instead on the darkness of his beard, the full lips, angular nose, and deep-set eyes. Hazel eyes laced with flecks of blue, green, and gold that reminded her of the Wasatch Mountains that surrounded them.

"What does P.D. stand for?" Elam asked. He spoke softly, but the rumble of his voice could have carried yards.

She cleared her throat before admitting, "Prairie Dawn."

She thought she saw the slightest lift to his eyebrows—as if she'd surprised him yet again.

"Pretty name."

P.D. grimaced. "Says the man who wasn't named after a Muppet."

That comment took him aback because his lips tugged at the corners. Not really a smile, but close. "And were you? Named after a Muppet?"

She shrugged. "Who knows? My parents were rather . . . unconventional."

And wasn't *that* the understatement of the year.

Elam was still holding her hand. The warmth seeped up her arm to spread through her body in a frisson of awareness. P.D. would have to be an idiot not to admit he turned her on—she'd have to be *dead* not to be turned on. But along with that awareness came the knowledge that the gaze he leveled her way could have been a huge, flashing sign reading: NO TRESPASSING!

And P.D. would never be the kind of woman who could convince a man like this to lower his defenses. That would take someone with infinite gentleness and patience. P.D. had never had time for either of those qualities. After clawing her way into mainstream America, she didn't have it in her to be docile and sweet.

Elam finally released her, then reached behind him to snag the T-shirt off his workbench. He dragged it over his head, but he really needn't have bothered. His chest was damp and the fabric was so well worn that it clung to every dip and valley of his body.

"Wild West Days start when?" he asked, but he'd directed the question to Bodey.

"Monday."

Less than a week away. Which was why Bodey had been scrambling for a replacement.

Elam turned to her. "Do you have an outline of the competition or a description of the events?"

"I've got a handbook with all of the rules and contest guidelines at Vern's. If you'll drop by tonight, around eight, I'll feed you and we can go through everything."

Hopefully, by having him meet her at her restaurant, she could cement their association in a casual enough setting so that she could banish her own lustful thoughts and concentrate on the business at hand.

"Fine." He was backing away, clearly finished with the conversation. "I'll see you there."

P.D. was more than willing to give the man his space for a few hours. He probably wanted to get as much work done as possible before the light failed him. Even better, he'd have a chance to dry off and put on a real shirt.

Maybe that way, when they spoke again, P.D. wouldn't come completely apart at the seams.

TWO

———•••———

ON his way to Vern's that night, Elam couldn't help making a slow "drive-through" of the ranch. Easing his pickup past the "Big House," where the Taggart family had lived for over a hundred years, and into the ranch compound farther on, he found himself automatically scanning the corrals with the mares and new foals, and the big barn, which Jace had recently had repainted a russet red. Slowing, he passed the pens of Angus cattle already sorted and waiting for a visit from the brand inspector so that they could be shipped to a ranch in Texas the following day. A little farther out was the pasture, where the colts waited for Elam's attention. Since he would be the one to break them, he spent most of his time there, familiarizing himself with each horse, learning their temperaments, and letting them grow accustomed to him as well.

A hint of dust warned him that someone was approaching from the canal road. When he saw Bodey's familiar flat-bed truck, he pulled to a stop and rolled down his window. Here on the ranch, there were few sit-down meetings. Instead, information was discussed and relayed from truck to truck or over meals—although Elam hadn't been around the Big House enough lately to catch many of those impromptu gatherings.

Bodey rolled to a stop. He grinned at Elam, one tanned arm draped across his window.

"You're on your way to Vern's?"

Elam nodded, slightly uncomfortable that Bodey knew so much about his movements.

"Please tell me you showered and shaved and—"

"Shit, Bodey. Mind your own business."

Far from looking cowed, Bodey's grin grew even wider.

"I just want to make sure you don't sully the Taggart name. You'll be taking my place, remember? And I have a certain reputation to maintain."

"Yeah, for being a pain in the ass," Elam muttered. But there was no sting to his voice. A person couldn't remain serious around Bodey for too long. He seemed to make it his mission to make the people around him laugh. "When's the semi coming in for the cattle?"

"Jace got a text saying they'd be here around noon. The brand inspector has already been notified. Then Maynard will be sending in a couple of semis for hay about two."

"And you've got everything set up for Sell Day?"

Each June, Taggart Enterprises hosted a Sell Day, when they auctioned off a portion of their quarter-horse stock and stud services.

"The auctioneer will be here around eight. Jace picked up the banners in town and he's going to get Barry to help attach them to the fence line along the highway tonight."

Elam nodded, checking the clock. "Let me know if you need my help with anything."

"Will do."

Shifting into gear, Elam pulled away, following the back access road to where it joined the highway. It took only a few minutes to make the short drive to P.D.'s restaurant, but with each mile, his tension ratcheted up a notch. As Elam eased his Dodge Ram into a parking space, every nerve in his body was telling him he'd made a mistake by coming to Vern's tonight. Already,

he had an itchy, anxious feeling, as if he were being watched.
Judged.

Pitied.

Bliss was his home, and in many ways, the people were his
family. He'd graduated in a class of little more than a hundred,
and between that, the close-knit network of farmers and ranchers,
and a community that took care of its own, there weren't many
strangers. Which was comforting . . . as well as a damned nuisance. Everyone knew everyone's business most of the time, and
he wished to hell that they didn't know so much of his.

He appreciated how everyone had rallied around him after
Annabel's death. And the way they'd given him a hero's welcome
when he'd returned two years later, after his stint in the hospital,
had been gratifying. But Bliss was a small town, and nothing
fueled a small town more than gossip. It had taken only one trip
to the grocery store for him to hear the whispers.

. . . medical discharge . . .

. . . wife . . . aneurism . . .

. . . out of the country at the time . . .

To think that his life had become fodder for tongue-
wagging had been more than he could take. So, soon after his
homecoming, he'd kept to the ranch or his cabin site. If he
needed supplies, he got them from the Big House or drove to
Logan.

What would the busybodies say once they heard that he was
reentering Bliss society by entering the very public Wild West
Games? As soon as folks realized he would be competing as
the partner to a woman as flamboyant as P.D. Raines . . .

Hell.

Elam sat in the truck for several minutes, a muted country
music station urging him to "Do the Dew" and his heart
pounding in his chest much harder than the situation
warranted.

He'd diffused bombs in Afghanistan, IEDs in Iraq, and
harbor mines in Yemen. He'd been in armed combat more
times than he could count, and suffered through the devastating effects of a missile attack, which had finally sent him

home for good. So why was he so nervous about walking into a restaurant and talking to P.D. Raines?

But even as he acknowledged his misgivings, Elam sat with his fingers drumming on the steering wheel and his "going to town" hat sitting on the console beside him.

He couldn't help wondering who P.D. Raines really was and what she meant to his brother. Bodey had introduced her as "his friend," but most of Bodey's ex-girlfriends were "friends," damn him. With that body of hers, she was Bodey's type. His younger brother liked his women on the voluptuous side, and P.D. definitely qualified. But Elam had no clue if Bodey had already pursued the woman or if he was patiently circling her, waiting to cut her from the herd of females that invariably flocked around him.

Damnit, not that it mattered. Elam wasn't about to put the moves on P.D. Raines—or on any woman for that matter. He merely wished he knew the score. The Taggart males didn't infringe on another brother's woman. Ever. Even if she was an ex.

Realizing that he was only avoiding the inevitable, Elam killed the engine. The resulting quiet after the rumble of the diesel motor was nearly overpowering. And silence of any kind hadn't been his friend for a very long time.

Sliding from the truck, he jammed his hat on his head, hit the lock button on his key fob, and shoved his hands into the pockets of his leather jacket.

The last time he'd been to Vern's, it had been a sleepy mom-and-pop diner—the perfect spot to grab a hamburger and a made-from-scratch milkshake. But judging by the vehicles crowded into the parking lot and the faint pound of music, P.D. Raines had made some real changes.

His boots crunched against the gravel as he crossed to the front door. Years of training had him automatically sweeping the shadows. But in the assortment of flashy pickups, dented farm trucks, minivans, and sedans, he saw nothing more threatening than a stray tabby cat packing a squirming kitten toward the privet hedge that separated the parking lot from the new dollar store next door.

Elam was nearly to the front entrance when the noise from inside filtered into his brain and he realized what he was hearing. Bluegrass. P.D. Raines had brought bluegrass music to Bliss, Utah. Granted, the folks around here were usually into country music—and pure Bluegrass was its mother genre—but Elam was still astonished. Especially since the lack of free parking spaces made it clear that the place was popular.

For several minutes, he gripped the door handle, an exuberant melody seeping into the cool night air. There was something about the melding of its boisterous accompaniment and soulful harmonies that pulled at his emotions, enveloping Elam in a wave of something that felt very much like . . .

Homesickness.

With only the door separating him from conversation and laughter and human companionship, Elam suddenly realized how long it had been since he'd spent time with anyone other than himself. Occasionally, he'd run into his brothers, or waved to someone as he barreled down the road on his way to the hardware store, but usually, he kept to his own self-imposed exile. It had been so much easier that way.

But tonight, it felt lonely.

Maybe his brothers had been right when they'd hinted that it was time for Elam to rejoin the real world.

Yanking at the door, he stepped inside and was immediately enveloped in warm air, a riff of fiddle and mandolin, and the incredible aroma of food. More than the addition of entertainment had changed at Vern's. He was sure he could detect the rich spices of BBQ sauce, the lower notes of roasted meats, and the sweet inexplicable tang of apples.

A divider made of reclaimed barn wood separated him from the rest of the restaurant. Benches lined either wall, and it was clear that there was a waiting list. Elam stepped toward a hostess stand cleverly fashioned from a sideboard like the one his grandmother had used to store her "best" silver and linens. A young woman dressed in a Western shirt with pearl snap buttons and tight denim jeans offered him a wide smile.

"How many?" she asked, picking up a clipboard. As Elam

had suspected, there were at least a dozen entries waiting for tables.

"I'm actually supposed to meet P.D.," Elam began. "I'm Elam Taggart."

The woman's grin became even more pronounced. "She had us hold a table for you." She grabbed a long menu and said, "This way."

He was led around the divider to the main room. Here in the dining area, the space had been completely transformed since he'd been here last. Gone were the vinyl booths and checkerboard floor, and in their places were rich wood and split logs. The furnishings felt familiar to Elam. As if he'd stepped into his own home. The floor had been built on several levels so that the tables circled a small dance floor, and at the far end, a makeshift stage had been erected to hold the live band.

The hostess took Elam to a corner table where a RESERVED sign rested against a mason jar full of black-eyed Susans. He shrugged out of his jacket and draped it over the back of a chair that could have been a part of an original farmhouse kitchen.

"What would you like to drink?"

It wasn't until that moment that Elam realized that he was hungry. Not just hungry, ravenous. Maybe it was the rollicking music, or the warmth of Vern's after too many nights camping out at the cabin in a sleeping bag. Or maybe it was the heavenly smells that kept wafting his way.

"Beer, please."

"Coming right up."

A glance at the menu soon had Elam's mouth watering. No lukewarm soup heated over a camp stove tonight. His only problem was choosing what looked best from a list of gourmet-sounding delights such as bison burgers with prickly pear cactus compote, grilled river-fresh trout with a lemon and dill sauce, and lamb fries with Dutch oven potatoes.

Good hell almighty, P.D. Raines was serving "lamb fries." In Bliss, Utah. And after a glance at the plates of some of his fellow diners, Elam could see that the crispy battered sheep testicles appeared to be a hit.

"Hi, there."

Elam looked up as his waitress appeared, setting a cold beer and a pair of glasses in front of him, one chilled, but empty, the other filled with ice water. She followed it with a wooden cutting board that held three small loaves and a ramekin of whipped butter.

"Tonight, we've got our famous house beer bread, a chipotle cheese corn loaf, and a seven-grain sweet bread," she said, pointing to each of the varieties. "Have you had a chance to decide what you'd like?"

"What's good?" Elam asked, his hunger seeming to gnaw in the pit of his belly.

She winked. "The lamb fries are a favorite for those hoping to get lucky," she said with a laugh, reminding Elam that many people considered the fare to be an aphrodisiac. "The steaks are always a hit. But I'd have to say my favorite is the bison burger."

"I'll take that."

She nodded, taking his menu and hurrying away.

The instant the woman left the table, Elam was reaching for the bread. Cutting a huge hunk of the first loaf, he slathered it in butter and took a bite.

He'd never had beer bread before, but it could have been manna from heaven for all he knew. Dense and slightly sweet, it had a homey flavor that could never have been found wrapped in plastic and sitting on a grocery store shelf. And if this first taste was anything to go by, no wonder there was a waiting list at the door.

Cutting himself another piece, Elam leaned back in his chair and allowed himself to look around, nodding to a few of the townspeople he recognized. Vaguely, he wondered where P.D. might be, but supposed that with business booming the way it was, she must be holed up in the kitchens or an office or—

His gaze fell on the band and he nearly choked on the piece of bread he was chewing. There, on the corner of the stage, a fiddler was jamming out a frenetically paced solo. Curly hair flying, body twisting and turning with the melody, P.D. Raines coaxed a ribbon of pure joy from the violin. Her eyes were closed, her mouth slightly parted—and there was such a look of rapture on her face that Elam would have thought the emotion was more in keeping with the throes of lovemaking than a public performance.

The thought hit him like a jolt to his gut, and he reached for his beer, averting his eyes as if he'd been caught glancing through a neighbor's window. But even after washing down his surprise, he found himself looking at her again. Closely.

When Bodey had introduced P.D. Raines to him this morning, Elam had been distracted—no, he'd been pissed. Like a bear hauled kicking and screaming out of his cave before his hibernation was finished, Elam hadn't been too intent on paying attention to the participants. He'd been more focused on making his displeasure known. If someone had asked him to describe P.D., he probably couldn't have said much beyond: "She's a woman. With brown hair. Or blond."

But now . . .

Hell. P.D. was tall and curvy in all the right places—a fact that was all too clear by the tight jeans and snap-front shirt that seemed to be a uniform here at Vern's. But while the waitresses managed to look cute in their getup, P.D. was all woman, with long legs, hips enhanced by a sparkling belt, and a full bosom beneath a shirt that must have been tailored to fit her shape. And her hair . . . her hair was nearly to her waist, falling into natural ringlets and waves in the shades of a new fawn—russet and gold with hints of auburn.

She was a country boy's wet dream to be sure—a city boy's, too. And for the first time in months, Elam found himself stirring at the mere sight of a woman. Holy, holy hell. He was supposed to partner up with . . . *that*? He was supposed to remain cool and businesslike with a woman who . . . who . . . probably played the fiddle the same way she would make love? With utter abandon?

"Here you are."

Elam started like a guilty teenager when his waitress set a plate of food in front of him. Taking his napkin, he subtly arranged it in his lap as the waitress explained, "The little pots next to the burger are the house's own stone-ground mustard, garlic and onion aioli, and the prickly pear compote. But I can bring you the regular store-bought condiments if you'd like."

Was she kidding?

"No, this looks great."

"Wave if you need anything else. In the meantime, enjoy."

Enjoy.

How could he not enjoy his meal with the scents rising from his plate, a cold beer in a frosty glass, and his own personal peep show mere yards away?

Trying to avoid staring at P.D. like the letch he evidently was, Elam loaded his burger with lettuce, tomato—and yes, onion. He sure as hell wasn't kissing anyone tonight.

But for some reason, the realization didn't bring him the reassurance that he'd thought it might.

After dipping his spoon in the compote and finding it to be tart and savory with quick bite of jalapeños and the slow heat of cayenne, he liberally dosed the top of his bun and jammed it over his burger. As he took his first bite, the juice and toppings began to run down the side of his hand—which in Elam's opinion was the hallmark of an excellent burger.

"The first taste is always the best," a voice said next to his table. "And judging by your expression, I've got you hooked."

WHEN Elam looked up, P.D. caught a glimpse of something raw and sexual in his eyes, and the effect was so startling, so powerful, that she nearly took a step back. But just as quickly, the searing heat was gone and his expression was carefully neutral again.

Unconsciously, he licked the side of his hand, then set the burger back on his plate. The sensuality of his movements, as well as the thought of that tongue licking other things—*her* things—had her sinking into the chair before she stumbled like a starstruck groupie.

"It's good," he said after swallowing. "Really, *really* good." Then he gestured toward the stage. "*You're* good. You run a restaurant *and* provide the entertainment?"

P.D. shook her head. "Occasionally, the band persuades me to join them, but otherwise, I listen like everyone else."

"It's a rare talent to play the fiddle like you do."

She shrugged. "My parents might have opted for homeschooling—when they bothered with any education at all—but they insisted I learn to play music. I was able to put myself through college by playing in honkey-tonk joints around the Midwest."

She was sure that Elam almost asked about her parents. Almost. But just in time, he seemed to realize she wouldn't give him any answers so he asked instead, "What were you studying? Music? Culinary arts?"

"Nah. I graduated with double degrees in physics and business."

"And you ended up in Bliss, Utah?"

His tone was so incredulous, she laughed. "It turned out that being stuck in a lab bored me. Since I'd traveled a lot as a kid, I knew I wanted to live in the mountains, so I came back to the place I felt most comfortable."

"Military brat?"

"Hippie hostage."

And with that, she condensed her crappy childhood into a few sentences, hoping he wouldn't ask any further questions about her "adventures" with Summer and River.

A familiar figure moved toward their table. "What can I get you, P.D.?"

P.D. smiled at Becky, one of her best waitresses, and said, "A cold diet soda, thanks."

"You're not going to eat?" Elam asked.

"No. I eat before the dinner shift, otherwise I'd be nibbling all night long. But you go ahead. You're probably starving after spending your day sweating on the job. Construction work must be really demanding."

Geez, P.D. Smooth, really smooth. You may as well have added, "With your muscles bulging and your chest gleaming."

Not for the first time, she rued the fact that her parents had fallen into a form of "free-range childrearing." P.D. might have roamed the country and wallowed in nature, but she still wasn't too adept at social skills. Especially small talk. Which was why most men didn't view her as "relationship material." Her background and awkwardness made her difficult to explain should dating ever reach the "meet the parents" stage.

Thankfully, Elam began to eat again, which helped to break his powerful gaze.

"So tell me about this competition of ours," he said between bites.

"I've got all the information in my office," she said with a jerk of her thumb in that direction. "Once you've eaten, we can go get the handbook so you can familiarize yourself with the rules. It's a bit like television's *Amazing Race*."

When Elam stared at her blankly, she could have kicked herself for being an idiot. He probably wasn't watching much television in a cabin with no electricity.

"It's a relay race, four days long. It involves negotiating our way from the Ridley Historical Farm near Logan to an, as yet, undisclosed spot in Bliss. According to the rules, we'll randomly be assigned roles—such as prospectors looking for a claim, or mountain men in search of rich furs."

"Schoolmarm and outlaw," Elam filled in smoothly.

And damnit, his idea sounded like a whole lot of fun.

P.D. cleared her throat of its sudden dryness as a host of images flooded her brain—Elam kicking down the door to a one-room schoolhouse while she trembled in the corner with something far more intense than fear.

Geez, P.D.

"Uh . . . yeah." She verbally stumbled, then quickly dragged her mind back to the topic.

Rules. Rules.

"Anyway, at the starting line, we'll be given a sealed envelope that will outline the first location we need to find. Our journey will be timed from the moment we receive the envelope to the point when we check in with a contest official at our destination."

His brows rose. "We're supposed to walk?"

"Some."

She leaned forward, propping her forearms on the table. For

a split second, Elam's eyes betrayed him, skipping down to her cleavage before steadfastly returning to her face. A warmth flooded through her chest as she realized Elam Taggart was probably a breast man, and he liked what he saw, even if he wasn't comfortable admitting that fact to himself.

"Modes of transportation could include buggies, wagons, horseback, railroad cars, or like you said, good ol' boots to the road. Then, once we get to our assigned spots, we'll be asked to perform a series of pioneer-related tasks appropriate to the locale. Most of the stops will include a gun range where we'll be tested on marksmanship, but we could also be challenged with roping and tying cattle, bronco busting, cooking—even panning for gold."

"So we're graded on our times?"

"Times, accuracy, and quality of performance. The rubrics they use to put everything into a numerical point system are located in the back of the handbook. From what I understand, they've had a huge response to the Games. The contestant roster was filled within the first week of accepting applications and there's already a waiting list for next year. They've got volunteers all over the county lined up to help take scores and times. Vendors have rented space at the historical farm. Several large businesses have become sponsors. And there's even a rumor that an indie documentary producer will be coming to watch some of the stages to see if it might be something they'd like to film next year."

Elam had all but wolfed down his burger and Dutch oven potatoes, and sensing he might still have a little room left, P.D. gestured to Becky. When the waitress arrived, P.D. asked, "Could you bring Elam a blossom? And if you wouldn't mind, could you go to my office? I left a pamphlet about the Wild West Games on my desk and I need to give it to Elam."

Becky smiled. "Sure. No problem."

Within seconds, Becky arrived with the rule book for the Games, a glass of soda for P.D., and a small cast iron skillet that she set in the middle of the table. In the center, nestled in a pool of lemon sauce, was a perfectly formed shell of piecrust shaped like a flower bud. A scoop of homemade vanilla-bean ice cream was beginning to melt beneath the heat of the pastry.

"You can take the rules with you and look them over in more detail when you've got a minute. But it boils down to following some commonsense safety precautions, especially on the gun ranges, remaining on our outlined routes and designated checkpoints, and using only the methods of transportation we've been assigned or earned through special bonus challenges. And there's to be no cell phones or modern technology. The competition will be stopped each night, which means we have to remain at the last checkpoint we've reached for the day. I guess they didn't want a bunch of teams stumbling around in the dark." She pointed to the dessert. "You'll want to dig in while it's hot," P.D. urged. "It's one of my latest concoctions."

Elam hesitated only a second before slipping the information about the Games into the pocket of his jacket. Then he cracked the blossom open with the tip of his spoon. He immediately released a fragrant puff of steam and a lava-like flow of cherries, blueberries, and apples. After combining the contents with a bit of ice cream and a dab of the lemon sauce, he took a bite.

"Oh, wow." He closed his eyes, and the look of utter pleasure had her body responding in ways that it shouldn't. For a moment, Elam's barely submerged anger at the world was displaced by a primal delight that had her thoughts roaming once again to sex.

Yeah, right. As if she had a snowball's chance in hell of inspiring Elam Taggart to taste anything but her food. She'd learned long ago that men who were as primitively masculine and dangerous as Elam were attracted to dainty women with blond hair and big blue Alice in Wonderland eyes. They gravitated toward delicate creatures who wore sizes that had no numbers to speak of, just lots of zeros. Females who needed to be protected from the harsh realities of life by a big, strong he-man who would wrap them in cotton wool during the day and silk and lace at night.

P.D., on the other hand, had already seen her fair share of the worst the world had to offer. With parents who were more concerned with free love and recreational medication, P.D. had discovered early on how to protect herself from her parents' so-called "friends" when they groped her in the dark. She'd learned where to scavenge food if she got too hungry, and the best places to curl up outside to sleep if the haze of marijuana got too thick in the bus. Most of all, she'd found out that there wasn't a damn thing a man could do for her that she wasn't perfectly capable of doing herself. Even if sometimes, deep down, she longed for someone else to help shoulder her burdens.

Just as she inwardly insisted that she would never actually surrender control to a man who would curb her independence, Elam extended one of his extra spoons.

"You're going to have to help me with this."

Her first instinct was to refuse. There was something intimate about sharing food with another person. It was one of the unspoken rituals of courtship. And there was nothing like that between P.D. and Elam. They had a . . . business arrangement of sorts.

But she couldn't deny that she wanted to share that intimacy with him. Even if it was only an illusion.

When she didn't immediately react, he loaded the spoon and held it toward her. And for an instant she could see all the wariness and pain that he carried with him like an unshakable burden. But there was something else there as well. The wish—the *need*—for human contact, however small that contact might be.

She leaned forward, accepting the bite, then drew back slightly, but only slightly, so that he wouldn't think that she was rejecting his gesture of . . .

Of what?

Friendship?

Because there could never be anything else between them. Not with the weight of their respective baggage preventing even the thought of anything more.

He held the spoon toward her, handle first, and wordlessly, she accepted his challenge. Then, they were finishing the dessert together, their spoons coyly darting and chasing across the plate until the last morsel was gone.

Finally, Elam sat back in his chair, lacing his hands over his taut belly. His posture was more relaxed than she'd ever seen—and she sensed that this was the first meal in months that hadn't come from a fast-food joint or a can. When he spoke, it was with the low, rumbling purr of a satisfied man. And what she wouldn't give to find out what other activities might satisfy him.

"So what do you need me to do?"

P.D. blinked at him, suddenly overtaken with images of Elam Taggart stripping the shirt from his body, then reaching out to do the same to hers. But with some difficulty, she remembered the gist of their conversation.

"We should probably practice some of the skills," she offered tentatively.

His eyes narrowed, more green than blue in the dim light of Vern's. "And?"

"And I've never fired a gun. Bodey was going to teach me, but . . ."

"What kinds of weapons?"

"Single-action revolvers, double-barrel shotguns, and rifles."

"Do they supply the weapons and ammo, or do we?"

"We have to supply our own. If you can give me a list, I'll make a trip to Cabela's to get what we need."

He shook his head. "I can handle that. Meet me at my place tomorrow morning, and I'll give you a crash course."

She felt a quick thrill at the thought of seeing Elam again so soon, even though she'd known spending time with him was inevitable.

"This may be a bit of an endurance test . . ." P.D. began. "I've been trying to walk and hike as much as my own schedule would allow."

"You think I'm out of shape?" Elam drawled, one brow lifting.

If there was one thing that could be said about Elam, it was that he was fit.

"No!" When the word emerged too forcefully—too "I am already hung up on the sight of your rock-hard abs"—P.D. tried to corral her thoughts. "No, I thought I'd better lay it all on the table so there are no surprises." She toyed with her spoon in a show of studied casualness.

"And?"

"Well, there is one more thing that hasn't been mentioned." He wasn't going to like it. Even Bodey had groused about the final requirement. "You'll be expected to . . ."

She paused, trying how to phrase the words, and Elam scowled, growling, "Expected to what?"

From his tone, he assumed he'd be required to do something horrible like arena sex or nude cactus jumping. But then, what she had to say might be even worse in his opinion.

"We have to dress up, right down to the underwear."

A look of utter horror crossed his features, and she nearly laughed, realizing that he'd leapt to conclusions. Clearly, he expected her to outline something outrageously out of his element like space aliens or Comic-Con characters.

Laughing, she said, "Relax. Since the Wild West Games are being held in honor of Bliss's sesquicentennial, we need to wear clothing appropriate for the period. For you, that's probably not much different than what you wear on the ranch: twill pants, a button-down shirt, maybe a vest. There's a final Cattle Barons' Ball. That night, there will be a costume contest, which is twenty-five percent of our score. For that you'll need something dressier, maybe a frockcoat or tails. I've got a friend who designs period clothing for the local SASS group—the Single Action Shooting Society? She said she'd be happy to supply us with what we need. Have you heard of SASS?"

She wasn't sure if Elam was familiar with the national shooting club that dressed in Victorian clothing and participated in staged shooting events, all in the hopes of gaining the winning time.

"Sure. Bodey's a member. I was, too, before I went into the military."

"So you've already dressed up before?"

He grimaced. "I wasn't as rabid about the costuming portion of the sport as some are."

So P.D. continued to push the requirement. "If you want, I could arrange for my friend Helen to meet us here tomorrow night. We could try things on in my office."

P.D. worried that she'd taken things one step too far. But shoot, it wasn't as if *she* were the one insisting on the costumes.

Fearing that Elam might refuse, she said, "If you'll do it, I'll throw in dinner. Every night for a week." Not wanting her offer to sound like the bribe it was, she hurried to add, "As a way to thank you for filling in for Bodey this way."

His lips twitched. Obviously, he knew when a carrot was being held over his head—or a bison burger, for that matter—but then he nodded, ever so slightly. "You've got a deal—even though you had to know I couldn't pass up food like this. Not after my own bad cooking."

The band was returning to the stage after its break. And even though it was nearly nine thirty on a weeknight, the crowd showed no real sign of moving on.

"What time do you want me to come to your place tomorrow morning?" She still couldn't believe that she was about to be tutored in the rudiments of shooting by Elam Taggart.

And why did the activity seem more tantalizing than it should have been?

"Whenever you want. I'm usually up by five."

She grimaced. "I'll be there around ten."

THREE

———•———

ELAM supposed that was his cue to leave. But he was so relaxed—so full of P.D.'s amazing food—that he found himself loath to move.

He couldn't remember the last time he'd felt so at ease, so . . . comfortable. Gazing around the dining room, he could see that he wasn't the only one. At least half of the diners had finished their food and were simply talking or enjoying the music.

Becky approached the table and cleared away their plates. "Hey, P.D., Bart said we're running low on straws—and some knucklehead put the box on the upper shelf. Again. Do you have any idea where the stepladder has gone?"

A crease appeared between P.D.'s brows, and Elam had the crazy impulse to smooth it away. "Crap. I took it home to replace some lightbulbs. Give me a second and I'll find something to stand on."

"Can I help?"

Elam hadn't been aware that he'd even thought the words until they emerged from his mouth.

P.D. grinned at him. "Would you? I'm tall, but I still can't reach the upper shelf, even on tiptoes."

"No problem."

Elam stood, weaving through the tables in P.D.'s wake. He felt a few sets of curious eyes following their progress, and a spot at his back prickled between his shoulder blades. But the sensation didn't bother him as much as it used to do. Maybe, after all this time, he'd become old news.

P.D. led him through the double doors into the kitchen, then turned right, heading to a corridor flanked on either side with doors. She chose the closest one and slipped inside, fumbling along the wall until she found the light switch.

As with many of the older buildings in town, there was only a single bulb in the center of the room—and the wattage couldn't have been very high because the space was illuminated in a faint golden glow that didn't quite reach into the corners.

P.D moved confidently through the rows of shelving holding bags, boxes, and cans of staples—sugar, flour, dried beans. She turned into an aisle dedicated to paper goods. Packages labeled PLACEMATS vied for space with those proclaiming COASTERS and NAPKINS.

"Yep. There it is."

She pointed to a box perched on the top shelf that displayed a graphic of a bendable straw. It was wedged close to the ceiling above a sack of granulated sugar.

"Who the heck put that up there? It's supposed to be in the next row," she grumbled.

She planted her hands on her hips for a moment, scowling up at the offending bag of sugar. The pose was comically mutinous—as if she were a general and one of her underlings had been discovered AWOL. But even as the thought flashed through his mind, Elam noted how the stance drew attention to the sparkling belt wrapped around her hips and the ripe fullness of her breasts pressing against her tailored shirt.

Ripping his gaze away from places where it didn't belong, Elam pointed to the sack. "Do you want me to get that down, too?"

Her smile was so sudden, so completely genuine, that Elam felt a sharp arrow of awareness shoot through his body.

"If you wouldn't mind. I'm a little OCD about my storeroom."

Since the space between shelves was limited, Elam had to squeeze past P.D. In doing so, his body brushed intimately against hers and his hand drifted to her waist, to that nipped-in spot above the glittering belt. His body reacted of its own accord, but he steadfastly tried to push the sensation away.

Hell Almighty. It wasn't as if he'd groped her.

Nevertheless, the skin wherever their bodies had glanced together began to tingle.

Ignoring his traitorous response, Elam wedged himself into the corner and reached up. His fingers were able to burrow beneath the box of straws so that he could nudge it forward enough to grab it with both hands. He turned to hand it to P.D. But he'd forgotten how close she was behind him.

As she took the box, their fingers brushed, and for some reason, time slowed for Elam. He became overtly conscious of the woman who looked up at him. Her eyes were alight with such inner peace and joy that Elam could barely believe such an expression was possible. In the dim light of the overhead bulb, her features were cast into light and shadow, playing up the delicacy of her features, the lake blue eyes, the smattering of freckles over her nose. Her lips were a perfect cupid's bow. And her hair . . .

She had the kind of hair a man would want to touch, to plunge his fingers into, to fan out over his chest.

Shit.

He wanted to touch her. His fingers twitched from the need. And as her eyes darkened, he knew he'd somehow telegraphed his thoughts. But she didn't back away.

She didn't back away.

Just once. What could it hurt?

The thought slipped into his consciousness like a traitorous spy. The air around them hummed with hidden electricity. And for an instant, the world could have melted away. There was only this moment, this woman, this want.

But then, he remembered how he'd come to be in this spot.

The Games.

Bodey.
You don't poach on a brother's girl.

P.D. knew the instant the moment between them was lost. He'd been about to touch her—she *knew* he'd been about to touch her. Then, in the blink of an eye, everything changed, the awareness dissipated as if in a sudden brief explosion.

And the stranger she'd met this morning was back.

Damnit. She'd wanted to feel his fingertips on her skin. She'd wanted him to touch her cheek, her hair. She'd wanted him to dip his head and kiss her. Even if he couldn't give her full-blown passion, she'd longed to have him brush his lips against hers. Just once.

He'd been about to do it. She wasn't so foolish or naïve that she could have misinterpreted his intentions. He'd been looking at her with such aching hunger that her breath had locked in her chest in case the wrong move, the wrong sound should break the mood.

Then his eyes had become suddenly shuttered and his posture grew brittle.

He turned away from her then, reaching up for the bag of sugar. His shirt pulled tight against his back and P.D. fought the urge to place her palm in the vulnerable crease of his spine.

His fingers wrapped around the plastic handle sewn into the top of the bag and he yanked. But rather than freeing the sugar from its perch, the handle suddenly tore free and a shower of granulated sugar poured down from above.

P.D. watched in disbelief as Elam was engulfed by the granulated waterfall. He seemed rooted to the spot until the glittering stream ran dry. But when he turned toward her, there was such a look of horror on his face that she began to giggle.

To her relief, Elam's face cracked into a smile. He shook his arms and twisted his head back and forth, and sugar went flying in every direction.

Still laughing, P.D. held up her hands in protection, her lashes squeezing closed. But when she looked up again,

Elam's shoulders and hair were still liberally dusted with sweet snow.

"Hold still," she ordered, brushing her hands over his chest and shoulders.

And in an instant, the intimacy between them was back.

P.D.'s ministrations slowed, but she didn't stop. Instead, her hands lingered over the task, absorbing the firm bulge of muscle beneath her palms, the crisp button-down shirt. Then, her fingers lifted to his hair.

In the muted gold light, she could see there were a few streaks of gray at his temples, and she had the inordinate need to touch them. The sugar was forgotten as she took a wavy strand between her thumb and forefinger and traced the entire length.

Elam grew still, so incredibly still—as if his life depended on his not moving. His eyes had grown dark, and P.D. wasn't sure if he even breathed as she lifted her fingers again, this time to his temple.

His expression held such a haunting mixture of emotions—grief, hunger, want—that she could have been melted on the spot from their power. But he didn't back away.

She took a tiny step forward. Another. And another. Framing his face in her hands, she lifted on tiptoe and pressed her lips against his, softly, fleetingly.

Elam could have been made from stone. Other than the sudden hiss of his breathing, he offered no response whatsoever. But she sensed no resistance either. So she kissed him again, tasting the sweetness scattered on his lips. Again, he remained still, so still. But his hand lifted to rest against her waist, then slid around to rest in the hollow of her back, pulling her infinitesimally closer.

As if she were dealing with a yearling colt that might never trust her again if she startled him, P.D. pressed a kiss to Elam's cheek, then his temple. This time, ever so slightly, he leaned into the caress.

Then, knowing that this was probably the first time that anyone had touched him this way since Annabel had died, she wrapped her arms around his neck in a loose hug and whispered against his ear.

"Have I told you 'thanks' yet?"

"For what?" his response was little more than a whisper.

"For helping me."

"I made a mess."

She couldn't resist stroking his hair. It was softer than she'd imagined. Silken. And the waves sprang back against her fingers.

"Not that. Thanks for helping me with the Games. I know it isn't exactly how you'd planned to spend your time next week."

His other arm wrapped around her as well, and for one brief instant, he hugged her tightly against him.

"You're welcome."

The words rumbled from a spot deep in his chest.

P.D. longed to kiss him again to see if he would respond this time. But instinctively, she sensed that Elam was still on edge, the past warring with the present. So she stepped back, and his arms dropped away.

Turning, she gathered up the box of straws. "Leave the sugar. I'll bring the stepladder back tomorrow and deal with it. In the meantime, I'll send one of the busboys in to sweep up the mess." She purposely kept her tone light and carefree—as if their embrace had simply been an inevitable way of conveying her thanks. If Elam knew how her attraction for him had suddenly blossomed tenfold, she feared it would scare him away for good.

Elam followed her out of the storeroom, ducking to brush even more sugar out of his hair.

Again, she laughed. "You're going to need a shower to get it all out, I'm afraid. Otherwise, you're going to be sticky all night."

Damn, damn, damn! Did that comment suddenly sound as suggestive to him as it did to her?

She led Elam back to the kitchen. The instant she stepped inside, Bart Crowley, her manager, rushed to take the box from her hands.

He glanced suspiciously at Elam. Normally, customers weren't allowed beyond the dining room.

Nevertheless, Bart gestured to P.D. "Can I talk to you for a sec?"

P.D. had hoped that business could take care of itself for a few more minutes, but she shouldn't complain. "Sure." She turned to Elam. "Why don't you go take a seat and listen to the music?"

Bart Crowley let the door slap shut behind Elam's back before he asked, "Is that Elam Taggart?"

"Yeah, why?"

Bart's jaw flicked for a moment, but he quickly said, "No reason. I just haven't seen him around lately, that's all."

"What did you need?" P.D. prompted.

Bart jerked a thumb toward the back window, his features tight. "That line cook you fired last week? Eddie Bascom? He's been hanging around, insisting on talking to you."

P.D. sighed. "Is he still here?"

"No. I had a couple of the waitstaff run him off—but not before he kicked your garbage cans and beat the hell out of the Dumpster lid with a tire iron." Bart's look became ironic. "Apparently, he wants his job back."

Frowning, P.D. realized that by firing Bascom for stealing steaks from the freezer, she'd created more problems rather than solving them. She'd agreed not to press charges against him if he left quietly, but now it appeared that she would have been better off turning him over to the sheriff.

"Let me know if he shows up again. And if he causes trouble, call the police."

After checking the morning's produce orders and making a few additions, she turned back to the dining room in time to hear the melancholy strains of a song twining into the air. One that had been written by the guitarist, Manny Zarate, when his daughter Annie had left for college. A hush settled over the patrons as the lead singer began the familiar ballad.

Soft and sweet like a lullaby,
She came to me 'neath a summer sky,

Filled my life with immeasurable grace,
With a gentle smile and a hint of lace.

P.D. was washed in a wave of horror.

No. Oh, no! Elam's late wife was named Annabel. And Annie's full name was...

Annabel, oh, Annabel. What I'd give for one more smile,
Or to sit and talk to you for a while.
Annabel, Annabel where did you go?
Won't you come back home for the winter snow?

She rushed to the swinging doors, intent on doing something—*anything*—to stop the emotional train wreck that was about to happen. But she'd taken only two steps before she saw through the window that Elam had grown still in his chair. The color had leached from his face, leaving the darkness of his hair and beard in such sharp contrast that he could have been carved from marble.

Never in her life had P.D. seen such utter devastation settle over another human being. In the space of a few bars of music, he became a ghost of the man he'd been mere minutes before—and in that instant, she knew, without ever being told, how much he'd loved his wife. How much he continued to love her.

She taught me how to live and love, Like an angel sent here from above.

As the rest of the lyrics flowed into the dimly lit restaurant, P.D.'s sole aim was to stop the music—even if she had to interrupt the band with a bogus announcement. But she'd barely made it into the dining room when she saw Elam lunge to his feet. Despite her promise to feed him for a week, he threw several bills on the table, grabbed his jacket, then strode from Vern's with ground-eating strides.

P.D. hurried to follow him at a more casual pace, not wanting to draw attention to his exit with her own panicked reaction. But by the time she reached the main entrance, Elam's pickup was already on the highway, his lights glowing blood red in the darkness.

*   *   *

ELAM drove without seeing, needing to outrun the storm of emotions that hurtled toward him like a tidal wave. For months, he'd managed to lock things away, to dwell in the here and now and ignore the specters of the past. Then, in one unguarded moment . . .

He'd heard his wife's name being sung to him in the darkness of a crowded room.

He took a corner wide and fought for control, even though he wanted nothing more than to drive, farther and farther, until he managed to outrun his own memories. His fingers gripped the wheel until he feared either his bones or the plastic would snap. He didn't know where he was going, but he was going there fast. And once he got there . . .

He needed to tear something apart, beat out the frustration that simmered beneath the surface of mundane everyday chores. He wanted to exorcize the gnawing loneliness eating at his gut until he feared that he would never really sleep again, never laugh, never love . . .

The thought seared through him like a lightning bolt and he slammed on the brakes, skidding onto the shoulder. Dropping his head, he hunched over the wheel, breathing hard, trying not to remember Annabel.

Her sweet musical laughter.

Delicate features.

And the hair that ran through his fingers like corn silk.

Most of all, he missed the way she burrowed under his arm in the middle of the night, curling up in a tight ball like a kitten, one hand always flung out to touch him, as if she feared he would be spirited away. And heaven only knew he'd been gone too much during their ten-year marriage. He'd probably spent half of it deployed in the Middle East. But even when he was far from home, he'd known that Annabel was waiting for him. She was there in the daily letters she sent, the stolen phone calls, and the funny care packages with her horrible cookies.

Until three years ago.

Then, she suddenly wasn't there. Wasn't anywhere. She was just . . . gone.

He'd spoken to her on Skype mere hours before her death. They'd argued about what colors to paint the master suite in the Big House. And even though he'd groused at her selection, he'd let her win. Because she was like a little bird, nesting, waiting for his imminent return.

So when he'd come home—a journey he didn't even remember—he couldn't believe she was dead. There had to be a mistake. Annabel was out there somewhere, waiting for him.

Elam blinked against the tears—the damned tears that never solved anything. His chest grew so tight that he had to gulp for air, but he still refused to give in. He'd spent plenty of solitary nights, hiding from his brothers, weeping in the darkness. And it hadn't changed a thing. Annabel was still gone. Even worse, the memories of the time they'd spent together were fuzzing around the edges. Bastard that he was, he could remember the day that they married. And the first time he'd held her in his arms.

But he couldn't seem to remember what she liked for breakfast or her favorite television shows. And was that threadbare cotton nightie she wore in the heat of summer pink or white? The trivial minutiae of their lives together were seeping through his hands like sand, and he found it harder and harder to pull the images back.

Suddenly, the grief he'd held at bay for so long flooded his body, filling him with an exhaustion that made breathing too much of an effort. Closing his eyes, he vainly fought to forget the stolen moments in P.D.'s storage room. The touch of a woman's lips upon his own, the caress of velvety fingers. In an instant, Annabel's image was superseded by that of another woman. One who was tall and strong, with breasts that would more than fill a man's hands, and hips that would easily straddle his as she rode him.

Elam tried to push the thought away—tried to remember his wedding night and making love to his wife under the stars. But much like the song he'd heard, he'd been robbed of her presence so long he couldn't seem to connect with Annabel's spirit anymore. At least not enough to comfort him during the long, solitary hours.

And heaven help him, even though it felt like a betrayal, he longed for a woman he'd met only that morning to touch him again.

P.D. rushed to her office and closed the door behind her. Pacing behind the desk, she flung herself into her chair and reached for the phone she kept in the lap drawer. But as soon as she punched the Power button, she wilted.

Who was she going to call? She didn't have Elam's number—and she couldn't call one of his brothers. What would she say?

Have you seen Elam? Is he upset? Really, really upset?

She tossed the phone back onto the desk, pressing a finger to the ache forming between her eyes.

Suddenly, all thought of the Wild West Games faded in importance. She'd heard enough of the stories from Bodey to know how worried the Taggart brothers were about their eldest brother. And she'd always thought their concern was an overreaction.

Until tonight.

She had to do something. She had to make things better somehow.

Jumping to her feet again, she snagged her purse and stormed out of the door. After locating Bart in the kitchen, she asked, "Can you lock up for me tonight?"

Bart look alarmed. "Is something wrong?"

Too late, P.D. realized that she'd never asked anyone else to lock up for her. She'd always been there until the last table had been wiped down and the final car had left the parking lot. Then, she oversaw the receipts and the closing up herself.

"No. Not really. I'm coming down with a lousy headache."

"I've got some ibuprofen in my locker."

"No! No." She sighed. "Maybe I'm coming down with something."

P.D. didn't know why she felt it necessary to lie to her

manager. But she didn't want to explain herself, and she didn't want anyone knowing where she was going. *Sheesh*. The town grapevine would have a heyday with that.

"Would you mind?" she asked again. "My keys are in my desk drawer. If you could add up the receipts and put the night's earnings in the deposit box at the bank on your way home . . ."

"Sure. No problem."

P.D. squirmed a little when Bart seemed touched by her trust in his abilities.

"Thanks."

Before she was required to explain anything more, she dodged through the rear delivery door and scrambled in her purse for her keys. Climbing into her truck, she revved the engine and waited for the stuttering grumble to grow even. Then she backed out and turned onto the highway.

She wasn't sure what she intended to do. It wasn't conscious thought, but instinct that caused her to drive south. Before she knew it, she was turning into the winding gravel lane that led to Taggart Hollow.

At first, she drove slowly, afraid that she might catch up to Elam—and wouldn't that be swell? He'd think she was checking up on him. But after flicking off her lights, and easing around the corner toward the Big House, she was able to see that Elam's truck was nowhere to be found.

Just in case, she parked her vehicle near a copse of aspen by the side door. Then she took the steps two at a time and knocked softly on the screen.

She'd always loved the Big House. The structure was quintessential turn-of-the-century farmhouse with a wide wraparound porch, ornate timber arches and dormers, and a river rock foundation. Earlier Taggarts had planned on housing several generations within its walls, because it was one of the largest homes that P.D. had ever seen. Nevertheless, it looked as if it had grown out of the earth rather than being built.

A light flicked on in the kitchen and she heard uneven footsteps approaching. *Thump-tap. Thump-tap.* Thank heavens. Bodey.

The door swung wide and Bodey's brows rose in surprise when he saw P.D.

"Isn't it about closing time at Vern's?" he asked, opening the screen for her to come in.

"Yeah. I asked Bart to lock up."

Bodey's eyes narrowed. "That's not your usual routine. Is something wrong?"

"No . . . yes." She sighed. "I don't know."

He motioned toward the table. "You want something? Beer? Soda? Coffee?"

Her nerves were already jangling with caffeine but she still said, "Have you got any Diet Coke?"

"Yeah, sure."

He swung toward the counter and took a glass from the cupboard, filled it with ice from the freezer, then snagged a beer for himself and a can of soda for P.D. Then, after handing them to her, he maneuvered gingerly back to the table.

As P.D. sank into a chair, he hooked one for himself and leaned his crutches against the polished wood.

"So what's up?"

She took her time pouring her drink into the glass, then finally admitted, "Elam came to Vern's to talk about the Games."

Bodey frowned, the beer bottle hovering in front of his mouth. "He didn't back out of the deal, did he?"

"No. At least I don't think so. At least . . . I hope he doesn't . . ." Realizing she was making a mess of things, she asked, "Would you happen to have his phone number?"

Bodey grimaced. "Elam doesn't have a land line up to the cabin and he stopped using his cell once he came back to Bliss. Said he needed his *privacy*." He took a swig. "What he really meant was that he was tired of people asking how he was doing."

"Oh." P.D. used the tip of her finger to poke at the ice in her glass.

"*Should* we be asking how he's doing?"

"I—" P.D. exhaled a puff of air and said, "I don't know. It's a long story."

Bodey shrugged. "I've got nowhere to go since I've been sidelined from the next few Cattle Cutting events. Even if I did, I couldn't get there fast," he said, slapping the orthopedic boot.

"Well," she drawled, searching for the right way to explain the evening's events. "He came into Vern's and I fed him."

"Always a plus."

"Then we talked about the Games."

"Was he grousing about the competition?"

"No. Not really."

"That's good." He suddenly grinned. "What did he think about the costume requirement?"

Her breath escaped in a semblance of a laugh. "He wasn't thrilled, but he didn't balk too much."

Bodey crowed in delight. "Maybe it will inspire him to shave off that beard and trim his hair. He looks like a raggedy sheepherder who hasn't seen civilization in a while."

P.D. had known Bodey long enough to realize that, to those employed in raising cattle, being called a "sheepherder" was cutting criticism.

In her opinion, Elam didn't look "raggedy" at all. There was something wild and untamed about his current look, but she wasn't complaining.

"So . . . what happened?" Bodey prompted.

"I got called into the kitchen for a few minutes," she said, neatly avoiding the encounter in the storage room.

"And?"

In a rush, she said, "And the band started playing Manny's song, 'Annabel.'"

Bodey froze with his beer partway to his lips, then whispered, "Shit."

"I'll say."

"I'm assuming Elam didn't take it well?"

She shook her head. "He went white as a ghost, then left Vern's like his seat was on fire."

Bodey shook his head, staring sightlessly ahead of him. "Hell. Maybe I shouldn't have pushed him into helping."

"But he seemed fine up until then."

Bodey set his bottle on the table and leaned forward to rest his elbows on his knees, seeming to examine his laced fingertips.

"It's been three years since she died." He cleared his throat. "When he came home for the funeral, Elam was devastated." Bodey looked up to meet P.D.'s gaze. "I swear, Annabel was the only girl he ever dated. As far as he was concerned, he loved her so much the sun rose and set in her eyes."

P.D. felt a twinge of jealousy, then a twinge of pain. No one had ever cared for her like that. Not even her own parents.

"After the services, Jace and I tried to talk him into staying with us as long as his leave would allow. But the minute the Navy would let him work again, he headed back to Afghanistan." Bodey's voice grew husky. "I honestly thought they'd be sending him home in a box. He was so angry . . . so . . ." Bodey scrubbed his face with his hands. "I can't tell you how relieved we all were when we found out he was coming home. He was injured, sure, but he was alive."

Silence throbbed in the kitchen until P.D. was compelled to ask, "So what do I do now?"

Bodey swore under his breath. "I don't know. Just . . . act like nothing has happened. That would be my best piece of advice. Getting him involved in the Games has been the first thing to get Elam off that damned mountain since he came home."

She nodded, gathering her purse and standing. "Thanks, Bodey."

She was at the door when Bodey spoke again.

"You've caught his eye, P.D."

She whirled to face him, gasping. "What?"

"Don't play coy. We've been friends for too long. For a minute this morning, Elam was looking at you like you were a tall drink of water and he was a thirsty man."

She flushed, hoping that Bodey hadn't seen her own hungry glances.

"Be careful. I thought he was finally ready to move on. But if what you said was true . . ."

"You've got it all wrong, Bodey. He doesn't look at me any differently than he would any other woman."

"Uh-huh."

Again, she felt the heat rise in her cheeks and she prayed that Bodey wouldn't sense that she and Elam . . . that they'd . . . that . . .

"This time, it isn't Elam I'm worried about," Bodey continued. "It's you."

"Honestly, Bodey—"

"Just don't expect too much of him, okay? You want to have some fun . . . fantastic. But I wouldn't count on his being able to offer you much more. Elam might be one of those men who can only commit once in his lifetime."

She waved a dismissing hand toward Bodey—as if to say he was being totally ridiculous. But as she pushed her way out into the cool night air, she couldn't entirely will away the twinge of regret that settled in her chest.

Because Elam wouldn't be the first person in her life to kick her butt to the curb as soon as he was tired of her company.

ELAM straightened from the ornate wrought-iron railing he'd been attaching to the rear deck and reached for the Styrofoam cup of coffee he'd left sitting on the edge.

In an instant, he became aware of the cool night breeze, the rumble of the generator, and the glare of the spotlight that illuminated the work he'd done. He'd been keeping a punishing pace, trying to push all but the most rudimentary thoughts from his head. But as he set down his drill, it wasn't the finished length of railing that captured his attention. Instead, it was the silence. The stillness. The sense of being alone.

Wiping his brow with his sleeve, he dragged air into his lungs and glanced at his watch. Only eleven. And another solitary night stretched ahead of him.

Elam swore, suddenly conscious of his aching muscles and the fact that this house might be nearly finished, but there was no electricity—and the only nod to comfort was an air mattress and a sleeping bag.

Sighing, he dumped the contents of his coffee cup onto the

ground. Right now, he'd kill for a hot shower and a comfortable bed.

Almost as soon as the thoughts sifted through his brain, he realized that both of those things could be easily obtained. All he had to do was make a trip down the hill to the Big House.

In the past, he would have resisted the urge—at least until morning after everyone had begun preparing for the day. But tonight, he found that the glittering lights in the valley below beckoned to him, reminding him that his solitude was self-imposed. Besides, he'd promised to help P.D. learn how to shoot. And for that, he'd need to gather some supplies.

Killing the generator, he wrestled his keys out of his jeans pocket and climbed into his truck.

Elam could have made the trip blindfolded. Even as a kid, this spot on the hill had been his own special haunt when he needed to think things through. But tonight, he found himself taking the trip in reverse, returning to the valley nicknamed Taggart Hollow. A low moon provided enough light for him to see the familiar layout of the ranch. The house was the centerpiece, and beyond it was the modern barn, corrals, and paddocks that Elam's father had finished just before his death, and the huge metal equipment building they referred to as "The Shed," which Jace had constructed only a few years earlier.

Elam slowed the truck and paused to enjoy the view. Even though he took this same route several times a day, he felt as if he was seeing the compound with new eyes. The Taggart Ranch had been home to the family since Josiah Taggart, freshly discharged from the Union Army, joined the railroad crews and followed them west. After the meeting of the rails in Promontory, he'd found himself tired of the grind of laying rails. With little more than his horse, a rifle, and fifty dollars in gold in his pocket, he'd headed toward the mountains he'd grown to love.

According to legend, the moment he'd entered Taggart Hollow, he'd known he'd found his home. And when he'd made a trip to Bliss and seen the woman behind the counter of the land office, he was sure he'd found his mate as well. But his bride-to-be hadn't been so easy to convince. So he'd built her a cabin in a stand of trees near the creek and courted her with wildflowers and snippets of poetry. Their home—or the "Little House," as it was known—still stood a few hundred yards away from the rest of the compound, shaded by pines and willows that had grown to gigantic proportions.

Since then, each generation had added to the holdings. Josiah's sons had farmed, clearing the land and adding acreage. Elam's great-grandfather had added cows, making his fortune when cattle was king. He'd commissioned local artisans to build the "Big House," a huge Craftsman Era dwelling rich with hand-carved details, river rock foundations, and lodge pole beams. He'd brought a bride home from England, shocking the community with his choice of an aristocratic "foreigner" rather than a local girl, but it was soon clear it was a love match. When the stock market crashed and beef prices plunged, he'd lost nearly everything. Somehow, despite the strictures of the Great Depression, he'd still managed to hold on to the land.

Their grandfather had served with distinction in World War II, survived time as a POW, and fallen in love with a schoolteacher from New Zealand, who'd also been interred. Bringing her home to the peace of the mountains, he'd doubled their acreage yet again and brought the ranch back into the black.

Even Elam's father had drawn his inspiration from the land and his college sweetheart—a woman he'd courted for three years before her parents would allow her to marry. Anticipating the day he would bring her home as his bride, he'd renovated the Big House, bringing it into the modern age. Then, he'd done the same for the family business, increasing the amount of cattle they ran by purchasing more pastureland, especially for summer grazing, as well as stud and training services for their purebred quarter horses.

Putting the truck into gear again, Elam eased down the winding road, clattering over the bridge that spanned the creek. Despite the upheaval and tragedies that had befallen the family in the last few years, Taggart Enterprises was still going strong. When their parents had been killed, Jace had somehow been able to take over their father's duties as ranch manager, as well as overseeing the crop production, which fed their stock. Although young, Bodey had assumed most of the responsibilities in caring for the horses and cattle. Sure, since leaving the military, Elam had come to work with the colts every day. But as he pulled up next to the house, he realized that he might have shown up, but his head hadn't been in the game.

That needed to change. He was a part of this family, but he was also a partner in the family business and it was time for him to pull his weight.

Despite the late hour, lights were blazing from the kitchen windows. As Elam stepped through the door, Bodey looked up from the stove. The scent of searing meat filled the room.

Elam crossed to peer over Bodey's shoulder. "You think it's dead yet?" he asked wryly. As usual, Bodey was burning the shit out of a T-bone steak.

Bodey regarded him with surprise. "What brings you here?"

Elam's brows rose. "Any reason why you don't want me here?"

"No, I—" Bodey swore when popping grease splattered on his hand. Reaching for a fork, he transferred the meat onto a plate.

As he reached to turn off the burner, Elam deftly snagged utensils from a nearby caddy, then swiped the plate and moved to the table.

"What the hell, Elam?" Bodey groused when he discovered his missing food. "I thought you ate at Vern's."

"That was hours ago and I'm hungry again," Elam said, then realized it was true. Something in P.D.'s food must have kick-started his appetite because the sight of the steak was making his stomach grumble.

Bodey opened his mouth to argue, then sighed, turned the burner back on. Reaching into the fridge, he grabbed the package of steaks wrapped in plastic and white butcher paper.

The swinging door to the kitchen flapped open and Jace stepped through.

"Might as well cook one for me, too," he said, his long limbs eating up the distance to the sink, where he began washing his hands. "Whoever the hell tracked grass all over the rug had better start wrestling with the vacuum. The cleaning lady just came yesterday and those cattle buyers are going to have to come into the house to finalize the paperwork."

He looked expectantly at Elam, then Bodey. "Well? Any confessions?"

"Barry did it," Elam said automatically, just as Bodey parroted the same thing. But Elam caught the way Bodey nudged his dirt- and grass-covered boots farther under a chair.

"What are you doing here?" Jace asked Elam as he reached for a towel.

Elam lifted his hands. "Geez, do I need an engraved invitation?"

"No. Bodey just said that—"

Bodey slapped Jace on the shoulder, then quickly returned his attention to the steaks he'd placed in the pan.

Elam's eyes narrowed. "Bodey said what?" he asked suspiciously.

Jace had never been much good at hiding his thoughts—and clearly something was up, but Jace merely said, "He said you'd be taking his place in the Games—which is great. P.D.'s a good friend."

Friend?

Or *friend*.

Elam couldn't tell anything from either brother's expression. Jace adopted such a look of innocence that a choir boy would have been proud. He seemed overly concerned with wiping the last drop of moisture from his hands while Bodey was completely absorbed in his duties as a chef.

"What's going on?"

"Mmm?" It was Bodey who looked up. "Nothing. Just haven't seen you here at the Big House much lately."

"I came to get some weapons and ammo so P.D. and I could practice in the morning. Do you mind if P.D. uses your gear, Bode?"

Bodey shook his head. "No. Not at all. Knock yourself out."

Since his brothers were still acting weird, Elam added, "And I decided, while I was here, that I'd grab a hot shower and crash in a real bed. Any objections?"

As if the words broke the odd tension in the room, his brothers suddenly relaxed.

"Hell, no," Jace assured him. "Come morning, you can help Bodey with the vacuuming."

Then the good-natured ribbing began as Jace opened the refrigerator to gather steak sauce and a tub of salad, ranch dressing, and several bottles of beer. But as their voices rose, Jace quickly held a finger to his lips. "Damnit, keep it down. You'll wake up Barry."

"Maybe he'll want Bodey to cook him a steak, too," Elam offered.

Bodey rolled his eyes.

Jace adopted a look of horror. "Shit, it took me an hour to get him to go to sleep!"

Elam felt his lips lift in a ghost of a smile even as the weight in his chest seemed to ease. But Bodey couldn't help himself. As he slapped a plate with a still steaming steak in front of Jace, he said, "Then you'll have to read him another bedtime story. So what?"

Jace's eyes narrowed and he lifted his fork in warning.

"Damnit, if either of you wake him up, I'll be sure to let him know that both of you blamed him for the grass. Then I'll suggest the three of you stay up for a *Star Wars* marathon."

This time, it was Bodey who assumed a patent look of horror.

And for the first time in as long as he could remember, Elam suddenly felt . . . at home.

FOUR

———◆———

P.D. didn't know what she should expect as her pickup bounced and jounced over the ruts leading to Elam's cabin the next morning. Several times, she'd chickened out about coming up the mountain at all. She'd even called Bodey to tell him to get word to Elam that she wasn't able to meet with him. But she hung up before he could answer his phone. Bodey had advised her to act as if nothing had happened, so she was going to have to go through with their plans whether or not Elam was still in the mood to give her a shooting lesson.

Once again, she'd screwed up her courage enough to drive through Taggart Hollow. But this time, rather than turning at the Big House, she took the service road leading up to Elam's cabin.

As she rolled to a stop and leaned forward to peer through her cracked windshield, the yard looked empty. There were no tools scattered on the workbenches or a shirt discarded in the warmth of the late-morning sun.

Damn. She'd probably chased the man off for good last night—and she had no clue how to undo the damage. Should she apologize for the random song the band had decided to play? Or should she beg him to give her another chance to . . . what? Be his friend?

As she sat there, the sunlight reflecting off the dented hood of the secondhand truck she'd bought to haul produce from local farms to Vern's, she wasn't even thinking of the Wild West Games anymore. Yeah, her half of the possible prize money had seemed like a perfect way to pay for a much-needed addition to the kitchen, but she'd always known that winning was a long shot. And now, remembering Elam sitting in the darkness, the blood draining from his features, was enough to make her reconsider.

It had been a stupid idea. Stupid, stupid, *stupid*! She might be able to keep her backside on a horse and hike the foothills, but she sure as hell couldn't handle a team or shoot a—

A loud metal bang and the jolt of her tailgate being dropped made her jump. When she glanced in her rearview mirror, she caught sight of Elam hefting a heavy metal box into the bed, then a padded rifle case.

Relieved, she saw that she'd overlooked Elam's truck. The shiny silver Dodge Ram was parked in the shade of a stand of aspens next to an older Ford with a toolbox in its bed. Without a word, Elam made another trip back to the Dodge, grabbing another weapons case from the backseat of the extended cab, and a second ammo box. He threw them into the bed with the others, relatched the tailgate, then rounded the truck and wrenched open the door.

"Morning," he said as he folded himself into the passenger seat.

P.D.'s heart began pounding like crazy in her chest, and she had to fight to keep from grinning. Although Elam was still quiet, reserved, he showed no other signs that he'd been driven from her restaurant the previous evening.

"Morning."

Elam wore a cowboy hat low on his brow, casting his face in sharp planes and angles. To her delight, she could see it wasn't a "fancy" hat like those worn by city folk—with their seven-hundred-dollar flashy boots and their stiff, ill-fitting cowboy hats—who came to Bliss to hunt or fish. Elam's headgear had obviously been worn well and often, probably more for work than for town since the brim was streaked with dust, and a darker ribbon of color next to the band showed where the hat had faded in the sunlight. He slouched in his seat and pointed to the dirt track that headed higher into the foothills.

"Head up that way," he said. "There's a natural berm toward the top that we can use for target practice."

She put the truck in gear, carefully maneuvering through the ruts caused by spring rains and the heavy trucks that had delivered supplies for the cabin. Once they passed Elam's house and began to climb, the surface grew smoother and she was able to go a little faster.

"What's this?" Elam asked, gesturing to the cooler that sat between them on the bench seat.

"Lunch."

One of his brows rose, drawing attention to those changeable hazel eyes that were more gold and green today.

"Are you trying to make me fat?"

She allowed her grin to slip free. "I promised to feed you."

"Dinner. You promised dinner."

Her stomach fluttered in anticipation. Did that mean he was still planning on coming to Vern's later? If so, she was going to have a word with the band. Tonight, they would play nothing but happy, happy, happy songs.

"I didn't want you fainting from hunger with a loaded pistol cradled in your hands," she said—and why, oh why, did the words sound so dirty the minute they fell from her lips?

He eyed her for a moment—as if he, too, had made the ribald connection—but thankfully, he let the comment pass. "So are most of the recipes at Vern's yours?"

"About half," she admitted. "I've got a great chef I persuaded to move here from Logan. He was ready to leave the rat race of a college town. But I love to experiment with sauces and pastries."

"You do good work." He lifted the lid and peered inside, revealing the ice packs, boxed lunches, and bottles of soda. "It smells good," he said, closing the cooler again.

"Peppered turkey on homemade sourdough bread, my

famous crock-aged pickles, a three-cabbage slaw, and Smack-Yo-Mama chocolate cake."

This time, both of his brows rose. And—*yes!*—some of the tension eased from around his mouth.

"Smack . . . what?"

"You know. 'It's so good you'll—'"

"Smack your mama," he finished. "Where on earth did you learn to cook like that?"

P.D. shrugged, slowing for a sharp turn. "You might say that my parents were throwbacks to the seventies flower-power movement. We traveled the country in an old school bus that they'd painted in psychedelic colors gathered from the cast-off bins of local hardware stores. Summer and River Raines, my parents—and yes, those were their real names—weren't too fond of work, but they loved to barter. So now and then, when money was tight, they'd offer to wash dishes or clean tables for food. I was exposed to a lot of regional cooking and produce, and I paid attention. Plus—" She stopped, wondering if she could offer him a more painful kernel of truth. But after witnessing his own naked anguish the night before, she knew she deserved to give him at least that much. "There wasn't a whole lot to eat when I was growing up, so I became horribly preoccupied with food. I pored over recipes in the newspapers like other kids read the comics."

The air between them pounded with the intimacy of her confession, but thankfully, Elam didn't offer any pity for her sucky childhood. She couldn't have borne that. Instead, he said, "And before you knew it, cooking became so much more fun than the physics lab."

"Exactly."

The road widened in front of them, exposing a sandy bluff where the vegetation had sloughed away. They weren't the first people to use the area for target practice, because a pair of half-ton straw bales had been propped against the slope and scraps of paper targets fluttered in the breeze.

"Is this it?"

"Yeah. Pull over there." He pointed to a spot near a copse of scrub oak.

After she'd parked the truck and killed the engine, he motioned for her to join him at the back of the truck. "What do you know about firearms?"

He was watching her so intently, she feared her inexperience might disappoint him.

"I know which end to avoid."

She thought she saw a glint of humor in his eyes, but his lips remained grim. With his overgrown hair and beard, and the hat pulled low over his hawk-like brow, he looked like . . .

He looked like a brooding hero from the historical romance novels tucked away in her desk drawer.

"That sounds like a good place to start," he said in answer to her comment.

He handed her two bent pieces of wire and a paper target with concentric rings in varying shades of black and gray. The whole thing was smaller than a dinner plate—and the bull's eye was a little bigger than a fifty-cent piece.

"You think I'm going to hit this?" she asked skeptically.

"Yup."

"You're crazy," she muttered under her breath. Clearly, he thought she'd exaggerated her inexperience. But she obediently marched toward the straw bales and tacked the targets in place with what looked like a pair of overgrown hairpins. Then she turned back, took two steps . . .

And stumbled to a halt.

"Lord a-mercy," she whispered under her breath.

Elam Taggart stood before her, the embodiment of every cowboy fantasy she'd ever entertained—and she wasn't talking about a modern "ride the fence line with an ATV Ranger" kind of cowboy. She was talking about a bodice-ripping, gun-slinging, blazing, historical romance hero with a capital *H* kind of cowboy.

In the scant amount of time it had taken her to prepare the target, Elam had shrugged out of his Carhartt jacket to reveal that he was dressed in a button-down Western shirt that he'd carelessly rolled up to his elbows. And once again, she was struck by the elegance of his hands, the dark hair that dusted his forearms. Over his shirt, he'd donned a leather vest so supple and well worn that it fit Elam's chest as if it had been painted on. A hundred years ago, a gold watch might have dangled across his flat stomach, but a pair of safety glasses had been tucked into one of the many pockets instead. A leather belt had been threaded through his jeans, and she'd bet the oval buckle had been a prize from a rodeo or cow cutting competition. But even more astonishing—and arousing—was the intricately tooled leather holster slung low on his hips. As P.D. watched, Elam bent to adjust the thigh string around a pair of black jeans that coated his lower half like a second skin.

God bless America! If this was how good Elam looked in his own clothing, Helen was going to have a field day dressing him for the Wild West Awards Banquet.

Unaware of her regard, he turned away, opening one of the weapons cases to remove a pair of beautiful pearl-handled Rugers and slide them into place. P.D. knew they were Rugers—expensive Rugers—because she'd been poring through a backlog of SASS *Chronicle* magazines that Helen had provided so P.D. could familiarize herself with the period clothing and accessories she would need for the competition.

Elam glanced up, then motioned for her to join him. "Get over here."

She stumbled toward him, then cursed herself for having all the grace of a newborn colt. Good gravy. If she couldn't look at him now without becoming all wobbly, how was she supposed to endure four days of this man in period costume?

Elam retrieved another holster from the case. "You can use Bodey's getup for now."

P.D. was immediately inundated with horror. *Crap!* Bodey was as big around as a beanpole. What if it didn't fit? The last thing she needed was to pull attention to the fact that, as her mother was fond of saying, she "had an Amazon's physique with sturdy peasant birthing hips"—which was Summer Raines's way of saying that P.D. was too tall, big chested, and voluptuous for her own good.

Elam bent toward her, looping the heavy leather belt around her hips—and miracle of miracles, he could actually fasten the damn thing well in the middle of the array of holes. As he bent to secure the buckle, Elam's fingers brushed against her body, low on her belly, and she prayed he couldn't feel the way her muscles twitched in reaction. *Damn.* She'd worn an old T-shirt, anticipating the dust and gunpowder they would encounter. What she hadn't counted on was the way her nipples began to harden beneath the fabric.

He stood and turned his back to her, and P.D. exhaled in a rush—not realizing that she'd kept air trapped in her lungs all that time. But her relief was short-lived when he faced her again, handing her a pair of amber protective glasses and spongy earplugs.

"Put these on."

She donned the protective gear while Elam did the same. Then he grabbed another set of Rugers from the padded case and shut the lid. "These are Bodey's as well." He slid one of the pistols into the holster, then shifted so that he was beside her, their shoulders brushing.

"This particular pistol has a capacity for six bullets, but for safety's sake, you only want to load it with five. Keep the empty chamber under the hammer."

He could have been speaking Greek—and her confusion must have shown, because he handed her the pistol. "Let's start with the basics."

With the Ruger unloaded, he showed her how to hold the pistol with two hands, arms extended. Patiently, he explained the mechanics of the gun and how to aim. Then, filling a leather pouch at the back of his holster with bullets, he led her to a spot about twenty feet away from the target.

"You need to stand like this."

He demonstrated the stance she should take—one foot forward, the other slightly back—and had her practice sighting in on the target and dry-firing the weapon. Then, he handed her five bullets.

"Load it like I showed you."

Nervously, she released the cylinder, slipping the bullets into place, and then carefully shut it again so that the hammer was even with the empty chamber.

"Now, get a bead on the center of the target."

She raised the gun, but Elam stopped her, stepping behind her and encircling her with his own arms to correct her position. For the life of her, the fact that she held a loaded firearm wasn't nearly as disconcerting as the way he leaned in toward her, his chest nudging her back, his arms sure and strong around her, his hips pressed against her buttocks. And he smelled good. It wasn't fair that this man could smell so good—especially since they'd been out in the sun for an hour and she'd begun to "glow" a long time ago.

But what was really pitiful was that she couldn't allow herself to sink into the sensual storm of sensations. Not when she knew that Elam's grief was still so raw that she could have been a post rather than a woman. He wasn't ready to hold anyone in his arms, let alone someone like her. Someone who was so clearly . . . not Annabel.

Even though she couldn't bring herself to regret that kiss.

And she prayed he hadn't regretted it too much either.

"Now squeeze the trigger slowly. Don't jerk it. Just squeeze," he said against her ear.

Lordy, Lordy, how could the rumble of his voice and the tickle of his breath be so arousing?

Get a grip, P.D. Get a grip.

"Is it going to be loud?" she whispered, somehow loath to do anything noisy or boisterous that might force Elam to step away.

"A little. But the earplugs will take care of most of it."

She fought to keep the sights lined up even as the unaccustomed weight of the pistol fought a war with gravity. Elam steadied her with one palm under her hand and the other beneath her arm.

"Ready?"

She squeezed her eyes closed in anticipation of the noise and felt Elam's lips against her hair. "Open your eyes. You can't see what you're shooting at with them scrunched shut like that."

P.D. forced herself to look down the barrel again, line up the sights, and . . .

Bam!

She squeaked when the pistol reared back. The scent of cordite teased her nostrils, bringing with it faint memories of Fourth of July fireworks and sparklers. Squinting, she looked at the target. There, in the upper-right corner was a neat black hole.

"I hit the target," she whispered in disbelief. "I hit the target!"

She turned toward Elam, but he held her tightly in place. "Do it again. Empty your rounds, but make sure to carefully aim each shot."

P.D. did as she was told, the black holes marching closer to the center until the last one was slightly off center. Crowing in delight, she intently listened to Elam's instructions as he showed her how to clear the brass and reload. Soon, she was using both pistols, drawing first one gun from her holster, emptying it, then moving on to its mate.

They shot the Rugers for nearly an hour before Elam thought she was competent enough with the pistols. Then he brought out a Henry rifle with shiny brass accents, and the lessons began again—how to load, aim, and fire; how to safely carry the weapon; how to reload on the fly. Then, after at least a dozen targets had been shredded and another one tacked to the bales, he brought out the shotgun.

The first ram of the butt against her shoulder was enough to convince P.D. that she was "not a shotgun kind of gal." But by the end of Elam's tutoring session, she could load, aim, and fire with relative competence. At least for a beginner.

But when Elam pinned a set of targets to the bales and emptied both pistols, a rifle, and the double-barreled shotgun in a matter of seconds, she knew she was in the presence of a master. Even more telling, she was completely turned on by a man who could handle his weapon properly. Pun intended.

It was hours later, when the ammo containers were empty and the ground was littered with brass, that they were forced to stop. While P.D. gathered the casings, Elam stowed away the weapons and their holsters.

"How about lunch in the shade of the cabin?" Elam suggested. "That way we can wash up."

Since her hands were grimy from powder and the

ever-present blowing dust, she nodded in agreement, tossing him the keys. "You drive."

She didn't want to admit it, but after so many hours holding the heavy weapons, her arms felt like overcooked spaghetti.

But Elam obviously knew what was going on. "You'll be sore tonight, especially the shoulder that's been absorbing the shock of the shotgun. Normally, I wouldn't have kept you at it so long, but you seemed to be enjoying yourself."

P.D. laughed self-consciously as she sank into the passenger seat. "My peace-loving, PETA-promoting parents would die of shock and horror if they ever found out how I spent the afternoon. As far as they're concerned, the Republican Party is the Antichrist and the NRA is the devil's legion. Woe to anyone who even thinks of owning a weapon."

Elam laughed. He actually laughed. Granted, it was a little rusty sounding—a grunt of humor. But his lips twitched. And for a moment, the shadows eased from his eyes.

Then he started the truck and offered, "Imagine what they'd do if I took you hunting."

AFTER washing up at the pump, P.D. and Elam spread a checkered tablecloth and the food P.D. had brought on the front deck overlooking the valley, then settled with their backs against the wall, legs extended. P.D. handed him what looked like a white shoebox, but when Elam opened it, he found a thick sandwich, a tub of coleslaw, a pair of pickles sealed in plastic wrap, and a see-through container holding a thick slice of cake.

"The bright green pickle is one of my Super-Sour Dillies, and the smaller one is the Hot and Sweet."

"You made these?"

"Mmm-hmm."

Elam settled the box on his lap, suddenly ravenously hungry—which was strange. Until meeting P.D., he couldn't remember the last time he'd consciously wanted food. He'd worked hard and eaten by rote. But since she'd come along, he walked around with a growling belly that couldn't wait for another one of her meals.

He unwrapped the sandwich and took a big bite, then closed his eyes at the succulent combination of peppered turkey—not from a package, but sliced off the bird—bacon, lettuce, and something sweet and spicy he couldn't identify.

"What's on this?" he asked around a mouthful of food.

"Cranberry jalapeño jam."

"Wow."

She laughed at his tone of reverence and he took another bite, chancing another surreptitious glance at P.D.

Damn, if she wasn't pretty—but not with the artificial painted beauty of a fashion model. She was the poster child for the Girl-Next-Door with eyes the color of a summer sky and those freckles across her nose. She'd worn her hair in a long braid that morning, but the wind had played havoc with the style, teasing the fawn-colored curls free to frame her face. Near her temple, there was a streak of cordite, probably from trying to tame a strand behind her ear. Her cheeks were pink from the sun and the breeze and her sheer excitement at having conquered her fear of firing a weapon. For a minute, Elam couldn't think of a damn thing but her smile.

But what really intrigued him was the streak of iron buried beneath her softness—as if the world had pushed her down a time or two, but she'd bounded to her feet again, ready to push back. Somehow, he sensed that she didn't do anything half-hearted. She would love as hard as she argued—and the makeup sex would be just as riotous.

The mere thought caused his gaze to dip down to the fullness of her breasts. The T-shirt she wore was old, baby soft, and clung to every curve and valley. He wondered if she knew that with that shirt on, he could see a hint of lace rimming the cups of her bra. If he looked hard enough, he might even see the rosy tips of her nipples.

Whoa.

Elam slammed his thoughts back into line and forced himself to look up, up to where she regarded the valley with an expression of . . .

Contentment. And guardedness. As if what she saw was too good to be true. He wondered if the childhood she'd spent on the road had left her wondering if anything was truly "permanent."

When she turned toward him, Elam quickly took a bite of his sandwich, knowing instinctively that she wouldn't be comfortable with how easily he'd read her thoughts.

"So I might not have to get you a costume after all," she said with a slow smile. "Once you strapped your pistols on, you looked ready to go."

There was something about her expression and the way that her own gaze feathered over his shirt and jeans that made Elam realize she hadn't been completely unaware of his inspection. He fought the sudden heat that streaked into his groin as she held his gaze, revealing that his attraction was far from one-sided.

Shifting uneasily, he tried to remember what she'd said. For the life of him, he felt as clumsy holding up his end of the conversation as a teenager at his first dance. Finally, remembering she'd been talking about his clothes, he took another quick bite to hide his hesitation and shrugged. "It's not anything I wouldn't wear to work on the ranch," he said once his mouth was clear enough to speak.

"Even the guns?"

"Well, maybe not the guns."

"Have you got a pair of chaps?"

Again, there was a note to her tone, an intensity that left him feeling like he was missing something. This conversation wasn't merely about his wardrobe. But for the life of him, he couldn't fathom why the exchange had begun to thrum with the slow heat of sexual awareness. "Sure. You want me to wear those, too?"

The color in her cheeks intensified and her gaze bounced away. "Why not?" she said, lifting her shoulder in a careless gesture.

Her response was so casual that Elam felt a rush of awareness, his skin prickling as if suddenly coming alive, his heart seeming to flip-flop in his chest.

P.D. Raines was turned on by his cowboy gear.

He was about to embark on a close-contact, Victorian-inspired romp in the woods with a woman who already wanted to eat him alive with her eyes—and he was only dressed in jeans and a cotton shirt. What would the addition of a pair of chaps, suspenders, and a leather vest do?

Elam cleared his throat. "What are you planning to wear?" he asked, taking a long swig of his soda.

Her nose wrinkled and she squinted up at a pair of fluffy clouds that were inching their way toward the sun. "The usual pioneer-bride ensemble. Long skirt, blouse. Pantalets. Corset."

Elam choked on his soda, then couldn't catch his breath and coughed some more. Dear God in heaven. P.D. Raines was already stacked like a brick outhouse. The thought of her breasts contained by a frilly corset . . .

He couldn't stop coughing, and P.D. finally leaned over to slap him on the back.

"Who knew the thought of me in costume could bring you to your knees?" she joked.

She had no idea how close she'd come to the truth. And when he finally stopped choking long enough for her to lean back, unwrap her pickle, and slide it into her mouth to suck on the end . . .

The rush of pure, unadulterated sex that raged through his body was so intense that he had the overpowering urge to sweep the food away and pin P.D. to the wall.

She must have caught a portion of his thoughts, because she glanced at him, then blushed furiously, and threw her pickle back into the box.

"I probably should get going," she said hastily.

Elam stopped her headlong departure by reaching out to lift one of the errant curls away from her forehead. The strand had a will of its own, wrapping around his finger, flashing copper in the sunlight. He became entranced by the color, the texture, the weight of her hair. And then, unable to stop himself, he skimmed the back of his knuckles down her cheek.

P.D. leaned into the caress, her eyes closing as she savored the contact. He wanted to kiss her—more than he'd wanted anything in a very long time. But even as he bent forward, reality loomed over him like a vulture. This was Bodey's girl.

Bodey's. And he was about to kiss her, here, in Annabel's favorite spot.

The thought was like a dousing of cold water. Elam snatched his hand back as if it had been burned. He must have tugged her hair because P.D.'s eyes flew open and he watched a montage of emotions cross her features: desire, surprise, and then humiliation.

Jumping to her feet, she gathered up the cooler and her own lunch box. "I guess I'll see you tonight."

"Tonight?" He couldn't tow his thoughts into line. Not when he was reeling beneath the impression that he should have kissed P.D. when he'd had the chance and let the consequences be damned. The last thing he wanted to do was hurt or embarrass her.

"Helen will drop by Vern's to help us with our costuming around eight and you'll want to grab a bite to eat first," she continued, her tone too bright.

"Sure." Elam nodded absentmindedly, but his attention was on the blush staining her cheeks and the wounded shadows that darkened her blue eyes. She couldn't possibly know why he'd pushed her away at the last minute.

He opened his mouth to explain, but P.D. was already backing away from him to the roughed-out staircase. She hadn't even bothered to grab the tablecloth, which still held part of his food.

"Bye, then."

Shit. Before he could even react, she'd bolted. Dropping the remains of his lunch into the box, he rushed to follow her, catching her wrist just as she opened the truck door to throw the cooler inside.

"Look, I'm sorry, but I—"

Before he could say another word, she launched herself into his arms, her mouth touching his—and it was as if a match had been touched to gasoline. Elam clutched her tightly against him, his lips slanting over hers as he pressed her back against the side of the truck. Her mouth opened, and his tongue plunged into her silken warmth. Passion flared through him like a wildfire, and he ground his hips against hers, one hand dropping to cup the luscious weight of her breast.

Dear God.

God.

She moaned against him, fighting to pull him even closer, her fingers gripping at his back, tunneling beneath his vest. More than anything, he wanted her to reach beneath his shirt and caress him, skin to skin.

But nearly as quickly as she'd thrown herself into his arms, she pushed him away.

Elam stood trembling like a kid on a first date, tongue-tied, not sure what to do. So he began with, "I'm sorry, I—"

P.D. held up a hand to silence him. "Don't. Just . . . don't." She stared down at the toe of her shoe for the longest time, then she slid into her truck and slammed the door.

He felt a moment of inexplicable panic. "I'll see you to-night, then."

When she met his gaze, he could see the determination in the crystal blue depths. Even more, he read an expression that looked very much like a dare. "*I'm* sure as hell not about to run away."

Then she revved the engine and drove down the hill.

FIVE

———•◦•———

F OR several long moments, Elam stood in the grip of P.D.'s
challenge. His body still pounded with the effects of her
nearness and his brain . . .

Well, his brain didn't know what to make of her. For too
long, he'd been slogging through his days like a bad-tempered
bear, and most people had been willing to give him his space.
But P.D. Raines was intent on testing the emotional bulwarks
he'd constructed. And her skirmishes, far from being the gentle
probings he'd encountered from a few of the braver women in
town, were nothing short of full-frontal attacks. Literally.

And damned if it hadn't left him with the urge to pump
his fist into the air in triumph.

Cursing softly under his breath, he moved through the trees
so that he could catch one last look at her truck as it barreled
around the turn at the base of the hill, then threaded the narrow
bridge over the river at near race car levels.

If she weren't Bodey's girl . . .

No. He couldn't go there. He wouldn't. Nothing broke the
bro code.

But as he returned to the cabin to clean up the remains of

their meal, he couldn't deny that he suddenly felt . . . as if he could breathe again. And damned if he wasn't tired of struggling—with his grief, his emotions, and even this damned cabin. Where only hours ago, he'd looked upon his attendance in the Wild West Games as a chore to be finished, he now relished the mental challenge, the physical demands, the . . .

The intriguing woman who would be alongside him.

Hell. He couldn't start thinking like that. He was going to have to spend every waking minute with P.D. Raines. And he couldn't start looking at her as a . . .

A woman.

But how in heaven's name was he supposed to ignore that fact when she was so . . . so . . .

Hot.

A grunt of humor emerged from his throat, taking him by surprise. Hell, yes, she was hot. Hot to look at and hot in his arms. But that didn't make it a good idea to even consider going down that road. She was probably one of his brother's ex-girlfriends— and wouldn't *that* make family gatherings awkward.

Hey, Elam, I've seen her naked.

Good hell Almighty! Why was he even thinking about such a thing? He wasn't planning on dating the woman. He would help her win her freaking Wild West Games and then they'd probably never see each other again.

Yeah, right.

In a town the size of Bliss, they were bound to bump into each other—and why, oh, why did that thought lead to an entirely different interpretation of "bumping into each other"? Did he honestly think he'd be able to keep his hands off her while they competed?

"You're a dumb ass, Elam," he muttered to himself. But this time, by focusing on the absurdity of his situation, the tightness eased from his chest and he took a deep shuddering breath, and another. And another.

And suddenly, he was out of his head and more in tune with things he'd forgotten to notice—the warmth of the day, the satisfaction of a good meal, and a hard-on that wouldn't quit.

He was committed to the Games, he reassured himself.

And there'd be hell to pay if he tried to back out. Bodey would ream him a new one.

But even as he insisted such a thing to himself, he realized that he wasn't even tempted to renege on his deal with P.D. Somehow, disappointing P.D. carried more weight than disappointing his brother. So that meant he and P.D. were stuck with each other for the duration.

And why, oh, why, did that cause "little Elam" to perk up again in joy?

Moving quickly, Elam gathered up the rest of the picnic items, carefully folding and stowing P.D.'s tablecloth in his truck so that he could return it later that evening. Then, reaching across the cab to the jockey box, he riffled through the receipts and weigh slips until he found his cell phone and the car charger. Revving the Dodge, he waited for enough power to operate the device and then quickly called Russell Branson, an old friend from high school who had a construction business.

Russell answered on the first ring. He apparently had caller ID because he said, "Elam, you son of a bitch. I was beginning to believe you'd forgotten how to use your damn phone."

Elam felt an unaccustomed tugging at the corners of his lips. "I guess all this clean living has gone to my head."

"Next, you'll be telling me you're Amish and you haven't bothered to connect the power to that hut you're building on the hill." There was a pause, then, "You *haven't* connected it yet, have you?"

"It's got power."

"Bet the wiring's done but you've still got nothing more than a generator going to charge your tools."

"You got me there." Elam tapped his thumb nervously on the steering wheel. "Actually, that's why I'm calling. I wondered if you had any time in your schedule? I'm about sick to death of this project, and I was hoping you could finish it up for me."

There was a moment of silence. Two. Three. Elam lifted the phone away from his ear, wondering if the call had been dropped, but then he heard Russ laughing and exclaiming, "Fuck, yeah! I told you I'd help when you started digging your hole, if you remember. It took you long enough to call."

"Yeah, well . . ." Uncomfortable with explaining his reasons, Elam said, "I don't know when you'll have a minute—"

"I'd reschedule all my projects if I needed to, but as luck would have it, the house my crew is working on has some drainage issues. For the past two days, an excavation crew has been pissing around up on the bench. In the meantime, my men have got their thumbs up their asses. How about we get going tomorrow morning?"

"That would . . ." Elam fought an unfamiliar tightness in his throat. "That would be great. Can you recommend a decorator as well?"

"Don't want to spend your time picking out paint chips and carpet samples, huh?"

"You know me. I'd rather have my head stapled to the floor."

Russ offered a blazing expletive in agreement. "Tell you what . . . my sister-in-law Noreen has been helping us out with that kind of thing—and she's really good at what she does. I'll have her gather her crap together and we'll all meet you in the morning. Then you can get on to doing whatever it is you need to be doing."

"Thanks, Russ. I owe you."

He'd no sooner ended his call with Russ than Elam dialed the number of the Big House. This time, it rang several times before an eager boy-man voice said, "This is Barry Taggart from Taggart Enterprises. Bodey's gone and there's no one here but me and Jace, and Jace is in the bathroom. He's swearing—even though he's told me I'm not supposed to swear. Ever. He must have eaten too much chili. How may I direct your call?"

Somewhere in the background, Elam heard Jace shouting back, *Damnit, Barry, don't tell them that!*

"Tell Jace to relax, Barry. It's Elam."

"Elam?" Barry echoed excitedly. Then, without backing away from the mouthpiece, he bellowed, "Jace! It's Elam! Elam's on the phone! I don't think he cares what you're doing in the bathroom!"

"Barry, try not to yell," Elam reminded his younger brother.

"Oh. Yeah. Sorry." But even after the reminder, his voice

remained an ear-splitting level. "Elam, are you coming to see me? I haven't seen you in a long, long, *long* time."

In truth, it had been less than three days, but to Barry, who'd suffered brain damage in the same accident that had killed their parents and little sister eight years ago, days were often confused with an eternity. As his little brother hurried on to tell him about the litter of kittens they'd found in the barn loft, and the trip on horseback to check on the summer pastures, Elam realized that even though he regularly came to the ranch to work, he hadn't really interacted with Barry much. He'd unconsciously isolated himself from his brothers as well as from the community.

As Barry continued his ecstatic monologue, Elam felt a wave of shame. After his return home, his brothers had been there to support him all along, and he'd withdrawn from them. Even when his actions had proven painful to them, they'd allowed him his space. But it was clear from Barry's reaction at least, that they hoped that he'd soon change his mind.

"Hey, Barry," Elam interrupted. "I'm coming down to the Big House to pick up some of my gear. Do you want to get a treat from the Corner?"

The "Corner" was nearly eight miles away and was one of Bliss's few gas stations and convenience stores. Barry loved the place because it had a small lunch counter in the back. Over the years, it had become the hangout for farmers and ranchers who needed something quick and hot to eat.

"Can we?" Barry asked excitedly. "Really? Can Jace come?"

"If he wants."

"And can we ride in your new truck?"

Elam's truck was a year old, but it would remain "new" to Barry until Elam purchased another one.

"You bet."

"I'll get my boots on!"

"No, wait! Barry?" The phone clattered, and Elam realized that Barry had abandoned it in favor of getting ready for the outing. Luckily, he must have been caught in the act because Jace's voice could be heard growing closer.

"Barry, did you hang up . . . No. You didn't. Hello, Elam."
Jace's voice rumbled with barely concealed surprise. Clearly,
he hadn't expected to hear from Elam so soon after their impromptu, late-night dinner.

Elam quickly explained, "I made the mistake of inviting
him to go to the Corner before telling him to give you the
phone."

"I hope you're already on your way here, because he's hop-
ping around the living room, trying to—Barry, put your socks
on first! You can't put your boots over bare feet!" Jace's tone
returned to normal. "What's up?"

"Hey, I don't want to interrupt if you've got important
business in the bathroom."

Jace choked on an expletive. "For your information, I was
in the bathroom cleaning up all the mud"—his voice rose
pointedly—"that a certain somebody left when he tried to wash
his irrigating boots in the tub!"

Not for the first time, Elam was struck by the way Jace had
slipped into a father role with their youngest brother. Barry
would turn sixteen this summer, but he required the supervision
of an eight-year-old. Jace's parenting skills might be a little
rough around the edges, but he was carefully straddling a line
between sibling support and parental authority.

"This can wait," Elam said.

"So can the mud. What's up?"

"I . . . uh . . ." It had been so long since he'd asked for anyone's help that Elam felt suddenly awkward. Even his voice
emerged with a rusty rasp. "I've called Russell Branson about
doing the finishing work on the cabin. It's about time I wrapped
up that project and spent more time working at the ranch."

There was a pause, then, "That sounds good. Real good."
There was no hiding his brother's pleasure at the idea.

"Anyway, I wondered if you'd mind checking on things
while I'm gone."

"No problem. Barry would get a kick out of riding up that
way. He's always happiest on the back of a horse."

"Thanks. I appreciate the help."

"All you have to do is ask."

Elam's throat tightened, but before he could think of a response, Jace suddenly swore and shouted, "Barry! Not those boots! I haven't got the mud off the—" He broke off what he'd been about to say. "Five minutes. You'd better be here in five minutes. Because if you aren't, Barry is probably going to meet you halfway."

P.D. wasn't sure what kind of mood Elam would be in when she saw him next. She still couldn't believe she'd driven away after uttering a remark that could only be interpreted as a flat-out dare. She'd probably sent the man fleeing into the hills.

But even as she tried to reassure herself that he'd responded to the kiss—in fact, he'd damn near come unglued when their lips had met—she couldn't help thinking that she'd plunged impetuously into a situation she might not be equipped to handle. But damnit, she hadn't been able to keep her hands off him another second! After a day spent with his arms around her, steadying her aim, she'd been wound tighter than a guitar string.

Which left her with two distinct consequences to her actions: Elam would back out of their agreement; or she'd be spending four days with him on the mountain fighting to keep her hands off him all over again. Either way, things were bound to get awkward. Really, really awkward.

"He's here."

"What?" P.D. had been so deep in her thoughts, she hadn't heard the door to her office open. Becky, one of her waitresses, leaned her head inside.

"Elam Taggart is here. So's Helen. They met up in the parking lot."

As quickly as she'd appeared, Becky disappeared again. With the weekend crowd, Vern's was filled to capacity and the waitstaff were busy. Because of that, P.D. had arranged for dinner to be laid out in her office, where she and Elam could have a few minutes of privacy. But Helen had arrived early, snatching away the chance for P.D. to talk to Elam before their costuming session.

"Damn, damn, damn," she whispered under her breath. She'd hoped to give him room to renege on their deal if he was determined to do so. But Helen would catch one look of him and start matchmaking.

Crap!

P.D. heard the rear service door open and Helen's familiar voice echoing off the walls.

". . . a sight for sore eyes, Elam Taggart! I swear, after a week of my husband's shooting buddies loading brass in my garage, I could use a change of scenery."

P.D. jumped from her office chair, nearly sending it crashing backward. "Crap," she muttered under her breath as she glanced in the mirror, then winced. Her cheeks were overly pink from an afternoon spent in the sun. Even worse, she hadn't thought to repair her makeup or run a comb through her hair.

Quickly, she smoothed a hand over the tresses, drawing them to the nape of her neck and twisting them into a knot. Then, she scrounged in her desk drawer for a pair of warped hairpins, just as Helen burst into her office.

"Look who I found in the parking lot," she exclaimed.

Elam stepped more hesitantly into the room, and suddenly, the walls shrank. P.D. saw the way his eyes roamed the small space, taking in the battered antique swooning couch and wooden dressing screen in one corner, the overstuffed leather wing-back chair and turn-of-the-century wood filing cabinets in the other, and the sturdy oak partners' desk and slag glass lamp that took up most of the remaining floor space. Then he looked at P.D. and she knew that somehow he'd interpreted the antique pieces for what they were, a symbol of her need for permanence. A place to belong.

Helen dropped a voluminous red-and-black carpetbag on the couch and quickly enfolded P.D. in a hug. "Land sakes, it's good to see you!"

"How have all the SASS shoots gone this spring?"

"Good. Really, really good. Winter Range nearly wiped out my stock, so I'll have to get sewing," Helen said, referring to one of the Single Action Shooting Society competitions held each year in Arizona. "Now, let's get the two of you measured. I was hoping I could stay a little and chat, but I promised Sydney I'd be home in an hour. We've got grandchildren coming to spend the night."

She whirled to face a bemused Elam, eyeing him up and down with a keen eye. "Well, God Bless America," she muttered under her breath.

P.D. felt her cheeks flame, even though she knew there was no way Elam could interpret the true sentiment behind the remark.

Without another word, Helen turned to her carpetbag, and much like Mary Poppins, she opened it wide to remove a tape measure, clipboard and pen, several pairs of twill pants, a half-dozen linen shirts, a pin cushion, and a pair of scissors. Moving toward Elam, she kept up a running monologue on the well-being of her nine grandchildren while she quickly took Elam's measurements and relayed them to P.D., who wrote them down on a form mounted to the clipboard.

P.D. tried to concentrate on the task. Really, she did. But her eyes kept straying to Elam's lithe frame as Helen's hands roamed freely over the planes and angles. What P.D. wouldn't give for an excuse to do the same.

Finally, just when P.D. feared she would spontaneously combust, Helen handed the trousers and shirts to Elam, then added suspenders, bright yellow sleeve garters, and a vest, and told him to try them on.

"I think they'll do fine. But I'll need to mark the hems."

To P.D.'s estimation, Elam was looking a little shell-shocked. His gaze ping-ponged from P.D. to Helen as if they expected him to strip there and then. "Is there a . . ."

"There's a restroom down the hall to the left," P.D. said, throwing him a lifeline.

When he disappeared, Helen cast P.D. a knowing look. "I remembered him being a dish, but . . . Holy moley! Is that what the Navy does to a man?"

"*Shh!*" P.D. said quickly, rushing to close the door. "He'll hear you!"

Helen laughed. "I'm sure he's used to female admiration by now." She returned to her carpetbag. "Strip."

"What? I can't—"

"He's not going to come barging in without knocking. And I've only got a few more minutes to get this done before Syd lights a distress flare. He's Super-Grandpa if he's only got one or two kids, but if I don't hurry, the nine of them will have him duct taped to a chair before he can say 'Boo!' And while Elam's clothing is merely a matter of finding something premade that fits, I've got your ball gown to make, and for that, I need your measurements in the corset. So strip."

Sighing, P.D. reluctantly shucked off her boots and jeans. Then, after donning the camisole Helen handed her, she stripped off her bra from underneath and threw it onto the pile forming on the swooning couch. Helen withdrew a frothy confection made of red and black jacquard silk and lace, wrapped it around P.D.'s body, and fastened the hook-and-tab metal busk down the center front. Then, she moved to the back and began yanking on the laces.

Grunting, P.D. gripped the edge of the filing cabinet to keep from being yanked onto her backside. Listening for the telltale sound of boots in the hall, she impatiently endured the process until it felt as if she'd been encased in an iron band and couldn't take a deep breath. She opened her mouth to complain that there was no way on God's green earth that she was going to wear anything that tight, but then she caught a look of herself in the mirror.

"Pretty good, huh?" Helen said with far too much satisfaction.

P.D. wasn't going to argue with her. The corset had cinched her torso into a wasp-waist hourglass. And her boobs . . .

There was no disguising how "well endowed" she was in this contraption.

"Does it have to be this tight?" she panted, even though her own vanity begged her to leave it as it was.

"Only for the banquet. I've got a regular coutil working corset for you to wear in the competition."

"Yippee," P.D. offered with lightly veiled sarcasm.

"Beauty is pain, sweetie," Helen offered. Moving to her carpetbag again, she withdrew several black ruffled petticoats and dropped them over P.D.'s head.

As she marked the placement for the buttons, P.D. asked, "How on earth do you carry all that crap in one bag?"

But before Helen could answer, there was a knock. P.D. opened her mouth to tell Elam that she and Helen would be with him in a minute, but before she could utter a sound, Helen reached out and threw open the door.

P.D. watched in horror as the barrier swung wide. But then, she caught sight of the man framed in the threshold. With his dark hair and beard, linen shirt and twill pants, ruffled arm garters, and suspenders, he could have been liberated from one of her beloved period novels.

He held out the vest in Helen's general direction, saying, "This is too big. I think I'd rather wear the leather one I use for shooting."

But even though the words were directed at Helen, Elam's gaze had latched on to P.D., who stood dressed in nothing but a pair of petticoats, camisole, and a nineteenth-century over-bust corset.

Her cheeks felt as if they'd caught on fire as he looked down, down, down, taking in every inch of exposed flesh, every silk-covered curve, the fullness of the ruffled underskirts. The scorching heat of his scrutiny could have rivaled the touch of his fingers for intimacy. When his gaze moved back up again to linger on her breasts, she found it even harder to breathe. Unwittingly, in that quick sweep of his eyes, he'd ignited a smoldering fire deep in her belly. And judging by his own expression, Elam wasn't thinking of his wife or his grief or his lonely cabin on the hill.

He saw only her.

Only her.

And he wanted to touch her. With his hands, with his mouth.

If Helen hadn't been there, P.D. knew without a doubt that he would have closed the distance and thrown her on the swooning couch—and P.D. would have convinced herself that his passion was enough, even if it were only temporary. But he managed to restrain himself beneath the eyes of their un-witting chaperone.

"You look . . . beautiful," he said, his voice gruff.

For a moment, the words shimmered in the air in front of

them, as brittle and fragile as glass. And in that instant, P.D. knew that she was in deep trouble. Elam Taggart was unlike any man she'd ever known—dark and brooding and powerful. He should have come with a flashing sign that read DANGER to women like her. Hell, she'd had less than a half-dozen relationships, none of them long-term. Inevitably, the men she dated soon settled into two categories. Either they began to look upon her as a mother confessor to their woes . . .

Or they would decide she was too "rough around the edges" for anything even close to a commitment and they would break her heart.

Without question, Elam fell into the latter category. As much as she might want to dive headfirst into a passionate romp with this man, he was still negotiating his way out of the grieving process. And as any fool knew, if she allowed the attraction between them to blossom, she would become his "rebound" relationship. He would gain his emotional footing and then move on to someone who was perky and blond and the life of the party. Beautiful people attracted beautiful people—and Elam was drop-dead gorgeous, so he would need a stunner for his arm candy. That was the way the world worked. Besides, there was also the fact that he was Bodey's *brother*, and you didn't date your best friend's brother.

But even as she mentally listed all the reasons why getting involved with Elam Taggart was a really, really *bad* idea . . .

She couldn't deny that she wanted Elam to keep looking at her the way he was now.

"One more thing," Helen said, turning back to her bag. Reaching deep inside, she withdrew a brocade vest and a woolen frock coat.

"How do you get so much crap in that thing?" Elam asked with a suspicious frown, unknowingly echoing P.D.'s same question.

"Magic," Helen supplied with an infectious laugh. She motioned for Elam to come closer. "Everything else fit?"

He nodded.

She peered at his feet. "Those the boots you plan on wearing?"

He rocked back to squint at his shoes. "What's wrong with them?"

"Not a thing. You'll need something worn and dusty and covered in cow shit to give you an added authenticity. I'm hoping you have something better for the ball."

"How much better?"

"Maybe it's time you got yourself some new boots," she said cheekily as she scooped the shirts and pants out of his arms. Then she tossed an order in P.D.'s direction. "Shoot, I forgot. Grab that tape measure and take his inside and outside leg measurement for me, will you please?"

P.D.'s cheeks flamed so hot she was amazed her hair didn't catch on fire. "Me?" she squeaked.

"Yes, you. I don't have a mouse in my pocket."

P.D. waited until Elam was distracted with the vest Helen handed him, then threw her friend a murderous look.

Helen's broad grin confirmed that Helen hadn't forgotten to take the measurements at all. She'd decided that subtle matchmaking wouldn't be nearly as much fun as throwing P.D. at Elam's feet. Literally.

Kneeling on the floor, P.D. tried to ignore her suggestive position. She stretched the tape measure from his waist to a point an inch off the ground, then twisted to write the number on the clipboard. Geez, the man had great legs. Great thighs, great calves, great butt.

Great package.

Stop it!

"Can you, uh . . ." She motioned for him to part his legs more.

He widened his stance to "parade rest." Damned if he didn't look down at her through lashes that were darker and thicker than any man's had a right to be.

Suddenly, P.D. realized that from his vantage point, he had a perfect view of her breasts straining against the cups of her corset and the deep valley of her cleavage. And he didn't seem inclined to look away. Even more telling, a pronounced bulge pressed against his fly.

Air became an even more precious commodity as she fought to get enough oxygen past the tightness of her corset.

But there was no avoiding the necessary intimacy as she pressed the end of the tape measure against his crotch and measured to the proper hem length.

Did he notice the way her fingers lingered of their own volition? Could he guess that she wanted to wrap her arms around his thighs and press herself to his warmth?

The thought had her leaping to her feet. But when she tripped on the flounces of her petticoat, Elam quickly snagged her elbow, pulling her against the solid strength of his body.

"My work here is done," Helen proclaimed, her tongue-in-cheek comment rife with amusement. "I've got to get back to the house or Sydney will have my hide."

P.D. managed to yank her gaze away from the hard planes of Elam's chest. "But what about the frock coat?"

Helen's eyes twinkled. "I'm sure it'll be fine. If not, let me know. I'll pick up your costume pieces tomorrow morning."

She scooped up her belongings and dumped them higgledy-piggledy into her carpetbag. "Don't worry about me, I can find my way out." Then, laughing at her own private joke, she swept out of the room, snapping the door shut behind her. From the other side, P.D. heard her blithely add, "I'll leave the two of you to get out of your things."

The receding tap of her shoes was soon punctuated by the slam of the delivery door. Then a silence settled into the office, thick and heavy and warm.

Six

P.D. looked up to find that Elam was still watching her, his eyes hooded, a muscle twitching in his jaw. She feared that Helen's parting salvo had pushed him too far—that he would recognize her friend's maneuvers as those of a married woman still so deeply in love with her husband that she felt it her Christian duty to ensure that all of her single friends were matched up two-by-two.

But when P.D. feared that Elam had reached his snapping point, he surprised her again. He snapped, oh, yes, he snapped. But not with anger. Instead, he reached up to cradle her head between his palms while, at the same time, he pushed her back, back, against the edge of the desk. Then, just when her knees gave way and she sank onto its hard surface, he bent to crush his lips to hers.

Like a match to kerosene, she opened her mouth to admit his sweeping intrusion. Her arms swept around his waist, feeling the bunch of his muscles as he bent over her, straining to taste her very essence. Then he reached to pull her up against him, one of his broad hands curling around her thigh and lifting it high until she wrapped her foot around the corded muscles of his leg and pressed even more intimately against him.

There was no hiding his arousal now. She could feel the length of him straining against the buttons at his fly. P.D. ground herself against him, seeking to ease the ache settling deep within her. This time, the corset wasn't to blame as she panted against him, desperately trying to drag air into her lungs as his kisses strayed to her cheek, her jaw, then down the line of her neck to the soft mounds pressing against her camisole.

Her eyes closed and her whole being centered on that point of contact. She'd never been kissed by a man with a beard, and she found the sensation more arousing than she could ever imagine. Where the hair on his head was silken and soft, his beard was at the same time crisp and feathery, providing so many delicious sensations as it rasped across her breasts that she writhed against him, little kittenish sounds of pleasure and distress bursting unbidden from her throat.

Elam must have heard them because he lifted his head. His expression was filled with something akin to wonder. As she watched, the color of his eyes changed to the deep molten blue of the secret hot spring she'd discovered deep in the woods up Wilson Pass.

He drew back, tracing her cheek with the backs of his fingers. His thumb reached out to follow the lower curve of her mouth and she surprised him by lightly nipping the pad.

He bent toward her again. But this time, his kisses were slow and lingering. He seemed to be learning the contours of her face, her lips, her mouth, through feel alone. Then he moved lower, trailing sweet nibbling kisses down her throat to her collarbone.

P.D. couldn't be sure, but she thought he took a moment to taste her. Then his calloused palm swept the strap of her camisole aside and he pressed a slow kiss to her shoulder.

Unbidden, her arms wrapped around his waist, holding him tightly against her.

"What are we doing, Prairie Dawn?"

She'd always hated her name and bristled whenever it was used. But coming from his lips, the words sounded like a continuation of his caress.

She didn't know how to answer, so she remained silent, her head tucked beneath his chin, where she could hear the *thump, thump, thump* of his racing heart.

P.D. knew she was playing with fire. There were a thousand reasons why she shouldn't get involved with Elam Taggart. But at the moment, she couldn't think of a single one. His arms felt so right around her. And the warmth of his body eased an inner chill that she'd carried with her for far too long.

But then, to her infinite regret, Elam pressed a kiss to the top of her head and took a step back.

"I think I'd better go," he murmured.

Sure she'd heard him wrong, P.D. frowned, gripping the folds of his shirt as if to keep him there. "Go?"

He nodded. "If I stay . . ." He bent to brush a kiss over her forehead, her temple. "I'll be laying you down on that swooning couch and we'll be here 'til morning."

She opened her mouth to argue that such a thing might not be such a bad idea, but his lips moved to whisper across her cheek and then her lips. But when P.D. would have returned to the passion they'd shared only a few moments ago, he broke the contact and whispered next to her ear, "And I'm afraid I came to this party unprepared. It's been . . . a long time."

It took her a moment to fathom his meaning, and damned if her cheeks didn't burn with another telling blush when she realized that Elam was confessing to her that his most recent sexual partner had probably been his wife.

This time, when he backed away, she didn't stop him—even though her fingers twitched with the need to do so. But she wasn't any more prepared than he was.

Elam scooped up the clothing that Helen had brought, allowing the untidy bundle to fall strategically over the obvious shape of his erection.

"I haven't fed you," she whispered belatedly, scrambling for a reason to make him stay. "You must be starving."

He paused, bending to press another quick kiss to her lips, then murmured, "You have no idea."

Then, before she could think of another way to delay his retreat, he let himself into the hall and closed the door behind him.

She couldn't help running to the back window so that she could watch him stride through the gloom toward his truck. When the Dodge roared past, she suddenly felt as young and giggly as a teenager watching her prom date disappear in the darkness.

But the euphoria drained away as the silent shadows slipped back into the corners of the room, reminding her that she was alone. With them came her own doubts.

What was she thinking? That she could fall into this man's arms without regrets? He was on his way home, back to his cabin. Back to the memories of his wife.

Maybe if P.D. was more like Annabel, they could have had a chance. But from the stories she'd heard, the two of them were polar opposites. And from her experience, men were born with an attraction to a certain type. They might stray occasionally out of curiosity, but they always committed to the same kind of woman.

From what P.D. had been told, Annabel was next to perfect. So girly and feminine and delicate. No doubt, she'd made Elam feel like a manly-man in his need to protect her.

P.D., on the other hand, was wild and stubborn and too independent for her own good. If there was protecting that needed to be done, she would do it herself. Otherwise, she would feel smothered. After years of fighting for her dreams beneath her parents' indifference, she would never surrender herself to another person's control.

So there she had it. Even more reasons to keep him at arm's length.

But as she turned to remove her Victorian garb in favor of well-worn jeans and a T-shirt, she was already anticipating the next time she'd see Elam Taggart.

ELAM pulled his truck up to the front of the Big House and strode to the front door. Since Russ would be finishing up the cabin in the next few weeks, Elam figured he might as well start hauling some of his personal stuff up the hill. He'd already made calls to the various utility companies. He should have water and electricity connected by midday and a natural gas tank hooked up by the end of the week.

Anticipating the amenities, Elam had stopped at the grocery store on the way home. He'd forgone anything that had to be refrigerated, but he'd stocked up on some staples and canned goods as well as some junk food for Barry or Jace should they drop by. He figured he'd better have something in the house just in case.

But even as he made the preparations for visitors, he knew deep down that he wasn't thinking about the welfare of Russ or his brothers, but of a blue-eyed woman with freckles on her nose. *Geez.* Who knew freckles could get him in the gut?

Opening the screen door, he called out, "Hello?"

Instantly, he heard the thunder of footsteps coming toward him from the back of the house. He barely had time to brace himself before Barry ran toward him full force.

"You're back!"

"Hey, Barry."

Barry barreled into him, wrapping his arms around Elam's waist. "Please say you'll stay with me. Please."

Elam frowned. "What's going on?"

"Jace has to go change the water and I don't want to go."

"Why not?" Usually, Barry would fight to spend time outside.

"'Cause he washed my boots and now they're wet inside."

"O-kay," Elam said slowly.

Jace ambled into the hall, rolling his eyes. "He forgets that he started the job. In the tub."

"Where are you watering?" Elam asked.

"Down on Angle field and over on 62," Jace said using rancher code for the appropriate areas. "Normally, I'd have the hands do it, but there's a dance at the armory so I gave them the night off."

Most of the hired hands were teenagers or in their early twenties, so a community dance would be a hot gig in the area.

"You want me to change it?" Elam asked.

"Nah." Jace sat on the hall bench and began pulling on his

boots. "It would take longer to explain what we've been up to than to do it myself."

"I'll stay with Barry, then."

Jace had been stamping his foot more firmly into his footwear, but he looked up and squinted at Elam in surprise. "You sure?"

Once again, Elam realized that it had been a long time since he'd spent so much time at the Big House. He usually came in, grabbed something to eat or spoke with his brothers on ranch matters, then left again as soon as he could.

Elam nodded. "Barry looks like he could use a whoopin' on the Xbox until bedtime."

Barry began to hop excitedly. "Can he, Jace? Please?"

Jace rose to his feet. "Sure. That would be"—he paused, then his eyes crinkled in a smile—"that would be great."

IT was pitch black in her office when P.D. awoke with a jerk, her heart pounding, her hair spilling around her face onto the desk blotter under her cheek.

Crap.

She'd been so wound up after Elam had left—so jittery and antsy and aroused as hell—that she hadn't gone home after closing up Vern's. Instead, she'd decided to get caught up on bookwork in her office.

Tugging on the chain of the slag glass lamp, she squinted against the harsh brightness, peered at her watch, and groaned. One in the morning. Too early to get up for good, and too late to drive home, take a shower, and climb into bed for a decent night's sleep. Glancing at the swooning couch, she supposed she could crawl over there and pull the afghan over her shoulders. It wouldn't be the first time she'd slept at Vern's—and it probably wouldn't be the last. But the piece of furniture hadn't been restored yet, and the springs sometimes poked through the upholstery.

A rattling noise came from the direction of the delivery door and P.D. froze, suddenly realizing that it had been a similar sound that had yanked her from her sleep.

Pushing herself to her feet, she reached behind the filing cabinet and grabbed the metal baseball bat that had been given to her by a concerned line cook years ago. Even as she wrapped her fingers around it in a death grip and her heart began thudding in her ears, she found herself wishing that she had something more threatening at her disposal.

Like one of Elam's pistols.

Or his rifle.

Or the man himself.

The jiggling came again—and even though she knew the industrial deadbolt she'd installed would discourage even the most determined of thieves, she couldn't prevent the roaring of her pulse as she carefully opened the office door and padded down the hall.

"Bad idea," she whispered to herself, knowing she should stay in her office and call the sheriff, but unable to keep herself from moving closer to the source of the noise. "Bad idea, *bad idea*."

She had the fingers of both hands wrapped tightly around the cushioned grip of the bat. She raised it high over her shoulder as if awaiting delivery of a blazing fast ball. From the other side of the door she heard a muttered curse, then drunken laughter receding into the background.

Kids. Nothing but kids.

Her breath emerged in a whoosh and she lowered the bat, leaning over to gulp air into her lungs. She needed to call the sheriff, all right, but only to warn him that there was probably a keg party somewhere nearby.

P.D. had just straightened and begun the trek back to her office when a crash came from the kitchen around the corner. Anger bubbled inside her as she realized the kids must have circled around to try a new tack on getting inside. But as soon as she'd pushed through the double doors, she was assaulted by a wall of heat and smoke from a fire that was raging toward her.

"No, no, *no*!"

Throwing a hand over her nose and mouth, she raced toward the fire extinguisher bolted to the wall, knowing even as she reached for it that it was too late for such a puny defense.

ELAM let his voice trail into silence, then waited.

One second.

Two.

Three.

When Barry didn't stir, Elam leaned forward to pull the blanket more securely around his brother's shoulders. Then he marked the page in Roald Dahl's *Charlie and the Chocolate Factory*, flipped off the lamp, and set the book on his brother's nightstand.

For long moments, he remained in the huge wooden rocking chair. The piece was an artifact from all their childhoods. Some of Elam's earliest memories were of his mother sitting in the chair, reading them stories or comforting them when they were sick. And now, even though Barry was in danger of growing out of his childhood bed, the rocking chair remained, a symbol of comfort to a teenager who would remain a boy and the love of a mother whom he couldn't really remember.

Idly pushing against the floor with his toe, Elam began to rock, absorbing the creaks that were as familiar as breathing. His brother was hell on wheels when he was awake, but in this unguarded moment with the faint beam of the nightlight washing his face, Barry looked sweet and innocent and little-kid-lovable tucked beneath his Spiderman sheets.

The door to the hall opened with a soft squeak—one that Jace refused to oil because he said it was his "Barry alarm."

"He looks all cute and cuddly, but I can assure you it's an illusion. As soon as he wakes up, he'll be chasing frogs and trying to teach that damned goat of his to pull a wagon."

Elam's lips twitched at the mental picture Jace painted.

"You take good care of him, Jace." Elam pushed himself to his feet. "I should have been more help to you."

Jace shrugged. "You've had a thing or two on your mind."

"It's time I gave you a hand."

"I'll send him your way every now and then as soon as you're done with the Games."

Elam didn't doubt that he would.

Barry frowned in his sleep and twisted to lie on his stomach, dragging the blankets with him so that his feet dangled off the edge.

"He'll need a new bed soon," Elam remarked.

"You can help with that, too," Jace said good-naturedly.

This time, Elam laughed, a low rusty-sounding half grunt that underscored how long it had been since he'd found anything amusing. He bent to readjust Barry's covers, then swore, saying, "Where did you find footie pajamas his size?"

Jace grinned. "P.D. gave them to him for Christmas."

The two of them moved into the hall, then down the ornate narrow staircase that generations of Taggarts had tread for more than a hundred years.

"Thanks for staying through the movie marathon," Jace said as they reached the main level. "I don't think I could have handled one more viewing of *Star Trek: Into the Darkness* on my own."

"Thanks for grilling the steaks."

As they crossed into the bright light of the kitchen, Jace threw him a knowing look. Outside in the darkness, moths threw themselves with suicidal abandon against the window. The soft thumps provided a staccato accompaniment to the emergency scanner chattering to itself on top of the refrigerator. Since Jace worked every other weekend as an emergency EMT, the sporadic radio traffic made a familiar white noise in the background.

"You seem to be getting your appetite back," Jace said as he grabbed a couple of beers from the fridge. Pulling a chair away from the worn farmhouse table, he twisted it around backward and draped his arms over the back, extending a bottle toward Elam.

Elam shook his head, knowing he still had the drive home, but even more, knowing he needed a clear head to think things through once he was on his own again. "The way P.D. has been feeding me, I'm going to need to start running an extra mile in the morning."

Jace twisted the top off his own drink and took a long draft. "A few pounds wouldn't hurt you."

And there it was, the glint of concern in Jace's eyes. But this time, rather than feeling uncomfortable beneath his brother's regard, he felt . . . fine.

"Where's Bodey?"

Jace shrugged. "Catting around, most likely. He's been after one of the waitresses at Vern's and I don't think she's putting up much of a fight."

Elam stared down at the dusty toes of his boots. "So he and P.D. . . ."

Jace laughed. "He calls her his sister from another mother." Jace shook his head. "I don't know what his problem is." He waved his bottle in the air to punctuate his disbelief. "That girl is pretty, smart, and talented as hell, but he can't seem to see her as anything more than a buddy."

Elam's heart began a slow measured beat in his chest.

"So she's not . . . an ex."

"Hell, no. He's too stupid to see what a great thing he has right under his nose." Jace broke off, his eyes narrowing consideringly.

Not wanting Jace to get the wrong idea—or any ideas at all—Elam pushed himself away from the counter. "Well, I'd better head back up the hill. I'm supposed to meet Russell in the morning."

"You could bunk here again."

Elam shook his head. "Thanks, but not tonight. I've got some stuff in the truck that I need to get inside the cabin before I turn in."

"'Night, then."

"'Night, Jace." Tossing an absent wave at his brother, Elam strode through the house and into the cool evening air. He paused a moment to make sure that the ties he'd thrown around the boxes loaded in the back were still secure, then shooed away Bitsy, Barry's pet pygmy goat.

"Get out of here," he growled good-naturedly, "or I'll have you made into chops and slapped on my grill."

The goat merely looked up at him hopefully, wagging her triangular tail as if she were an eager puppy, her rotund figure blocking his way to the door.

Knowing that the goat probably had an IQ higher than his own—and that she would not be dissuaded with false promises—Elam reached into the bed of the truck, where he'd placed the box of groceries. Ripping open a bag of corn chips, he scattered them on the ground.

Bitsy bleated in delight—and damn if it didn't sound like she was offering her thanks.

"You're welcome, you little extortionist."

Elam was just swinging into the cab of his truck when Jace suddenly burst through the screen door, drawing Elam's attention with the same piercing whistle he used to alert the horses that feeding time had finally come.

Rolling down his window, Elam paused with his hand on the gear shift.

Jace ran toward him, his feet bare beneath the hems of his jeans.

"There's been a call over the scanner. P.D.'s restaurant is on fire!"

Elam didn't even wait for his brother to close the distance between them. Throwing the truck into drive, he jammed his foot onto the accelerator, causing a spray of gravel that sent the goat scampering for safety.

"Make sure P.D. is all right," he heard Jace shout after him. "Sometimes she spends the night on the couch in her office!"

Elam threw a hand out of the open window to show that he'd heard, then urged his Dodge even faster down the lane.

P.D. stood with her arms wrapped around her body, the strobing lights from the fire engines and police cars whirling in the darkness like the beams of alien spacecraft. The entire scene had been surreal from the moment she'd confronted the flames in the kitchen. But now, the situation was bordering on the absurd.

True to the workings of a small town and a primarily volunteer staff, there were no fewer than three fire engines, a paramedic truck, and two ambulances. There were three Sheriff's Department cruisers, a member of the Highway Patrol, and even a representative from Animal Control. Then, as if that weren't enough, half of Bliss's population had a police scanner in their homes and her parking lot was filled with cars and pickups belonging to those who had come to see if they could "help" or take a look. Apparently, since nothing much happened in Bliss in the middle of the night, no one wanted to miss out on the action.

P.D. didn't know if she should be grateful or embarrassed. She should have called 911 immediately. But like an idiot, she'd thought she could put out the flames with the fire extinguishers. After she'd emptied the first one without making a dent in the inferno, she'd tried the second extinguisher. It was only after that had proved ineffective as well and she'd begun to feel light-headed from the smoke that she'd realized an accelerant must have been used.

Thankfully, the Fire Department had been able to beat down the flames before they could move beyond the kitchen into any of the other rooms. Now they were picking through the embers and pulling down ceiling tiles and wallboard to ensure that there weren't any unseen dangers that remained.

George Hamblin, the local sheriff, strode toward her, the lights glinting off a belt buckle the size of a dinner plate. "We've got a witness over there who saw a couple of figures running across the street about the time you think the fire started. They were being chased by the neighbor's dog. He got a good look at their car, so I'll see what I can do to track it down. Like you said, I think a couple of drunken teenagers might have been responsible."

George regarded her with the quiet somber eyes of a basset hound, and with his pronounced jowls and the scruffy beginnings of a beard, P.D. wouldn't have been surprised if he'd suddenly begun to bark.

Lordy, she was tired. Tired and punchy and running on the remaining fumes of adrenaline.

"You'll probably have to close down for a while to make repairs."

A tightness gripped her throat when she thought of the lost revenue and the employees who would be without pay in the meantime. In an instant, her mood swung from weary silliness to crushing defeat, leaving her without the ability to speak, so she merely nodded. Thankfully, her insurance agent had been among the gawkers. She'd already spoken to him and a call had been made to an emergency restoration service. A cleanup crew and a pair of security guards were on the way from Logan to begin the process of bringing Vern's back to working order as soon as possible.

"P.D.!"

Twisting, P.D. saw Helen making a beeline toward her with such speed and determination that the crowd parted to avoid being mowed over. In her wake, following much more slowly, was her husband, Syd, who carried two camp chairs and a thermos.

Helen quickly embraced her, then stood back to study her face. "Lord-a-mercy, are you all right? You look white as a sheet."

P.D. nodded then said, "Hello, Syd," to the tall, quiet man behind her friend. With his full beard and waxed mustache, he could have walked out of the pages of a Louis L'Amour novel. But his looks were deceiving. Behind his eyes was the wicked brain of a chemical engineer. Before his retirement, he'd been part of a team at ATK in charge of making the solid rocket boosters that put the space shuttle into orbit.

"What a shame," he said, squinting at the scorched area of the wall outside the kitchen window. "Is there much damage?"

"I—I don't know yet. They're telling me I can't go back in until morning, just in case they need to take care of any hot spots."

Helen made a *tsk*ing noise with her tongue. "Didn't I tell you she was probably here when the fire started?" She squeezed P.D.'s arms, then motioned to Syd. "Why don't you set things up while I take her home, honey?"

P.D.'s sluggish brain fought to make sense of the words. "I

can't go home. There's a cleanup crew coming and I'll have to notify my employees and . . ."

Helen patted her shoulder as if she were a particularly dense child. "We'll shoo away the rubberneckers and serve as welcoming committee to the restoration people. Shoot, with as many times as my basement has flooded in the past ten years, I know them all by name. As for your employees, the grapevine has probably already taken care of notifying them. Nevertheless, I've got a cell phone and I'm sure I can make some calls."

P.D. hugged her arms around her torso. Although the evening was warm enough, she was beginning to shake uncontrollably. "No, I've got to board up the broken window and . . . and make sure no one tampers with anything or gets inside until the damage can be . . . can be documented and . . ."

Her voice began to tremble in time with her body. Worse yet, she felt as if she might burst into tears. And she couldn't do that—she *wouldn't* do that. She didn't cry in public. Ever. She didn't cry. Ever. Nothing could be solved by tears. She'd learned that lesson the hard way.

She watched in astonishment as Syd unfolded the chairs and took a seat, stretching his long legs out in front of him as if he'd planned all along to spend the morning sitting in the middle of a messy crime scene watching the stars.

"But your grandchildren . . ."

"Are asleep and being watched by their uncle Mark until their parents come to get them in the morning." Helen squeezed her hand. "We'll take care of everything," she said, gesturing to Syd, who proceeded to unscrew the top of the thermos.

Helen threw a large purse—an only slightly smaller version of her magical carpetbag—onto the empty camp chair. Opening it wide, she removed a pair of mugs, a bag of miniature marshmallows, and a box of granola bars before slinging the strap over her shoulder again.

"Syd will keep an eye on things until I can drop you off and come back." She patted her bag. "Let me have a word with the sheriff, then we'll go. I'm packing, so you don't need to worry about our security."

The remark should have made P.D. laugh. There was no

need for Helen to announce she was "packing." Helen was always packing: a revolver in her purse; a pistol in her minivan; and on special occasions, a derringer in her garter or corset holster. But the humor of the situation suddenly escaped P.D. as the last of her control seeped away like fine sand.

Not wanting Helen to see how close to tears she was, P.D. averted her gaze and scanned the crowd. It was then that she saw a familiar Dodge Ram skid into one of the few remaining parking places in the lot. As soon as the engine had been killed and he'd slid to the ground, Elam began searching the crowd.

P.D. stood frozen, waiting for the moment when his eyes would find hers. And she wasn't disappointed. As soon as their gazes locked, her pulse flip-flopped in anticipation and the pounding at her temples eased.

He turned to grab something from the back of the cab. Then he was striding toward her, weaving his way through a crowd that was finally beginning to disperse.

"Well, now, I've got Sydney settled and had a word with George and the fire captain, so everything's arranged. All that's left to do is get you home," Helen said from somewhere behind her shoulder.

P.D. watched Elam's familiar silhouette weaving through the chaos. He murmured something to the deputies who were stringing up crime scene tape in a large circle around the restaurant. Then, he was dipping beneath the flimsy barrier and closing the distance with his ground-eating strides.

"Look who's here," Helen murmured.

But P.D. barely heard her as Elam stopped and asked, "You okay?"

She nodded, clenching her jaw to keep her chin from crumpling. She'd known the man less than forty-eight hours, yet she longed to lean into him, to draw the warmth of his body into her own.

"You cold?"

Again, she dipped her head, not trusting herself to answer without bursting into tears. He held out his hands, revealing the heavy Carhartt jacket he'd taken from his truck.

"Put this on." Elam stepped behind her to help her slip her

arms into the sleeves, then left his hands, warm and heavy, on her shoulders. When she shivered, he stepped closer and drew her back to rest against him, offering her the heat from his own body.

"Hello, Helen. Syd."

"You're just in time. I was about to take P.D. home. She's dead on her feet after all this."

"What happened?"

P.D. forced herself to speak. "Kids. They had a snoot full of liquor and decided to play with matches."

"Looks like more than matches. Is there much damage inside?"

"I won't . . . I won't know until morning. But I think . . . most of the fire was confined to the kitchen. I don't know if any of the appliances can be saved. The Sheetrock and the flooring will have to be replaced. The wiring might have to be redone. Everything will have to be scrubbed and repainted, supplies restocked, c-carpets cl-cleaned—"

Helen stopped her with another squeeze of her hand. "But not tonight. There's nothing more you can do tonight." She made a gesture toward Elam with her chin. "Take her home, Elam."

"Yes, ma'am. I intend to."

SEVEN

———◆———

ELAM took P.D.'s hand. Lacing his fingers between hers, he led her through the darkness and the well-wishing townsfolk to his truck. To her surprise, he didn't take her to the passenger side, but opened the driver's door and leaned inside to lift up the center console so that she could slide through from his end. But the truck had been jacked up so high, she wasn't sure if she could climb in. She was just too, too tired.

She needn't have worried because Elam wrapped his arms around her, lifted her up, and then took his place beside her. When she would have slid to the opposite door, he stopped her, reaching for the center seat belt and securing it before tunneling into his pocket for his keys and revving the engine. Then, draping his right arm around her shoulders, he pulled her close to his side while he used his left hand to flip on his lights, adjust the heater, and then put the vehicle into gear.

As they pulled away from the restaurant, taking the winding lane that would lead them to the main road and away from the whirling cacophony of lights, the dark summer night settled around them. Stars winked like scattered fairy dust on a velvet blanket. Gradually, P.D.'s trembling ceased, aided by the proximity of Elam's body and the soft caress of his fingertips on her arm. Funny, how she could feel the caress even through the thickness of his jacket.

"You'll have to tell me where to go."

"I live in the old Francom house. Do you know where that is?"

"Yup."

P.D. closed her eyes as exhaustion threatened to pull her under. Shifting, she rested her head in the hollow of his shoulder. The rumble of the truck, the steady *thump, thump* of Elam's heartbeat beneath her ear, and the faint irregular melody of a country-western ballad on the radio were melding together into their own unique form of lullaby.

She was well on her way to falling asleep when the sudden silence of the Ram's engine caused her to start. As her eyes blinked open, she realized that she was home.

Elam slid out. Then he reached in to push her hands aside when she clumsily tried to release her seat belt. Finally, he lifted her to the ground, keeping her in the protective lee of the door. Framing her face in his broad palms, he brushed aside the stray strands of hair with his thumbs.

"Are you sure you're all right?"

She nodded. "I'm just tired. Really . . . *really* tired." Again, the tightness gripped her throat. But after averting her gaze from the sharp planes of his face etched by the weak dome light, she was able to say, "Thanks for the ride home."

P.D. expected him to move out of the way, but Elam continued to brush the ridge of her cheekbones with his thumbs. And damned if she didn't want to lean into that caress and soak it up like a wounded cat.

"I . . . uh . . ." she began, then stopped again. She'd been about to tell him that she could handle things from here, and that he ought to head home while there were still a few hours of sleep available to him. But he must have read her thoughts because he leaned down to press his lips to the top of her head.

"I'm not going anywhere," he said lowly. Then, taking her hand again, he led her toward the front door.

* * *

ELAM didn't need a crystal ball to tell him that P.D. had expected him to drop her off and then disappear into the night. But there was no way he was leaving her. Not when her eyes were wide and shadowed, and she huddled like a wounded little bird in the bulky confines of his jacket. Damned if he knew why, but the moment he'd heard about the fire, his heart had begun pounding with the same fierce jolt of adrenaline that he'd felt countless times when he'd been sent to diffuse an IED. He'd only known P.D. for a short while, but the thought of her being hurt or injured . . .

He wasn't above admitting to himself that he'd been scared shitless.

Even now, as he drew open the ornate wooden screen to the simple little bungalow, his hands shook ever so slightly.

"Key?"

She shook her head. "This is Bliss."

P.D. reached out to twist the knob and stepped inside.

"Damnit, P.D., you don't lock up your house?" he groused as he followed her inside.

"Why? No one in Bliss locks their doors. The landlords didn't even have a key to give me. It was lost several renters ago."

"You should at least have a deadbolt."

"I keep telling myself to get one, but then I forget. I can lock things up while I'm on the inside, just not while I'm on the outside."

"That doesn't make a lick of sense."

"So sue me." She was feeling her way through the dark. "Wait there. This old house doesn't have a light switch by the door for some reason, so I'll have to turn it on from the other side of the room."

Elam waited as he'd been told, allowing what little moonlight remained to slip through the screen. Then, with a *snap*, light from an overhead bulb chased away the gloom.

Elam quickly shut them inside and fastened the lock.

"What? Are you afraid someone's going to sneak inside?

Everyone is down at the restaurant gawking. There's no one left to bother us."

Her blithe disregard for her safety was arousing Elam's inner "caveman." But rather than argue with her, he simply decided that he'd head to town sometime soon and buy a set of new locks himself. Besides, she looked like a gust of wind could knock her down. Even worse, she stood in the center of her living room, too exhausted to string a coherent thought together.

"Why don't you get out of your things and into a hot shower?" he said as he drew his coat from her shoulders.

She looked down at herself as if suddenly becoming aware of her sooty clothing. Then her nose wrinkled. "Are you trying to tell me I stink?"

At the faint resurgence of her usual feistiness, he smiled. "No. But there is a certain *eau de campfire* about you. And if you climb into bed like that, you're bound to wake up with your sheets smelling like a BBQ pit."

She snorted, but he'd managed to chase a few of the shadows from her eyes.

He nudged her toward the hall. "Go on. While you're doing that, I'll fix you something to eat. Then you can go to bed."

She made a face. "I'm not hungry."

"No, but your body is hovering on the edge of shock, so it will take the edge off." He grasped her shoulders and turned her toward the shadowy doorways he could see. "Now, go."

"Can you cook?" she argued as she headed toward a room at the far end of the hall.

"I haven't starved yet," he called after her.

"*Yet*," she argued back as if she were aware of the twenty pounds he'd dropped since leaving the Navy.

He remained where he stood until he heard the slamming of drawers, then the hiss of the shower. Then, turning, he surveyed the room before him.

The décor was like nothing he'd ever seen before—except perhaps for P.D.'s office. Muted shades of taupe and ivory blended with at least a dozen variations of white with little pops of jadeite green and pink and blue. It was at once elegant and casual. And soothing. Most of the furniture was old and repurposed, the wood painted or slipcovered. Overall, the pieces looked well loved and comfortable with a hominess that could only come from a woman's touch. Nevertheless, it was still a room where a man wouldn't feel awkward kicking off his boots and resting his feet on the oversized ottoman-like coffee table while he relaxed and watched television.

Moving to the small kitchen, he flipped on the light and nearly laughed out loud when he found a continuation of the scheme. But here, there more obvious dashes of color. A retro, fifties-style stove and refrigerator in jadeite green were the focal point of the minuscule room, as was an Arts and Crafts breakfast table and four chairs.

After searching through the cupboards and the shelves of the refrigerator, Elam realized that most of the ingredients were above his skill set. So he settled on cereal, thick slices of bacon, and eggs.

By the time he heard the water turn off, he was ready to dish up the food. As soon as he heard the whisper of P.D.'s feet on the carpet, he grasped the plates and turned.

For a moment, he was struck dumb at the picture in front of him. P.D. stood fresh-faced and vulnerable in a pair of over-sized men's flannel pajamas, her damp hair streaming in wild ringlets down her back. She could have been a little girl coming to say good night if it weren't for the very womanly body limned by the soft fabric of her nightwear.

"What?" she demanded, looking down.

"Nothing. You look . . ." He scrambled for an appropriate description. Somehow *hot as hell* didn't seem appropriate, so he quickly substituted, "Shorter."

She blinked at him in confusion. "Shorter?"

He gestured to the hems puddling around her feet to waylay her suspicions, then wrapped his foot around the leg of a chair to pull it out for her. "Sit."

P.D. took in the box of Cap'n Crunch with Crunch Berries and laughed. "I thought you said you were cooking?"

"I cooked."

He set a plate of eggs and bacon in front of P.D., then took the seat at right angles to hers.

"You put cheddar cheese on the eggs."

Elam glanced up, wondering if she was "anti-cheese" or something. But she eyed them with an expression close to wonder.

"Never could stand a naked egg. That's how my mother got me and my brothers to eat them when we were little."

"You must miss her," P.D. said softly.

For the life of him, Elam couldn't remember the last time anyone other than his brothers had acknowledged Maureen Taggart's passing, and for some reason, it touched him.

"Yeah. Yeah, I do." He waited, his fork poised over his own plate while P.D. took her first bite. When she closed her eyes with an unconscious "Mmm" then licked the back of her fork, he couldn't prevent the jolt of arousal that shot into his gut.

"What about you?" he asked, knowing this was not the time or the place to give in to his baser instincts. "Do you see your folks much?"

P.D. grimaced. "Not unless I happen to intersect one of their 'Interstate Rambles,' as my mother calls them." She took another forkful of egg. "My parents seem to be constantly chasing the weather. If it's too cold, they move south. If it's too hot, they go north. If it's too windy, they head west."

Elam's brows rose.

"My mother lives in fear of Tornado Alley since what little televised news she sees is full of trailers being swept away by floods or fires or gale-force winds. But she'd rather see their bus blown away to Oz than put down roots somewhere in a real house."

When she frowned, poking at the yoke of her egg, Elam realized that he'd unwittingly hit a nerve. "It must have been tough for you as a kid with all that moving."

"Yeah."

Then, as if the admission were somehow a betrayal, she pasted a too-bright smile on her face. "You, on the other hand, must have been in kid heaven with your own room, horses, siblings, and acres of land to explore."

He smiled, realizing that Bodey must have been talking about the family. "Yeah. It had its perks. Still does."

As if the sharing of confidences was still too new, too awkward, they both turned their attention to their food. But even though a silence descended on the kitchen, it was a comfortable one. Elam didn't feel the need to search for something to say. He absorbed the peaceful hum of the refrigerator and the faint tick of a clock from deep in the house. After all the time he'd spent on his own, he couldn't account for the way P.D.'s nearness was easing kinks of tension he hadn't even known existed.

After their meal was finished—Elam eating two bowls of cereal to P.D.'s one—he nodded toward the back of the house. "Get to bed. I'll clean up."

She opened her mouth to argue, but was interrupted by a ferocious yawn.

He laughed, urging, "Go on. When I'm done, I'll crash on the couch."

"But . . . my couch is . . . your feet will probably hang off the edge."

He began gathering their plates in a stack. "I've slept on far worse," he offered ruefully.

She took two steps back, paused, then reversed her course until she was standing in front of him. Then, before he knew what she was about to do, she knelt down until they were at eye level.

"Thank you, Elam," she whispered.

The plates were abandoned as she wrapped her arms around his neck and kissed him on the cheek, the jaw, and then his lips. The caress was tentative and sweet, like the brush of butterfly wings. Then, without a word, she hugged him close, her arms tight, her body warm and feminine and still bearing the scent of lemon soap . . . and some kind of shampoo that smelled like it came from a candy dish.

Elam's heart ached at the simple gesture, at the emotional contact that he'd only ever shared with his wife. As much as he longed to sweep P.D. into his arms and carry her into her bedroom, he couldn't bring himself to do it. In her office hours ago, he would have taken her on the swooning couch if he'd had a condom at hand. But their coupling would have been nothing but an expression of lust and sex—great sex, but just sex.

Now, with his senses absorbing the nuances of her breasts flattened against his chest, the fuzzy fabric of her pajamas, the still-damp riot of her hair, he knew that he wanted more than a physical release. He wanted to wallow in everything this woman aroused in him—frustration, delight, arousal, and a he-man protectiveness that he couldn't tamp down.

But the timing wasn't right. Not yet. While he'd spent time with Barry at the Big House, he'd realized there was still a part of him that wasn't ready to let go of his memories of Annabel. And he couldn't do that to P.D.

As if sensing he would take things no farther, P.D. gradually released him and straightened, self-conscious. Offering him a faint smile, she fled from the room with a halfhearted, "'Night."

He could have kicked himself for the flash of hurt he was sure he'd seen in her eyes. But even as he pushed to his feet to follow her, he lost the nerve. What was he going to say? *I still think of my wife when I'm in your arms?*

Shit, shit, shit.

Turning resolutely toward the sink, he washed the dishes and returned them to their proper cupboards. He wiped the stove and put away the cereal—even took the time to rearrange the refrigerator shelves to military precision. Then, knowing he was merely delaying the inevitable, he turned off the light and went through to the living room.

While he'd been finishing up, P.D. had doused the overhead light and turned on a lamp near the couch. Pillows and blankets were piled on the armrest as well as a folded towel and facecloth and a new bar of soap. Lifting it to his nose, he smelled the same citrusy scent that had clung to P.D.'s skin.

Grabbing the towels, he padded toward the bathroom, where he cleaned up for the night. He was walking back when he realized that the door to P.D.'s bedroom was open. Moonlight slanted through the mullioned panes of the sash windows to paint her bed in a patchwork of light.

Despite the warmth of the evening, P.D. had pulled the covers up to her chin. He could see her huddled in a near fetal position, as if she was still cold.

Sensing his regard, she rolled over and blinked at him.

"I set some pillows and blankets on the couch," she whispered, despite the fact that they were the only two people in the house and he wouldn't have faulted her if she'd wanted to shout.

"I saw. Thanks."

She didn't move and he couldn't bring himself to back away.

After several moments with only the ticking of the clock to rattle the silence, Elam braced his hands on either side of the doorway. "Having trouble falling asleep?"

She nodded, frowning. "Every time I close my eyes, I keep seeing that fire. If I hadn't been there—"

"But you were," he interrupted, not wanting her to go down paths of worry she didn't need to tread. Sighing, he hooked the heel of his boot with the toe of the other and began tugging his feet free. Then, crossing the room in stocking feet, he climbed onto the huge brass bed, drawing her against him spoon fashion. After running a soothing hand down her hair, he held her close until her bouts of shivering stopped and she began to relax.

"Elam?" she murmured, her voice already heavy with sleep.

"Mmm."

"Thanks . . . for everything . . ."

He smiled against the top of her head, knowing by the slow cadence of her breathing that she had finally dropped off for good. "No problem, Prairie Dawn. It's been no problem at all."

THE next morning, P.D. awoke by degrees as if her consciousness were a piece of driftwood being slowly pushed to shore. When she finally blinked and stretched, her body felt stiff and sore, but her mind was clear—revealing how long it had been since she'd really, *really* slept.

Stretching her arms over her head, she turned, feeling the pillows beside her—not really remembering why, merely sensing that she was missing something . . .

And then she remembered Elam climbing into bed behind

her, holding her close whenever her dreams threatened to be tinged with fire, until, finally, the horrors of the evening faded beneath the warmth of his body and a sense of well-being.

Blinking against the light streaming through the window, she rubbed at her shoulder. There was a bruise from the recoil of the shotgun, just as Elam had predicted. And yes, the clothes she'd left in the hamper did lend a slight *eau de campfire* to her bedroom. She'd need to throw them in the washer before she went to Vern's.

Vern's.

Her eyes strayed to the clock, bounced away, then returned again in disbelief like a rebounding Ping-Pong ball when she realized it was one o'clock.

One *p.m.*?

As if hit with a jolt of electricity, she kicked against the covers and scrambled from the bed like a crazed jackrabbit. Rushing to the window, she looked outside, noting that shadows were already beginning to creep across the lawn and through the trees.

Holy, holy *hell*!

She rushed into the bathroom, wincing at the tangled mass of her hair. It had been a mistake to go to bed without braiding it first, but she dragged a brush through the knots, then drew it back into a ponytail. She kept her makeup simple. Then, with an eye toward the mess she would encounter at Vern's, she dressed in something easy to clean: jeans and a Farm Girls T-shirt emblazoned with FARM GIRLS HAVE NICE CALVES.

Opening the door to the hall, she peered gingerly in both directions, wondering if Elam had stuck around. But the house was quiet. Too quiet. And damned if she didn't quite know how she felt about that. She wouldn't have expected him to hang around this long. But . . . it was disconcerting that he hadn't at least said good-bye.

As she made her way into the kitchen to grab something to eat, she stopped short, laughing out loud. On her kitchen table was a potted plant with a scrap of paper held to one of the branches with baling twine. Bending forward, she read the nearly illegible scrawl:

Thought you might need cheering up.
Couldn't find flowers, so I bought you this.

E.

Bewildered, she looked at the marker sunk in the dirt. A lemon tree. He'd bought her a lemon tree.

There were blooms on the end of each of the branches, and when she leaned forward to smell them, she was enveloped in a heavenly scent.

P.D. couldn't account for the way the unusual gift made her feel as if she were being lit from the inside out. He must have noticed that her favorite soap had a citrusy scent. To her, nothing smelled more like liquid sunshine than a lemon. And it didn't escape her that after he'd left for the morning, he'd taken time out of his busy schedule to buy the tree, then had returned to leave it on her table.

Had he also taken the time to check on her while she'd been sleeping?

Lord, please tell me I wasn't drooling or slack-jawed.

Buoyed by Elam's thoughtfulness, she set the tree on a table by the front window. It was only as she was stepping outside that it dawned on her that, since Elam had brought her home the night before, she was essentially marooned without a vehicle. But even as she stutter-stepped to a halt, she saw her rattle-trap truck waiting in the driveway. Apparently, Elam had been even busier than she'd supposed.

Her smile grew even wider when she noted that Elam had washed the vehicle and vacuumed the interior—a monumental feat for this rusty bucket of bolts. She could definitely get used to this treatment.

But her good mood began to seep away with each mile closer to Vern's. Now more than ever, she was going to need the prize money from the Wild West Games. Where she'd once hoped to use the cash to expand the kitchens, now she might need it to recoup any expenses the insurance wouldn't cover.

With so little time before the Games would begin, she

needed to check on the restoration people, arrange for security while she was gone, and start checking her supplies. Most of her fresh ingredients would probably be tainted with smoke. She would have to determine how long Vern's would need to remain closed, then reorder staples, produce, and perhaps even meat.

Her mind was already forming a mental list as she checked her watch and pushed the truck to its top speed of fifty. But with everything she'd prepared herself to find when she turned down the lane, she hadn't expected to see a parking lot full of cars.

As she pulled into one of the spaces, she saw Helen hurrying toward her.

"Hello! How are you feeling?"

Bemused, P.D. gestured to the scene around her. "What's going on?"

"We've had a few friends drop by and offer their help."

"But—"

"The restoration crew has already soaked up the water left by the fire department. They've got fans set up to dry out the moisture that has seeped into the walls and woodwork. They were going to bring in a contractor next week to deal with the electrical repairs and patch up the walls. Then they'll bring in a paint crew and a flooring company. In the meantime, we've got more volunteers than we can handle, so I put them to work carrying out the tables and chairs in the dining area so they can be scrubbed and dried in the sun."

"I don't . . . I don't know what to say," P.D. said weakly.

"Don't say anything. Come eat."

Belatedly, P.D. realized that the banana she'd meant to bring with her had been forgotten in her haste to leave the house. But when she saw Syd stretched out in his camp chair keeping watch over a line of squat black Dutch ovens, her stomach suddenly rumbled. "Oh, no, you didn't."

"We did. Dutch oven potatoes, chicken and dumplings, and even my famous chocolate cherry cake. Give us a minute to set up a table to hold the plates and cups."

Helen hurried toward Syd, but P.D. remained behind. She wouldn't be able to eat anything until she'd taken a look inside.

When she glanced up to see Elam striding from the building with an armload of scorched two-by-fours, she couldn't prevent the flutter of anticipation that settled deep in her belly. One that was quickly followed by awareness when he looked her way and smiled.

He threw the refuse into a skip that had been parked near the back door, then walked toward her. There was such power and effortless grace to his movements that gooseflesh pebbled her arms and her heart skittered against her ribs. He could have been the cover model for *Western Male* with his boots and tight jeans, faded T-shirt, and leather gloves. Instead of his usual cowboy hat, he wore a baseball cap embroidered with the logo for Taggart Enterprises.

As if sensing her gaze, he lifted the hat away and swiped at the sweat on his brow with his wrist. His hair was shaggy and tousled, needing a trim. But she didn't mind. In fact, she would have given anything at that moment to run her fingers through the waves, but he quickly replaced his hat.

"Hi there," he said, tugging a pair of work gloves from his hands. Again, she was struck by the strength in those digits, the slender concert pianist finesse of his movements. How could the mere sight of them turn her on?

"Sleep well?"

"Yeah. Thanks."

"Good."

She gestured to the people moving in and out of her restaurant. "How did this happen?"

"Small-town gossip, I suppose." He tucked his fingertips into his pockets. "Apparently, they're worried this little accident could play havoc with the daily special."

Dear heaven above, did he have any idea how sexy he looked? His clothing coated his body like a second skin, revealing musculature that would have done an underwear model proud. Since she'd seen him last, he'd trimmed his beard close to his face, and the tidier lines highlighted his angular features and high cheekbones. Today, his eyes were blue and green with flecks of brown. Faint lines fanned out from the corners of his eyes and the angle of his lips had softened.

"How about you?" she asked. "Did you sleep well?"

His expression was boyishly sheepish. "Yeah. Better than I have in a long time."

The remark sent a rush of pleasure spilling through her veins. Silence twined between them, warm and sticky and fraught with awareness.

"I . . . I should probably check on the progress inside," she said, feeling suddenly tongue-tied. If there weren't so many people around, she would have thrown herself at Elam. But she didn't want to frighten the man off with such a public display.

"Food's ready!" Helen called.

"Go ahead," Elam said, tipping his head toward the rear door. "I'll get you a plate."

"Thanks."

When she would have brushed past him, he snagged her elbow and pulled her back. Then, before she had a clue what he was up to, he bent and lightly brushed his lips over hers.

"Don't be too long," he murmured before releasing her.

And the last thing she saw before she headed inside was Helen's enthusiastic thumbs-up from the other end of the yard.

EIGHT

———•◆•———

THANKS to Helen and Syd's impromptu Dutch oven lunch, the parking lot outside Vern's soon took on a festive air. The tables and chairs from the dining room which had been brought outside to be washed were quickly put to use. Someone with a jacked-up Ford and a killer sound system had opened the windows and put on an old Brad Paisley CD. One by one, the volunteers made their way past the squat Dutch ovens and loaded up their plates, then gathered in groups to talk and eat.

Since everyone had been drawn outside, it didn't take long for Elam to see that P.D. still hadn't emerged from the building. So after setting their plates down in a shady spot, he headed back inside.

As soon as he stepped into the kitchen, he was assaulted with the smells of smoke, burnt wood, and scorched plastic. The dampness left from the fire hoses added an unpleasant humidity to the air as the heat from the day tinged the moisture with smoldering undertones.

Without electricity, the interior was dim, but it only took a moment for Elam to find P.D. She stood in the center of what would have once been the prep area. Although her back was turned to him, he ached to see the dejected slump of her shoulders and the way she'd wrapped her arms around her waist in an unconscious self-comforting gesture.

For a woman who had always been so self-assured and full of life, she suddenly looked tiny and vulnerable and oh, so alone. Suddenly, Elam realized that this was more than a setback to her business. To P.D., this was her home, her baby. Judging by what little she'd told him about her childhood, she'd fought tooth and nail to bring Vern's to fruition, and now those efforts lay in ruins at her feet.

His boots crunched over broken glass and bits of metal as he moved toward her, but she obviously didn't hear him. Her head dropped and he thought he heard her breath catch. The sound affected him more that he would have thought possible, squeezing his heart even tighter because he, more than anyone, understood the devastating loss she was experiencing.

Without a word, he wrapped his arms around her and drew her back against his chest. He pressed a kiss to her hair. "It can be fixed," he whispered.

The words were her undoing. Her chest suddenly heaved with huge sobs.

Turning her in his arms, Elam held her tightly, sensing that this show of emotion was as painful for her as its roots. She displayed a brave face to the world, but he doubted that anyone in Bliss had ever seen her cry.

At a loss for how to help her, he drew on his own experience, knowing that there were no words that could make things better. Yes, Vern's could be brought back to life. But it would not be an easy task and the weeks spent in repairs could hit P.D.'s expenses hard.

But what was even more devastating, he was sure, was the emotional cost. She'd lost a portion of her dreams for the future. She had no idea who had done this or why, and a little part of her would always be on guard. Even worse, this moment would be imprinted in fear on her brain so that a hint of smoke from the farmers burning their ditches in the spring or the fields of stubble in the fall would have her searching through the restaurant to make sure things were safe.

Elam bent toward her, enfolding her as tightly as possible in his embrace, feeling her tears moisten the front of his shirt and wishing there was more he could do for her. But as quickly as the storm of emotion rushed over her, it soon ebbed, leaving her trembling, her hands gripping handfuls of his shirt.

When he lifted her chin to wipe away her tears, she tried to shy away, obviously embarrassed.

"I—I never cry like that," she offered in quiet defense.

Elam brushed her hands aside and pulled the hem of his shirt out of his pants to dry her cheeks. "I do."

He hadn't meant the words to be uttered aloud, but they left his lips of their own volition.

She grew still, her eyes brimming again. "I'm so sorry," she whispered.

He let his shirt drop and framed her face with his hands. "I'm not." His throat grew dry and his voice husky, but he forced himself to say, "If you have to cry when something's gone . . . it meant something."

Her face crumpled again and he damned himself for adding to her distress. But she nodded, trying to smile amid the tears. Then she threw her arms around his neck and held on to him with the fierceness of a survivor to a life raft.

"Thank you, Elam."

"For what?"

"For being here."

He buried his face in her neck, whispering, "Where else would I be?"

BY the end of the day, the news P.D. received wasn't good. The kitchen was a total loss and would have to be gutted and rebuilt. Although the contractor was willing to squeeze her into his schedule as soon as possible, the water damage caused by the fire hoses could require several days to dry out. The process couldn't be rushed or mold could develop, unseen, behind the walls. That meant that repairs would be delayed for at least a week and Vern's could be closed for nearly a month.

Thanks to the help of the volunteers, the damaged Sheetrock

and part of the ceiling had been removed to the studs to facilitate the process. Huge fans and dehumidifiers had been situated around the kitchen, and the area was sealed off as much as possible. A team of college students from Logan manned the restoration company's power cleaners, scrubbed and polished the hardwood floors, then manhandled the furniture back into the restaurant. By sunset, when the last of the volunteers had left, everything had been stored safely away.

After exchanging a few last-minute instructions with the security guards who'd shown up minutes earlier, P.D. walked to her truck. More than anything, she wanted to turn around, head back into Vern's, and make everything perfect again. But she'd done everything she could until things dried out.

Her manager, Bart Crowley, waited by his own car, his thumbs hooked into the pockets of his jeans. Bart had been with her from the beginning. He was an unassuming man with a receding hairline and a slight paunch. But what he lacked in excitement, he more than made up for in dependability.

"Are you sure you don't want me to take that meeting with the contractor in the morning? You look beat."

She rubbed at the kinked muscles in her neck. "No. I need to be here. You'll have enough on your hands once I'm gone for the Games. I'll give all the employees a briefing on the situation tomorrow. After that, most of the supervision will be left up to you. With any luck, they can start rebuilding before I get back. I've left you detailed lists and drawings since I'd like a slight change to the layout we used to have. I've also left an inventory list for you and the other employees. We'll have to check all of our supplies for smoke damage and make a report to the insurance of anything we need to replace. I've been told that even things that were stored elsewhere in the building, like napkins and placemats, could smell smoky, so they'll have to be tossed. Our suppliers will deliver replacements as soon as we have a tentative opening date. As soon as we physically can, we'll want to start reloading the shelves and—"

Bart touched her arm. "Don't worry. I know what you want me to do."

She sighed, attempting to ease the knot of tension in the

pit of her stomach. "You're right. I guess I'm nervous about being out of touch for few days."

He patted her arm reassuringly. "Guess that prize money is even more tempting now, isn't it?"

P.D. offered him a neutral smile. She was uncomfortable discussing finances with any of her employees—especially since she still didn't know how much the repairs would drain her savings once insurance kicked in their share. Nearly half of all restaurants folded within the first year. Vern's was doing better than most, but she couldn't pretend that this setback wouldn't be a blow to her bottom line.

"Thanks for staying late, Bart."

"I couldn't leave you alone here."

"I appreciate it."

He dropped his arm and moved around his car. With his door half open, he paused. "Can I interest you in a cup of coffee somewhere? Or a soda from the Corner?"

It was no secret that Bart was sweet on her. He'd been trying for several months to get her to go out with him. So far, she'd kept things professional. Although Bart was a nice guy— divorced with a pair of six-year-old twins who sometimes met him at the restaurant—P.D. made it a strict rule not to mix business with pleasure. Until now, she'd managed to deflect his tentative overtures by insisting that she didn't have time for a relationship.

So what had Bart thought when he'd seen Elam bend to kiss her?

Her cheeks grew hot at the memory, but she shook her head. "Thanks, but no. I'm beat. I'm heading straight home to bed."

He looked at her hard, debating whether or not to ask if she planned to sleep alone. A muscle ticked at his cheek, but he offered her a bland, "'Night, then," and slipped into his car.

She waited until his Chevy cleared the parking lot before starting her own truck. Her muscles throbbed from lifting and scrubbing, but her brain couldn't seem to settle. She felt restless and antsy, as if caffeine were coursing through her veins—even though she'd been careful to drink only water throughout the afternoon. Maybe, after sleeping so late, her body wasn't ready to settle down.

Turning onto the road, she pointed her truck toward home. She wasn't really hungry. Not after Helen and Syd's Dutch oven feast. But she could throw in a load of laundry—especially the things that smelled of smoke. She had a basket of clothes that needed ironing and she could always scrub the bathroom. If she wasn't tired enough to fall asleep by then, she could see if there was a movie on one of the cable channels.

But as she eased into the drive and killed the engine, she remained where she was, listening to the soughing of the breeze through the trees, and the chirp of crickets, wondering why she felt a moment of disquiet.

Her eyes flicked to the inky panes of her windows and she wished she'd left on a light. That was one aspect of living alone that she'd never really liked. There was nothing so sad, so lonely, as a house that waited in absolute darkness.

Her fingers curled around the steering wheel and her heart lurched in her chest, then began to pick up speed. Was it the fact that her restaurant had been attacked, and Elam had suggested she install deadbolts, that had her suddenly seeing shadows moving behind the curtains and in the trees?

Damn, damn, damn. Why was her fertile imagination the one thing that her parents had insisted on developing?

Gooseflesh crawled up her arms to the nape of her neck, and before she consciously acknowledged what she was doing, she'd started the engine and backed out of her driveway. Even as she cursed herself for being a fool, she stamped on the gas, gaining speed.

She told herself she'd drive down to the Corner and grab a soda or top off her tank with gas. A few minutes among other people would be enough to chase away the heebie-jeebies. But her truck seemed to have a mind of its own, continuing down the road until she woke from her mental fog and realized that she'd turned down the lane that led to Taggart Hollow. Up ahead, a fork in the road mocked her with her own intentions. If she went left, she would climb the hill to Elam's cabin; right would lead to the Big House.

If she went to Elam with her fears, he might fold her in his arms and allow the heat of his body to seep into her own. Better yet, he might dip his head and . . .

Disgusted with her lack of control where Elam was concerned, she swerved to the right. Perhaps an hour with Bodey would help her calm down. Even more, she might be able to purge herself of the rush of pleasure she felt whenever she thought of Elam's very public kiss in Vern's parking lot.

Had he been claiming her as his own? Or merely telegraphing his decision to abandon his solitary life?

Stop it!

Why couldn't she enjoy whatever he was willing to give her rather than overanalyzing every aspect of their relationship? If they could call what they'd shared so far a relationship.

But even as she insisted there was nothing formal between them, she was flooded with memories of the way he'd held her in the ruined kitchen. Neither of them could say they were "just friends."

Stop!

Pulling onto the gravel next to the house, she killed the engine, slammed the door, and stalked up to the front door. Bodey would set her to rights. He'd tell her she was seeing shadows and chasing the wrong man. He'd never been one for bullshit. He'd let her talk things out, listening intently to everything she had to say, then he'd set her straight with a few blunt words.

She punched the doorbell and waited impatiently. She probably should have called first. Bodey might not even be home. He and Marci, one of her waitresses, had been circling each other for the past couple of weeks.

Footsteps approached from the other side of the door. Not Jace's. Jace's footfalls were long and rangy and usually filled with impatience. These were measured, nearly silent.

Crap!

The door opened to reveal Elam on the other side of the threshold and her mouth immediately went dry. He wore nothing but a pair of Navy sweatpants slung low on his hips. His skin was slick with sweat. With his bare feet and damp, tousled hair, there was nothing to remind her of a historical cowboy here, only pure, modern male.

When he saw her through the screen, he smiled, pushing the door wide. Then he propped a hand on the jamb, and deviant that she was, she enjoyed the ripple of muscle the simple action revealed.

"Hey." He appeared as self-conscious as P.D. felt. Not quite meeting her eyes. Between them shimmered the memory of their shared pain.

If you have to cry when something's gone . . . it meant something.

Suddenly tongue-tied, P.D. realized that her own storm of emotion had probably brought Elam's grief to the fore. Had he been haunted by memories of Annabel for the rest of the afternoon? Had he talked himself into taking another huge, emotional step back from P.D. in the intervening hours?

She shoved her hands into her pockets and rocked back on the heels of her boots. If he only knew how much effort it took not to launch herself into his arms.

Sheesh, he probably thought she was some desperate woman, so addicted to the excitement of his touch that she was hunting him down like a wild animal.

"I-is Bodey here?"

Great. Subtle. Now he'd think she was hunting his brother down as well.

"No. He and Jace are at a canal board meeting. I stayed here to use the weights and watch over Barry. He shouldn't be too long, though." He stepped back. "Come on in."

"Oh. I . . ." She hesitated on the doorstep, knowing that she should make up an excuse that didn't sound too lame and go home. But her body, traitor that it was, moved forward.

Elam stepped aside enough for her to pass through, but her skin absorbed his heat as she walked by, and that, more than anything, settled the jangle of her own nerves.

"Where's Barry?"

"Upstairs playing on his Xbox. He has exactly seven minutes left of the hour he earned doing chores and nothing short of nuclear war will blast him away from the controls."

She chuckled, knowing exactly what Elam meant. Left on his own, Barry would spend every minute of every day playing video games. But since Jace had designed a token system around his chores and schoolwork, every second he earned was doubly precious to him.

As soon as she stepped inside, Elam closed the door. Then he was standing directly behind her. So close. So very, very close, that she could feel his breath stir her hair.

"Was there something specific you needed from Bodey?"

P.D. swallowed against the dryness settling in her mouth. "I . . ."

She wanted him to touch her, to grasp her shoulders or slide his arms around her waist. Belatedly, she wondered if he could hear the want echoed in her voice.

"No, I . . ."

P.D. finally turned, and as she'd thought, Elam stood merely a hairsbreadth away. Up close, the curves and planes of his body were mind-boggling. Her fingers twitched with the need to re-assure herself that he was truly flesh and blood and not some creation carved from marble.

Her mouth grew dry as dust and she unconsciously licked her lips, then cursed her actions when his attention centered on that point with laser-like efficiency.

"A-actually, it's your fault . . ." she whispered vaguely.

"My fault?"

"That I'm here."

"Oh? Why's that?"

Was he leaning closer? Please, please let him be leaning closer.

"A-all your talk about . . . l-locks and deadbolts . . . I think I spooked myself going home."

Yes. *Yes!* He dipped his head, his gaze still trained on her lips as if he needed to see her tasting each word.

"I . . . I kept seeing shadows . . . everywhere . . . and I . . . I . . ."

She couldn't seem to remember what she wanted to say. She couldn't remember anything except the memory of his lips on hers.

Then he finally closed the distance between them, swooping in to kiss her. She sighed, surrendering immediately to his caress. There was no need for him to bid entry, because she willingly opened to him, matching thrust for thrust, parry for parry.

She felt herself being moved backward until her back lay flush against the wall. She welcomed the firm support since it allowed Elam to sidle up next to her, his thighs weaving tightly between her own. He planted one broad forearm on the wall, while the other slid behind her nape, cradling her skull as he plundered her mouth.

Finally, finally, she had the freedom to explore the firm groove of his spine, the flat planes of his shoulder blades, and the molded curves of his biceps. Then her fingers were trailing over his pecks, the flat nubs of his nipples. He reached low to grasp her buttocks, pulling her on tiptoe so their hips meshed together, ridge to valley, hard to soft.

Elam gasped against her, dragging air into his lungs in hungry gulps while she panted in an effort to relieve her oxygen-starved body.

"God, what you do to me," he whispered against her nape.

She smiled, her fingertips digging into his shoulders. In this moment, she could almost believe this passion was enough. *She* was enough.

"It's mutual. I—"

"Elam!"

Elam froze, swearing under his breath when the distant shout was followed by the thump of footfalls heading toward the stairs.

"Elam, the timer went off. Can I have another fifteen minutes?"

"Yeah, Barry! Go ahead."

There was a beat of silence, then, "Really?"

Clearly, Barry had anticipated more of a fight.

"You can have fifteen minutes, but you've got to change into your pajamas first."

"Oh-*kay*!"

The thunder of footsteps headed away again, followed by

a slide across the hardwood floor near the back of the house, where Barry's room was located.

Then, Elam was smiling at her. "I guess we'd better cool things down," he said.

She nodded, even though she would rather protest.

"I'll . . . uh . . . I'll go take a quick shower and change back into my jeans and T-shirt. As soon as Jace or Bodey gets back, I'll follow you home and check things out for you."

Huh?

With great effort, she remembered what had brought her to the Big House in the first place—an uneasiness about returning to the dark, empty bungalow alone. But she was beginning to wonder if that had only been an excuse her unconscious mind had fabricated so that she could begin a search for Elam. Now that she was wrapped in his arms, she knew that nothing short of his embrace would have satisfied her.

In an effort to retain at least a shred of her pride, she nodded, wondering if he would escort her home . . .

And stay.

BY the time Elam had changed, Jace's truck was rumbling into the garage. P.D. heard Elam briefly talk with him. Then he was striding toward the front door.

"Let's go."

He opened the screen for her—and sucker that she was, that unconscious gentlemanly act made her heart do somersaults in her chest.

The air outside was balmy, but dry. Overhead, the stars glittered in an indigo sky and the swing-shaped moon was half hidden by the mountains. But even in the limited light, P.D. saw the way Elam tucked something into the back of his waistband, then smoothed his shirt over the top.

"Are you packing?" she asked.

"I'm usually packing." He reached to open her car door. "I'm ex-military. We tend to be a suspicious bunch."

"You and Helen," she mumbled under her breath as she slid into her truck.

"I'll follow right behind you, but don't get out of your car until I look around."

She opened her mouth, feeling a little foolish that he was willing to go to such measures to ease her fears. He was probably going to assume she was a hysterical female who jumped at her own shadow.

But as she pulled into her driveway, a frisson of gooseflesh raced up her spine and she had the distinct, unsettling sensation that she was being watched.

Elam pulled in behind her, leaving his lights on. But as he stepped out of the truck, he grew suddenly still and doused them. Then, he was reaching behind him to pull out a pistol and level it in front of him.

It was clear from his stance that he knew how to use the weapon—and whoever had been lingering near the house must have thought the same thing because a shape dislodged from the bushes to her left, banged into the garbage can, then started running toward the trees.

Elam immediately gave chase, tearing through the bushes at top speed. He was closing the distance between them when both shadows disappeared into a copse of sumac.

P.D.'s heart was pounding so hard that it threatened to leap out of her chest. More than anything, she wanted to dodge out of the car and go running to Elam's defense. But she'd promised she would stay where she was. And with Elam armed, it would be stupid personified if she started chasing after him in the dark.

She waited for what seemed like hours—although the car clock revealed it was less than five minutes. Then Elam jogged back into sight. Holding his pistol by his thigh, he took the steps to her house two at a time, disappearing for another few minutes. Soon, she saw a series of lights being switched on as he retraced his steps to the front of the house. Then he returned to open her door, holstering his pistol behind him.

"W-who was it?" she asked, her pulse still pounding in her ears.

"I think some kids have been using a little clearing in the trees as their hangout spot. I chased whoever it was as far as the canal road, but the culprit had a car waiting and disappeared before I could catch him. Looked like a dark, beat-up sedan. The clearing is full of old beer bottles, cigarette butts, and a cache of girlie magazines."

"Do you think it's the same kids who started the fire?"

Elam shrugged. "I suppose it's possible. I'll let the sheriff know about it in the morning. I'm sure he'll want to keep a close eye on the spot for a while."

He took her hand, helping her stand, and then escorted her to the door. But when she thought he would leave her to return home, he followed her inside.

"You still have the pillows and blankets from last night?"

She motioned to where they were stacked on the arm of the couch. "You're going to stay?"

The timber of her voice emerged with a hopefulness that she hadn't meant to reveal, but she didn't think she could sleep alone in the house after everything that had happened.

He took her shoulders and turned her to face him. Then his hands looped around her back. "Yeah. I'm going to stay. On the couch."

She opened her mouth to suggest an alternative, but quickly changed her mind. It was clear that he'd considered the same arrangement. But there was also a storm of indecision raging in his eyes.

His touch had the opposite effect on her, stilling her panic and bringing a peace that she didn't quite understand. But while she was willing to experiment to see where these feelings might take her, she could tell from his expression that he'd begun to overthink things again.

And for once in her life, she was willing to be patient.

Rising on tiptoe, she briefly pressed her lips to his. "Thanks, Elam."

Before she could back away, he bent, deepening the kiss, wordlessly relaying to her that his reluctance had nothing to do with her and everything to do with him.

When he released her, she smiled and cupped his cheek with her hand to show she understood. "Sweet dreams," she murmured, then stepped out of his arms and moved down the hall.

* * *

ELAM wasn't sure why he let her go. He wasn't sure why he felt so conflicted. He was a widower, damnit, not a eunuch. No one would fault him for starting a relationship.

A relationship. That's where they were headed—if they weren't there already.

The thought didn't scare him as much as it might have done a week ago. He was attracted to P.D. Hell, he only had to be near her a few minutes before he wanted to haul her into his arms.

But as his desire for P.D. grew, his memories of Annabel were slipping out of his grasp. Even though logic told him it was natural, that nothing could eradicate his feelings for his wife, it felt . . . disloyal.

He sat on the couch long enough to pull off his boots and socks, then, heading to the bathroom, he used the bar of P.D.'s lemon soap to wash up. But when he walked out again, turning off the light, he couldn't stop himself from lingering opposite the door to P.D.'s room. She must have been exhausted, because she was already asleep, one arm unconsciously flung out toward him, the palm open, the fingers curled beseechingly.

Elam was suddenly suffused with the need to touch that hand, to absorb the warmth that only another human being could offer. He was so tired, emotionally and physically. He didn't want to run from the past anymore, nor did he want to avoid the future. So tonight, he wouldn't think about any of it. He would simply do what felt right.

Padding into her room, he set his pistol on the nightstand and carefully slid into the bed. P.D. remained asleep, but she sighed, rolling toward him until her head rested on his shoulder and her arm wrapped around his waist. Then she became boneless, melting into him as if she'd done it a hundred times before. And damned if he didn't feel his own body draining of tension as well.

How he'd missed this—not just having a woman in his arms, but the warmth of another person, the anticipation of the next encounter, the melding of purposes. So why, even after all this time, did he feel a niggling of guilt that the woman in question wasn't his late wife?

Logically, he knew that no one would fault him for moving on with his life. Annabel had been gone for three years—and even the hardest soul would have agreed he'd deeply mourned her passing. He'd had more than one person suggest that he begin dating, marry again. He was young; he deserved love in his life, a family.

But all of those arguments couldn't seem to fill the ache that lingered in his heart. He'd loved Annabel most of his life. From the moment she'd entered his kindergarten classroom, clutching her mother's hand, Elam had felt a tug of affection. In middle school, his crush had deepened, and in junior high school, she'd been the first girl he'd ever asked to dance. When she'd agreed, he'd thought he was the luckiest kid alive—especially when he'd realized that his feelings were reciprocated. They'd been high school sweethearts, and when he'd joined the Navy, she'd been his staunchest supporter. He'd married her as soon as he'd made it through basic training. When they were together, it was like a honeymoon all over again. And when he was deployed, she wrote and called as often as possible.

Probably he'd been selfish. He'd loved his job, loved the adrenaline rush it offered—loved the travel, the combat. He'd planned on retiring once he'd met his twenty years, so Annabel had followed him whenever possible. And when she couldn't be near, she'd returned to the ranch, where he knew his brothers would watch out for her. They'd both held fast to the fact that their separations were temporary. He and Annabel would have their whole futures together.

If he'd only known that life could reach out, grab you by the balls, and bring you to your knees.

If only . . .

Would he have done anything differently?

The thought was sobering. Now he could see that he'd been a selfish bastard, focusing on his career first while Annabel had patiently supported him from thousands of miles away. He could tell himself that the decision hadn't been his alone, and that Annabel had been the first person to urge him to continue his training. He could even believe that the Navy had made him the man that he'd become, the man Annabel had chosen to love.

But deep down, he wondered what he would have done if Annabel had made him choose between the Navy and her. Would he have been happy staying on the ranch, stewing over what it would be like to travel farther than the state line? Or would his wanderlust have ruined his marriage?

P.D. stirred, burrowing more securely into his side, and Elam felt his throat tighten as he realized that this was the moment, the precise instant, when he had to decide the course of the rest of his life. He'd loved Annabel, body and soul. But she wasn't coming back. And he wouldn't allow himself to get involved with another woman if he couldn't fully commit to her. It simply wasn't in his nature. Bodey might play the field and leave bruised hearts strewn in his wake. But Elam had always been the sort who gave his attention to only one woman at a time.

His chest tightened. Logically, he knew the answer: that it was time to move forward. But saying good-bye to the woman who'd been his sweetheart for more than half his life wasn't that easy.

The song he'd heard only a few nights ago seemed to weave through his head. At the time, the melody had almost crushed him. Then, it had begun to haunt him—so much so, that a search on the Internet had yielded a filmed performance of the ballad on YouTube. But two lines began to echo over and over in his head.

I know she's in a happier place,
With constant sunlight on her face,
Someday she'll visit us, this I know . . .

And it was then that the tightness eased from his chest and he was flooded by a sense of peace that he hadn't felt in a very long time.

Us.

It was as if, in that whisper of thought, Annabel herself had uttered the words. She wouldn't have wanted him to be alone. She would probably have scolded him for taking so long to work his way out of his despair.

His eyes stung with moisture, but this time they weren't tears of sadness. Instead, after he wiped away the damp tracks, he tangled his fingers in the riotous curls spilling over his chest and fell asleep.

NINE

————•◦•————

P.D. woke with a curious sense of *déjà vu*. The light slanting through the curtains revealed that it was late, although she hadn't slept into the evening like the day before. A glance at the clock revealed that it was afternoon—past the time she was usually beginning her day at the restaurant.

Normally, she would have been in a panic, but she'd slept so soundly and felt so refreshed that she pushed away the niggling guilt and stretched instead, enjoying the warmth of the featherbed and the softness of her pillow. Turning to her side, she closed her eyes again, trying to remember something of her dreams. Her body hummed with curious electricity, as if the overtones of her midnight fantasies had been slightly erotic. She felt her cheeks grow hot, knowing that Elam had been a major part of them all. But when her eyes flickered open and she saw the indentation of a head on the pillow opposite, she realized that the warmth she'd imagined next to her hadn't been a dream.

The next wave of heat to suffice her body was filled with wisps of her own phantom desires, but it was quickly replaced by a wave of consternation. *Please, please, don't tell me I groped him in my sleep!*

Crap!

P.D. threw the blankets back and scrambled for her clothes. She dressed in record time, all the while listening for any signs of life elsewhere in the house. But when she emerged into the living room, it was empty. The sheets and blankets she'd provided for Elam were still folded neatly on the arm of the couch—providing further evidence that he'd slept with her. And in the kitchen . . .

Another note.

She hurried to the table to find a terse message and a small bundle of keys.

It's Sell Day at the ranch, so I'll be in touch. In the meantime, use these.

Elam

Lifting the keys, she turned them over, having no clue what they might open. As much as she might secretly relish the thought, she doubted they were to his cabin. But after pocketing them and hurrying to the front door, she suddenly understood. He'd replaced her hardware with shiny new knobs and deadbolts.

She stood for long moments, staring at the pretty brass turnings, absorbing the fact that Elam hadn't just picked utilitarian items. No, he'd carefully chosen designs that would reflect the eclectic period-inspired furnishings of her home. They looked solid and effective, yet somehow delicate.

And why did his thoughtfulness, his obvious care for her safety, cause her heart to melt as if he'd given her diamonds?

Grabbing her purse, she stepped outside and quickly secured the deadbolts. As she hurried down the steps, her heart lurched a little when she saw a pickup at the curb, but she came to her senses when she realized that it was Bodey's vehicle.

He stepped out of the truck and hobbled toward her, this time on a walking boot rather than with crutches.

"Elam said you had some trouble here last night," he said as he rounded the hood.

She nodded. "He thinks I've got some kids using the back field for a drinking spot."

"Yeah. He let the sheriff know about it early this morning. Since he's helping with the auction, he asked me to stay here until you left, just in case they came back for their stash."

Again, she was inundated by a strange pleasure. She'd spent so long taking care of herself, of relying on her own ingenuity to solve her problems, that having someone else concerned about her welfare was disconcerting and . . . wholly wonderful.

She pointed to Bodey's boot. "It looks like you're making progress."

He scowled down at the offending orthopedic device. "Not enough, in my opinion."

P.D. suddenly realized that he blamed himself for putting her in the lurch. "You still want to do the Games."

He eyed her sheepishly. "Hell, yeah. It sounds like a lot of fun. And I feel bad for saddling you with Elam."

"We're actually . . . getting along," she said as blandly as she could muster, hoping she wouldn't get struck by lightning for the gross understatement. She'd spent the night in Elam's arms twice in a row—even if she couldn't completely remember one of them.

Bodey leaned back against his truck. "You'll be careful, won't you?"

"Of course. I don't plan on shooting myself if I can help it."

Bodey eyed her for several long seconds beneath the brim of his cowboy hat. "I mean you'll be careful with Elam. He's had a hard time of things these past few years. I was beginning to believe we'd never see him crack a smile again. But lately . . ."

He left a wide opening for her to comment, but she refused to take the bait. She'd never been one to kiss and tell, and she certainly wasn't going to share details with Elam's brother.

But her silence gave Bodey all the answer he needed because he grinned broadly, saying, "That's what I thought." Then, offering her a two-finger salute, he limped his way back

to the driver's seat, climbed into his truck, and drove away
with a mocking, "Don't have too much fun, y' hear," floating
out the window.

THE weekend passed in a blur. But to P.D.'s consternation,
she didn't see Elam again. She'd spent Saturday meeting with
her insurance representative, her banker, and her employees
while Elam had been busy with a Sell Day of yearling colts.
Sunday had been spent with Helen finalizing the details of
her costumes.

But by Monday morning, the first day of the Wild West
Games, P.D. felt comfortable enough with leaving Vern's in her
manager's capable hands. It would still be a few days before the
fans could be removed. As soon as the insurance company's
contractor was given the go-ahead, they could begin the rebuilding process. With luck, the painters and flooring people
could begin soon after P.D. returned from the Games.

She was lucky. Insurance would pay for most of the stag-
gering expense of restoring the restaurant to full operation.
But with her deductible and some of the items not covered,
she would still have to come up with more money than she
wanted to think about—which made the prize money offered
by the Games that much more tantalizing.

Please, please let us win.

As she paced in front of her living room window, waiting for
Elam's truck to appear, she had no doubts that Elam could hold
up his end of the bargain. He excelled in everything she needed
in a partner—athleticism, a keen mind, an ability to survive
outdoors, and shooting skills that could rival Wild Bill Hickock's.
She merely hoped that she could keep up with someone who was
clearly at the top of his game. Let's face it, most of the time, her
"aerobic exercise" came from running the restaurant. She'd rather
surf the Internet than run. And she sure as hell wasn't a camper.
In her opinion, "camping" was being forced to stay in a hotel
without room service. But knowing the rigors of the Games,
she'd spent the past few weeks walking every night. She'd gone
to a local gym whenever possible, and taken several hikes in the

hills. She could only hope she'd done enough to keep up with Elam, who was clearly a natural athlete.

"Just please don't let me embarrass myself in front of Elam too badly," she whispered in hasty prayer.

She'd been about to add an addendum—"and please keep me from any unladylike sweating, swearing, or shooting myself in the foot"—but Elam chose that moment to swing into the drive.

Grabbing the carpetbag that held only her most necessary supplies, she hurried outside, carefully locking the deadbolt and pocketing the keys. Truth be told, she still forgot half the time, but she didn't want Elam to think she didn't appreciate his gift.

"What's this?" he asked when she handed him the carpetbag.

"Helen let me borrow it so that I'd have period appropriate luggage."

His brows rose as he tested its weight. "I thought the Games were only four days long."

"They are."

"Feels like you have enough for four weeks."

"I only brought what was absolutely necessary."

"Uh-huh."

Before she could stop him, he opened the bag and dumped the contents onto the hood of his truck. A frothy pile of pantalets, camisoles, and petticoats lay jumbled up with her toiletries, an extra pair of shoes, and thigh-high cotton hose. Even though the garments were far from titillating, her cheeks heated.

"You won't need these, or these, or these . . ." He dropped the carpetbag on the ground and began throwing items inside—shampoo, conditioner, petticoats, camisoles, and pantalets. When he'd finished, she was left with only one change of underthings, socks, and a brush to comb her hair.

"You've got to be kidding."

"We're only going to be out there four days, P.D."

"What if I get cold?"

"We'll build a fire."

"What if I get dirty?"

"You're going to get dirty. That's why I let you have an extra set of underwear. If you absolutely need to, you can wash your stuff in whatever water we find and wear the extra set while it dries."

She narrowed her eyes. "You want me to beat my clothes against a rock?"

"If it makes you happy."

P.D. fought the urge to argue. "What about you? What are you bringing?"

Elam reached into his pocket and withdrew a toothbrush. "That's it."

"You can't be serious."

"First rule of hiking: If *you* take it; *you* carry it. I've done worse in the military. This is a walk in the park."

She looked down mournfully at the carpetbag and her supplies. She thought she'd been so careful to keep things to a reasonable minimum. But she'd also thought Elam would volunteer to carry her bag.

"What are you going to do if *your* . . . underthings need to be washed?"

"Go commando."

Her mouth opened, but no sound emerged. The sudden image of Elam naked flashed into her head and she was struck dumb.

When Elam continued to wait for a response, she said softly, "I don't want to stink."

Elam sighed, then bent to snatch up a wrapped bar of her favorite soap. After sniffing it, he shoved it into the same pocket as his toothbrush.

"I need something to carry these in," she said grudgingly.

He reached into his tool box and removed a canvas sack that had probably held potatoes or seeds a million years ago. Reaching inside, he removed a set of screwdrivers and gave her the dingy drawstring bag.

She opened her mouth to state the obvious: that it was dirty and hardly a fitting container for her clean underthings. But knowing her objections would probably be overruled, she sighed and did what she'd been told.

Returning to the house, she threw the carpetbag inside and relocked the door. Then, she marched toward Elam, wondering if going without the niceties of life was worth the chance at ten thousand dollars.

But the thought had barely formed before her brain insisted: *Hell, yes!*

She was about to climb into his truck—why on earth were men determined to make such a task as ungainly as possible for women?—when Elam stopped her.

"Wait a minute."

He took the smaller canvas bag from her hand and threw it onto the seat. Then, he turned her to face him, his arms sliding around her waist.

He wanted to kiss her. Right now.

There was a questioning glint to his eyes—and she wondered how on earth he had gained the impression that he needed to ask. But not wanting to scare the man, she placed her hands on his chest.

He took a step forward, two, until their legs were entwined, their hips brushing. A thrill of awareness rushed through her when she realized that Elam was already partially aroused. Was there a woman alive who wasn't turned on by knowing she had that effect on a man?

His hands slid around to link at the small of her back.

"This probably isn't a good idea since we're already running late," he murmured, leaning closer until his lips brushed the shell of her ear. The warmth of his breath sent a cascade of gooseflesh down her arms. "But I'm not inclined to do what's best."

He took his time, running his lips and nose so lightly across her forehead and temple that she might have imagined the caress if she hadn't been so attuned to his warmth. Then, he continued moving down, down, licking her cheek with the tiniest flick of his tongue so that her breath came in irregular pants. She shifted anxiously when he bypassed her mouth altogether and blazed a trail along the stalk of her neck. Her head fell back like a daisy heavy with dew. Here, he became bolder, sucking, nipping, until she felt as if her knees might give way.

Lordy, he was a great kisser—and she'd obviously been dealing with amateurs before. He took his time, exploring each dip and hollow as if he searched for something precious. He tasted her, tested her, nipped and suckled, until she thought she would go out of her mind—especially when he reached the notch between her collarbones and paused there, smiling against her skin. It was then that she realized that she'd spritzed perfume in that spot right after leaving the shower.

"I like that," Elam said. "You smell like summer."

A tiny corner of P.D.'s brain made a mental note to buy another bottle, or two, or a gallon of her favorite scent.

Finally, finally, he lifted his head. P.D. was able to part her lashes under the drugging power of his kisses, but she was glad she did because his eyes seemed to smile at her, crinkling in the corners. He was enjoying himself—enjoying her.

If only this could last . . .

Then, he finally bent to touch his lips to hers, softly, gently, before inviting her to open her lips for his tongue.

P.D. willingly complied, sighing into his mouth when he deepened the caress, standing on tiptoes so that, this time, she was the one to increase the contact between them. She wrapped her arms around his neck, meeting him taste for taste. And when he pressed her back against the side of the truck, she whispered, "Yes, yes."

Elam's kisses became more intense as he ravished her mouth. Cupping her buttocks with his broad palms, he lifted her more firmly against his arousal.

She drew back far enough to murmur, "Mmm, I like *that*."

Elam laughed. Dear sweet heaven, the man nicknamed Desperado, the great stone-faced recluse she'd met only a few days ago . . .

Laughed.

And then, before she could fully absorb how his features completely changed in that moment, his phone rang.

Elam sighed, resting his forehead against hers. "Hell. I knew there was a reason why I shouldn't have started using my cell again."

"You could ignore it," she said against his lips.

"Except the only people who know I'm available by cell phone are my contractor and my brothers."

He shifted enough to grab the phone, but didn't let her loose. Punching the call button, he barked, "Yeah."

P.D. couldn't hear much of the low voice on the other end, but the humor she'd witnessed was instantly gone as Elam frowned and said, "We're on our way." Then he ended the call and glanced at the screen, swearing.

"That was Bodey wondering where we are. They're starting to gather up the contestants. We have to get going."

THE words had barely left his mouth when P.D. turned to clamber into the truck. She squeaked when Elam planted a hand beneath her butt and gave her a boost.

P.D. probably wouldn't say so herself, but in Elam's opinion, she had a great ass, round and firm and filling a man's hands to perfection. Until today, he'd always seen her in jeans that hugged her body and teased a man with what he would find if he peeled the layers away. But this morning, she wore a high-collared cotton shirt and a full pleated skirt with rows of tucks around the hem. Covered from chin to ankle, she should have appeared demure, but the nipped-in waist and high bust-line caused by the corset she wore made Elam's imagination run wild.

Forcing his mind onto getting them both to the historical farm before they were disqualified, Elam surreptitiously adjusted his hard-on to a more tolerable spot.

Beside him, P.D. laughed. "Down, boy."

He shook his head, his lips twitching. "You are downright incorrigible, you know that?"

"But you admire that quality."

And it was true, Elam thought, the sentiment racing through him like a bolt of lightning. He loved the way she said whatever came into her mind, the way she lived life to the fullest. He envied her courage in displaying her emotions without a filter. Every obstacle she encountered was met with a passionate response that spoke more about her character than anything else.

Elam lifted his arm and wrapped it around her shoulders, drawing her close. Just as he'd expected, she melted into him, one of her hands resting on his thigh.

He fought to keep his attention on the road as he was hit with a burst of need. Somehow, by giving himself permission to wholeheartedly enter into a relationship with P.D., he was swamped by his hunger for her. It was why he'd avoided seeing her until now, knowing that he wouldn't be able to keep his hands off her. And damnit, if they weren't already late, he would have been tempted to find a private access road somewhere and slake his hunger.

Shit, had he grown so selfish over the past few years that he couldn't think beyond his own wants? Yeah, P.D. was attracted to him, but that didn't mean she was ready to climb into bed with him.

Like hell. He wasn't so far gone that he didn't know when a woman was attracted to him—and he was pretty sure she'd be agreeable if he suggested they take things to the next level.

Wouldn't she?

Damn, it had been so long since he'd been with a woman that he felt as randy and unsophisticated as a kid from high school. He'd debated with himself for hours about whether or not to include several condoms in addition to his toothbrush. At the last minute, he'd stuffed them into his wallet. But when he'd seen no such precautions in P.D.'s bag, he'd chickened out of informing her of the fact. If he mentioned it now, he was going to come off looking like a jerk who'd taken her acquiescence for granted.

Shit, shit, shit. How in hell did Bodey always manage to come across so smooth?

He felt a pressure on his thigh and roused from his thoughts. P.D. was watching him with concern.

"Is something wrong?"

"No, I . . . I'm just worried that we won't get there in time," he said, hoping she hadn't read even a portion of his thoughts.

But it was clear she hadn't believed his excuse.

P.D. knew the moment that Elam checked out on her, and she damned herself for not holding her tongue.

Down, boy.

Geez. Had she really said that? She needed to think before she opened her mouth. Annabel had probably been more circumspect, more genteel. A lady through and through. She'd probably been schooled in manners from birth.

P.D., on the other hand, had been schooled in survival. Unbidden, she was flooded with a montage of images from her childhood: searching through Dumpsters behind the grocery store for food; trembling beneath her father's grip when he was in one of his drug-induced rages; running out of a filthy gas station restroom where she'd struggled to wash her hair, only to discover that her parents had forgotten she was there and had driven away without her.

Biting her cheek, P.D. forced the bitter memories away, refusing to let herself imagine how different Annabel's upbringing might have been to her own. It would have to be for her to feel so content and secure in Elam's love.

But P.D. wasn't Annabel—didn't want to be Annabel. From what she'd been able to gather, Annabel had been shy and quiet. She taught first grade most of the year and puttered in her garden during the summer. She baked her own bread, sewed her own clothes, and volunteered at the hospital. She was a member of the Library Board and the Women's League.

She was the antithesis of P.D., who spent nearly every waking minute trying to get her restaurant off the ground.

But that was okay. P.D. was proud of her accomplishments and the life she'd made for herself. Even more important, she'd walked into this knowing that any relationship she and Elam might share would be brief and passionate. A bursting flame to bring back to life a man who would then move on to someone more his style. Because he could never love someone like her as much as his perfect Annabel.

So why, if she knew all that, was she having a hard time coming to terms with it?

As they rounded the bend, the Ridley Historical Farm came into view. It was a full-blown anachronism built on the edge of a busy freeway. Split rail fences, huge barns, and a quaint little town made from historical buildings had been rescued from demolition, reassembled, and then restored on the site.

A wide banner proclaiming THE OFFICIAL STARTING POINT OF THE WILD WEST GAMES! had been strung along the top of the arched entrance to the parking lot.

"Holy moley!" P.D. exclaimed as she saw the lines of vehicles. "Everyone and their dog must be here."

After going up and down the rows, Elam finally managed to find a spot near the back fence.

Not even waiting for Elam to bring the rig to a full stop, P.D. slid across the bench seat and jumped to the ground. For now, she would keep things simple and let Elam take the lead. She'd concentrate on the Games and only the Games—and not on the fact that she was competing with a ghost and there wasn't a damned thing she could do about it. She had to live with the fact that Elam might take a step back now and again. And she understood his situation. It was logical that he would still be chasing memories. But she was finding that jealousy wasn't reserved only for the living.

Rushing to gather their things, P.D. lowered the tail gate and began pulling the rifle cases and ammunition boxes toward her. But damn his hide, Elam came right up beside her and reached out to still her hands.

"Wait. Before we get mixed up with everyone at the starting point . . ."

He grabbed her by the elbows and forced her to face him.

"I've got something I need to say. Just to make things clear between us."

His features were so serious that P.D. immediately stilled, wondering what could be weighing on his mind so heavily. But before she knew what was happening, Elam pushed her back against the tailgate and swooped in to cover her lips with his own. This time, there was no finesse, no lingering kisses, no exploration. This time, it was an invasion, pure and simple, a blatant display of raw sex and emotion with no holds barred.

As if it were a match held to kerosene, P.D. exploded, wrapping her arms around his neck and throwing herself more tightly into his embrace, answering his raw desire with her own. It was only when his hands slid down to cup her buttocks, lifting her against the blatant evidence of his arousal, that his lips

tore free long enough for him to gasp, "I want you to know that
I'm not . . . that I . . ." He ruefully shook his head. "Shit, I don't
know how to be cool and . . . I don't know . . . *modern* . . . about
all this. But . . ."

He laughed and his eyes became suddenly soft and, oh, so
heated.

"Damnit all to hell, P.D. I'm crazy about you. I can't keep
my hands off you—which isn't going to help us win the prize
money if I can't even get us to the starting line on time."

*He was crazy about her? Wow. No one had ever told her
that he was* crazy *about her.*

She met his gaze then—met the blatant desire and fierce
hunger. This time, there wasn't a shred of regret in their blue-
brown depths.

When he saw that she believed him, he leaned to rest his
forehead against hers.

"When I get quiet like that . . . I'm not pushing you away,
P.D. Just the opposite." He paused, his eyes flooding with a
heat that she could scarcely believe was aimed at her. "And
this time I've come prepared."

TEN

PASSION shot through P.D.'s core like a bolt of lightning.

"Contestants, will you please gather on the boardwalk outside the Photo Emporium . . ."

The distant announcement caused Elam to swear even more colorfully. After one additional quick, hard kiss, he gathered up the ammunition buckets while she scrambled to take the rifle cases. Then, as if the chirp of the car alarm were a starting pistol, they raced toward the main square.

As they neared the rendezvous point, they were surrounded by crowds of people. Many of them had entered into the spirit of the Games by wearing historical garb. Little girls in ruffles and pantalets, with their hair twisted into braids, waited in line for the face painting booth or the puppet show, while the boys played hide-and-seek in the crowd with hand-carved pop guns. The teenagers were a little less exuberant, most of them in jeans and T-shirts, while the braver sort sported costumes with the jarring addition of ear buds dangling from their shirt collars.

Spying a familiar figure near the bandstand up ahead, P.D.

waved to Helen. She and her husband stood resplendent in their finery, Syd with a top hat, frock coat, and walking stick, and Helen in a beautiful sprigged bustle gown and parasol.

Bodey stood beside them, looking much like he did any day, a cowboy through and through. He'd added suspenders and arm garters in an effort to make his tight jeans and button-down shirt look a little more historically accurate, but the orthopedic boot ruined the effect. Jace hadn't bothered. His garb was Modern Cowboy—snap-front shirt, worn jeans, and his "going to town" boots. He leaned against one of the hitching posts, scrolling through his phone, his hat low over his eyes as he searched for a number. Barry, on the other hand, had gone all out, dressed tip to toe in fringed buckskins with a raccoon-tail hat tipped rakishly over one eye.

"They're here!" Barry shouted.

Before Jace could stop him, Barry ran to greet them, relieving P.D. of her rifle case. Secretly, she was grateful. She'd never realized how heavy the weapons would be. No wonder Elam had insisted she lighten her load.

Their greetings had hardly been made before the contest organizers appeared to hustle Elam and P.D. away to the Photo Emporium on the corner.

"Your picture will be used for news coverage as well as public announcements around town. While you're waiting, you'll need to read through these permission slips and waivers. Make sure the emergency contact information and spellings are correct."

It seemed odd to be perusing sheaves of laser-printed paper and signing them with ballpoint pens while standing in the midst of a reconstructed pioneer town. But P.D. managed to skim through the information and offer her approval, even though Elam was only a hairsbreadth away and his words kept echoing in her brain.

And this time I've come prepared.

Was it possible to suffer from emotional whiplash by inwardly insisting on caution, then racing back to full-throttle euphoria in the space of a few seconds?

"Next!"

She roused to her surroundings when Elam touched her elbow.

"That's us."

They were ushered into the cool interior of the Photo Emporium. Hundreds of props—hats, fans, parasols, dresses, and jackets—lined one far wall. On the opposite end, an elaborately painted Victorian background had been placed behind an ornate, straight-back wicker chair.

"Names," a woman with a clipboard prompted.

"Prairie Dawn Raines and Elam—"

At Elam's pronouncement, the woman peered at them over her bifocals and interrupted, "Real names."

"That is my real name."

The woman glanced at them again, then at her roster. Finding P.D. on the roster, her eyes widened, skipped toward P.D. again, then at Elam.

"Huh." She pointed to a basket filled with sealed envelopes. "Pick one of the colored envelopes. Throughout your journey, you need to make sure you always choose that particular colored envelope. This will guarantee that you fulfill all of your challenges in the proper order. Failure to do so could lead to a disqualification or penalty. Do not open this morning's envelope until you are told to do so."

"Yes, ma'am."

Elam burrowed into the pile to grab a yellow envelope from the bottom, then tucked it into his back pocket.

The woman handed them a pair of arm garters. Sewn to them were embroidered patches displaying the number seven.

"These are your contestant numbers. They must be worn at all times or you could be disqualified. Throughout the competition you will be monitored with or without your knowledge, so keep them visible."

P.D. and Elam exchanged glances. P.D. nearly giggled aloud at Elam's look of barely concealed horror. Clearly, he'd been planning on making his move sooner rather than later.

"Move to the photo area, please," the woman ordered curtly before barking, "Next!"

With a hand at her back, Elam ushered P.D. forward. He was

told to sit on the chair, back rigid, hat on his knee. Then, P.D. was positioned slightly behind him, her hand on his shoulder.

"We want these photos to look as historically accurate as possible, so no smiles, please. Hold as still as you can, just as if you were posing for a box camera."

P.D.'s fingers unconsciously tightened on Elam's shoulder. Once again, she was struck by the latent strength, by muscles honed to tiptop condition. But it wasn't the upcoming competition that stuck like a burr in her consciousness. It was the thought of smoothing the shirt from his body and kissing him, right there, in the hollow of his shoulder.

The lights flashed and the camera made a muffled *snuffle-snick*.

"Once more."

Flash! Snuffle-snick.

"Okay, head out the rear and circle around the building to the front again. Across the street, you'll see another contest volunteer by the door to Miller's Mercantile. He'll give you the next set of instructions."

Elam jumped from the chair, donning his cowboy hat again. Snagging P.D.'s hand, he led her out into the sunshine.

"No one said anything about a bunch of damned Peeping Toms watching us—and I read the rules cover to cover."

P.D. giggled. "Did you really think they'd take it on faith that the contestants had followed every instruction?"

Elam only grimaced. "Then I guess you and I are going to have to get creative, because I don't think either one of us is going to be able to wait that long for a little . . . privacy."

P.D. opened her mouth to disagree, but she couldn't. She wasn't sure if she could keep her hands off Elam another hour, let alone days.

Since there was a queue outside the mercantile, Elam helped her slide the arm garter over her blouse, then she did the same for him, purposely letting her fingers trail over each hollow and bulge of his forearm and bicep. She knew she was playing with fire—especially when his eyes met hers and smoldered from within—but she didn't care. For the first time she felt his whole-hearted response.

P.D. wasn't sure what had happened to put Elam so at peace with himself, but she was glad. Since he'd laid his feelings on the line, he seemed more at ease than she'd ever seen him, and more . . . present. As if he was living in the "now" and not pre-occupied with the past.

"Next!"

They took their place in front of a balding gentleman dressed like a shopkeeper with a crisp bibbed shirt, arm garters, and a green butcher's apron. He handed them a stack of gold pieces of cardstock printed to look like coins, and green rectangles labeled WILD WEST BUCKS, as well as an inventory of goods being offered for sale.

"You have exactly twenty minutes to peruse the list of possible supplies that can be found in the mercantile, hardware store, or livery stable. Bottled water will be made available to you at each of the checkpoints, as well as one lunch and ingredients for one dinner, but you're on your own for the rest. After purchasing your supplies, come back to me so that I can record your time, then report to the starting line in front of the bandstand." He lifted a stopwatch and said, "Go!"

P.D. didn't even bother to waste valuable time. "You have more experience in this kind of thing than I do. I'll get the weapons and ammunition to the bandstand and start taking them out of their cases. Meet me there."

Elam dodged into the mercantile without even perusing the list. Lifting her skirts, P.D. raced back toward Elam's family. To her relief, she noted that their guns had already been unpacked and their allotted ammunition for the day loaded into their belts. Helen helped P.D. don her holster, pulling it low on her hips.

"Make sure you drink water whenever you can and take regular breaks from the hikes. It's supposed to be hot the next few days. You don't want to get sunstroke."

Which P.D. quickly translated into: *We both know you're not used to this long-distance stuff, so take it easy.*

"Hopefully, I won't be the first casualty on this adventure."

Helen looked at a point over P.D.'s shoulder, and then grinned. "Oh, I doubt you'll be the first. The Butterman twins have entered—and they're seventy if they're a day. Besides, it looks like Elam has everything figured out to your advantage."

P.D. turned to find Elam heading toward her on horseback and immediately most of her nerves fled.

"You got a horse," she breathed in wonder as he stopped the animal in front of her and dismounted.

"Took more than half our money, but since it was one of several being offered, I figured we could use the advantage."

"What else did you get?"

"A pan, mess kits, a little feed for the horse, and a few basics for us." He gestured to the bulging saddlebags and a rolled-up blanket that he'd tied to the back of the saddle. "I kept fifty bucks in reserve just in case they require us to purchase something along the trail."

When she peeked into the bags, P.D. could see that Elam hadn't been kidding about only getting a "few basics." There was a package of jerky, another of dried fruit, canned pork and beans, a compass, a knife, a pan, a can opener, a ball of string, and a pair of fishhooks attached to a scrap of fabric. The other side held a canvas sack labeled OATS, another containing baking mix, a tiny container of salt, and chunk of raw sugar.

Her stomach rumbled at the lack of "real" food. She was used to walking into the cooler of her restaurant and choosing from a plethora of culinary supplies. This didn't look like enough for a snack, let alone several days.

"Don't worry," Elam said next to her ear. "I won't let you starve."

"I've had your cooking, remember?" she said. "And I don't see any Cap'n Crunch."

Elam laughed, sliding a rifle into a side holster below the saddle, then he circled the animal to put the shotgun on the opposite side. After he'd assured himself that the weapons were safely stowed away, he returned to strap on the holsters that Bodey held out to him, while Jace tucked the rest of their ammo into the saddlebags.

"If you'll give me your keys, I'll drive your truck back home," Jace said. "We'll have it ready for you at the end of the contest."

P.D. clutched the halter lead, hungrily drinking in the sight of Elam as he tunneled into his pockets and tossed the fob toward his brother. Then he wrapped the leather belt around his hips and tightened the thigh string. At long last, he pulled his hat down tight, buttoned his leather vest, and took the reins.

"Do you want to be in the front or the back?" he asked.

She considered her options, but decided it would probably be easiest for Elam to maneuver if she rode behind him and wrapped her arms around his waist.

"Back."

Elam swung deftly in the saddle, taking a minute to adjust the angle of the weapons. Then he reached down to her.

P.D. had thought it would be a struggle to get on the gelding with the cumbersome addition of her skirts, but Elam swung her easily onto the mount behind him and waited while she settled on top of the bedroll.

"Ready?"

"Yeah."

She wrapped her arms around his taut waist. He laid his own hand over hers, squeezing. Even through his leather gloves she could feel the warmth of his skin.

"All set?" Bodey asked.

"Yeah. We're good."

Bodey held up the bag with P.D.'s belongings and Elam tied it around the pommel of the saddle.

"Are you gonna win, Elam?" Barry asked excitedly.

"We're sure going to try, Barry."

"Will you bring me back a present?"

"It's not that kind of trip, Barry. But if I see something in my travels that I know you'll like, I'll bring it back to you."

Barry grinned and said, "All right, Elam! Bring me something good!"

"Are you sure you have everything?" Helen said, snapping open her parasol to shade her eyes from the sun.

P.D. nodded. "As much as we're able to carry, anyway. Somehow, I don't think we'll be lucky enough to keep the horse for the whole trip."

"Watch out for snakes."

P.D. had been adjusting her skirts and Helen's comment made her look up so fast, she startled the horse. "Snakes! Is it snake season? What kind of snakes?"

But before she could get an answer, Elam nudged the horse forward and eased toward the starting line at the end of the historical town's main street. A red ribbon had been stretched from the apothecary on one side to the livery stable on the other.

As the last of the contestants took their places, P.D. could see that at least thirty couples had decided to vie for the ten-thousand-dollar prize. Besides Elam and her, there were several teams on horseback, one with a team and a wagon, and a pair of elderly women who had opted for a carriage.

"They won't get very far with that if we're sent into the mountains," Elam murmured. "There aren't too many trails wide enough for a buggy."

From what P.D. could see, she and Elam were definitely traveling the lightest, and she hoped that the tactic would be to their advantage.

From the bandstand, the mayor rang a huge metal triangle with a ball-peen hammer. Immediately, the crowd hushed.

"Do we have all of the contestants at the starting line?"

The mayor was answered by a volley of shouts and whistles. The man, dressed in a top hat, frock coat, and elaborately embroidered vest held up a hand for silence. "Welcome one and all to the first Wild West Games. We hope it will prove to be an annual event."

Again, he waited politely for the applause and cheers to subside. Then, he said, "I'm sure you're well aware of the rules and regulations of the contest—after all, you signed your names saying you'd all but memorized them when you plunked down your two-hundred-dollar entry fee."

Elam glanced over his shoulder. "You paid two hundred dollars to enter?"

She nodded. "Bodey paid his half. He kept telling me that we'd be an unbeatable pair."

"What do you think now? Think we can win?"

She offered him a slow smile. "Oh, yeah."

His eyes crinkled at the edges and he turned back to listen

to the rest of the mayor's review of the rules. Finally, after warning them to wear their numbers at all times, and reiterating that they would be monitored throughout the competition—with or without their knowledge—the mayor said, "Please find the envelopes you were given at the Photo Emporium, but keep them sealed for a few minutes longer."

P.D. pulled the yellow envelope from Elam's back pocket.

"In your envelopes, you will find a set of instructions to guide you to your first checkpoint. There are a half-dozen versions, so *don't* follow your neighbors."

Like a true professional, the mayor waited for the titter of laughter to fade.

"Remember that over the next few days, you'll be led over pillar and post. Although you won't necessarily start at the same point, you'll all complete a similar course. You may even cross paths with your fellow contestants now and again. Keep to your own clues . . . and may the best team win."

With that, the mayor lifted the ball-peen hammer.

"On my mark . . ." He paused dramatically, then brought his hand sweeping down. "Go!"

The hammer had barely touched the iron when Elam spurred their mount into a gallop. P.D. held on for dear life as the horse sprang into motion in a single bound.

"Open up the envelope, P.D.!"

She wasn't sure how she was supposed to do that *and* remain seated, but she finally tore it open with her teeth, then wedged it between their bodies so that she could pull out the paper.

"We're supposed to find Wilson's Mill. They've only given us a crudely drawn map with some vague compass markings."

"Which way?"

"West. Near as I can tell, it's up in the foothills near the service road to the television towers."

Elam altered their course, urging their mount to even greater speed. P.D. held on tight, pressing her cheek against his back. Even through the layers of his clothing, she could feel the muscles of his shoulders grow taut with his efforts to control the horse.

At first, the terrain was fairly flat, but the ground soon began to rise. Time and time again, Elam found his way blocked by lengths of fences strung with barbed wire. But finally, he located a dirt access road that led into the hills.

"Where to now?"

P.D. had wrapped her arms around him so tightly that the map was crumpled against his waist. Forcing herself to loosen one hand, she peered over his shoulder while Elam squinted from beneath his hat, then surveyed the terrain ahead, adjusting his course south.

"Look for a river, stream, some kind of water. The trees should be thicker near the banks."

"There!" P.D. pointed to a spot to their right.

Elam reined the horse toward the water, and then, when the foliage proved to be too thick to ride along the bank, he plunged into the middle and began heading upstream.

After a few hundred yards, they were able to see a set of structures up ahead.

"That must be it," Elam stated.

As they grew closer, they could see that a plywood "water wheel" had been placed next to the river, along with a canvas scrim, which had been painted to look like a small rock building. A sign emblazoned on the side proclaimed, WILSON'S MILL.

Finally, the bank opened up to a shady meadow and Elam was able to spur the horse into a canter toward a pair of officials who waited next to a makeshift hitching post.

Just as the horse was reined to a halt, a flash of movement from the trees caught P.D.'s attention. Turning, she realized that another set of contestants were racing toward them.

"Elam, look!"

They'd barely come to a full stop when Elam reached for her arm. "Hurry and dismount."

Grasping Elam's forearm, P.D. slid to the ground. As soon as her feet had touched the earth, Elam slid down beside her.

"Let's go!"

They raced to the officials, who recorded their time. Then they were handed a sheet of paper with their instructions for the course.

Elam scanned the contents. "We have to chop a log in two,

pan for gold in the river, and then complete the shooting stages."

P.D. had barely digested the sequence of events when Elam took her hand and ran to a set of crossed two-by-fours set up next to the scrim.

"Do you want to go first?"

P.D. shook her head. She needed a minute to get her "land legs" again before she handled an ax.

Elam grabbed the handle, which had been propped up next to a pile of logs. Motioning for P.D. to stand back, he took his stance, then swung the ax in a high arc, burying the blade into the wood.

If they hadn't been in a hurry to finish as much as possible before the second pair of contestants arrived, P.D. knew she would have thoroughly enjoyed watching Elam work. There was something primitive and inherently male about the bunching of his shoulders and arm muscles as he swung the ax over his head again, and again, and again. The log thumped and shuddered with each strike until, finally, after less than a dozen hacks, the wood splintered and cracked in two.

Handing P.D. the ax, Elam quickly set another log on the stand.

"Think you can handle it?"

P.D. nodded, saying, "Oh, yeah."

Unbeknownst to Elam, she had plenty of experience cutting wood. One of the main sources of heat in the bus that had served as her childhood home had been an old potbellied stove piped into the back window. Once her parents had found a spot to stay for a few days, a few weeks, a few months, it was P.D.'s job to gather wood and fuel from the surrounding area and light the stove.

Grasping the ax, she planted her feet firmly apart and swung into action.

Although her movements weren't as powerful as Elam's, she made good progress, focusing on making the wound larger with each strike of the blade. Soon, her muscles burned with the effort, reminding her that it had been a long time since she'd engaged in this activity. But after only a few minutes, she planted the killing blow and the log plunged to the ground.

She turned to find Elam grinning at her, his hands on his hips—and she was momentarily struck to the core with the way his joy lit his features in a way that she'd never seen before.

"Brains *and* brawn," he said with obvious approval. "Remind me not to tick you off."

She laughed, propping the ax back where they'd found it.

Next, they rushed to the stream, where another official waited with two shallow metal pans.

"There are small rocks painted gold and hidden somewhere in the sandy bank. You need to find two of them," the man stated.

Elam grabbed one of the pans. After removing his holster, boots, and socks, he plunged into the water, beginning the search. But P.D.'s shoes proved more cumbersome. Since she was wearing period-inspired boots that laced up past her ankles, it took forever to get them loose enough to remove. Then there were her stockings, which came past her knees. As she bent to roll them down, she noted that Elam was momentarily distracted by her inadvertent striptease.

Finally, after she'd bared her legs, she set her holster next to Elam's, tucked her skirts into her waistband, and waded into the water.

She hissed when the cool stream hit the heat of her soles, but quickly bending to her task, she scooped up a panful of silt and gravel, swirled it around to investigate what she'd uncovered, then discarded the contents and began again. Behind her, she could hear the *thwunk, thwunk* of the other team beginning to chop their first log.

She was just bending to scoop up a mound of silt when she saw a dull gleam in the blackness of the mud. Reaching down, she grabbed a handful of slime and rocks, then allowed the moving current to sweep the mud away.

"Aha!" she crowed in delight, holding her palm out to the judge. There, amid the useless rubble, were two golden rocks.

"Done," the man proclaimed. "Move to the shooting range."

Elam grabbed her hand, tugging her back up to the bank. Scooping up their belongings, he pulled her toward the last obstacle that remained.

While P.D. rearranged her skirts and donned her holster again, Elam stood barefoot in front of a loading table that marked where they should stand. Metal targets shaped like various woodland animals were arranged in front of a natural berm caused by a rocky jut of land leading down to the stream. An official wearing a huge cowboy hat and furry chaps read from a script.

"In this sequence, you will use only your pistols. Winter is falling and you need supplies for the cold weather. Beginning with the squirrel, shoot each of the animals, small to large. You will receive a thirty-second penalty for each target missed. If you hit them all on the first try, ten seconds will be subtracted from your score as a bonus."

Elam didn't even bother with his boots and socks. Strapping on his holster and donning his shooting glasses and earplugs, he waited for P.D. to do the same, then adopted a shooting stance in front of the table.

"Ready?"

"Ready."

"The range is hot!" the official shouted, holding up a small red flag. Then, "Go!"

Elam swiftly loaded his revolver, then in a series of bangs and metal pings, he emptied both pistols. Within seconds, he'd finished, reholstered his last weapon, and held up his hands.

"Clean course! Next," the official barked.

P.D. had only been given enough time to adjust her holsters before it was her turn. Remaining barefoot, she took her place next to the table, carefully counting out ten bullets and setting them on the surface.

"Remember," Elam said from behind, his voice muffled through her earplugs. "Take your time, aim, then squeeze. Don't try to rush things. It's better to hit your target by being methodical than to hurry and make mistakes."

P.D. nodded.

"Ready?"

"Yes."

"The range is hot!" The official waved the flag, then lowered it again with a curt, "Go!"

P.D.'s fingers were trembling as she opened the cylinders one by one, sliding the bullets into the chambers, then seating the hammer against the empty chamber as she'd been taught. Lifting the pistol, she pointed in the direction of the squirrel and squeezed the trigger.

There was the *bang* of the gun, but no resulting *ping* of the target, indicating that she'd missed.

"Remember to line up both sights," Elam said calmly and quietly from behind.

She nodded, moving the pistol to a target shaped like a rabbit.

Bam . . . ping!

She couldn't prevent a tiny squeal of delight.

"Great! Now do the others."

She honed in on the raccoon.

Bam . . . ping!

Gaining confidence, she moved to the goose, bobcat, mountain lion—*ping . . . ping . . . ping*—finally finishing with the deer and the moose.

The last tinny *ping* faded away as the official wrote down her score. "One miss, nine hits. Go to the official at the hitching post and get your next challenge envelope."

ELEVEN

REACH Miller's Summit by nightfall. The distance must be completed on foot.

When she read the note, P.D. resisted the urge to curse. Barely. She'd only been in her period garb for a few hours, but she could already feel the effects of the layers of clothing and the stricture of her corset. Granted, she hadn't laced it too tightly, knowing that she would be required to perform a variety of physical activities. But she could feel the sweat pooling beneath her breasts, and the boning dug into her waist whenever she tried to bend.

How on earth had pioneer women gotten anything done?

But when the next pair of contestants moved on to the stream to pan for "gold," she knew that she couldn't spend her time wishing for a modern brassiere.

Taking the envelope with their instructions, they hurried back to their mount. At least they weren't forced to forfeit the horse. The animal was still available to carry their supplies.

A huge plastic tub filled with ice had been loaded up with bottles of water. Elam handed two of them to P.D., then filled the saddlebags with as many as he could fit inside.

"Drink," he ordered as he also placed water bottles in the bag that held her clothing.

P.D. didn't need more urging than that. She drained the first bottle, not realizing until then how thirsty she'd become.

As she began on the second bottle, Elam did the same. Then, checking the coordinates on the map with the compass from his pocket, he gestured to the north.

"That way."

After dumping their empty bottles in a garbage can, they each grabbed another full bottle and hurried to put as much distance between themselves and the first station as they could.

"Do you think the other contestants will have instructions to come this way as well?"

Elam shook his head. "Doubt it. They've got to mix up the order of all our tasks or it would be too easy for one team to follow another."

For some reason, P.D. felt a small measure of comfort in that fact. It was disturbing enough to know that contest officials would be monitoring them. But to think that the other contestants would be within shouting distance as well seemed intrusive.

Especially when she was entertaining some very carnal thoughts about her companion.

Knowing that she needed to keep her mind away from that tempting track, P.D. asked, "So why'd you join the Navy? Seems to me, you couldn't get much more landlocked than Bliss, Utah."

Elam grinned. He was nursing his water with one hand and holding the reins with the other.

"I wanted to blow stuff up."

She blinked at him for a moment, then said, "Pardon?"

Elam veered toward a faint track worn through the underbrush—probably the path left by deer or other animals looking for water.

"Both of my grandfathers were veterans of World War Two. Grandpa Jackson fought in Europe, but Grandpa Taggart, who lived in the Big House with us, fought in the Pacific. I grew up listening to stories of his escapades in the Navy." He shrugged. "Let's just say that the seeds of a career at sea were planted pretty early."

"So why the EOD?"

Again, Elam's smile was all-knowing. "One summer, Grandpa Taggart decided to widen our service road leading up to one of the summer pastures. My grandfather was never a patient man."

Somehow, P.D. knew where this was heading.

"So he decided to blast his way through with dynamite."

"And you . . ."

"I was his . . . helper of sorts."

Her mouth dropped open. "How old were you?"

Elam's eyes crinkled at the corners as he thought. Lifting his hat from his head, he swiped away the sweat beading his brow, giving P.D. a tantalizing glimpse of his tousled hair.

"Twelve."

"Twelve! And you were handling dynamite?"

Elam laughed at her horrified outburst. "I didn't handle the dynamite itself—"

"I should hope not," she muttered.

"I just set it off."

She gaped at him and he paused a moment, his eyes glinting with delight.

"You should have seen it! Grandpa Taggart was sure that the hillside was mostly bedrock, so he set a few extra charges. As soon as I lowered the plunger, *bam!* Half of the mountain disappeared in a shower of dust and rocks. The shock wave threw me onto my ass and I was nearly buried in dirt."

She gasped. "Were you hurt?"

"Just a few bumps and scrapes. Grandpa ended up with a black eye from a stray rock." He chuckled softly. "One of the best days of my life. I couldn't wait to blow something else up. But when we got home, my mother and my grandmother lit into Grandpa something fierce. It was clear that if either of us was ever found in a similar predicament again, there would be hell to pay." He shrugged. "So I figured that if Grandpa could learn stuff like that in the Navy, I was going to get the same kind of training. As soon as I could, I enlisted."

"And did you? Learn how to blow things up?"

"Sure. But I soon found I liked ensuring that things *didn't* blow up even more."

"Is that how . . . you were hurt?" she asked tentatively, hoping that he wouldn't balk at the more personal question.

He shook his head. "I was blown up having a beer."

Her brows rose.

"I was in the Officers' Club enjoying my time off and watching some football when a missile hit nearby." He instantly sobered. "I was lucky—broke some ribs, suffered burns and lacerations from the shrapnel. Some of the other men were in much worse shape. But when I developed nerve damage, they eventually sent me home."

The climb was becoming steeper, robbing P.D. of her breath, so she allowed the conversation to lapse. Thankfully, after touching upon what must have been painful memories, Elam focused on the task at hand rather than the past.

It didn't take long for P.D. to see that Elam was in his element. While she fought to gulp air into her lungs, he could have been strolling down a country lane. As the course grew steeper, his leg muscles bunched against the dark twill of his trousers. If not for the patches of sweat beginning to form on his shirt, she might have thought that he expended no energy whatsoever.

P.D., on the other hand, was beginning to struggle in earnest. The full skirts were hot and cumbersome—but even worse, they made traversing the uneven terrain awkward. The high-top boots she wore offered no real traction, so for each step she took, she slid a few inches back. But her pride pushed her forward. She couldn't let Elam know that she was flagging. Not yet. Not when they only had a few hours of daylight to reach the summit.

So when the ground momentarily leveled out and Elam led the horse into the shade of a stand of scrub oak, she didn't realize at first that he meant to stop.

Elam gestured to a large boulder just off the trail. "Have a seat there. I'll just water the horse."

"No, I can go on. I—"

Elam reached out to cup her cheek with his palm. "I know. You'd go on until you dropped. But the secret to this competition is pacing. If you expend all your energy the first day, you'll have nothing left to run on but fumes. We'll take a twenty-minute break, then we'll get back on the trail."

Realizing he spoke from experience, she sank onto the rock.

"Drain another bottle of water."

"But . . ."

"We need to keep hydrated. There will be another water station at the top of the summit when we check in, so we can replenish our stock there."

He handed her a bottle from their saddle bags and she quickly twisted the lid, then began drinking with hungry gulps.

Elam took another bottle and dragged the hat from his head. As she watched, he upended the liquid into his hat and offered it to their horse. After the animal had drunk its fill, he dumped what little remained in the bushes and set his hat in a patch of sunlight to dry. Then, he grabbed another bottle for himself.

P.D. nearly forgot her own thirst as she watched him tip back his head and drain the bottle. Despite her weariness, the sight of his taut flesh and the bob of his Adam's apple was enough to make her flush with a warmth that had nothing to do with the heat of the day.

After he'd finished drinking, she quickly looked away, not wanting Elam to catch her gawking at him. But he must have sensed her regard because he tucked the empty water bottle back into the saddle bags and retrieved another one. This time, however, after he twisted the cap, he dumped a small amount of water onto a bandanna that he'd shoved into his back pocket. Then he crouched in front of her and dabbed the wet cloth over her face.

"You should have brought a hat."

"There's a bonnet folded up in my pocket. Helen made it for me."

"Why aren't you wearing it?"

"It makes me look . . . dorky."

Elam draped the damp bandanna around the nape of her

neck, maintaining his hold on either end. "You could never look dorky." His voice deepened and he began to pull her inexorably closer by twisting the bandana corners around his fingers. His eyes centered on her lips and his tone dropped to a husky whisper. "You are so freakin' beautiful."

Then his lips were on hers, softly, sweetly. But his gentle foray lasted only a few tantalizing seconds before she leaned into him, responding wholeheartedly. The embers of their attraction exploded between them and they strained to erase the scant distance between them.

Elam's tongue bade entrance and she opened her mouth to his intimate caress, knowing that he was feeling his way back into his future as a single man. The thought that he would choose *her* to begin those forays, that he was "crazy" about *her*, was as heady as his touch. She leaned into him, eager to show him through her own response that she was just as crazy about him.

His lips grew even more forceful against hers and his hands looped around her waist to pull her closer. P.D. wrapped her arms around his neck, reveling in the heat of his body, the strength of his arms. She'd never encountered anyone who could make her feel like this—giddy and excited and so instantly aroused that it was a wonder that she didn't burst into flames.

She drew back only when the need for air superseded her need for Elam. But he wasn't dissuaded. His lips trailed down, down, past her jaw and lower to the edge of her high-neck blouse. Then, with one hand, he began releasing the buttons, one by one, his tongue blazing a trail with each inch that was revealed.

It was only when he reached the ribbon woven through the eyelet beading of her chemise that he paused. His breathing was ragged, the warm puffs slipping into the hollow of her cleavage.

Then, just when she wondered what Elam would do next, he rested his forehead against her breastbone. Unable to stop herself, she buried her fingers into the damp, tousled waves of his hair.

"Much as I would like to continue this," he whispered against her, "I think that our twenty minutes are up."

She made a soft mewl of distress and he chuckled, lifting his head.

"We've got about an hour until sundown and only a few more miles to go. Then we can make camp for the night."

Much as she wanted to argue, to tell him that she no longer cared, the need for her share of the prize money loomed above her.

"Only a few more miles," he murmured, kissing her quickly, powerfully. Standing, he pulled her to her feet. "Let's get there as fast as we can."

THEY reached the summit well before sundown. P.D. supposed their excellent progress had less to do with their will to win than their wish to camp for the night. After racing to the official charged with taking their time, they were told to bed down in a clearing a few hundred yards away. At six in the morning, their next task would be delivered to them.

While P.D. gathered firewood, Elam removed the gelding's saddle and bridle, and rubbed him down with a handful of grass. Then he led the animal to the trough of water provided for their use before tying the animal to a tree, where it could graze.

When he returned, P.D. had stacked the firewood in a circle of stones she'd moved to the center of their camp. She was attempting to light the pile with a match when he intervened.

"You need to start with some dried weeds and kindling first." After gathering what he needed, Elam struck another precious match from their stash and touched it to a mound of foxtails. Patiently, he nursed the tiny flame into a small blaze, then began adding dried twigs and sticks until the fire had grown large enough for one of the smaller logs P.D. had found.

Now that the sun had gone down, the temperature was falling and the breeze off the mountain was cool. P.D. wrapped her arms around her waist and huddled closer to the fire. Glancing her way, Elam took one of the blankets from their bedroll and wrapped it around her shoulders. He paused there, his hands firm and strong.

P.D. glanced up the hill to where the timekeeper had pitched a pup tent and was settling in for the night. Thankfully, an outcropping of rocks and sumac offered them a small measure of privacy.

"He can't see us," Elam murmured, wrapping his arms around her waist, his breath warm against her ear.

"It still makes me nervous."

Elam pressed a kiss against her neck. "Right now, the only thing he's going to see is a pair of weary contestants rustling up something to eat."

"Like what?"

"Rummage through our supplies. Use one of the cans of beans, and see if you can't find something to go with it. I'll be back."

He kissed the top of her head, then strode away, disappearing into the trees a few yards away. Figuring that he might be "answering the call of nature," P.D. figured that she'd better take advantage of the few minutes she'd been left alone. Heading in the opposite direction, she hurriedly took care of her own needs. Then she returned to use some of the bottled water to wash her hands and face until she felt a little less grimy.

Searching through the saddlebags, she withdrew the beans, the can opener, and then the pan. Then, frowning at the meagerness of their meal, she ran a quick eye through the rest of their supplies.

After opening up the beans, she set the can on a flat rock in the fire to heat. She reconstituted some of the jerky with water and stirred it into the beans. Then she mixed a small amount of baking mix with sugar, water, and raisins to make drop biscuits, which she scooped, one by one, onto their single pan.

Keeping one eye on the biscuits, she scouted the area, finding sorrel and dandelion greens, which she might be able to use to augment their meal.

But where was Elam?

As if hearing her thoughts, Elam stepped from the trees. Dangling from his fingers were a pair of speckled trout.

"How in the world did you manage to get those so far up the summit?"

He winked. "Easy. I headed back down to the stream where we were panning for gold."

P.D. stood with her mouth agape. She was more out of shape than she thought.

Elam glanced at the food she'd already begun to cook. "Looks good." He held up the fish. "What do you want me to do with these?"

P.D. shuddered. "You'll need to clean them."

He laughed. "What? You're a big, bad gourmet cook and you've never cleaned a fish?"

"I've cleaned plenty. That doesn't mean I have to like it."

Still chuckling, he took the fish to a spot away from the camp and made quick work of cleaning them, then returned. P.D. seasoned the fish with a small amount of their precious salt and stuffed them with the greens for flavor, then removed the biscuits from the pan and replaced them with the fish.

Darkness had fallen by the time everything had finished cooking, but P.D. didn't care. After the day's strenuous work, she felt as if she were about to eat a banquet. But what made it even better was the way Elam took a bite of his fish and sighed in delight.

"You constantly amaze me," he said, fixing her with a warm gaze. "Here we are, under the most primitive conditions, and you still manage to come up with a gourmet meal."

"Not quite gourmet, but it will scare the hunger away."

They ate in companionable silence for a few minutes before P.D. spoke again. "What do you suppose they'll throw at us tomorrow?"

Campfire illuminated his features into golden planes and velvet hollows.

"They've brought us up to the summit, so I suppose we'll have to go down the other side."

She sighed heavily, wondering how she would find the energy. She was utterly exhausted—so much so, that her limbs felt as if they were made of rubber. Her feet were sore and beginning to blister on the heels and toes. Her skin prickled with the beginnings of a sunburn—and she knew she must look a wreck.

Elam rose, reaching for her mess kit.

"Spread the bedrolls out. I'll take care of the cleanup. You go rest."

"But—"

"Go, P.D."

She didn't have the energy to argue. Not really sure how the bedrolls should be arranged—together or separately—she was too exhausted to decide. So she laid them side by side next to the fire, then kicked out of her boots and crawled beneath the covers. She would relax for a few minutes. Then, she'd scramble up the energy to wash her face and brush her hair.

Just a few minutes . . .

ELAM returned later to find her fast asleep, one of her hands tucked under her cheek, the saddlebags her makeshift pillow. In the firelight, he could see that her cheeks and nose were overly pink and the wind had made a wreck of her hair. She had a smudge of flour on her forehead and her shirt was streaked with gunpowder and dust.

But she had never been more beautiful to him than she was at that moment.

He waited for the pain to come, the guilt. But what he felt was a tenderness that he'd never thought to experience again.

Tugging off his boots, he positioned his bedroll closer to hers and slipped beneath the covers. As if she'd been waiting for him, P.D. sighed and rolled into his arms, then fell back asleep.

He smiled, stroking her hair and pressing a kiss to the top of her head.

"Sweet dreams, Prairie Dawn."

TWELVE

"**E**LAM!"

Elam jolted awake, his hand automatically reaching for his sidearm. When he encountered a handful of dirt, his eyes sprang open.

But he wasn't in his quarters in Afghanistan. He stared at nothing but the blue sky.

A face swam into focus above him, and he slammed into the present when he recognized P.D.

"What's wrong?" he croaked. He couldn't remember the last time he'd slept so soundly. Usually, his internal clock awakened him long before dawn.

"Someone stole our horse." She leaned close to whisper, "And my underwear!"

Sitting up, Elam wiped a hand over his face, scrubbing away the last vestiges of sleep.

"Are you sure?"

"Yes, I'm sure," she hissed. "I wanted to wash up and change my clothes. Last night, the bag was still hooked around the pommel of the saddle. But when I went looking for it, the horse and the tack were gone."

Elam peered around their camp, verifying her claims. "Do you think it's part of the challenge?"

"They haven't brought us our envelope yet."

He grimaced. "So maybe we've been sabotaged."

Her eyes widened in horror. "They have my underthings!"

Elam laughed. "It's not as if they stole your real clothes. If anything, they stole Helen's underwear."

She punched him on the shoulder. "That's not the point."

The sound of heels crunching in the gravel warned them that someone was approaching. P.D. straightened, trying to smooth her hair, then stamped her foot, muttering, "They stole my brush, too, damn them."

"Morning, folks." The rotund volunteer who had taken their time the night before glanced at a huge pocket watch that dangled from his leather vest. He slapped an envelope against his leg, waiting for the appropriate moment. "What happened to your horse?" he asked idly.

P.D. looked like she was about to explode so Elam said, "It must have wandered off."

"Along with its saddle and bridle," P.D. muttered under her breath.

"Shame." Suddenly, the man sprang into action, handing the envelope to Elam and backing away. "Good luck to you both!"

Elam tore into their clue. "We need to find Black Bart Mines due west."

"Do we have the compass?"

"It's in the saddlebags along with our supplies and ammo. Do we still have the saddlebags?"

"Yes. I grabbed them last night for a pillow."

"Good girl."

"The weapons were on the ground next to us, so we've got them, too." She sighed. "Elam, can we do this on foot? Or will I slow things down too much?"

Elam rolled to his feet and offered her a searing kiss. "We have our wits and each other. That's all we need. And you haven't slowed us down at all."

She took a deep breath, gripping her hands in front of her.

"Okay. You're right. I've spent weeks getting as ready for this as I can, so feet, don't fail me now."

He grinned at her little pep talk and gestured to the bedrolls. "Help me get everything gathered together, then we'll hoof it out of here."

They were able to don their holsters, pack up their gear, and leave camp within ten minutes—although P.D. continued to grouse about her missing clothes. With no horse, Elam knew that the trip would take double or even triple the time it would have with a mount. The two of them would have to move as quickly as they could. But Elam doubted that P.D. was up to a punishing pace—especially with a rifle and shotgun to carry.

After yesterday's punishing hike up the mountainside, P.D. was flagging, so Elam did his best to keep her going, and damn it all, she gave him everything she had. Heading down the summit helped to some extent. But the shoes they wore weren't optimal for the terrain. So Elam shifted the rifle to the same shoulder as the saddlebags and took P.D.'s hand to steady her. Then, knowing he needed to get her mind off her pounding pulse and the heat of the day, he asked, "So why were you named Prairie Dawn? There has to be a story to it."

P.D. grimaced. "Supposedly, I was born in South Dakota just as the sun broke through the clouds."

"Supposedly?"

She grimaced. "I'm not sure if that's the real reason or if I really was named after the Muppet character. My mother was a fan. I wouldn't have been surprised if the sight triggered her memory somehow. To make matters worse, my parents didn't believe in formal medicine either. So no one was called in to help with the birth—which also meant there was no legal documentation. Later, they couldn't remember exactly where or when it happened, just that it was morning, sometime in the first week of April." She winced. "I can't tell you how much grief that cost me later when I needed a birth certificate."

Although her comments were offhand, Elam sensed a hidden pain behind the story she told. Good hell, her parents didn't remember the day she'd been born? How could you forget something like that? And what about birthday parties and celebrations to make her feel valued and special?

But when Elam opened his mouth to ask, he caught the brittleness of her expression. Instinctively, he realized that she'd probably told him more in the last few minutes than she'd ever told anyone else. But she didn't want his pity. And *that* was something he understood all too well. So when he spoke, he purposely kept things light.

"Could have been worse," he said.

Her brows rose. "How?"

"They could have named you The Badlands or something."

She laughed, and her guardedness disappeared. "True."

He helped her climb down from a large boulder. Then, when she would have continued down the slope, he stopped her, turning her to face him.

"I like it. Your name." Unable to help himself, he framed her face with his hands. "It suits you."

She stared up at him with disbelieving eyes, and he brushed his thumbs over her cheeks.

"It's feminine and fanciful and full of joy. Just like you."

Lord, she was pretty. Even with the beginnings of sunburn and her face beaded with sweat, she made his heart beat faster—and he wasn't quite sure what to do about it. Now that he'd given himself permission to go wherever his emotions might take him, he couldn't help thinking that things were proceeding way too fast. He'd courted Annabel for years, taking his time, feeling his way.

But with P.D., he wanted to jump in headfirst. He wanted to wallow in her joyful nature and drown himself in her passion. But he couldn't help thinking that anything that burned so white-hot was bound to peter out just as quickly. And wouldn't that be a shame.

He bent, brushing her lips with his, needing to drown out the voice in his head that insisted that this romance with P.D. couldn't last. She leaned into him immediately, her hands on his chest, their warmth burrowing straight through to his heart. Even so, a taunting voice inside his head chanted: *It'll burn out soon . . . it'll burn out soon . . .*

His arms swept around her waist and he hauled her against him, trying to deny the fear that rushed over him. He'd already survived the death of one relationship. Could he really handle that again? Could he bear having P.D. tell him that they should "just be friends" or that she was ready to move on? Because he knew that, deep down, she was as free-spirited as her name. She would have to be, given the nature of her upbringing. Sure, she was fond of Bliss and determined to make Vern's a success. But there would come a time when she would want to try something else, somewhere else.

Someone else.

And Elam's days of wanderlust were gone. He'd seen enough, done enough, to know that this was where he belonged. If anything, the last year his roots had sunk even deeper into the soil of his birthplace. Now, more than ever, he wanted to spill his sweat into the land and the horses and the honest toil of making the ranch a success. He wanted to see the march of the seasons in the crops they grew and the ever-changing weather.

Drawing back, he stared down into P.D.'s bemused gaze.

"You are so beautiful," he whispered, knowing he would probably get hurt in this affair.

P.D. shook her head infinitesimally. "No."

"Yes." Then he kissed her again, harder, fiercer, willing away the demons that told him he could never be enough for her and denying the chattering fear that warned him that none of this was real.

She must have sensed his desperation because she wrapped her arms around his waist, clinging to him, imparting the warmth of her body into his, easing that icy sliver of dread that warned Elam that nothing this good could survive for long.

Then, breaking their kiss, he tucked her head under his chin, willing his pulse to ease and the pounding desire to ebb.

"We've got to get going," he whispered.

She nodded against him. "I know."

But he continued to hold her, imprinting the feel of her into his brain, knowing that whatever pain and loneliness might come in the future, he had today. And he wasn't going to throw it away.

* * *

P.D. was sure she was on her last legs when, finally, their goal appeared up ahead.

Black Bart Mines were actually the property of the Mickelsons, Clive and Sandy, who were regulars at Vern's. As soon as P.D. and Elam burst through the main gate, their time was taken by a woman dressed in Scarlett O'Hara finery.

"Great time!" she exclaimed. "You have thirty minutes for a food and bathroom break before reporting to the shooting range behind the barn."

Sandy Mickelson beckoned to them from the front porch of her home. "Come in out of the sun, you two."

P.D. seriously wondered if she would have the strength to go even that far. But somehow, with Elam towing her forward, she managed to step inside the sprawling home.

"They have central air," she sighed with reverence as a cool blast hit her cheeks.

Elam laughed.

"The bathroom is down the hall to the left," Sandy continued. "I've left clean towels and washcloths on the counter if you'd like to wash up. When you're done, there are sandwiches and drinks for you in the kitchen. Tables have been set up on the patio and there's a set of instructions for the shooting sequence on each table."

P.D. didn't need any further bidding. She hurried down the hall while Elam stowed their weapons and saddlebags.

As soon as she'd made use of the toilet, P.D. opened the spigot wide, letting the water run cool. She splashed the liquid on her face and hands until she'd eased the heat of her skin. Then, she used a washcloth to get as much as the griminess off as possible before patting herself dry. Finally, she spied a brush and made quick work of her hair, plaiting it down her back.

When she emerged again, she found Elam leaning against the wall opposite the door.

His eyes crinkled in the corners as he smiled. "Feeling better?"

"Much."

She allowed him to take her place in the bathroom and hurried to the kitchen, where the food awaited.

Spread out on the counter were thick sandwiches wrapped in plastic; small bags of chips; bowls of macaroni, potato, and green salads; and tubs filled with ice, soft drinks, and water bottles.

Heaven.

P.D. loaded up her plate and snagged a bottle of soda, then headed outside onto a shady patio where several card tables had been arranged.

There were already a few teams of competitors present, finishing up their meals. P.D. worried that it might be a sign that she and Elam were really far behind in their times, but as she sank into a chair, she realized she couldn't worry about it now. She and Elam only had a few minutes to eat before they would have to be on the road again.

Elam appeared a few minutes later. Like her, he'd taken the time to clean off the dirt and sweat. His hair was wet, as if he'd plunged his head into the running water, and fresh tine marks showed that he'd also taken advantage of the brush.

"The food looks good," he said as he sank into the chair next to her.

"It's wonderful." P.D. sighed as she took a bite of potato salad.

Elam chuckled. "Tired of frontier cooking already, I see." But as soon as he bit into his sandwich, he began to eat with the same uninhibited enjoyment.

As they consumed their meal, they noticed that one of the contest volunteers would appear at the side gate and yell out the names of a pair of contestants, presumably to take them to the shooting range.

"So what do we do next?"

P.D. grabbed the laminated set of instructions and read the scenario printed at the top. " 'Black Bart Mines has just been attacked by outlaws who are determined to steal the precious silver that is about to be shipped to Denver. You must protect your cargo at all costs as well as escape the cave-in caused by the gun battle.' "

She looked at the accompanying chart. "There are five

targets shaped like outlaws"—she squinted at them—"or Scooby Doo, it's hard to say."

Elam laughed.

"Anyway, we shoot them with pistols, left to right, then right to left." She read the rest of the instructions. "Then, there are metal plates on a spinning target. We each have to shoot two of them off with the rifle. Last, there's a pop-up series with the shotgun." P.D. peered up at Elam, who had eaten his fill and now leaned back with his hands laced over his taut stomach. "What's a pop-up?"

"You shoot a release button, which launches something into the air. Then you hit that as well."

She blinked at him and winced. "Great. I can barely hit a nonmoving target with the shotgun."

"You'll do fine. Just keep your eyes on your sights." He gestured to the paper again. "What's the deal with the land-slide they mentioned?"

She flipped to the back side. "It's hard to tell from the drawing, but it looks like they have several archways that are filled with big rocks and we have to move enough of them to get through."

"Any specific instructions?"

She skipped down to the words underneath. "'Use your wits to create an opening large enough to crawl through. Once on the other side, you'll be handed your next challenge envelope and will continue your journey.' There's a picture of several tools available: a pickax, shovel, or a sledgehammer." Her eyes widened as she continued to read. "'The first team to breach the landslide with a time under five minutes will be given a horse and buggy!'"

Sandy Mickelson happened to come by at that moment and reached to collect Elam's empty plate. "Teams have been trying for two days to win the buggy, without much success. It's actu-ally a concrete panel that's been painted to look like rocks. Frankly, I think Clive is up in the night if he thinks anyone is going to get that buggy," she said, referring to her husband, who was one of the contest organizers.

P.D. sighed. The food and rest had brought some life back to her body, but she didn't know if she had the strength left to swing a sledgehammer.

Elam abruptly stood. "I'll be right back. I'm just going to gather our things. Our thirty minutes are just about up."

As he disappeared, P.D. hurried to finish her food. She wasn't about to leave a single bite on her plate—not when their next meal would probably be jerky and raisins.

She was just pushing her empty plate away when Elam reappeared. She paused in chewing, noting that their saddlebags looked bulkier than before. But before she could ask about it, a man dressed all in black with a huge Yosemite Sam mustache appeared next to the patio gate and called out, "Taggart and Raines!"

"Good luck to you both," Sandy called out with a wave as they followed their guide.

They were led past the house, the barn, and a handful of other outbuildings to where the property butted against the hillside. Hurrying to the loading tables, they were briefed once again on the shooting sequence. They were allowed to have their weapons preloaded to start, but were told that the time would consist of the total amount for both shooters to clear the shooting range and make their way through the "landslide."

"Do you want to go first or last?" Elam asked.

"Last."

He nodded and they both loaded their weapons. Since the rifle and shotgun would have to be reloaded after Elam had shot, P.D. volunteered to be in charge of the shotgun while Elam took care of the rifle.

"Ready?" Elam asked when the preparations were finished.

She nodded.

Several men ran onto the course to reset the targets from the previous contestants. Elam took P.D.'s hands and held her gaze. "Remember to aim, line up both sights, then squeeze the trigger. Take your time and breathe."

"Aim, sight, breathe," she repeated.

"When we get to the landslide wall, I want to you hang back so you don't get hurt."

She frowned, sure she hadn't heard him correctly. It would take both of them to get through the concrete. "What?"

"Trust me. Hang back by the edge of the range, okay?"

"Sure." P.D. was still confused, but she was willing to do what Elam had asked.

"You folks all set?" the official asked. When Elam nodded, the man barked, "Eyes and ears."

Elam and P.D. both donned the provided safety glasses and earplugs.

"On my mark," the man said.

Elam nodded, his hands held at the ready next to his holsters, the rifle and shotgun on the loading table.

"The range is hot!" the timekeeper shouted. Then, "Go!"

Elam was the consummate soldier, whipping out the first pistol, sighting, *ping, ping, ping,* then moving on to the second. As soon as he'd slid the second Ruger into his holster, he was reaching for the rifle.

At the far end of the range, a contraption much like a Ferris wheel loaded with metal targets spun in a slow circle. Elam was supposed to hit two of them.

Ping! Elam hit the first target dead-on, causing it to fall from its position, *clang!*

Ping-clang!

He set the rifle aside and grabbed for the shotgun. Toward the side of the range was a round metal target that had been painted red. Elam shot at the target, hitting it and causing a metal object to be flung high into the air. *Ca-chick.* He ratcheted the second shell into place and shot.

Too late, P.D. realized the metal object was a can of soda, which exploded when Elam shot it, sending a spray of sticky liquid in all directions.

"Damn waste of a good Pepsi!" someone shouted from the sidelines, where onlookers had gathered to watch.

But P.D. didn't bother to see who'd spoken. She grabbed the shotgun and inserted two shells. As soon as Elam had set the rifle back on the loading table and backed away, she stood in position and shouted, "Ready!"

"Go!"

P.D.'s movements were much slower and more deliberate than Elam's, but when she hit the first target, the second, the third, some of her tension eased and her confidence grew.

She emptied her pistols without a miss and moved on to the rifle. Since the target was spinning, she had to aim and judge the movement at the same time. She missed the first one.

"Breathe," Elam murmured behind her.

She took a steadying breath, then, *ping-clang*. She took another breath, *ping-clang*.

Quickly, she set the rifle on the table and reached for the shotgun. After ratcheting the shell into place, she aimed at the red target. *Bam!*

The shotgun kicked back against her shoulder, but there was no time to think about it as the shell ejected from her gun and the pop flew into the air. She quickly readied her weapon, and just as the can was beginning to fall, she pulled the trigger.

Her aim wasn't quite as good as Elam's. She winged the edge of the can, causing it to fall to the ground then spin around in a circle as the carbonated liquid streamed out of the hole like flame from a bottle rocket. But she'd hit it!

The instant she'd finished, Elam scooped up their saddle-bags from the ground and raced toward the "landslide" wall. Just as he'd asked, she hung back as he ran past the tools and knelt in front of the wall. With his back to them all, she couldn't see what his was doing, but within a few seconds, he was grabbing the saddlebags again, and racing back toward P.D.

"Fire in the hole!" he shouted.

The timekeeper stood slack jawed. "What?"

"Duck!"

Elam barely had time to issue the order before a huge explosion rocked the ground and the concrete wall instantaneously turned to dust, shooting dirt and debris in all directions.

P.D. quickly shielded her face, then began to giggle. Elam had somehow blown up the wall. He'd *blown it up*!

She turned to find Elam laughing behind her, admiring his handiwork. The wall was completely gone—as was a good portion of the ground and the frame that had once held it.

The timekeeper stood transfixed, bits of dirt clinging to his mustache. Suddenly, he remembered his job and pushed the plunger. Wiping the dust from the timepiece, he coughed and choked out, "Two minutes and twenty-two seconds."

P.D. squealed, clapping her hands. Elam caught her around the waist and whirled her in a circle. Then, letting her slide down the length of his body, he kissed her hard and said, "Let's get our buggy and the next set of instructions and go."

ELAM grabbed their things, then raced toward the buggy and horse tied in the shade next to the barn. He wanted to get out of here before someone realized that he'd stolen some simple household items, a pop bottle, and fertilizer from the barn, and used it to fashion his own personal IED.

They were just rolling past the barn and beginning to pick up speed when P.D. shouted, "Stop!"

The horse sidestepped skittishly and Elam automatically pulled back on the reins. They hadn't even come to a halt yet when P.D. dodged from the carriage.

"What the he—"

He bit off the exclamation he'd been about to give when he saw P.D. marching toward a pair of contestants who were just now dismounting in front of the Mickelson house. Elam swore when he realized they were riding the horse that he and P.D. had bought with their Wild West Bucks the day before. The drawstring bag with P.D.'s belongings was still slung across the saddle horn.

Before either of them knew what was happening, P.D. stormed toward them in full fury. But only Elam seemed aware of the peril that was about to befall the team dressed in Mountain Man finery. By the time they became aware of her presence, it was too late.

"You, there!" P.D. called out, nearly spitting out the words in her fury.

The taller of the men jabbed his partner in the ribs to get his attention.

Elam wouldn't have been surprised if steam started pouring out of P.D.'s ears. Her cheeks glowed red with righteous indignation as she stopped in front of them and planted her hands on her hips. For one brief instant, she looked like a warrior princess, her braid swinging, her breasts thrust forward by her corset, her waist seeming impossibly slender.

"Lose something, missy?" the taller of the two asked, snickering.

She wrenched the reins out of the man's hands. And when he laughed again, she slugged him in the stomach.

The man doubled over and Elam winced in sympathy—even though he probably wouldn't have been as charitable as P.D.

"Touch my underthings again, and I'll make you a eunuch," P.D. proclaimed to the pair of men dressed in buckskins. Then, spinning on her toe, she marched back to the buggy, tied the horse to the side, and climbed back into her spot.

"Remind me never to get you angry," Elam murmured, trying not to laugh at the saboteurs with their dazed expressions.

"Damned Skippy," P.D. said with a huff. "Now let's get out of here."

They were a good mile away before Elam dared to say, "Feeling better?"

Her posture was still ramrod straight. She whipped around to look at Elam, her eyes still flashing.

"They cheated."

Elam didn't bother to point out that using an explosive device wasn't exactly playing by the rules either. He valued his health too much.

"I could excuse stealing the horse," she continued. "Almost. But to steal my belongings . . . my *underwear* . . ." she finished in a fierce whisper. She speared Elam with a gaze full of blue fire. "What would you have done if they'd stolen your underthings?"

Elam didn't even hesitate, saying, "Shot them."

P.D. pointed at him with a finger. "Exactly!"

Again, Elam fought the urge to laugh. And it was in that moment, with P.D. folding her arms in satisfaction and nodding her head in emphatic agreement, that Elam realized he was having fun. Damn it all to hell, he was having the time of his life. He couldn't even remember the last time that he'd laughed so much. This whole situation—P.D., the competition, the test of wits—was the most damn fun he'd had in years.

Pulling on the reins, he brought the buggy to a stop, then reached to pull P.D. close, kissing her fiercely, tasting her lips, but more. Absorbing her love of life, her passion, her willingness to fight for what she believed in. When he drew back, she stared up at him, bemused.

"What was that for?"

"You are so fucking amazing."

A slow, self-conscious smile spread over the lips he'd just kissed. "You're just saying that because you don't want me to slug you."

"Yes, that's true."

Her mouth dropped in indignation. Then, when she realized he was teasing, she slapped him on the arm.

Elam lifted her chin. "But you *are* amazing."

This time, it was a blush that stained her cheeks, and he suddenly realized that she probably wasn't used to receiving compliments. Further proof that the world was full of idiots.

Elam kissed her again, then again, then drew back to say, "Thank you."

Her brows rose questioningly. "For what?"

"For bringing me on this little adventure."

Her grin was lopsided. "From what I remember, you didn't have a whole lot of choice."

"Maybe, maybe not. But I'm glad I came." He hesitated before adding, "I'm glad I could share this with you."

For once, P.D. seemed at a loss for words. She waited for him to qualify the statement, to temper the intimacy of his sentiments. When he didn't, her breath escaped in something akin to a sigh of wonder.

"I'm glad I could share this with you, too."

THIRTEEN

———•◆•———

AFTER another sweet, sweet kiss from Elam, P.D. gestured to the envelope in her hand.

"I guess we'd better make sure we're headed in the right direction."

Elam nodded, but the way he zeroed in on her lips made it clear that wasn't his primary focus.

She ripped open the clues, then smiled when she read them. "This time, I know where we're going." She gestured to a gravel access lane up ahead. "Head north."

Even towing the extra horse, they were able to move at a fast clip down the canal road. Twice, they were forced to a stop when they were jolted into the modern world by asphalt intersections and late-afternoon traffic. But after turning onto another gravel path, they were swallowed up by lush farm ground again.

Green wheat fields bobbed in the wind, the stalks heavy with kernels that would soon turn to gold. Other plots had new shoots of corn bending like seagull wings toward the sun. But P.D.'s favorites were the acres of canola with their bright yellow blooms.

"It's so pretty here," P.D. murmured, feeling something akin to reverence.

"Is that why you decided to live in Utah?"

"Partly. But I suppose it had more to do with the fact that, when I was about seven or eight, my parents stayed for a month in the campground. There was a library nearby—"

"I know the one."

"The woman in charge knew I wasn't a resident."

"That would be LaVerna Wamsley."

"I think I lived in that library for several days. I'd never known such a place could exist. I started with *A* of the picture book section, and I was bound and determined to reach *Z* before my parents pulled up stakes. After I'd been in there several times—spending hours and hours there—she gave me my own laminated library card and allowed me to take two books home each night."

"That sounds like LaVerna. She kept me supplied with Louis L'Amour novels through most of junior high."

"I'm sure she broke a dozen rules giving me that card, but she made me a reader for life."

"She's still around, you know."

P.D. breathed, "Really?"

"Sure. She's probably in her eighties now. She lives with her daughter, LaVae, in a little house about three miles away from the ranch. I'd be happy to take you there sometime. She'd get a kick out of seeing you again."

P.D. shook her head. "I doubt she'd even remember me."

"Oh, she'll remember you. She never forgets a reader or their favorite books." He bumped her shoulder with his. "Wanna go?"

"Sure."

There was a fork in the road and P.D. pointed to the right. "That way."

An old frame house appeared in the distance. It had probably been built more than a hundred years ago. The paint had long since disappeared and the porch was sagging in the middle. The clapboard walls looked as if a good puff of wind could collapse the whole structure.

"The old Colby place?"

"Is that what it's called?" P.D. had come here several times to gather wild asparagus from the ditch banks.

"When we were kids, we all believed it was haunted. At school we used to dare one another to sleep overnight here."

"Did you do it?"

He shot her an "are you kidding me" look. "Several times."

As they neared the house, they saw one of the contest volunteers sitting in a camp chair beneath a huge orange umbrella. Elam drove straight toward her, not even bothering to get out of the buggy.

"Afternoon," called a woman in a sunny yellow Civil War–era day gown. As she stood from the chair, her hoops ballooned into shape. Peering under her bonnet, the woman checked the numbers on their armbands and wrote the time in the log book. Then, she handed them a piece of paper, a paperback book, and two pairs of scissors. "Good luck to you. You're going to need it— most of the contestants have struggled with this challenge. As soon as you've gathered everything, bring them back to me to be checked, and I'll write down your time."

Elam handed the items to P.D., then touched his hat with his fingers. "Thank you, ma'am."

Allowing the horse to meander forward, he asked, "What does it say?"

P.D. glanced at the book, *A Guide to the Flora and Fauna of Utah*, then at the instruction sheet.

"'Medical professionals of the nineteenth century were few and far between, so many of the original settlers relied on cures involving natural remedies of tonics and poultices made from local plants and herbs. Below is a list of twenty such plants. You must locate and provide a small clipping of fifteen varieties.'"

"Do you know anything about these herbs?" Elam asked.

She scanned the list. "Some. There are a few that I've cooked with before and some that my mother used to make teas." She handed the paper to Elam. "What about you?"

He looked over the paper. "Maybe half a dozen. I can sure as hell identify dyer's woad. It's toxic to our crops."

"Tell you what . . ." She took the paper and ripped it in

half, then began wrestling to do the same with the binding of the paperback.

Elam's brows rose. "Don't you think they'll want their book back? In one piece?"

"I'm sure they have more." She finally tore the tome in two and handed Elam the front half. "As soon as you've found eight of them, meet back here."

"Do you want the buggy?" he asked.

"Are you kidding? I can't drive the thing—and I doubt I can get on the other horse without a boost." She squinted at the surrounding area, then pointed toward the mountain bench. "I'll head toward that little pass there, you go the opposite way."

He nodded and she jumped from the buggy. Since they hadn't been given a shooting sequence, she removed her holster and the heavy pistols and set them on the seat next to Elam. Then, she resolutely strode toward the foothills.

"Wear your hat!" he ordered.

She dragged the sunbonnet out of her pocket and plunked it on her head—feeling like the dork of the year. But she knew the wisdom of wearing it, so she securely tied the ribbon under her chin.

"Sagebrush will be easy," she muttered to herself. The area was covered in the stuff.

She used the scissors to snip a twig from a bush and tucked it into her pocket.

"Sunflower, also easy." She marched toward the fence line, where the waving yellow blooms beckoned to her. The stem was sticky against her fingers once she'd cut it loose and she reluctantly put it in her pocket as well.

"Sorrel, sumac." Squinting, she realized that most of the sumac was high on the bench. She'd rather not go on a hike if she could avoid it. Sorrel, she'd recognize if she stumbled across it.

Realizing it would be easier to study the unfamiliar plants first, she spent at least a few minutes dog-earring the pages and reviewing the pictures. Then, reluctantly, she looked up the hill. At least with the sumac, she knew where to go.

Gathering her skirts, she wrestled her way through the barbed wire fence, wincing when her hair caught, and began to scramble up the slope. After riding in the buggy, her thigh and calf muscles had tightened up, and they screamed at the renewed exercise. Her heels were chafing against her boots, and P.D. winced again, realizing that she'd have full-blown blisters by the end of the day. What she wouldn't give for a hot shower. Or a long soak in a tub. A bed.

Time alone with Elam away from prying eyes.

Her heart flip-flopped in her chest and she paused, gulping air into her lungs. If it weren't for the threat of being watched by the contest observers, P.D. had no doubts that she and Elam would have had sex by now. Heck, they might have even found a way to make love last night, if she hadn't stupidly fallen asleep before Elam had joined her in the bedroll.

Heat plundered her veins at the mere thought of Elam's hands roaming her naked flesh. What she wouldn't do for an hour of privacy. Three times now, she'd awakened and realized that she'd spent the night sleeping in Elam's arms. Only sleeping. And each time, her half-remembered dreams had left her itchy with echoed passion and feeling unfulfilled. She could only imagine how much more powerful the reality of his caresses could be.

So what had happened to loosen the grip of Elam's grief? A few days ago, there wasn't a popsicle's chance in hell that Elam would even kiss her, let alone make love to her. But now, every look, every touch, every caress radiated his desire for her.

P.D. couldn't fool herself into thinking that she'd been solely responsible for banishing Elam's ghosts. After all, Bliss was filled with women who were prettier and more feminine than she'd ever be. If all he'd needed were a few stolen kisses and a night or two in a woman's arms, there would have been dozens of volunteers over the past three years.

She looked over her shoulder at the valley below, finding Elam a few hundred yards north, where he was hunched over a bush. Sunlight glinted off his scissors as he cut a sample. Then he stood, his back broad, his feet braced apart in an unconscious show of strength.

Maybe it was the distraction of the Games, or the physical challenges being thrown at them. Or perhaps it was the way he'd begun to interact with his family and the community again.

Whatever the reason, she was glad that he had found some peace with himself and the past—at least for the time being. P.D. wasn't foolish enough to think that he'd finished mourning. There would always be triggers—anniversaries, holidays, snatches of music, the scent of Annabel's perfume.

P.D. herself had only to smell the mixture of diesel exhaust, woodsmoke, and snow to be thrust into the past. In an instant, she was six years old again, huddling outside in a sleeting storm under the faded pink polka-dot umbrella that had been given to her for Christmas. What she'd really wanted was a doll, but when her parents had gone to the thrift store, they'd bought her the umbrella instead. She remembered sitting on a warped picnic bench, trying to ignore her parents' drunken argument behind the foggy windows. They were talking about her, and she'd begun to hum to herself to drown out their words.

. . . your fault that we're saddled . . . brat . . .

. . . you were there . . . conceived . . .

. . . should have kept driving . . . left her there . . .

P.D. had insisted to herself that the umbrella was far more useful than a doll, especially in the storm. But she couldn't completely drown out the knowledge that she would have willingly sat uncovered in a blizzard if she could only have a semblance of a loving friend. Even an imaginary one.

Geez. Why was she thinking about that now? Hadn't she put all of that behind her? She'd risen above the challenges of her birth and made something of her life.

Challenges? Was that what she was calling them now? Why couldn't she be honest with herself? Her childhood had been riddled with neglect and abuse by the very people who should have loved her most. And somehow, in showing her the best way *not* to treat another human being, they'd left her . . . broken.

The thought was so unguarded, so stunning, so . . . painful . . . that P.D. whirled to continue her climb and stumbled instead.

No, not broken. She refused to believe that. *Flawed* was probably a better term. She was educated and successful. She had a thriving business and a comfortable home.

She just didn't seem to have what it took to keep a man's interest for more than a few months.

But she couldn't think about that now. She wouldn't think about it.

Shaking herself loose from her memories, P.D. continued her climb. As she grabbed for handholds among the scrub, she scoured the path for plants on the list—and her efforts paid off.

"Yarrow," she muttered under her breath, snapping off one of the tufted yellow blooms. "Aha! Queen Ann's lace." She was halfway to her quota.

As she paused to put the snippings in her pocket, she realized she should have brought a bottle of water with her. The late-afternoon sun radiated off the rocks and seemed to simmer through the layers of her clothing. Beneath her bonnet, she could feel a rivulet of sweat trickling from under her braid and running down her back.

Turning, she glanced down into the valley again. Elam was much farther away now. He'd tied up the horse and buggy and seemed to be wandering in aimless circles. Great. That meant he was having trouble finding items from his list.

P.D. turned to continue her ascent, then paused when she heard a rustling in the underbrush above her. She halted, remembering Helen's warning about snakes.

Her heart began a slow pound, and she wondered if she should abandon her search and return to the valley floor. She was incredibly thirsty, and there'd been a huge tub of iced water bottles near the front stoop of the Colby house. She could always get Elam to ride the horse up the slope to get the sumac. The last thing she needed was to run head-on into a rattler.

But she was almost there. And the rustling noise had seemed . . . larger . . . than a snake. Maybe it was a deer or . . . or a porcupine. That was possible. She'd seen porcupines waddling their way across the highway not too far from here.

P.D. moved even more gingerly, peering around boulders and avoiding the clumps of bushes where a rattlesnake might have gone for shade. At long last, she was able to climb onto an outcropping of rock within arm's length of the sumac. Turning, she surveyed the trail she'd made, but thankfully, it was free of any "critters." She should be in the clear on the way down.

After taking a few minutes to rest in the shade, P.D. cut off a branch of the distinctive sumac leaves—then crowed in delight when she saw a copse of scrub oak, which was also on her list. In the autumn, the two types of trees would turn the mountainside to scarlet, but for now, the samples brought her closer to her goal.

Afraid of leaving the safety of the rock, she leaned over as far as she could, finally managing to grab a leathery leaf from the scrub oak. Then, wobbling, she righted herself, and shoved her prize into her skirt. She glanced around—in case there might be other plants she needed. But when a breeze suddenly chilled her clammy nape and the hairs rose on her arms, she realized that she wasn't about to head into the trees to look for anything else.

Turning to face the valley, she balanced on the boulders again, mentally plotting the best route for her descent. But just as she was about to jump onto the path, something hard whacked her on the back, and she was suddenly pitching forward.

For a moment, P.D.'s arms windmilled frantically as she tried to gain her balance, but there was no way to correct herself. She fell hard, her head striking the ground, her hands pinned awkwardly underneath her. Then, she was rolling down the hill, gravel and scrub scraping at her skin and clothing, her eyes squeezing shut against the dust and the sickening revolution of sky, dirt, sky, dirt, sky.

At long last, she came to a stop, wedged up against a clump of tumbleweed that prickled and stung.

For several seconds, she couldn't move, couldn't breathe. Then, as if reminded that her body required air, she took a huge gulp and opened her eyes.

The mountain dipped and swayed, and she quickly squeezed them shut again. But in that fleeting moment, she thought she saw a shape slipping back into the clump of trees at the top of the hill.

THE shadows were beginning to lengthen when Elam finally found the eighth plant sample on his list. Rolling all the cuttings into the paper, he inserted them in the remains of the guide book and shoved the whole thing into the back of his waistband. Then he walked toward the spot where he'd left the two horses to drink and graze on the ditch bank. Thankfully, a farmer downstream had begun his water turn, allowing Elam to take care of the animals.

Tying the mount to the buggy again, Elam climbed onto the narrow bench seat and turned back toward the Colby house. Hopefully, P.D. had already finished finding her cuttings and they would be done for the day.

But as he rode back toward the dilapidated building, all he could see was the contest volunteer calling out to a new pair of contestants who were jogging toward her. Damned if the woman didn't look like an inverted buttercup being beset by a pair of flies. But there was no sign of P.D.

Elam lifted his hat and wiped at the sweat hovering near his eyes, then jammed it onto his head again. He scanned the open field and then the hill beyond.

Nothing.

A cold trickle of foreboding began at his scalp, then swept down the length of his spine. He'd been in the military too long to ignore his instincts. Urging the horse into a trot, he hurried toward the volunteer, who was just sending the next set of contestants on their search.

"Have you seen my partner? Has she checked in with you?"

The woman lifted a hand to shade her eyes. "No. Sorry."

"When did you catch sight of her last?"

She grimaced. "I couldn't say. I've had two more sets of contestants come through. In between their arrivals, I was reading a book."

"Thanks."

Elam knew that he probably shouldn't leave the buggy unattended. They'd already had a pair of contestants steal their horse. The buggy would provide an even bigger temptation. But the sudden pounding of his heart warned him that there were more important things at stake.

Handing the volunteer the book and his cuttings, he said, "Check these off. I'll be back."

To her credit, the woman didn't seem too upset about the ruined book. She turned it over in her hand as if it were a grubby curiosity, but then she took a pen from her clipboard and wrote his number on the rolled-up paper.

As she returned to her camp chair and umbrella, wrestling with her hoops so that she could settle into the narrow seat, Elam tied the buggy to one of the few remaining support posts of the Colby house and swung himself into the saddle of the other mount instead.

"Don't let anyone mess with the buggy," Elam said to the woman as he rode past.

She lifted a distracted hand in his direction, but she appeared more intent on checking off the plant cuttings that he'd brought to her.

Elam spurred his mount into a trot, heading in the last direction that he'd seen P.D.

He tried to tell himself that there was no need for alarm. P.D. had lived in the area long enough that she couldn't really get lost. All a person had to do was climb one of the hills and take a look around. Bliss was just east of here, and the network of roads leading in and out of town were easy to see. If all else failed, she could find a canal and follow it downstream. He was blowing the whole thing out of proportion. For hell's sake, there were a hundred logical reasons for her disappearance. She could be watering a bush or sitting in the shade where he couldn't see her.

But the thoughts didn't ease the knocking of his heart against his ribs or the twisting sensation in his gut.

Bringing the horse to a halt, he stuck two fingers in his mouth and whistled sharply, then called out, "P.D.!"

But there was no movement that he could discern.

Scouring the dirt ahead of him, he finally found evidence of her trail. She was heading toward the bench.

Riding the fence line, he located a spot where he could pass through with the horse. Then he went back to the place where she'd scrambled through the barbed wire. P.D. had caught her hair on one of the barbs and the distinctive curly strands waved in the breeze.

"P.D.!" He listened, not sure if there was an answer or not. As day bled into evening, the ever-present breeze that blew into the valley from the north was beginning to pick up again, rustling the foliage around him.

Elam pointed the mount up the hill.

"Prairie Dawn, can you hear me?"

And then he heard it, a small cry from up above.

Spurring his mount in that direction, he hurried up the rocky slope.

"P.D.?"

Finally, he heard her voice.

"Here!"

His heart had changed gears from a slow thud of dread to a quicker thump of relief. But Elam didn't allow himself to analyze the sensation. Instead, he nudged the horse slightly to the left. Then, after making his way around a crop of boulders, he finally saw P.D.

She sat with her back propped up against a rock, her sunbonnet hanging at a lopsided angle from her neck. Her face was scratched and streaked with blood and a lump on her forehead was turning purple. Her clothes were dirty and torn. But what caught him in the gut was her woebegone expression.

Elam had seen gravely wounded men in action. He'd taken his brothers to the emergency room with broken bones and deep gashes. But none of them had ever affected him as much as finding P.D. hurt and bedraggled.

Her lower lip trembled betrayingly as he swung from the saddle.

"What happened?" he asked as he took some water from the saddlebags and rushed toward her.

"I—I fell."

He sank onto his knees beside her, his pulse still beating an uneven tattoo as he twisted the cap off one of the bottles.

She took it, drinking greedily as he dragged the bandanna from his pocket and used the other water bottle to dampen it.

Gingerly, he began wiping the blood and grit from her face. Thankfully, most of the scrapes and cuts were superficial, but the welt on her forehead had a deeper cut and he was concerned she might have a concussion.

"We need to get you to a doctor."

She shook her head. "No. No doctor."

"Why not?"

"Because it would disqualify us from the competition."

"P.D., you should be examined—"

"No!"

When Elam regarded her in exasperation, her chin wobbled again and her eyes brimmed with tears.

"I need that prize money, Elam," she whispered, obviously embarrassed. "If not, I don't know how I'm going to come up with enough cash to make the repairs at Vern's."

Elam wanted to insist that no prize money was worth her health, but she gazed at him so piteously, so upset that she'd been forced to reveal her tenuous financial situation, that he folded her into his arms instead. P.D.'s own hands whipped around him, gripping him as if he were a lifeline.

"I bet the contest people have a medic on call who can come to us. But we've got to get you off this hill. Can you stand up?"

She nodded into his shoulder, but she didn't release him. So, tamping down his worry, he held her tightly, absorbing her trembling until it ceased.

"Elam?" she whispered.

"Yeah, baby," he murmured, still rubbing her back with long, soothing strokes.

"Elam, I think someone pushed me."

He eased his hold enough to look at her, sure he hadn't heard P.D. correctly.

"What?"

She smoothed her hair out of her face with her hands. "I think someone pushed me."

Elam could scarcely credit the hot anger that roiled through his frame. "Who?"

A look of relief raced over her features. "You believe me?"

He lifted her chin. "Why wouldn't I believe you?"

She shrugged. "It sounds crazy. I didn't see anyone—and it doesn't make sense that anyone could be there. But I'm sure I was pushed."

"Where were you?"

She pointed to a knot of sumac near the summit. "Up there by those boulders."

"Wait here." Elam handed her the second water bottle, then mounted the horse, urging it farther up the slope. He could see where P.D. had landed and his gut lurched, but he forced himself to move on. Once at the sumac, he dismounted and headed into the tangle of branches. It was easy to see that the area had been disturbed. There were hoofprints and boot marks in the weeds. And someone had carelessly discarded a candy wrapper and an empty soda can. The garbage didn't look weathered enough to have been here long.

Elam's jaw clenched. But when his eyes fell on a heavy branch that had been tossed onto the boulders where P.D. must have been standing, a slow rage rose inside him.

Someone had been here, all right. And they'd taken that branch and swung at her as hard as they could.

Elam bit back a searing expletive. Who the hell would do such a thing? Surely not one of the observers that the contest organizers had warned them about. Another contestant?

He thought of the man that P.D. had accosted at the previous challenge. He'd taken a hit to the gut, but he hadn't appeared overly put out by it. If anything, he'd seemed to think her reaction was funny. But had he decided to take his own brand of retaliation? If so, how could he and his partner possibly have made it this far on foot? And why was there no evidence of a second man?

Which left him with an even more serious possibility. The fire at Vern's, the figure he'd found lurking at her house . . .

Did someone have a private grudge against P.D.?

The thought caused his anger to settle into his chest like a lump of hot coal. His eyes were already intently searching the countryside, the Wild West persona from the Games disappearing beneath years of training as a soldier. If it weren't that the competition was so important to P.D., he would pull up stakes, notify the authorities, then take her somewhere safe.

But he couldn't do that. Not when the prize money was so important to P.D. and Vern's future. He would just have to stay more aware of his surroundings and keep her as close to him as he could.

Elam threw the branch onto the ground and strode back to his horse. Right now, he needed to focus on what was critical: getting P.D. some medical attention. Then he could report the incident and let the contest people decide what to do. But if it turned out it was another contestant . . .

Heaven help the man, because Elam was going to pound him into the ground.

P.D. waited patiently while Elam investigated the area. The trembling had begun to subside beneath the throbbing of her head and the dozens of stinging cuts and scrapes. But worst of all was the tightness that gripped her throat and the burn of moisture at the backs of her eyes.

She never cried. Never. But she was tired and hot and hurt and she couldn't afford any setbacks in the competition.

Her eyes skipped up the hill and she took comfort from Elam's strength. If anyone could get her through this, it was this tall, tough cowboy. And that thought alone was enough to shock her to the core. In the past, she'd always maintained her emotional distance. It wasn't that she consciously held people at bay. It was just that, after spending most of her life moving from place to place, a part of her was always preparing for the next set of good-byes. Partings were painful enough. But if you truly cared about a person . . .

They were gut-wrenching.

So P.D. had learned early on to keep things casual. Even with Bodey—whom she'd considered the closest friend she'd ever had—there had always been a hidden line of defenses. There were intimacies she'd never shared and confidences that she'd never allowed.

But with Elam, she'd unwittingly bared it all—her pain, her vulnerability, and her wounded pride. He'd seen her at her best and at her worst. And miracle of miracles, he hadn't pushed her away. Instead, he'd willingly accepted all of her baggage while sharing his own.

She heard the horse approaching and looked up, expecting to see Elam regarding her with barely concealed pity. P.D.

was crazy to think that someone had pushed her. The notion defied all logic.

But what she hadn't thought she'd find was his face set in fierce lines of fury and concern. He could have been wearing a neon sign blaring, NO ONE HURTS WHAT'S MINE. And his blatant display of possessiveness was completely at odds with the closed-up, stoic stranger that Elam had been the first day they'd met.

"You were right. Someone was there."

P.D. hadn't even considered how she would react if her fears were confirmed. But she hadn't thought she would burst into tears. Nevertheless, as she pushed herself to her feet, she started to sob.

In an instant, Elam was there, folding her into his arms, one broad hand resting tenderly at the back of her head.

"We need to get you to a doctor," he whispered, his voice thick with worry.

"No, I . . . I don't even know why I'm c-crying . . ."

She never let anyone see her cry.

"You've been hurt, P.D. It's natural. Just let it all out."

She wrapped her arms around Elam, knowing that she could sob the night away if she wanted, and Elam wouldn't think any less of her. He didn't see her tears as a sign of weakness. He understood her chaotic emotions and allowed her the release, free from censure. And that, in itself, brought more tears until she felt as if she were cleansing her soul of years of apprehension and regret.

When she grew calm again, she felt his mouth against the top of her head. "P.D., I think you have a concussion or—"

She stopped him with a finger to his lips. "No. I'm fine." She stared up at him through lashes that were still beaded with moisture.

"But you—"

This time, she kissed him, softly at first, then more purposefully.

"We need to—"

"Shut up and kiss me, Elam."

He needed no second bidding. He took her lips with a hunger and ferocity that matched her own. And when it became clear that she was answering him move for move, his arms swept around her waist, pulling her even more tightly against him.

Passion tinged with relief raged over them both as his tongue swept into her mouth. Sensation took her by storm as their legs wove intimately together and his hand cupped her buttocks, grinding her to his arousal.

Her own hands swept over his back, then lower, tunneling beneath his belt as far as she could reach, digging into the tight muscles of his butt, wishing that she had more access.

"I should take you to a hospital just so I could get some time alone with you," he gasped against her lips.

P.D. laughed. "I could almost, *almost*, go for that."

Elam lifted his head. He was breathing hard and he made no effort to hide the fact. "When I couldn't find you, I was scared shitless," he admitted.

She frowned. "Why? We weren't apart all that long."

"You're always so . . . in control, so . . ." He rested his forehead against hers. "I just knew something was wrong."

She allowed herself a small smile. "I would have crawled down eventually."

"Don't talk like that." He kissed her again, fiercely. Then he backed up, pulling her toward the horse. "Let's see if they have a medic who can take a look at you."

"Elam," she protested as he lifted her into the saddle. "That really isn't necessary."

"Yes, it is," he growled, swinging up beside her.

"But the plants. I only found six."

"To hell with the plants."

"Elam—"

He silenced her with a kiss to the curve of her neck. "Just . . . do it for me. All right? Then I promise to find the rest of the damned samples."

She sighed. "All right."

IN the end, a call for a "medic" resulted in three ambulances, a paramedics' vehicle, a fire truck, and several EMTs in shiny pickups with flashing headlights—all of them arriving at the Colby house in less than fifteen minutes.

Under normal circumstances, P.D. would have been mortified that a call for help had resulted in the arrival of half the volunteer services of the county. But with Elam hovering over her, and one of the men congratulating P.D. on "livening up an otherwise slow evening," she decided that she wasn't going to worry about the fuss she'd caused. It was more important that she be cleared for "active duty" so that she and Elam could continue the game.

To her surprise, it was Jace who ambled toward her, carrying a medical case.

"So what has my lunkhead of a brother done to you?" he asked as he knelt in front of her and pulled a stethoscope from around his neck.

"What are you doing here?" P.D. asked.

"I've been volunteering my time today as part of the Games. I was just about to go off duty when I got the call. So far, all I've seen is heatstroke and mosquito bites, so this should shake things up." He listened to her heart, front and back, then wrapped a blood pressure cuff around her upper arm. "I thought I told Elam to take care of you. He doesn't seem to be doing a very good job."

Elam scowled at his younger brother, but didn't speak since Jace was observing his watch and slowly releasing the pressure.

"Looks good," Jace said as he wrote down her vitals on a chart. Even P.D. could see her blood pressure was only slightly elevated.

Jace took a penlight from his pocket and said, "Look straight at me." He flashed the light in her eyes. "Look up."

P.D. followed his instructions to the letter, feeling an itching need to get going. While they'd been dallying with the medical teams, one of the groups had already checked off their plants and another was racing toward the woman in yellow.

"What's your name?"

She jerked her attention back to Jace.

"What? You know my name."

"Just answer the questions, please."

"Prairie Dawn Raines."

"The month?"

"June."

"And are your intentions toward my brother honorable or dishonorable?"

"Jace," Elam growled in warning.

Jace winked at P.D. "*His* reaction time seems normal." Jace ripped open a packet of antiseptic cloths and began wiping the scratches and abrasions. "This might sting."

P.D. hissed and Elam immediately bristled. But before he could say anything, Jace said, "Don't you have something better to do?"

When Elam would have barked at his brother, P.D. grasped his hand and squeezed. "Go see if the samples we gave them were okay, then get whatever else we need so we can get out of here as soon as they're done."

"Sounds like a good idea," Jace said soothingly. Then, glancing up from his work, he offered, "She's fine, Elam. No sign of concussion. You'll want to keep your eye on her for the next twenty-four hours. If you see anything out of the ordinary, you can call us back again. But I'd say she'll just be stiff and sore for a day or two." He tucked the soiled wipe into a waste bag in his kit, then reached for a clean one. "This is going to take a while, so go finish up what you need to do. By the time you get back, I should be done."

Elam remained where he was until P.D. squeezed his hand again.

"Please? I'd like to get out of here." They were losing time and daylight, but that was only part of her concern. Whoever had pushed her could still be in the area.

And it was that last confession, that she didn't want to linger in a place where someone had purposely brought her harm, that finally convinced him. Jamming his hat on his head, he leaned down to plant a swift kiss on her lips, then strode away.

Jace waited until his brother was out of range before allowing a slow smile to split his features.

"So that's the way the wind blows," he murmured.

P.D. damned the slow heat that spread into her cheeks.

"Do you mind?"

Jace shook his head. "Nope. I'd say it's about time he got involved with someone." Jace's smile widened to a grin. "And I can't think of a nicer person for him to choose."

Her embarrassment turned to shyness, causing Jace to laugh.

"Why, P.D. . . . I do believe I've finally rendered you speechless."

FOURTEEN

———◆———

E LAM came racing back just as the last of the EMT vehicles crawled down the lane. Slapping the cuttings into the volunteer's hand, he didn't even pause in his stride before heading toward P.D., who waited in the late-evening shadows of the old house's portico.

"And?" he asked peremptorily.

"I'm fine. Bumps, bruises, cuts. Nothing that won't heal within a few days."

"What about the head?"

He sat down on the narrow front steps next to her, lifting away the ice bag she'd been given to counteract the swelling.

"It's fine, but I was warned it might turn several shades of purple by dark."

There was a gauze patch covering the deeper cut, so Elam couldn't examine it himself. But since Jace had been the one to take care of P.D., he was satisfied. "Did you tell them you were pushed?"

She looked away, then shook her head. "No."

Elam opened his mouth to chide her, but held himself in check when she fiddled with the edge of the ice pack.

"Why not?"

"It sounds stupid and paranoid and . . ." She shrugged. "I just want to get out of here. I don't want to spend the next hour or two answering questions."

Elam instinctively wanted to raise holy hell about the whole situation, but he reined in his natural reactions.

With Annabel, he'd been prone to White Knight Syndrome—rushing in to save the day, overcoming obstacles in a way that he considered best, but never really listening to what Annabel wanted. It was one of the few things they'd argued about. Annabel would spend the time he was overseas asserting her own independence, only to have him arrive home to "fix" everything without even asking. In doing so, he'd unconsciously undermined her decisions and made her feel helpless.

P.D. was asking him to let her make up her own mind. She wanted him to trust her decisions. And even though he might want to surrender to his Inner Caveman and drag her to safety, he couldn't do that to her.

"Okay," he said slowly. "But if anything else happens, we report it."

She grinned and threw her arms around his neck. "Thank you."

When she would have backed away, he held her tightly, just for a few more seconds. He needed to feel her heart thud against his own to drown out the last of his misgivings. Sweet Holy Heaven Above. What would he have done if she'd been seriously hurt?

"All checked off."

Elam was forced to let go of P.D. when the woman in yellow approached. "Here's your next set of instructions. Good luck to both of you."

P.D. reached for the envelope and ripped it open, withdrawing a hand-drawn map with a compass rose at the bottom of the page.

"It looks like we're supposed to go to . . . Mirror Lake."

"What? Mirror Lake is in the Uintahs up by Monte Cristo State Park. That's at least a hundred miles from here." Elam took the paper and laughed. "Looking Glass Lake. That's the name of the fishpond by Henry Grover's summer cabin." He stood and took P.D.'s hand, pulling her from the stoop. "Come on. We can get there in twenty, thirty minutes."

Elam paused to touch the brim of his hat as they passed the volunteer—who was again struggling to tame her voluminous skirts so that she could sit in her shaded camp chair. "Thanks for your help."

She waved. "My pleasure. You two be safe, y'hear?"

"Yes, ma'am."

Elam helped P.D. into the buggy, and made sure the second horse was tied securely to the back. Then, he climbed in beside her and slapped the reins.

"Hi-yahh!"

The buggy jolted forward and he headed toward the lane that the emergency crews had taken. Once he reached the main highway, he turned west, keeping as far onto the shoulder as he could.

Now and again, Elam would hear a car coming from behind, but thankfully, the other drivers knew enough to slow down and give them as much space as possible so that the horses wouldn't be spooked. Nevertheless, he kept a tight rein on the mare in the traces until its skittishness disappeared along with each vehicle.

"Where'd you learn to drive a buggy?"

He grinned. "The annual Founder's Day Parade." He glanced at P.D., then back at the road. "You've seen how it works. Anyone who is *anyone* in the community is in the parade—at least that's what we thought when we were kids. Grandpa Taggart had an old wagon in one of the barns and my brothers and I would decorate it each year and hitch it to a team of his prized mules. Then we'd volunteer to carry one of the town dignitaries in the back. I think I was about twelve the first year."

"An early display of civic pride?"

"Not really. Jace and I figured that there'd be big bags of taffy being thrown to the spectators. If we drove the wagon, we were sure we could snag the leftovers."

"Did it work?"

He winced. "Yep. We had a grocery sack filled with candy

that first year—and I bet we ate most of it in one day. I still can't face a piece of taffy."

P.D. laughed—and shit, he loved the way she looked when she did that. Her eyes sparkled like clear blue water on a summer's day. And her face . . . the joy in her expression was contagious.

His gaze dropped to her lips as he felt a slow burn begin in the pit of his stomach.

"You are so beautiful," he murmured.

She looked away in embarrassment. "You keep saying that."

"Because it's true."

"That's not what I see in the mirror every morning."

Was she kidding him? Even with the scrapes and cuts and mottled patches of purple beginning to form on her face and arms, she was the most beautiful woman he'd seen in years.

"Maybe you need a new mirror."

"Maybe I just need you around more to make me believe it." She flushed as soon as the words left her lips. "Sorry, I didn't mean—"

He leaned forward to stop whatever she'd been about to say with his lips. When they parted again, he murmured, "Maybe you're right."

The approach of another car forced him to return his attention to the road. Dusk was falling and the vehicles had turned on their headlights. The horse grew more skittish as a set of glowing orbs approached from the opposite direction. And Elam soothingly called out, "Easy, girl. Nothing to worry about."

The highway suddenly dropped into a steep hill as the road swept down toward the winding path of the Bear River. The water was high with fresh runoff as the heat of summer melted the snowpack on the mountains. The sound of hooves against asphalt was soon drowned out by the rush of water.

It took all of Elam's concentration to keep the buggy in control down the slope, but finally, they reached the bridge spanning the water. With each minute that passed, the traffic grew heavier—probably due to the Movie in the Park being offered in town that evening—and Elam had to maintain a firm grip on the reins. But soon, they were heading up the opposite slope, their speed dropping to a slow walk as the mare struggled to surmount the steep incline. Once they were at the top, Elam allowed the animal to maintain an easy pace so that it could catch its breath.

"Are you sure you're headed to the right place?" P.D. asked.

"Pretty sure. Henry Grover was a good friend of my dad's. We used to meet at his cabin every Fourth of July for a picnic."

Elam glanced behind him, saw a pause in the line of cars, and moved into the road, then the turning lane. As soon as possible, he urged the horse onto a quieter street headed south. Here, houses with huge trees crowded in between the pastures and fields of corn and grain. But the horse appeared more comfortable on the shadow-dappled lane.

"Is there any more water?" P.D. asked, twisting to reach for the saddlebags.

"There should be a few more bottles. They might be warm. I didn't think to restock our supply while we were at the Colby place."

P.D. opened the flap, then grew very still.

"What's wrong?" Elam asked when she didn't immediately retrieve the bottles.

After a beat of silence, P.D. murmured, "You stole some sandwiches and chips."

From her grave tone, a person would have thought she'd just discovered that Elam had spirited away the Holy Grail.

"Well, yeah," he replied, his own tone rife with an implied "duh." "I wasn't about to eat beans and jerky if I could filch something else."

She grabbed a water bottle and again he saw the laughter dancing behind her eyes. "I knew there was a reason why I like you so much."

Again, his eyes zeroed in on her lips. "You like me, huh?"

She twisted off the cap and took a long swallow, then handed him the bottle.

"How much?" he asked before taking a drink.

"Just you wait and see."

The remark was so full of promise that Elam nearly choked on his second draft of water. Then, knowing he had to be off this damn buggy as soon as possible, he handed her the bottle and slapped the reins onto the horse's rear, urging it to a faster clip.

TWENTY minutes later, Elam turned the buggy down another gravel drive. Fields of wheat bordered them on either side. The wind ruffled the heavy tips until the fields resembled a green rippling ocean.

"You're sure this is the place?"

"Yep. We've got ground we lease just over there."

He pointed to several fields of grain and alfalfa.

P.D. remained skeptical since there wasn't any water in sight except for rivulets of ditchwater escaping from a series of cuts and flowing into the field ahead.

"Please tell me Looking Glass Lake isn't a flooded pasture."

"You're not high on patience, are you?"

She grimaced. "Not really, no."

"Then watch this."

The road passed through an open gate, then abruptly turned to the right. And there, opening up below them, was a tiny hidden valley thick with ancient willow trees.

Sensing that the end of the journey was near, the horse quickened its step, its ears flicking, its head bobbing. The buggy zigzagged down a winding track to where the gravel path abruptly ended in a pasture of tall grass. Elam followed a faint set of tracks around the trees, revealing a tiny cabin nestled up against the hill and, below it, a crystal-clear pond. A bright blue paddleboat bobbed in the water next to a wooden gangplank that ran a few yards into the pond. A rope swing swayed in the breeze, suspended from one of the overhanging branches. And a zip line had been strung from a tree across the pond to a post near the top of the hill.

"You've got to be kidding me," P.D. breathed. "How long has this been here?"

"Years and years. But not many people know about it. It's one of the best kept secrets in Bliss."

Elam rolled to a stop in front of a huge metal barrel that had been cut in half to form a trough. A pipe dribbled fresh water into the trough before the cool liquid overflowed into the pond.

"The water's pure as long as you drink from the pipe. It's brought in from an artesian spring." He stepped from the buggy, tying the horse to a hitching post near the trough. The animal immediately sank its velvety nose into the water and began to slurp noisily.

"Are you sure this is the place? I don't see any contest people."

"They've got to be here somewhere." As he untied the other horse so that it could also drink its fill, he called out, "Hello?"

There was a bang from behind the trees, and a few minutes later, a rotund man wearing a straw hat and overalls emerged from a path to the side of the cabin. "Hello, folks! Sorry for the delay. I had to avail myself of the facilities." He gestured a thumb to a tiny wooden shed on the hillside, one with a telltale crescent moon on the door. "Don't worry. I heard you comin' and made a note of your arrival time." He patted his bib pockets, one of which held a notebook and pencil while another displayed a watch chain hooked to a strap.

He hurried toward them, quickly washed his hands under the running water, then wiped them on the legs of his pants. "Hey, there! Miss . . . Raines, isn't it? I recognize you from Vern's."

"Yes." She shook his hand and allowed him to help her down from the buggy.

"Who won?"

P.D. struggled to comprehend his comment. "Sorry?"

He chortled and pointed to the bandage on her forehead. "Looks like you've been in a barroom brawl."

She laughed, saying, "I'd say the hill won the first round, but I intend to win the war."

"Good for you!"

At that moment, Elam ducked under the horse's neck and walked toward them. As soon as the volunteer caught sight of him, he blurted out, "Elam Taggart, you son of a bitch!"

Elam shook his outstretched hand. "Hello, Henry."

"You're looking fat and sassy."

"Thanks." Elam hooked a thumb toward the volunteer. "This is Henry Grover, P.D. This is his cabin."

"They twisted my arm, I can tell you. But the minute they offered to throw in a steak at Vern's, I had to give in."

"So what's the challenge?" Elam asked, leaning an arm against the horse's saddle.

"You have to send up a flare."

Elam squinched his eyes shut, pinching the bridge of his nose. "What the hell?"

"This is the Happy Home challenge, buddy boy," Henry said.

Elam sighed. "What does that mean? And what does it have to do with sending up a flare?"

Henry chortled and held up a warning finger. "Patience, or I'll add ten minutes to your time." Henry's expression was fierce, but then he looked at P.D. and winked. "Come on, you two. This way."

He led them to a grassy area between the house and the pond. With evening falling, the long shadows had bled together under the trees, creating a blessedly cool patch of shade.

"This here's the deal," Henry said, rocking back on his heels. "On that table there is a package of balloons, some old shaving soap, and a straight-edge razor. You have to blow up a balloon, tie it off, cover it in soap, and shave it clean."

"That sounds easy enough," Elam said.

Henry let out a bark of laughter. "Maybe so, but you ain't the one who's gonna do it. Since yer a *mixed gender* couple"—he made a face to show what he thought of the terminology—"*she's* gotta do it."

P.D. eyed the long, thin blade of the razor and was glad she only had to shave a balloon.

"After she's done with that, *you*"—he poked Elam in the side—"get to shear a goat."

Henry pointed to a pen of animals in the distance. Several dozen goats grazed in shadows. Unlike most of the local goats P.D. had seen in the area, these had long white hair that had matted into tufts and ringlets.

"Are those Willis's angora goats?"

"Yep."

"And he's letting us do the shearing?"

"The contest committee paid him for the wool in advance, so he don't care. As you can see, most of the shearin' that's been done so far ain't worth shit."

P.D. had to admit that many of the goats who'd already been cut looked like they had the mange. For the most part, they'd been relieved of their wool, but there were spots with longer tufts of hair—and even a few areas that hadn't met the shears at all. P.D. could have sworn that the animals gazed back at them in forlorn embarrassment.

"The shears you need are hanging on the gate support and there's an empty bucket to catch the wool. Bonus points may be awarded for how pretty the job has been done. Those bonus points will be awarded by yours truly."

Elam lifted his hat and raked his fingers through his hair. "Is that all?" he asked wearily.

"Nope." Henry pointed to a table under the eaves of the cabin. "After that's done, there's a bonus puzzler. You don't have to do it if you don't want to, but if you solve it within three minutes, you can shoot off a flare and the organizers will take twenty minutes off your time. If not, there's no penalty."

He walked them toward the table where there was a huge wooden bowl, a bin full of flour, a metal scoop, an old-fashioned grocer's scale, and two paper sacks.

"This here is a five-pound sack. If you fill it completely full, you'll have exactly . . ." He pointed to Elam for the answer.

"Five pounds of flour."

Henry cackled. "He's not as dumb as he looks, is he now," he said to P.D. with a wide grin. "The other'n is a three-pound sack." He pointed to the grocer's scale, which had two brass platforms balanced over a teeter-totter-type bar. On one of the platforms were several shiny metal weights. "Your goal is to come up with four pounds, in a sack. No more, no less. You can use all the flour you want, but you can only weigh the sack once." He fixed them each with a stern gaze. "Got it?"

"Got it," P.D. echoed.

Elam sighed, but finally said, "Sure."

"All right. Just let me get settled here." He sat down in an old metal porch chair that looked like a refugee from the fifties. He removed the pad and pencil from one pocket, made a note on a blank page, then removed his pocket watch from the other. He waited with the tip of his tongue peeking out of the corner of his mouth, then abruptly yelped, "Go!"

P.D. immediately ran toward the table of balloons, ripping open the package and selecting one. But when she tried to blow it up, she couldn't force enough air into the narrow opening to get it to expand.

"Here."

Elam grabbed a balloon from the package and quickly blew it up to full size, then twisted a knot in the end.

While he held the balloon, she grabbed the cup of shaving soap and ran to the trough, allowing a generous amount of water to dribble inside, then ran back to the table. Snatching the brush, she mixed the soap enough to cover the brush, and then began to coat the balloon.

"Make sure I can't see any of the green, or you've got to start over," Henry called out.

Sighing, P.D. became more deliberate, double-checking the balloon until she was sure that she had it completely covered. Then, she set the brush and soap aside, ignored the strop, and grabbed for the razor.

The instant she touched the razor to the balloon, it suddenly exploded, sending shaving cream and bits of latex everywhere. P.D. squealed, her face suddenly pelted with soap.

When she opened her eyes, she found Elam wiping white foam from his cheeks. His right hand still hung suspended in midair, holding nothing but the shattered stem from the balloon.

"Sorry," she said, tamping back a giggle. "I assumed the blade wouldn't be that sharp."

"Maybe you'd better check it," Elam said wryly.

She carefully raked her finger sideways over the blade, determining that the razor was very sharp indeed.

Elam blew up a bright red balloon and fastened the end.

"Careful this time."

"Copy that," she muttered.

She slathered the second balloon with soap, then grasped the razor. Taking a deep breath to steady her nerves, she placed a finger on the top of the balloon to hold it steady.

This time, she angled the blade more and carefully swiped down the length of the balloon. When she reached the bottom, revealing a swath of red, she let out her breath.

"Atta girl," Elam murmured.

Very carefully, she repeated the procedure. When she reached the bottom without mishap, she straightened and rolled her shoulders.

"If I can get through this, *I* might have to join the EOD," she muttered.

Elam laughed. "It is a bit like diffusing a bomb."

She readied herself for the next pass, but paused to shoot him a quick glance. "Why would you ever want to do something this nerve-racking for a living?"

His voice dropped. "Because the process feels so great. Your heart is pounding, your pulse is jacked up. Every sense is heightened. For a few short minutes, every ounce of your attention is focused on a single task until you can disable the ignition switch or force a safe detonation. Then . . . *bam!* In a single explosion, all your frustration and concentration explodes, leaving you panting and joyously relieved."

P.D. stared at him, wondering at what point his description had become loaded with sexual innuendo.

Bam!

Too late, she realized she'd let the blade hover too near to the balloon again.

Sighing, she wiped the shaving soap off her face. From the porch, Henry cackled in delight.

Chuckling, Elam reached for another balloon.

IT took four tries for P.D. to shave the balloon. When she finally managed to complete the task, Elam watched in amusement as she tried to "spike" the balloon on the grass and do a victory dance. He indulged himself in the sight for only a moment before grabbing her hand and pulling them toward the goat pen.

The shears they'd been given looked like old-fashioned lawn clippers and Elam feared that they would work about as effectively. But with P.D.'s help, they cornered one of the goats and separated it from the herd.

Spying a length of baling twine on the ground, Elam flipped the goat, bulldog fashion, and tied its hooves together.

"Are you supposed to do that?" P.D. asked when the goat bleated in distress.

"How the hell should I know? I deal with cattle and horses, not goats." He began cutting at the long wool. "Hold its head."

P.D. sank onto the ground and pillowed the goat's head in her lap, crooning to it like a baby. Although Elam knew that time was of the essence, he kept getting distracted by her lulling voice and the tender stroke of her hands against the goat's ears and nose. If the goat had been a cat, Elam knew it would have purred—and he couldn't blame it. He inexplicably wished that it was his head resting there and her hands were stroking him.

Which suddenly made him work at an even more furious pace. He wanted time alone with P.D., away from the pressures of the Games. And if cutting the fur off a damned goat was the price, he was more than willing to do it.

It was growing dark by the time he finished the last cut. After releasing the goat—who didn't seem too inclined to move—Elam pulled P.D. to her feet and grabbed the bucket.

"Let's go!"

They raced back to Henry, who was regarding them sleepily from his chair. He offered a perfunctory glance at the bucket of wool and made a notation in his notebook. Then, once they'd taken their place at the table, he glanced at his watch and said, "Three minutes! Go!"

Elam glanced at the flour, the sacks, and the scale and tried to summon his wits about him. But if the truth were told, he really didn't care what the answer to the puzzle might be. After the day he'd had, he wanted to haul P.D. into his arms and kiss her. No, he didn't just want to kiss her, he wanted to plunge headfirst into his hunger for her. He wanted to touch her, hold her—and yes, he wanted to make love to her. After the past couple of days together, his desire for her had grown to a fever pitch and he didn't know how much longer he could wait. The threat of being observed had lost much of its power beneath the want raging through his body. But there was also a part of him that was on high alert. After P.D.'s accident, he wasn't just worried about contest officials anymore. Either someone was out to hurt P.D., or there were contestants who were willing to go further than stealing a mount. That meant that Elam was going to have to keep his eyes open and trust in the instincts that had kept him alive overseas.

A part of him acknowledged that P.D. had started to talk her way through the riddle, that she was reaching out to measure flour into the sacks, but he couldn't concentrate on anything other than the sweet curve of her lower lip, the soft slope of her cheek. He wanted to touch her there, kiss her there—and more. He wanted to release the buttons to that schoolmarmish blouse to expose her delicate collarbones and the roundness of her shoulders. And if he went farther, undoing *all* of the buttons, who knew what he would find? He longed to discover the shape of her breasts mounded above her corset, the nip of her waist, and more.

He started when P.D. suddenly squealed and threw herself into his arms. Too late, he realized that she'd solved the puzzle and he hadn't even noticed how she'd done it. But his guilt was quickly swept away in a rush of awareness at the warmth of her body pressing into his.

Damnit! He had to get a grip on himself. Now wasn't the time to be thinking that way. Not with Henry present, the thought of other, unwanted intruders—and shit! The last thing P.D. needed after tumbling down that hill was Elam pawing at her. She had to be hurting like hell about now.

Even so, Elam couldn't prevent himself from closing his eyes and hugging her tight, just once, before letting her go.

Henry pushed himself out of his chair and handed Elam a flare gun, forcing him to let P.D. go.

"Now aren't you a smart cookie?" Henry said to P.D. "Only two groups before you have managed to solve the riddle."

Elam pointed the gun skyward and pulled the trigger. The flare streaked into the sky leaving a trail of smoke, then exploded like a new star that burned out as it fell to earth.

"I hear tell the local airport isn't too happy about the flares, but I tend to enjoy 'em," Henry said, looping his thumbs around the straps of his overalls. After the last of the red glow disappeared, he said, "Well now. That's it for tonight. I'll bring your next set of instructions bright and early tomorrow morning." He jerked a hand toward the willows. It was only then that Elam saw Henry's old Ford parked under the feathery fronds. "Walk me to my truck, Elam." He paused to grin at P.D. "And you have a good night, Miss Raines."

"Thanks, Henry."

Elam followed Henry to his vehicle, wondering if he'd heard Henry correctly and the older man truly intended to leave them alone.

"You're leaving?"

Henry's eyes narrowed and he pointed a warning finger his way. "Long as you'll promise, on your honor and your word as a Taggart, that you won't leave the premises or do anything against the rules of the competition." He looped his thumbs around the straps of his overalls. "See, I've been stuck here a couple of nights already and that ol' bed in there is playing havoc on my back. I got a hankerin' for a hot shower, some of my wife's good cooking, and an honest-to-goodness mattress." He sniffed. "If it were anyone else, I'd stay and watch 'em like a hawk. But I know a Taggart's word is his bond, so do I have your promise?"

Elam nodded, holding out his hand. "Absolutely."

Henry answered with a hearty handshake.

"Say, Henry, do you have any idea if there's anyone else in the area?" Elam asked, trying to pose the question as casually as he could.

Henry's eyes twinkled. "The nearest checkpoint is five miles away. The observer, Brandon Lasley, I hear tell, has had some . . . car trouble."

Elam stiffened, wondering if the sabotage was extending to the contest officials as well.

Henry cackled. "He's stomping mad. Seems his tires went flat—all four of 'em—sometime after your brother Bodey brought him something to eat. He can't prove it, but since he and

Bodey have been Cow Cutting rivals for years, he's swearing Bodey wanted to maroon him on Wilson Point for the night since there's a dance at the Bowery and he and Bodey are fighting for the affections of the same girl."

And Elam wouldn't put it past Bodey to stack the deck in his favor.

But then, Elam was struck by another thought. Wilson Point. There was no way Lasley could see into Henry's valley from there.

"If you're wondering about the other contestants," Henry said with a wink, "you all were the last ones to get buttoned down for the night. So . . . you've got the place to yourself for the night. Feel free to help yourself to the supplies." Again, he pointed a warning finger. "But no shenanigans. You stay within a hundred feet of the cabin or you'll have all our butts in a sling." He turned the key, stomping on the accelerator until the engine finally turned over. "I'll see you at first light."

"THERE'S dust, Jace!" Barry announced from the passenger seat. An excited bounce quickly followed. "It must be Henry!"

Jace pushed back his hat and yawned, waking from his doze. After signing off as a volunteer for the Games and picking up Barry from his Scout group, Jace had been watching a field of alfalfa and it was just about ready for him to adjust the dam and begin another set of water.

At least, that was his cover story. Truthfully, he'd been waiting for Henry to appear.

Turning the key, Jace flashed his lights. Within seconds, Henry stopped and rolled down his window.

"Did it work?" Jace asked.

Henry's chuckle came straight from the gut. "You bet. He looked pole-axed soon as I mentioned I was leavin' 'em alone."

"You're sure you can keep it from the contest committee? I wouldn't want to hurt their chances for the prize money."

"Hell, no one's gonna argue about givin' your brother and P.D. a little privacy—after all they've been through? It's not like they're goin' anywhere." He made a dismissing gesture with his hand. "How 'bout you? How's he gonna take it when he realizes you've been doin' a little matchmaking?"

"He'd better never find out," Jace said, putting the truck in gear.

"What's Elam not supposed to find out?" Barry asked wide-eyed from the passenger seat.

"Never you mind, Barry," Jace said.

"But I want to know," Barry insisted.

Henry chortled and explained, "He'd better not find out what happens when two lightning bugs are left shut up in a jar, Barry."

Barry blinked. "But there's no lightning bugs in Utah," he insisted.

Jace laughed. "There's a couple of 'em tonight, Barry."

His little brother's eyes widened. "Can we go see 'em?"

"Not tonight, Barry. Not tonight."

Henry chortled and put his truck in gear. With a wave, he drove away in a cloud of dust.

Jace headed in the opposite direction, his truck rumbling down the gravel road. And for a moment, just a moment, he was struck by a wave of sadness—and a healthy dose of sibling jealousy. What would it be like to have a woman regard you with so much naked emotion—love, desire, friendship—in her eyes the way he'd seen P.D. looking at Elam? Try as he might, Jace couldn't get a female past the friendship stage. Especially once they realized that the ranch, his brothers, and his guardianship of Barry all came as a package deal where Jace was concerned.

And he wouldn't change his situation for anything. Not even a woman.

He glanced at Barry with his gangly boy-man body completely at odds with the little-kid earnestness of his expression. For several long moments Barry stared into the darkness frowning, clearly trying to work out something in his head. Then he turned and asked, "Jace, what *does* happen when you put two lightning bugs in a jar?"

Jace allowed himself a slow smile. "Sparks, Barry. Lots of sparks." And suddenly, his bad mood drifted away as he chuckled. "And with a little luck, it will create some spontaneous combustion."

FIFTEEN

———•◆•———

THE hiccupping grumble of Henry Grover's truck had barely disappeared in the distance when Elam suddenly ripped off his holsters, then whipped his shirt over his head and threw it onto the ground.

P.D.'s jaw dropped. But by the time she could react, his fingers were already poised at the buttons of his fly.

"What are you doing?"

He spared her a glance. "I don't know about you, but I haven't had a decent shower in two days. I'm heading for the pond."

Elam shucked out of his pants, revealing a pair of period-style drawers that coated his butt like a second skin. But before P.D. could truly appreciate the scenery, he was running toward the gangplank. Launching into the air, he made a perfect shallow dive, disappearing beneath the glassy surface before reappearing again farther in the lake.

"Come on in!" he called, pushing the wet hair out of his face with his palms.

P.D. eyed the water, unconsciously licking her lips. "I can't swim," she finally admitted.

"What? Really?"

She nodded.

He swam toward her, then near the gangplank, he stood. Water rushed over his shoulders and chest, arrowing down to a point beneath the chiseled ridges of his abs. Where he stood, the water came to his navel.

"It's not deep unless you're in the middle."

P.D. didn't need a second urging. She set her holsters and pistols near Elam's, then quickly unbuttoned her shirt and her skirt, then wriggled out of her petticoats. When she straightened, she became aware of Elam's keen stare.

"What?"

He leaned back into the water, idly swimming away.

"Just enjoying the view."

She suddenly became aware of her corset, chemise, and pantalets. Although the attire covered most of her body, there was still something . . . suggestive about the period underwear.

The thought caused her to cross her arms over her chest. "What if there are observers nearby?"

Elam's smile was slow and intimate. "Henry assured me that the nearest Peeping Tom is five miles away on the wrong side of the hill. Besides, within an hour, it'll be too dark for anyone to see anything."

Privacy.

The thought brought an immediate rush of awareness. Deciding to test more than just the waters in the pond, P.D. dropped her arms and began to move with deliberate slowness, first tugging on the ribbon of her chemise.

"What if someone else shows up?"

"I don't plan on sharing the pond."

"Elam," she chided.

"No one's going to come. We were way behind on the Colby house challenge so we were the last of the teams to arrive at our checkpoint. The contest committee has kept us all buttoned up tight and in one place at night." When she still didn't move, he added, "There's no way Henry would have left us here if he was expecting someone else."

Her hands moved to the metal fasteners of her corset. Elam followed the movement so keenly, she felt his gaze like a brand.

"You're sure?" she asked as she unhooked the metal post from its eye.

Elam's Adam's apple bobbed. "Yeah. I'm sure."

She released the rest of the fasteners and tossed her corset into the grass.

The moment the stricture was gone, she sighed in relief. A cool breeze touched her hot flesh and she realized that she'd been wearing the rigid foundation for nearly two days—and it had been nearly that long since she'd had a bath.

Unwilling to wait another minute, she ran toward the pond, slowing down only when the cool water hampered her movements. Then she launched herself into Elam's arms.

What had been meant as a purely utilitarian gesture to keep herself afloat instantly became an explosion of sexual awareness. Elam's skin was slick and smooth as he wrapped his arms around her. She held on tight, and her legs drifted intimately between his. He was already aroused, and she smiled against his lips.

"Mmm. I like that."

Then, while he held her, she tugged her chemise over her head and threw it onto the bank.

"You're sure no one will come," she whispered one last time.

"They'd better the hell not, or I'll have to shoot them."

Giggling, she said, "Maybe we'd better wait. Just in case. I'm kinda hungry and—"

"I'm freakin' starving," he interrupted hoarsely, then captured her lips in a powerful kiss.

From that moment, there was no time left to think, only feel—the strength of his arms, the rasp of his beard against her cheek, the rough-slick texture of his tongue as he tasted her again and again and again.

P.D.'s eyes slammed shut as she focused her entire being on this moment, this man. Never had she felt so at home in another person's arms. There was no awkwardness, no self-consciousness.

Her fingers roamed over his cheeks, his shoulders, his back as he slanted his mouth over hers.

He drew back only when they were both gasping for air.

"It's about time," he said, his lips trailing down her neck. "I don't know if I could have lasted another day."

She laughed, wrapping her legs around his waist. "Are you sure about that?"

He groaned. "Oh, yeah."

His fingers reached for the button of her pantalets.

"Why, Mr. Taggart, whatever do you think you're doing?"

"You know what I'm doing."

"Such outrageous liberties."

"Hell, yeah."

He quickly shucked her pantalets, throwing them onto the bank. But when he would have reached for the buttons to his own drawers, she beat him to it, her fingers quickly releasing the fasteners. She spread her hands wide, smoothing the fabric away from his buttocks, allowing him to spring free. Then, it was her turn to sigh in relief as her hands closed around him, feeling the heat, the rigid strength.

"Damnit, I don't think I can hold on for very long," Elam whispered against her lips.

"Then don't hold on." She smiled against him. "We have all night."

As if the words were all he needed to hear, he strode from the water, her legs still wrapped around him. He reached for the trousers he'd abandoned on the bank, fumbling for a condom. But she was there already, helping him to ready himself. Then, he was laying her down in the verdant grass, and in one single thrust, he entered her.

P.D.'s head arched back and she gasped.

He was immediately contrite. "Did I hurt you?"

"No. Don't stop," she said frantically, drawing his hips back to meet her own. "It feels so good."

He began rocking against her, his face a study in pleasure and concentration. His wet hair hung down around his face, giving him a primitive air. He could have been an example of primordial man at his finest . . . or a cowboy of old, like the books she loved to read.

She tangled her fingers in his hair, drinking in his blatant desire, knowing that the intensity of his expression would live in her memory the rest of her days. No matter what the future might bring, no matter when they might part ways, she would remember the reverence, the joy, the utter passion that radiated from his face.

Finally free to explore the body that she had admired for so long, she roamed the curves and valleys of his chest, his shoulders, as if she were blind and he were Braille. His skin flowed beneath her fingers like hot silk, overloading her senses, making her wish that she could freeze this moment in time.

Saints above, please don't let him tire of her too quickly.

Because she didn't think she could ever grow weary of this . . . him . . . Every time she saw Elam, she would remember the strength of his embrace, the power of this joining.

P.D. held him even more desperately as their movements became frenzied, frantic, and the pleasure built to a fever pitch. Flinging his head back, Elam muttered a curse as his whole body began to tremble.

"I . . . can't . . . hold . . . on." His eyes squeezed shut. "You . . . feel . . . too . . . damned . . . good . . ."

"Let go, Elam," she whispered, knowing that his expression alone was enough to finish her off.

He plunged into her one last time, then cried out with the power of his release.

P.D. followed immediately on his heels, biting her lip to keep from crying out loud with the intensity of her orgasm.

When she finally became aware of her surroundings, Elam lay with his head cradled between her breasts, his wet hair cooling her hot skin.

He was still, so still.

In a rush, she realized that this was probably the first time he'd made love since Annabel's death. A wary chill crept through her body as she prepared herself for the inevitable hurt, knowing that he would probably experience a wave of guilt or a rush of old memories—and she couldn't fault him if he did. It would be natural for him to think of his wife at a time like this.

But he remained where he was, one finger lifting to trace idle circles on her side.

Closing her eyes, she allowed her muscles to become boneless as her heart eased from its thunderous pace. The emotions would come to him, she was sure of that. Maybe not right now, but soon. It didn't mean that Elam cared about her any less. She couldn't be jealous of a ghost.

She wouldn't.

But try as she might, she couldn't push away the fear that she would always come up short against Annabel Taggart.

Maybe so, but tonight, he's mine.

All mine.

Clinging to that thought, P.D. concentrated instead on the weight of his head between her breasts, the ragged cadence of his breathing. It seemed impossible, but she'd grown to care for Elam Taggart, battered heart and all. It didn't seem to matter that she'd only known him a few short days. It was as if her soul had known him forever.

So she would take whatever he could give her. Without regrets. Because somehow, he'd managed to touch a tiny corner of her heart that she'd never allowed any other man to breach. And she was more than willing to let that be enough for now.

Tonight, he was hers.

And she didn't plan on wasting a single minute.

It was much later when Elam murmured, "So how did you solve the flour thingy?"

P.D. peered at him through half-closed eyes. "Weren't you paying attention?"

His gaze dropped to her breasts. "Not really."

She tried to look stern and disappointed, but somehow she merely managed to appear . . . satisfied.

"I filled up the three-pound sack and dumped it into the five-pound sack. Then I filled the same sack again and dumped as much as I could into the five-pound bag. That left one pound in the bag. Then I emptied the five-pound bag and replaced it with the one pound left from the other container. Then all I had to do was fill the three-pound sack again and add it to the mix. That made the required four pounds."

Elam squinted at her. "You're pretty smart, you know, but there's one thing you still need to learn."

Her brows rose.

"Swimming," he supplied, enjoying the look of surprise that flashed across her features. "Come on."

HE dodged into the cabin to borrow a lantern so that they could care for the horses and then wash and rinse their clothes. Then, they returned to the cool waters of the pond.

Holding P.D. tightly to give her confidence, Elam taught her the rudiments of floating, and for the longest time, she lay on her back, looking up at the stars while the moonlight bathed her wet body in shimmery paleness.

Through it all, Elam drank in the sight of her, her lightheart-edness, her infinite joy. She'd responded to his lovemaking just as he'd thought she would—wholeheartedly, passionately, just as she attacked everything she did.

He waited for the guilt, the sense of betrayal toward Anna-bel, but the feelings never came. Yes, there was a twinge of nostalgia, of saying good-bye to what he'd shared with a woman he'd known most of his life. But he was at peace with his decision to court Prairie Dawn Raines.

Court.

Funny how that was the word that sprang to mind. An old-fashioned word for an old-fashioned man, he supposed. Or maybe it was the Games that had put him in a traditional frame of mind. But he realized the word suited him. He wasn't just drawn to P.D. for the sex. She was funny and smart and so full of passion—everything that had been missing from his life for so long. When they were apart, he couldn't wait to see her again. And when they were together, he didn't want her to go.

Elam knew that his brothers would caution him against jumping headlong into a relationship after so long without a woman in his life. Bodey, especially, would tell him to play the field, enjoy what feminine companionship Bliss had to offer. Hell, even Elam found himself thinking he shouldn't rush into anything approaching even a casual commitment.

But Elam couldn't even imagine looking at anyone else if P.D. was in the room. There was something so . . . *real* . . . about her. So . . . *right*. And at least for now, he refused to analyze the sensation. He was flying by the seat of his pants, following his instincts rather than his head.

In many ways, he regretted that the Games would soon be over. Only two more days. Two days with no outside interference for P.D.'s time. But as soon as the Games were finished, she would be consumed with repairs at Vern's, her job, and her life. There could even be other men vying for her attention.

That thought alone was enough to send a wave of possessiveness raging through him, but he forced it back, leaning over to brush his lips against P.D.'s.

Her eyes flickered open, her lips curving in a soft smile.

"I love it here," she murmured.

"Me, too," he answered, even as a part of him wanted to say, "I love it here with you." But he figured that would sound too sappy. Damn. If only he had Bodey's finesse in charming the ladies. "We probably should get you inside before the mosquitoes make a meal of you."

She grimaced, unconsciously scratching her thigh. Then her stomach rumbled and she laughed. "Apparently, the mosquitoes aren't the only ones who are hungry."

He kissed her again. "Then let's feed you, too."

She tried to sit up, floundered, and grabbed for Elam. His body instantly reacted, but he refused to give in to the hunger for her that still raged inside him. He'd feed her first. Then, they could make love again.

"There are towels in the cabin next to the sink. Not great ones, but they'll do until our clothes can dry." His gaze flicked to the willow overhead where P.D. had draped their things so they could dry by morning. "Shit."

"What's wrong?"

"My drawers. When you took them off me, I just kicked free. That means . . ."

She started to giggle, "That they're down at the bottom of the lake. Told you you'd need an extra pair."

Since they'd neared the bank, her toes hit the bottom and she wriggled free, moving to the shore. "See if you can find them. I'll gather the sandwiches from the saddlebags."

Still cursing, Elam dove under the water, feeling blindly with his hands—knowing it was probably a lost cause, but not relishing going commando with two days left in the competition.

He spent at least twenty minutes diving beneath the surface and returning again for air. In that time, P.D. had taken the saddlebags inside, dressed in her spare set of underwear, and returned to sit on the bank to watch him.

Finally, his fingers brushed against the waterlogged fabric, and he snagged them, then kicked toward the surface. By the time he waded out of the water, she was unabashedly staring.

The lantern rested just inside the cabin, but a beam of light bathed her in gold. And damned if she didn't look like the pioneer bride she pretended to be with the light piercing through the fabric of her chemise and pantalets, and her hair neatly plaited and held together with a scrap of ribbon. But it was the way she watched him, no holds barred, her eyes filled with raw desire for him, that nearly brought him to his knees.

"Nice tan," she said, indicating the demarcation line below his navel and the spot where the waistband of his jeans rested.

He was already beginning to respond to her blatant regard, but he managed to grin. "There are some things that shouldn't be hanging loose around power tools."

"Amen to that."

She stood, offering him a small washcloth. "Sorry, I used the towel."

He regarded the scrap of fabric. Throwing his underwear onto the ground, he growled, "Maybe I should use something else to dry myself off."

She squealed when he started to chase her. But her resistance was short-lived. At the steps of the cabin, she suddenly turned, jumping into his arms rather than running away.

He caught her easily, holding her tightly as she dipped her

head for a kiss. And there it was again, the thunderous need that rushed through him like spring runoff whenever she touched him.

Blindly, he carried her into the cabin and slammed the door shut with his foot. Then, he allowed her to slide down the length of his body.

"Hungry?" she murmured.

"Uh-huh." He kissed her again. He could tell that she was a woman who liked kissing. And there was a spot, just behind her ear . . .

Just as he'd thought, her eyes flickered shut and her breath escaped in a shudder.

"You are a dangerous man, Elam Taggart," she whispered. "My wild Desperado."

He chuckled against her neck, moving lower to the spot where her throat joined her shoulder. Another of the secret places that drove her crazy.

"That's what they used to call you in town," she said, the words barely audible.

"It sounds like something from an old John Wayne movie."

"Mmm." Her lashes were closed now. He loved that about her, too, the way she closed her eyes to heighten the experience. "Or my own private cowboy."

He laughed again. Dear sweet heaven above, before meeting her, he probably hadn't laughed in years. "Your what?"

She tugged at his hair, forcing him to lift his head. Her eyes were blue and sparkling in the lantern light.

"You know . . ."

Kiss.

"Save a horse . . ."

Kiss.

"Ride a cowboy."

Holy, holy hell.

Then she was pulling him toward the iron bedstead in the corner—not that he put up any objections. In fact, he didn't know how he was going to keep from exploding when she pushed him onto the mattress, then straddled his stomach.

When she bent to kiss him, the chemise gaped, giving him

a perfect view of her full breasts. Then, his eyes slammed closed as she kissed him—fiercely, hungrily.

His arms wrapped around her body, but she shook him free, sitting up, eyeing him with careful deliberation. Then she pulled at the ribbon of her chemise, allowing it to gape. There were tiny hooks and eyes that held it closed, and he forgot to breathe as she released them one . . . by one . . . by one . . .

The placket gaped open to reveal the ripeness of her breasts. She didn't bother to shrug out of the garment. Instead, her hands moved to the button at the back of her pantalets, leaning forward as she did to whisper against his lips.

"Did you know that Victorian women wore crotchless pantalets?"

He moaned at the mere idea.

"Just imagine. All that prim fussiness on the outside"—she pressed a kiss to his jaw—"all that repression"—she touched the tip of her tongue to his throat—"and underneath, sheer wantonness . . ."

Unable to help himself, he clutched at her, turning so that he lay above her. And then, they were fumbling to remove the lace-festooned underdrawers. But when he would have entered her, she forced him onto his back again.

She shook her finger, making a *tsk*ing sound. "I get to ride my cowboy, remember?"

He groaned, sure that he'd never seen anything so arousing in his entire life as Prairie Dawn Raines wearing nothing but a gaping chemise. Then, his eyes closed as she reached for a condom, readied him, then positioned herself above him.

In one slow thrust, he buried himself in her soft, slick heat.

Just as P.D. had promised, she began to ride him, slowly at first, then with wild abandon. When he would have assisted, she held his hands above his head, testing him to his utter limits, until finally, he felt her arch back and she cried out with her release.

His own was swift to follow as he bucked against her, his climax so intense that he literally saw stars behind his eyes. Then, from far, far away, he felt P.D. wilt, her body melting against his as if she were made of silk.

"Whoa, boy," she murmured almost unintelligibly against his chest.

Not even bothering to open his eyes . . . Elam laughed.

MUCH, much later, P.D. crawled from the bed and reached for the saddlebags. "Ready for a sandwich?"

She watched as Elam stretched like a languid cat, the muscles of his arms and stomach tightening deliciously before he relaxed again.

"I think we can do better than that," he said, rolling from the bed.

While P.D. set out paper plates and water bottles, Elam rummaged through the cupboards. He took out a bag of corn chips, a bottle of homemade salsa, two kinds of pickles, a can of olives, and a box of Twinkies. He set them on the table, then banged through several drawers before coming up with a can opener and utensils.

"It's not Vern's but it'll do for tonight," he murmured, pressing a kiss to her hair as he moved to the opposite chair.

P.D. groaned in sheer delight at the selection. "I've never been so happy to see junk food in my entire life."

As the lamplight flickered, they laughed and dined on their makeshift banquet. But once their hunger was slaked, a different hunger began to rise. One that P.D. could see blossoming behind Elam's eyes like heat lightning.

She'd just opened a Twinkie, and without thinking, she broke it in half, scooped out the cream with a finger, and slid it into his mouth. As he sucked it free, an answering tugging came from deep in her body.

"I do believe that you have thoroughly corrupted me, Mr. Taggart."

He smiled, finally releasing her finger. "I think it's the other way around."

She reached out a hand, pushing back a strand of his hair. Since their swim in the pond, it hung around his face in riotous waves.

Elam grimaced.

"I need a haircut. Badly."

She shrugged. "It's not exactly military issue. Some men like it long."

He frowned. "It's a damned nuisance."

"Then why did you grow it out?"

He seemed to consider his answer before saying, "I don't think it was a conscious choice. I think I was . . . hiding."

His stark honesty struck her to the core. There was such vulnerability to his answer, yet such strength. As if he trusted her enough to be privy to his emotions.

"I could cut it for you if you'd like."

His brows rose. "Would that be a good idea or a bad one?"

She pretended to slug him in the shoulder. "I used to cut my father's hair all the time. I mean, it won't exactly be a salon fluff and curl, but I can give you a standard male hairstyle."

"All right."

He'd surprised her by accepting, but now that she'd talked herself into the corner, she wasn't about to renege on her offer.

"'Course, then your beard will seem shaggy."

"We have a razor," he stated.

Her lips lifted in a slow smile as she remembered the single-bladed razor. Hadn't she read somewhere that one of the top male fantasies was to have a woman shave him?

It took only a minute to gather the scissors P.D. had inadvertently kept from the herb challenge, the shaving soap, strop, and razor. Moving onto the porch, Elam took a seat on the metal chair while she repositioned the lantern.

She ran a comb through his hair, gently separating the tangled strands. Then, she began to trim the long waves. Soon, her efforts became a kind of meditation as she absorbed the silky texture of his hair, the *snip* of the scissors, the whisper of the comb. Bit by bit, the tangled curls fell to the ground, the breeze stirring them beneath her feet. With each new section she removed, a whole new Elam emerged, one with blunt bone structure and deep-set eyes.

When she'd finished trimming his hair, she took several moments, staring hard, adjusting herself to the more powerful man who had taken Elam's place. But then again, she thought as her fingers smoothed the dark strands away from his brow, maybe that man had always been there, hiding, just as Elam had said.

If she'd seen him this way on that very first morning, would she have allowed Bodey to ask for his help?

No. Probably not. Because this was the face of a man who was definitely out of her league.

But even as the thought appeared, Elam linked his hands behind her back and looked at her, his eyes smoldering with awareness, and she was able to quickly reassure herself that nothing had changed. Just because she'd cut his hair, that didn't mean she'd altered the man inside.

But the doubts persisted as she rubbed the shaving soap on his cheeks and jaw. She inched closer, and he tipped his head upward, his throat smooth and vulnerable. After sharpening the blade, P.D. moved slowly, carefully, not wanting to cause him any undue pain, wanting to please him with her efforts.

But if she'd thought that the cutting of his hair had revealed a totally different man, she was completely unprepared for the one beneath the beard. Elam's jaw was square and firm. His chin revealed the faintest cleft in the middle.

And his mouth. How was she supposed to resist him now? Even knowing that someday he could break her heart?

Unable to stand it another minute, she didn't even bother to wipe off the rest of the soap. Instead, she bent to kiss him, needing to reassure herself that—even if they might eventually part—it wouldn't be tonight. Tonight, he was hers and she would absorb every ounce of joy and laughter and passion. Then, much like squirrels stockpiled food for the cold weather to come, she would store up her memories up for the emotional winter that was sure to follow.

When Elam lifted her and carried her into the cabin, she didn't protest. This time, their lovemaking was slow, each caress lingering and sweet. He memorized every square inch of her body, first with his fingers, then his eyes, his lips. When the lantern flickered and died from lack of fuel, he didn't pause, whispering sweet nothings against her skin. And when he finally slid inside her, he was determined to bring her to her release again and again and again. Until finally, when she was sure she couldn't stand another minute of pleasure, her body took over, exploding around him. Only then did he take his own release, his fingers laced with hers as he thrust deeply into her body.

Later, exhausted, she allowed him to draw her tightly against his chest. Her body pounded in an echo of her passion, and she discovered she didn't have the energy to breathe, let alone move.

"I don't want to fall asleep," she whispered, struggling to keep her eyes open, not wanting this evening to end. She didn't want to return to the real world with its distractions and responsibilities.

Elam stroked her back. "I know."

"Thank you, Elam." Weariness tugged at her, drawing her deep into its depths.

"For what?" she thought she heard from very far away.

"For"—she sighed—"you."

Sixteen

———————

I T was still dark outside when Elam awakened P.D. with a kiss on her shoulder.

"Unless we want to greet Henry in the altogether," he whispered against her silken skin, "we'd better get going. We've got the pond for washing and our clothes should be dry by now. But we've got to hurry."

Elam was sure that P.D. caught the wisdom of his words, but it still took several minutes for her to roll out of bed and follow him outside. He was already in the water when she touched a toe to the ripples and shivered.

"It's better to surrender all at once rather than a little at a time."

She gingerly waded into the water.

He swam toward her, wrapping his arms around her and pulling her into the middle of the pond. She rested her head on his shoulder, her eyes closing again. Elam loved that about her, the way that she curled into him for warmth and for comfort. The way there was no artifice to her emotions, no coyness, no hidden agenda.

Which left the possibility of hurting her that much greater.

He was ready to see where things could go between them, sure. But when it came to something more . . . permanent.

He couldn't do that again. He could never do that again.

"Come on," he murmured. "Wake up."

He took the bar of lemon soap he'd brought with him into the pond and held it under her nose.

"We have about ten minutes before it starts getting light."

She made a sleepy sound deep in her throat. Then the citrus scent pierced the fog of her weariness, because she suddenly jerked her head up. "When will Henry be here?"

"Any minute."

Her feet suddenly churned and she grabbed the soap. She washed haphazardly, then tossed him the bar.

Elam barely managed to catch it since all of his attention had been on watching P.D. Enough light had begun to peek over the horizon that he could see the velvety expanse of her skin and the waves of her hair spread over her back. But when she hurried onto the bank and gathered the tresses over one shoulder to wring out the water, Elam swore. Stretching across her shoulder blades was the huge blue-black shape of a bruise.

When she looked at him in surprise, he became acutely aware of the scrapes and cuts and bruises that covered her whole body.

He left the water in ground-eating strides. "Geez, P.D. Why didn't you tell me you'd been hurt this badly?"

He gingerly traced the bruise on her back, then wrapped his arms around her waist and pulled her against him. "If you'd told me—"

"If I'd told you, you would have kept me at arm's length," she said, twisting to face him. "And that was the last place I wanted you to be."

She rose on tiptoe, and try as he might to control himself, Elam felt an immediate response. But the low rumble of a distant engine spurred them both into action.

Elam, who was used to being called into action at a moment's notice, was the first to dress. He helped P.D. to lace up her corset again, then ran interference while she ducked into the cabin to finish putting on her clothes.

Within seconds, Henry's truck turned down the lane. With what Elam knew was deliberate slowness, Henry parked under the willows, giving Elam enough time to tidy up outside and pack their things into the saddlebags. When he finally approached the cabin, Elam had donned his holsters, stowed their belongings in the buggy, and was hitching up the horse.

"Ollie-ollie-oxen-free!" Henry called out.

"Morning, Henry."

Henry altered his course away from the building and approached Elam.

"How was your night?"

The old dog was fishing, but Elam refused to take the bait. "We slept well, thanks."

Henry chuckled. "I hope not."

Before Elam could respond, he waved a familiar yellow envelope in the air. "This is for you." He lifted his pocket watch and squinted. "Just about time."

Elam finished hitching up the buggy and moved to their spare mount.

"Only two more days," Henry said, making idle conversation. "Then, whatcha plan on doin'?"

After throwing the saddle blanket over the quarter horse, Elam shot him a glance. "What do you mean? Same as usual. Work on the ranch will be heating up and there'll be a whole new set of colts to break."

"Life's not just 'bout work. You should know that by now."

Elam couldn't prevent a quick glance toward the cabin. "I know that, Henry."

"Just so's y'do." He slapped the envelope against his thigh. "And don't forget what yer grandpappy told you when you were learning to ride. If you get bucked off, y' get right back on. Otherwise the fear will cripple you."

Elam wasn't sure what Henry was leading up to, but thank heavens, P.D. burst from the door.

"Hey, Henry!" She rushed toward them, shoving the last of their things in the saddlebags. "We used some of your food, so I owe you dinner as soon as Vern's is up and running again."

Henry blushed and waved a dismissing hand. "Ah, shucks, you don't have to do that. But I'll let you!"

P.D. gave him a quick kiss on the cheek. "So what's our next challenge?"

Elam quickly threw the saddle onto the horse's back, quickening his pace. If they had to continue with the Games, then they may as well win. Because there was nothing Elam wanted more than to provide P.D. with the money she needed for her restaurant. Maybe then he could ease some of the strain that was beginning to settle in her eyes.

He slid the bridle over the horse's head, then double-checked everything. Then tying the animal to the buggy, he said, "All right, Henry. Let's have it."

Henry checked his watch again, waiting, waiting. Then he handed the envelope to P.D.

She ripped it open, reading, "'Your train is about to leave, so don't be late. Only one pair of contestants can board at a time. The number of minutes spent waiting for the next train will be added to your score. Hopefully, you've still got a few coins left to buy your fare.'"

"Hell, let's go!" Elam grabbed their things from the buggy and threw it around the horse's neck instead. Then he swung into the saddle and reached for P.D.

As soon as her arms wrapped around his waist, he urged the horse toward the hill.

"Yee-hah! That's the way to ride, Elam!" Henry called as they galloped away.

P.D. thought her teeth would be jarred from her head when the horse lunged forward, clawing its way straight up the side of the hill, rather than the winding road. But as soon as the mount found purchase on flatter ground, Elam spurred the gelding into a gallop.

Immediately, the ride became smoother, but after only one peek at the ground rushing by, P.D. screwed her eyes shut and clutched Elam's waist in a death grip.

She was still struggling with lack of sleep and sensory

overload from the night before. There was a part of her that insisted that none of it was real, that Elam hadn't made love to her with such tender ferocity.

But the evidence was there in the thrum of her body and in the carefully trimmed hair and shaved chin. As daylight broke, sunlight stroked cheekbones sharp as an ax and a jaw that could have been hewn from a block of wood.

What did a man like that see in her? Again, she was struck by the fact that men like this didn't gravitate toward women like her. As soon as they returned to their everyday activities and it became apparent that Elam had rejoined mainstream life, he would be beating beauties off his doorstep with a stick. And that was the way it should be. He needed to be living it up, indulging in his bachelor status, playing the field.

But as much as she told herself that she'd never expected a binding relationship with Elam Taggart, that didn't seem to make her feel any better. Too late, she realized that she'd let herself become too emotionally involved. She'd ignored her own warnings and wallowed in Elam's touch, his concern, his gentleness. Worse yet, a part of her soul which she had always kept hidden from the world had been awakened. She'd begun to feel, really feel. And all of those emotions revolved around Elam.

The thought took her by surprise and she tried to thrust it away, but once it had emerged, there was no denying the truth. She'd always thought that Elam was the one guilty of closing himself off from the people around him. But hadn't she done the same thing?

If her upbringing had taught her anything, it had made her see that loving someone didn't necessarily guarantee that they would love her back. She'd carried that lesson wherever she went. She kept to herself, made few friends, and moved to a new job, a new home, anytime she felt someone was growing too close.

Then, she'd come to Bliss. The moment she'd entered the valley, she'd felt a sense of peace. She hadn't felt the need to prove anything here. She'd been accepted for who she was, no questions asked.

Bliss was home.

Was that part of the reason she'd been able to trust Elam with her secrets? Was it because she'd sunk her roots deep into this place and knew that, no matter what happened, she would still belong? She had a house, a business. Friends. No, not just friends. She had family here. Helen was mother and sister combined. And the Taggarts?

Jace was her knight, showing up when her battery was dead or snow needed to be shoveled. Bodey was the closest thing that she'd ever had to a brother. He was her confidant, her cheerleader. Dear, sweet Barry was like a younger sibling, one to be spoiled and protected.

And Elam?

She cared for him.

Perhaps too much.

The thought pierced her heart like lightning, and she couldn't deny it. She could tell herself that they'd known each other only a short while. She could insist that real devotion didn't develop that fast.

But the truth was . . . she'd begun caring about him the minute he'd appeared on his deck the first day she'd met him.

"Almost there!" Elam called.

She nodded against his back, suddenly panicked. She wasn't ready for anything too serious. She had her restaurant to repair and expenses to recoup—both of which would take most of her time and energy in the coming weeks. And they were only halfway through the Games. She had to keep all her wits about her since she was going to need the money for Vern's now more than ever.

Peeking over Elam's shoulder, she could see the station ahead. The tiny building had once been a hub of commerce for the area, especially when sugar beets had been a key crop in the valley. But now, houses crowded close on all sides. The rail spur had officially been abandoned long ago by the railroad, but the tracks remained. And somehow, the contest committee had obtained a steam locomotive, a passenger car, and a boxcar.

"Are we really riding on a train?" P.D. asked in disbelief.

"It looks like it."

She could barely hear the words as the wind snatched them away.

"Shit! There's another group."

Squinting over his shoulder again, she could see a pair of men in buckskins racing toward the train from the opposite direction.

"It's the pair that stole our horse!"

Elam slapped the reins against the gelding's rump, but P.D.'s skirts probably dampened the effect. She groaned when it became clear that the men were going to reach the passenger car seconds before them.

"Damn, damn, damn!"

Elam was reining in the horse when P.D. suddenly remembered their instructions.

Hopefully, you've still got a few coins left to buy your fare.

"Go to the ticket booth," she shouted.

"Wha—"

"The ticket booth!"

Elam altered course, causing the horse to turn on a dime. As soon as they came to a stop, P.D. slid to the ground and grabbed the saddlebags.

She could hear a commotion near the passenger car, but she ignored it.

"How much?" she gasped to the woman behind the ticket gate.

"Ten dollars. If you don't have that much, you'll have to earn it by doing an extra challenge. If you have a horse or buggy, it will be another ten dollars to take them as well."

P.D. dug through the saddlebags—praying that the Wild West Bucks hadn't fallen out in their haste to pack things up before Henry had arrived that morning.

The other team was rushing toward her now, and she damned the way her fingers had gone completely numb and fumbly. But finally, she felt the betraying rustle of paper.

Hauling out the colored "coins," she paid for their fare and that of their horse. But she knew that they could still lose their chance to ride first.

"Get the horse on the boxcar!" she called as she ran toward the passenger car.

Elam had anticipated her orders. He was already leading the horse up a ramp and into the railway car.

"Just get on the passenger carriage," he said. "I'll be there in a minute!"

Lifting her skirts, P.D. rushed to the steps. She could hear the other men thundering toward her. Scrambling into the car, she rushed to the conductor, handing him the tickets.

The elderly gentlemen punched the tickets, then shouted, "All aboard!"

Immediately, the buckskin pair was stopped before they could climb onto the car.

Steam poured from either side of the engine as it began to *chuff, chuff* slowly at first, then more deliberately. Then, as if breaking free from the bonds of gravity, the car shuddered forward.

Elam. Where was Elam? Did he get trapped in the boxcar with the horse or was he still trying to make his way to join her?

"Wait! My partner!"

The conductor shook his head. "Sorry, miss. Once the train starts, there's no stopping it." He handed her an envelope, but for the first time, she didn't immediately open it. She had the ammunition and her pistols, but Elam had the rifle and shotgun.

The train was picking up speed, leaving the onlookers and the opposing team behind, but P.D. stood in a daze, feeling suddenly bereft. Without Elam beside her, working with her, spurring her on, she was immediately inundated with doubts and apprehension—and that fact was even more troubling. She'd always been a person who prided herself on being independent and resourceful. And here at the first setback, she longed for Elam's support? How had that happened?

But just as soon as she was filled with uncertainty, she pushed it away. Thanks to Elam's expertise, he'd brought them this far in the competition, and she couldn't let him down. They were still a team, even if they weren't together.

Ripping open the envelope, she quickly read the scenario.

The train is being watched by the infamous Hole in the Wall Gang. They've laid an ambush at Little Bear Canyon. You may have to shoot your way out of this one.

There was a drawing of the train tracks up ahead. She was supposed to hit each target in order. If she missed, she could try again, but there wouldn't be much time to reload. Glancing out the window, she could see that she had less than a mile to get ready.

With shaking fingers, she removed her ammunition and carefully loaded her pistols. She was just sliding the last Ruger into her holster when there was a loud *thump* behind her.

Glancing over her shoulder, she saw Elam on the outer platform. Hurrying forward, she opened the door.

"How did you—"

"I forgot the long guns and had to go back for them. By that time, the train had started rolling." He grinned. "I had to climb up the boxcar and swing myself over to this car. Trust me. It's not as easy as it looks in the movies." He spied the challenge paper on one of the seats. "What do we have to do?"

"Hole in the Wall Gang up ahead. Six pistol targets, two rifle, pop-up shotgun."

He squinted down the tracks. "I need to load. You take the pistols, I'll take the others."

P.D. had never gone first, but there was no time to argue. She could see the metal targets up ahead. She ran out onto the platform, unholstered her first weapon, and aimed carefully.

The train slowed to take the bend. She lined up her sights.

Ping, ping, ping.

There was a break. This time the targets were farther up the hill and staggered.

Ping, ping.

She quickly changed to the other pistol.

Breathe!

Ping!

"Good girl!"

She quickly switched places with Elam, taking the shotgun from his grasp. Whipping the rifle into position, Elam aimed.

And missed. Elam Taggart missed.

P.D.'s heart lurched into her throat, but he quickly recovered, trying again. Just before the target was out of sight, he shot again.

Ping. Ping.

He handed the rifle to P.D., taking the shotgun. This time, the target was on a faux water tower. Elam waited until the train drew as close to the target as possible. At the last minute, he shot the release mechanism.

Bang . . . ping!

A charcoal briquette launched into the air. Elam aimed, and fired.

Puff!

The briquette exploded into dust.

P.D. squealed, jumping up and down.

"Yes!" Elam gave her a high five, then hauled her close for a searing kiss.

"None o' that, now," the conductor said from the doorway. "Soon as the train stops, you have exactly one minute to get your things off the train. Anything not unloaded in that time stays on the train."

P.D. had barely met Elam's gaze before he was handing her the shotgun. "Can you bring the weapons and the saddlebags?"

She nodded.

"You're sure? It'll be a handful, but we need that horse."

"I can do it."

He kissed her again. Then, grasping the ornate ironwork on either side of the platform, he climbed onto the railing. "See you soon."

Her heart leapt to her throat, thudding behind her ears, as he jumped forward, grabbing the iron rungs bolted to the back of the boxcar. Only once she saw him reach carefully around the car and swing to the other side was she able to move.

Back in the passenger car, she carefully unloaded the remaining ammo from their weapons, returning it to the proper boxes in the saddlebags. Then, throwing the bags and the drawstring sack with her extra underwear over her shoulder, she grabbed a long gun in each hand.

The train was grinding to a slow halt.

"Good luck to you, miss," the conductor said, opening the door for her. "Once you debark, there's a volunteer waiting with your next challenge."

"Thanks."

She stood impatiently on the platform until the train came to a stop. Then she quickly jumped down and moved toward the waiting volunteer.

"Any other cargo?" asked a woman dressed in gauchos and a bolero adorned with elaborate cabochons.

"A horse."

At that instant, the door to the boxcar rolled open and Elam called out, "Grab the ramp!"

P.D. set the guns and saddlebags on a table provided and hurried to grapple the length of wood and put it in position. But the horse wasn't too keen on getting out of the boxcar now that he was in it. Even with Elam tugging on the reins, it was digging its heels into the wood, refusing to budge.

The train whistle blew.

"Ten seconds!" warned the volunteer.

At the last minute, P.D. whirled toward the saddlebags. Digging inside, she grabbed one of the plastic-wrapped Twinkies that she'd stuffed there that morning. Ripping open the plastic, she ran to hold it under the gelding's nose. In the movies, she was always seeing people feeding animals lumps of sugars. Hopefully, the animal could smell something in the Twinkie that might tempt him.

The whistle squealed again.

"Five seconds."

"Come on. Pretty please," she crooned.

The horse's ears twitched. Its velvety lips wrinkled. Then, just when it would have opened its mouth to nibble on the treat, P.D. backed away.

Miffed, the gelding reared its head, but finally followed.

"Grab the reins, P.D.!"

She reached for the strips of leather, pulling hard. The final squeal of the train sounded just as the animal cleared the ramp.

"All aboard!" the conductor called from the train.

Elam had time to throw the ramp back into the boxcar, but he didn't bother to close the door. Instead, he backed to safety while P.D. shamelessly allowed the horse to nibble on the Twinkie.

"Here you go, folks." The volunteer held out a fistful of colored envelopes fanned out like a poker hand. "Congratulations."

Elam snatched the yellow one. Inside was a crude document entitled "Land Deed" with another map.

Elam read the directions and sighed. "You know, I used to wonder why my ancestors traveled all the way from the fertile farmlands of Ohio to Utah, a spot that is basically an inhospitable desert."

He looked up at P.D., his expression rueful. "I'm beginning to believe they were just too damned tired to keep going."

P.D. laughed. "We're close to the end. Maybe two more challenges, three at the most."

"Then let's get this one over with."

SEVENTEEN

—◆—

B Y this time, lack of sleep had blurred reality to a point where the challenges had become . . . normal. More and more, P.D. felt as if she were disappearing into the fantasy of the Games. She was having a hard time remembering the responsibilities that awaited her—repairs at Vern's, her need for more cash. Instead, she was sinking into the role of partner and pioneer bride. And there was some danger to that.

Fantasy could never become reality.

As their horse skidded to a stop and P.D. slid to the ground, she forced herself to remember that none of this was real. It was merely a harmless game, a flirtation, a quick passionate affair.

"What do we need to do?" she panted, hoping that whatever was involved this time would keep them off a horse for a while.

Elam looked at the laminated scenario pinned to an old dilapidated cabin on the outskirts of the valley. "Plow a furrow between the markers . . ." Elam glanced at the field nearby and grimaced, then at the very modern awning that shaded a table with a variety of tools, foodstuff, and housewares they would need to complete their assignment. "Then we need to use the ingredients provided to make a meal with at least three items, one of which needs to be bread. For that bread, we are required to grind wheat for flour, gather eggs, milk a cow, churn at least a half cup of butter, and cook the loaf in the wood-burning stove—all of which will be graded on taste and originality."

"Good grief! The bread alone will need an hour to rise."

"Oh, there's more. Chopping wood, herding cattle . . ."

P.D. rubbed at her throbbing temples. "No rest for the wicked," she muttered.

Elam smiled, pulling her close. "And are you? Wicked?"

He looked at her with such hopefulness—such blatant awareness—that she couldn't resist and melted into his arms.

"I'm so tired. I just want to go to bed."

"So do I." But it was clear from the low rumble of his voice that he wasn't contemplating rest.

P.D. lifted her head enough to peer around them. "Shouldn't there be a volunteer somewhere?"

This comment caused Elam to look up as well. "Yeah. We've had one at each of the other stops. Maybe they're off watering the weeds somewhere."

"Maybe . . ." But P.D.'s uneasiness remained. She wanted credit for their times—and their food should be judged as soon as it was ready. Without a volunteer, there might be a problem.

"Let's just get this over with as fast as possible," she said.

"Sounds good to me." He looked at the list again. "Tell you what . . . I'll use the horse to take care of the cattle, haul a log closer for firewood, and bring you the milk cow." He squinted at her. "Can you milk a cow?"

She shrugged. "I've milked a goat before."

"Shouldn't be too different. You get the bread going since that seems to be the most time-consuming element."

"Okay."

As Elam took a lariat from the table and disappeared in the direction of the cows grazing in the distance, P.D. looked at the ingredients that had been left for her. There were basic baking supplies—yeast, sugar, oil, and shortening—as well as one cooler filled with meat. Examining the packages, she saw chicken, trout, bacon, and ham. In a second cooler she found hunks of cheese, vegetables, berries, and watermelon. Her mouth watered at the bountiful supply.

Examining the packages that had been opened, she could tell that most of the other contestants had kept things simple. The bacon was nearly depleted, as was the lettuce and watermelon. But P.D. knew it wouldn't take much more effort to roast chicken and vegetables along with the bread. She could also bake potatoes, and throw together a summer salad with lettuce, strawberries, and even some candied seeds.

For the first time since the competition began, P.D. felt comfortable with what she was being asked to do. While waiting for Elam to bring her the cow and firewood, she grabbed the glass canister of wheat and the hand grinder. Again, this wasn't beyond the realm of her experience. Her mother had once been on a whole-wheat, whole-grain kick, and P.D. was more than familiar with the grinder.

Although a recipe had been provided for the bread, she made a few adaptations. She had brown sugar, raisins—and yes!—a tiny container of cinnamon. It would be easy to make a cinnamon swirl loaf, which would complement the dense texture of the whole-wheat flour.

There was an apron hanging from a hook and she wrapped it around her body, then headed toward the temporary chicken coop, which had been erected in the shade of an old maple tree. After shooing the chickens out of the way, she checked through the straw, quickly gathering three eggs. Since they were clean and shiny, it was obvious that these chickens hadn't laid them. Which meant there should be a contest official somewhere.

Ducking out of the coop again, she shaded her eyes and searched the area. Elam was heading back, towing a cow with swollen udders, but other than that, she couldn't see anyone else.

Elam tied the cow a few yards away from where she was working.

"Everything all right?"

She smiled. "They've left enough supplies for a veritable feast."

"Hallelujah for that. I'll go get the wood so you can fire up the stove."

"Thanks."

When Elam disappeared again, P.D. quickly mixed together the bread dough. She worked from memory, using one of her own recipes rather than the one provided. With as much bread as she made at Vern's, she could do it by rote.

She left it to rise in a well-oiled bowl draped with a dishcloth and grabbed a bucket from the table. According to their instructions, they would only need enough to churn the half cup of butter. But she had no idea how much cream would separate from the milk, and the cow looked so miserable, she figured she may as well get as much as she could.

Wetting a cloth at the nearby pump, she washed the cow's udders, then pulled a chair close.

"Don't kick me," she warned the huge animal.

The cow twisted to look at her with thickly lashed eyes.

Gingerly, P.D. reached for the udders, but the cow stepped away, switching its tail.

"Come on, let me touch you. I'll help you feel better."

Again, P.D. reached for the udder. Since the sound of her voice calmed the animal, she spoke low, nonsense words to the beast until finally she was able to grab hold. Sheesh, this was nothing like milking a goat.

Resting her head against the animal's side, she squeezed.

Nothing happened.

She pulled.

Nothing happened.

"Are you crossing your legs or something?" she muttered, trying again. This time, a small dribble emerged from the end.

Adjusting her motions, she squeezed and pulled at the same time and was rewarded with a small stream.

"Yes!"

It didn't take long for her to finally get the hang of things. Granted, she would never break any land-speed records, but at least she would get the job done. Eventually.

She heard Elam return, heard the rhythmic *whack, whack,*

whack of the ax as he chopped wood. This was followed by clangs and bangs as he started a fire in the stove.

Since the cow was beginning to grow restless, P.D. concentrated on her work. She really wasn't in the mood to start the entire process over again if the cow accidentally tipped over the bucket.

She was concentrating on the *hiss, hiss* of the milk jetting into the bucket and the frothy bubbles rising around the rim when she became aware of footsteps running toward them. But when she looked up, it wasn't a volunteer, but another pair of contestants.

"Hey." A red-faced teenager stumbled into the camp followed by a taller gentleman, who looked so much like him, he could only be the boy's father.

"Where's the contest volunteer?" the father gasped.

"We haven't seen anyone."

"What?" He straightened, standing with his hands on his hips, staring out at the surrounding countryside. "Aren't they supposed to take our time?"

P.D. shrugged. Since she wasn't getting much milk anymore, she lifted the pail and untied the animal. Then, with a swat on its rump, she sent it back toward the other cows.

If P.D. were honest with herself, she was beyond irritated that another group had shown up at the same challenge. She and Elam had already done part of the work, gathering the wood and firing up the stove. Now this pair could ride on their coattails. But that wasn't what irked her the most. She resented any intrusion at all on her time with Elam. The end of the competition and the return to the "real world" were already breathing down her neck. Did she have to share these last few days as well?

Knowing that the arrival of another group could also compromise her supplies, P.D. draped a cloth over the pail and made room for it in one of the coolers. Then she quickly gathered all the ingredients she would need for their meal and piled them on one corner of the table.

"Nice dough," the father said, sidling up behind her.

"Touch it, and I'll shoot you."

He held up his hands in a defensive motion—especially

when she brandished the butcher knife in his direction. P.D. supposed she was overreacting, but she was suddenly in a really, really bad mood.

"Josh, why don't you start on the furrowing. I'll . . . uh . . . I'll go get us a cow."

The teenager ran toward the partially tilled field.

Grabbing the chicken, P.D. seasoned it with salt and pepper, then stuffed the bird with half of an onion, some carrots, and leafy celery. Using one of the tin baking pans, she set the bird in a bed of new potatoes, carrots, and turnips, then slid the whole thing into the oven.

There was no way to gauge the temperature of the old stove, but it felt hot enough, so she slammed the door closed. Then, since her dough hadn't quite doubled in size, she checked the milk.

A little of the cream had begun to separate, so she skimmed off what she could with a spoon, pouring it into a mason jar and securing the lid. Then, sitting on the stoop, she began to shake the bottle. There was no way she was going to take the time to use the paddle churn on the table, and this should work just as well. Maybe if she did several smaller batches, she could make the butter a little faster.

In the meantime, she could enjoy the scenery—and she wasn't talking about the Wasatch foothills.

After gathering the firewood and starting the stove, Elam had moved to the field. Stripping to the waist, he'd manned a strange-looking plow that was mounted to an iron wheel. But since the ground was untilled, he strained to dig the plow through the matted weeds and dry earth.

Sweat gleamed on his skin, highlighting the bunching muscles. His shorter hair lifted in the breeze, making her fingers itch to touch it. But his jaw, which had once been smoothly shaven, was already darkening with a day's worth of stubble.

P.D. smiled to herself. Lordy, he was a sight for tired eyes.

From somewhere behind her, P.D. heard the soft mewl of a cat. She glanced around the edge of the cabin, but saw nothing.

Checking the mason jar, she saw that she already had a

small lump of butter. Draining off the liquid that remained, she added a pinch of salt to the butter. Then, since her dough was ready, she set it in the cooler and moved back to the table.

Her movements were as familiar to her as signing her own name. She dusted the table with flour, and since no rolling pin had been provided, she patted the dough into a rectangle. Retrieving the butter, she spread a thin coat on the dough and layered most of the remaining brown sugar on top of that. Then she speckled the layers with raisins, rolled the dough into a log, and set the whole thing in a loaf pan that she'd greased with the rest of her butter. Topping it with a dishcloth again, she set it aside and checked the pail of milk.

This time, she was sure that she had enough to make the half cup of butter that needed to be checked off. Filling the mason jar again, she topped it with the lid, and began shaking it.

She was settling onto the stoop when the mewling came again. A little closer this time. Had the smell of the chicken and the fresh milk attracted a cat?

Still shaking the jar, P.D. pointed an accusing finger at the other contestant. "Don't touch my dough; don't touch the stove."

The poor man was probably wearing more flour than was in his bowl. "But I need to bake it."

"If you don't let it rise first, you'll have a huge hockey puck on your hands. Did you proof the yeast first?"

"Proof . . . what?"

She leaned forward, looking into his bowl. His dough was a gloppy mess.

P.D. sighed. "Start over. Put your yeast in the water with a little bit of sugar, then leave it alone for at least ten minutes."

He regarded her as if she were the pickiest woman on the planet, so she shrugged. "Frankly, I don't care if you start over or not. But eventually, someone is going to have to eat"— she pointed to the goo in the bowl—"*that*."

The mewling began again, and following the noise, P.D. set the jar on the corner of the table and rounded the cabin. Maybe there was a litter of kittens hidden in the bushes.

Moving as silently as she could, she peered into the bushes. She couldn't see any kittens, but . . .

On the other side of the bushes, she could see a flash of white.

The noise came again, closer. But this time, the sound caused the hackles to rise on her nape. Rushing around the bushes, she cried out when she saw a woman's shape crumpled on the ground.

"Elam!" she shouted. Then again, "*Elam!*"

Elam finally turned to look and she frantically gestured for him to follow her.

Racing toward the figure on the ground, P.D. gasped when she saw that the woman was dressed much like her in a dark skirt and a light blouse, her hair worn in a braid down her back. But when she drew closer, P.D. could see that the back of the woman's hair was matted with blood.

Kneeling on the ground beside her, P.D. felt for a pulse just as the woman made a soft keening noise.

"*Shh, shh*, help is coming," P.D. crooned.

Elam came flying around the end of the bushes, followed quickly by the other team.

"What happened?"

"I—I don't know. This must be the contest volunteer. She's been injured."

"Go see if you can find something clean that we can put on the wound."

P.D. ran back under the awning, searching through the supplies. She found a pair of clean flour sack dishtowels and used a knife to help her rip one so that she could tear it into strips. Then, grabbing a bowl and filling it full of water, she returned to Elam's side.

"What happened?"

He pointed to the bluff a few yards away. "Looks like she dragged herself from over there, so maybe she fell."

P.D. handed him the supplies and Elam gingerly began to wash the area enough to reveal a deep gash in the woman's scalp.

P.D. hissed, her stomach flip-flopping, and she was forced to look away. "She needs a doctor or a paramedic. She's going to need stitches."

"Yeah. She's still bleeding like crazy. The other volunteers were communicating by phone. Does she have one in a pocket somewhere?"

P.D. gingerly slid her hands into the pockets hidden in the side seams of the woman's skirt. The first one was empty, but the second one . . .

"Aha!" But as soon as P.D. lifted the phone free, she saw that it would be no help. The screen was shattered. Just in case, she pushed the power button, but nothing happened. "It's ruined."

Elam looked up at the father and his son.

"Oh, no," the older man said, shaking his head and backing away. "We're already way behind in our times and I heard from one of the volunteers that there are only a few minutes separating first place from last place. I'm not hiking to the nearest telephone and back again. That could be the end of our chances to win."

P.D. stared at them aghast. "Seriously? You're worried about your times?"

"Look, we got lost day before yesterday and we're still trying to catch up. And since there's no one to check us off here, we're moving on to the next challenge. We'll let the next group know what's happened. They can come back here and get things squared away again." He elbowed his son. "Josh, see if you can find the lady's clipboard. We'll grab our envelope and be on our way."

P.D. opened her mouth, ready to lash out at the man, but Elam stopped her with a hand on her arm.

"We're better off without them," he murmured, and P.D. realized he was right. This woman didn't need to hear their callous disregard of her injuries.

"What should we do?" she said softly.

"I'll need to take the horse and ride for the nearest house. It shouldn't be too far."

He squinted into the distance. They were in a part of the valley that was used for dry farming, and buildings of any kind were few and far between. He'd have to ride a few miles at least.

"Will you be okay if I leave you for a little while?"

P.D. realized that he was thinking about the unknown person

who'd pushed her down the hill the day before. But she made a shooing gesture. "Go. Go! I'll be fine until you get back."

"I don't want to move her since she might have a neck injury as well, but we need to get her out of the sun."

She urged him on. "I'll rig up something to shade her then use the cold water from the water buckets to wash her off and cool her down. The sooner we get her into an ambulance, the better."

Elam stood. "Are you sure? You need the prize money for Vern's and—"

P.D. cut him off before he could even finish. "I don't care. This woman needs help and I'm not going anywhere."

Elam leaned forward to kiss her hard and fast. "That's my girl."

He pushed to his feet and ran toward the spot where he'd left the horse tied to a tree. Swinging onto the saddle, he whistled and kicked the animal into a swift gallop. In a flurry of dust, he was gone, hoofbeats thundering into the distance.

The woman whimpered and P.D. hurried to gingerly touch her hand. "Don't worry. I'm here. I'm just going to get you some water, okay?"

The woman's lashes flickered and she looked at P.D. with glistening brown eyes.

P.D. squeezed her hand. "I'll be right back. I need to find something I can drape over you so you're not directly in the sun, then I'll get you a drink."

Racing back to the supply area, P.D. took several water bottles from the waiting bucket. There were no more clean dishcloths, so she slid the loaf of bread into the oven so that she could use the one that had been covering the dough. Then, knowing there was no way she could manhandle the awning behind the bushes, she grabbed a pair of long sticks from the pile of firewood and returned to the injured woman.

"I'm back."

P.D. skewered the sticks into the ground, then, since there was nothing else available for shade, she wriggled out of her skirt, draping it over the sticks and throwing the woman's upper body in shade.

A soft sigh of relief pushed from the woman's throat and she tried to turn, but P.D. stopped her. "*Shh*. You've got to stay still until the EMTs get here. You might have some injuries we don't know about, okay?"

An imperceptible nod.

Knowing the gravel and weeds must be biting into her cheek, P.D. shimmied out of her petticoat. Folding it into a makeshift pillow, she carefully tucked part of it under the woman's cheek and neck. "Better?"

Another nod.

P.D. opened the water bottle, then realized that it was going to be tricky giving the woman a drink when she was lying on her stomach. "Sorry. I need some ice. I'll be right back."

She ran to the supply tent again and grabbed a bowl, filling it with the half-melted ice from the water bucket.

"Okay, that should be my last trip for a while," P.D. said, sinking onto the ground. "I figured it would be easier for you to suck on the ice than drink. She held an ice cube next to the injured woman's lips and she greedily took it.

Dipping the dishcloth into the water, P.D. began to dab at the woman's face. She was covered in dust and smeared blood, and as P.D. wiped her clean, she could see her skin was red from sunburn. "I'm so sorry," P.D. whispered. "I heard you earlier, but I thought the noise was something else. I should have thought to investigate the sound earlier."

"Others?" the woman whispered. "Where . . ."

"Elam, my partner, has gone for help. He's got a horse, thank goodness, so it shouldn't be too long. The other couple . . ." P.D. searched the area, but couldn't see them. "Long gone, I guess."

The cloth had grown warm so P.D. rang out the blood-tinged water.

"Ready for more ice?"

The woman nodded. She was growing more coherent, which P.D. took as a good sign.

She slipped more ice into the woman's mouth, then, after biting at the dishcloth to form a small tear, she ripped it in two. Then, she folded the two pieces and poured fresh water on each half.

"What's your name?" P.D. asked, laying one of the cloths on the woman's forehead and the other on her nape.

Come on, Elam. Hurry!

"Jen . . . nifer," the woman mumbled around the ice.

"Hi, Jennifer. I always wanted to be named Jennifer. Really. I thought it was a beautiful, lyrical name." She added wryly, "A normal name. And it has so many great nicknames: Jenny, Jen, Gwen." She gave her another ice cube. "But my parents never did anything normal."

If only she had a watch so that she could check the time. It seemed like an eon since Elam had left, but it had probably only been a half hour, maybe forty-five minutes.

P.D. leaned close to check the woman's color. The alarming redness of her cheeks was ebbing and she blinked again, to show she was listening. All good signs.

"My name's P. D., short for Prairie Dawn."

This time the woman's eyes opened wide.

"I am not lying to you," P.D. said ruefully. "I wish I were."

The woman swallowed and said, "Isn't that . . . the name . . . of a . . ."

"A Muppet." P.D. grimaced. "Yes. But I didn't know that until I was older. Honestly, I don't know if my parents named me after the character on Sesame Street or some fanciful notion about the moment of my birth. I always hated the name. Kids could be especially cruel, and I'd deck anyone who dared to call me Prairie Dawn."

Inch by inch, shadows were creeping across the rock-and-weed-strewn ground, marking the slow passage of time. But the air grew even hotter, as if the earth was radiating the heat from its very core. P.D. looked up, scanning the distance, but she'd lost sight of Elam long ago, and she couldn't see a sign of anyone coming to their aid.

What if Elam can't find a phone nearby? What if he has to ride nearly to town?

Stop it! If there was anyone P.D. could trust to do the right thing, it was Elam.

P.D. removed the cloths again, wrung them out, and re-wet them with cool water. This time, after replacing the one on

Jennifer's neck, she used the other to pat her face, her arms, her hands, rinsed it, then lay it over her temple and cheek. Now that Jennifer was out of the sun, her skin was beginning to take on an alarming pallor.

Knowing that she needed to keep Jennifer distracted, P.D. continued to talk—saying anything that came to the top of her head.

"Elam seems to like my name," P.D. admitted. "Heaven only knows why. Every now and again, rather than calling me P.D., he'll use my full name." She leaned close to whisper confidentially, "When Elam says it"—her heart skipped a beat at the memory of him murmuring her name in the throes of lovemaking—"it makes me quiver inside, you know?"

The woman nodded.

"Have you got someone like that?"

Jennifer dipped her head again, her eyes growing luminous. "B-Bill."

"We'll tell the EMTs to give Bill a call. He can meet you at the hospital, okay?"

"Thank . . . you."

P.D. squeezed Jennifer's hand, realizing that she'd spoken more frankly with a stranger about her burgeoning emotions for Elam than she'd revealed to the man himself.

From far in the distance, P.D. heard a low blaring horn begin to wind up, growing louder and louder until the noise spread through the whole valley.

"Can you hear that?" P.D. asked excitedly. "That's the alarm at the firehouse. Elam must have finally found a phone to use. Help is on its way."

EIGHTEEN

———◆———

A TEAR gathered at the corner of Jennifer's eye and P.D. dabbed it away. Sure enough, the sound of the alarm was quickly followed by that of the firehouse in Belleville, then Abbington. True to form, the volunteer emergency crews weren't about to lose out on a chance at excitement, and they were summoning all the help they could muster.

"The cavalry is on its way," P.D. murmured, rubbing Jennifer's back.

As the distant sirens joined those of the wailing alarms, P.D. could feel some of the tension seep from Jennifer's muscles.

"Are you married, Jennifer?"

The woman's lips lifted in a semblance of a smile. "Fifteen . . . years."

"Kids?"

"F-five."

"Five! Holy moley! You must be a saint!"

A soft laugh pushed from Jennifer's lips.

"This is what you need to do," P.D. said conspiratorially, her gaze sweeping the horizon for emergency vehicles. "You might need some stitches—not many, mind you. But once they have you all fixed up and you're ready to go home, I want you to milk this injury for all it's worth, you hear. Honestly, you shouldn't be cooking—or cleaning—for at least . . . a month? Maybe two?"

The woman laughed again.

"I'd say any kind of vacuuming is a definite no-no, and heck, you probably should keep your feet up and do nothing but read novels until . . . August?"

Jennifer nodded. "I . . . think you're right."

The sirens were growing louder now. Within a few minutes, P.D. could see the plumes of dust. She stood, waving to the line of vehicles bouncing and jouncing down the access road until they veered into the scrub and headed straight toward her.

Within minutes, the scene resembled an anthill, with firemen and EMTs scurrying toward Jennifer. With each person that arrived, P.D. was pushed farther and farther away from Jennifer's side until she stood on the fringes of the crowd.

"Hey, P.D., nice getup!"

Looking down, she realized that, from the waist down, she wore nothing but her pantalets. Snatching her skirts from the ground where they'd been tossed to one side, she quickly redressed. Then, remembering the food in the oven, she rushed to pull out the bread in the nick of time and added more wood to finish the chicken. Clearly in the way, she grabbed a water bottle from its sea of melted ice and greedily drained it.

Before she knew it, Jennifer had been loaded into an ambulance and whisked away.

P.D. watched with a twinge of sadness, wishing she'd had a chance to say good-bye. She didn't want the woman to think she'd abandoned her.

A bowlegged gentleman dressed in a pair of ornate chaps with a waxed mustache that stretched past his ears strode toward her, spurs jingling.

"You the one who helped Jennifer?"

P.D. shook her head. "I just sat with her. My partner was the one who rode for help."

The man held out his hand. "I want to thank you for staying with her. I heard one of the other pairs of contestants just ran off."

"They . . . uh . . . they were worried about their times." Since she didn't want to be guilty of speaking ill of another group, she added, "There wasn't much they could have done anyway."

The man grunted, obviously not feeling so charitable.

"We'll have another volunteer here as soon as we can. Meanwhile, I can pass off your objectives."

P.D. shrugged. "I suppose." It took her a moment to reconnect to the original purpose of her being in this spot. "I think Elam finished the field, I'm not sure. The chicken's on the stove. Might be a little overdone. The bread has cooled and is ready to slice. I . . . uh . . ." She scrambled to think straight while her eyes kept scanning the road for Elam. "Oh, yeah, the cow is back with the others we were supposed to separate from the group. The butter might have melted . . ."

The man waved a dismissing hand and handed her a familiar yellow envelope.

"Hell, I don't care. You've gone above and beyond the challenge. I'll be sure to let the committee know. Jennifer is my daughter-in-law, y'know."

"No. I didn't know."

The man held out a hand. "Will Tompkins."

P.D. recognized the name as one of the committee chairmen and major donors of the prize money.

"P.D. Raines," she said as she shook his hand.

"The lady that owns Vern's?"

She nodded.

"Mind if I have a taste of your food?"

"No, I . . . I think someone was supposed to judge it."

The man rubbed his hands together. "Then, I guess that would be me."

P.D. found that she didn't even have the energy to "put on a good show." Instead, she watched the flotilla of emergency vehicles and pickup trucks disappear in the direction of the hospital. Then her gaze returned to search the horizon for Elam.

It was nearly twenty minutes later when she saw him

walking down the access road, leading the horse behind him. She stood, shading her eyes, watching until he was a few hundred feet away, then moving to meet him halfway.

"What happened?" she asked, gesturing to the horse.

"Horse threw a shoe right after I managed to find a phone. I had to walk back."

"There's food waiting." She looked behind her to where Will Tompkins had pulled up a camp chair and was eating. "I think."

"What's next?" Elam said wearily, gesturing to the yellow envelope she still held.

"I—I don't know. I didn't open it." She slipped a thumb beneath the flap, then pulled out the letter inside. "Wildfire. We need to travel to the safety of Little Dodge." She squinted at the map. "Little Dodge seems to be the fairgrounds on the outskirts of town."

Elam offered a muttered oath, and P.D. suddenly understood the cause. Since their horse had thrown a shoe, the journey would have to be made on foot. It was at least ten miles to town.

"We might as well eat first," P.D. said, squinting at the growing shadows. "It'll be cooler then."

Elam nodded. "That sounds like the best idea we've had all day." He tied the horse to a tree and began to remove its tack. "See if you can't find something we can use to water him."

P.D. returned to the supply tent, and seeing nothing else, she grabbed the pail of milk from the cooler and dumped it into the weeds. Then she filled the bucket with water from one of the melted tubs and brought it to Elam.

Elam had just finished rubbing the horse down. He lengthened the rope so the animal could reach a patch of grass and set the bucket down, holding it steady until the gelding had drunk its fill.

Then, standing, he slipped an arm around P.D.'s waist.

"Hello, Will," he said as the other gentleman wiped his mouth with a paper napkin and stood.

"Elam Taggart! I don't think I've seen you in a coon's age."

"More'n likely." Elam sank into one of the remaining camp chairs.

P.D. quickly loaded a paper plate with chicken and roasted vegetables, then cut a slice of bread from the loaf.

"Didn't know you were paired up with the owner of Vern's," Tompkins said as he settled back with a contented smile. He patted his belly and tipped his hat to shade his eyes from the dipping sun. "She's a mighty fine lady."

P.D. expected Elam to explain he was a last-minute substitution, but Elam said instead, "Yeah, P.D. and I have been seeing quite a lot of each other lately, and I'm not dumb enough to stop."

Tompkins chortled in delight, removing his phone from his breast pocket. "Can't say I blame you. Especially with the way she cooks. I don't doubt she's made the best meal yet at this particular challenge. I've been hearing from Jennifer that she's been growing a little weary of undercooked bacon, overdone eggs, and the worst bread it has ever been her misfortune to eat."

He was talking and texting at the same time and P.D.'s fingers twitched in her sudden wish for modern conveniences—phones, gas ranges, and jetted tubs.

"How is Jennifer? Any word?"

"Just got a text a few minutes ago. My son's with her now. She's going to need about a dozen stitches and they're going to watch her for a while, in case she has a concussion. They're pushing the fluids, too. Can't tell you how much I appreciate the two of you helping her the way you did."

"Did she say anything about what happened?"

Will frowned. "Yep."

Now that her adrenaline was wearing off, P.D. was nearly overcome with weariness, but she made a plate of food for herself as well. But even once she'd taken a seat next to Elam, she could do little more than pick at the chicken.

"Did you see anyone around camp when you rolled in?" Will asked, obviously choosing his words.

Elam met Will's gaze with a piercing look of his own, then shook his head. "No, why?"

Will's brow creased in anger and frustration. "Jennifer thought she heard someone in the camp before you came. She went out toward the bluff to investigate, and next thing she knew, some rocks broke free and tumbled down the hill. One of them hit her in the head before she could get to safety."

P.D.'s gaze shot to collide with Elam's, but Will continued, "A few of the first responders had a look at that bluff and the spot where Jennifer was injured. Said there were boot prints up on top. We've had some problems with a few of the competitors sabotaging other groups. We've had two groups disqualified already. I'd sure like to know if someone did this on purpose."

"I don't think there was anyone else here when we arrived," P.D. said. "The other group didn't show up until at least an hour later."

Tompkins's lips thinned and his brows creased in a frown. "Don't s'pose you'd like to tell me who that second group might be, would you? I'd like to know why they left without botherin' to help with the situation."

Elam and P.D. exchanged glances.

"Does it matter?" Elam asked.

"Not in the grand scheme of things, but I wouldn't mind knowing for my own personal satisfaction."

P.D. imperceptibly shook her head. Somehow, "snitching" on the father and son duo felt a little too unsportsmanlike for her.

"Let's just leave things the way they are," Elam murmured, seeming to tacitly agree with her view on the situation.

Tompkins nodded. "Fair enough. But I have taken it upon myself to confer with the other committee members and we're all in agreement. Due to the fact that Jennifer was incapacitated before she could mark down your arrival and check off your progress, I've been given the go-ahead to tell you both that, as per the written rules of the game, we're giving you a time equal to the fastest one recorded for this particular challenge to date. And in light of Jennifer's reports on the god-awful food she's already eaten, I am hereby declaring your meal the best—which comes with a bonus prize."

P.D. knew she should be celebrating, but the thought of walking to "Little Dodge" dampened her enthusiasm.

"I don't suppose it would be a new pickup," Elam said wryly. "P.D. could use one of those."

She met Elam's grin and somehow managed an answering smile.

"No, but you might find it just as nice."

Tompkins lifted a hand to point down the road and P.D. twisted to see what had caught his attention. When she focused on an ornate stagecoach barreling toward them, her mouth dropped.

"I sent a text to ol' Elijah Walker, the curator of Buggy Town Museum. Told him we'd be needing his services today rather than tomorrow." Tompkins stood and grabbed for a bottle of water. "He's been giving rides at the Fair Grounds all week and he's ready for a break. The coach is a little slower than your horse would have been, but I didn't think you'd mind."

"Thank heavens," Elam said as the conveyance rolled toward them, drawn by a double team of shiny black Clydesdales with silky tufted hooves.

"Hey there, Elam!" the driver called out.

"Elijah! Good to see you."

Elijah cackled in open delight and pulled on the reins, bringing the vehicle to a stop right in front of them. "I bet it is! I sure as hell wouldn't want to be hoofin' it back to Bliss. Climb aboard and you can ride in style."

When Elam looked toward the trees, Tompkins said, "Don't worry about your mount. I'll have a trailer brought out and return him to his owner. Meanwhile, enjoy your evening. I'm much obliged to you."

P.D. scurried to collect their saddlebags while Elam gathered their weapons and bedrolls. Then, they clambered into the swaying stagecoach.

As soon as they were settled, Elijah shouted, "Hiyah!" and they were underway.

Elam groaned, leaning back and stretching his legs out so that his feet rested on the opposite bench. "I have never been so glad of a ride in my entire life."

"Me, too." P.D. sighed.

There was a beat of silence where they both wearily enjoyed the rocking of the coach and the breeze passing through the windows. Then Elam said, "I've always wondered what it would be like to make love in a stagecoach, but darlin', I'm just too damned tired to find out."

P.D. smiled, realizing that it was their lovemaking all night long that was the primary source of his weariness. She leaned into him, and Elam immediately wrapped his arm around her, drawing her onto his chest.

"You're still the best cook around," he murmured.

"And you're an incredible rider."

His chest rumbled with laughter. "Pun intended?"

Her cheeks raged with sudden heat. But then, feeling daring, she drew back to meet his gaze.

"Pun intended."

He pulled her up so that his lips could brush against hers, once, twice. For a moment, his tongue plunged into her mouth for a quick, fierce caress. Then he drew back again, his eyes closing. "Sorry, hon'. Too damned tired."

But P.D. didn't mind a bit. She rested her head against his chest again, hearing the *thump, thump* of his heart, then the almost imperceptible snore as he fell asleep.

Then she let her own eyes close, her lips settling into a satisfied smile.

THEY were awakened by a discreet cough.

P.D. started, abruptly becoming aware of her surroundings. She shook Elam.

"We're here." Her voice was husky from sleep.

"Where exactly?" he mumbled.

"I don't know."

She shook him again and this time he opened his eyes. "What do you suppose we have to do now? Bear baiting? Rattlesnake taming?" He scrubbed at his face. "What I wouldn't give for a few hours of interrupted sleep."

"Don't you mean *un*interrupted?"

His gaze held hers, becoming suddenly hot. "Not exactly."

He stooped to make his way out of the door, then turned to help P.D. to descend as well. But it wasn't until she was on the ground and looked up that P.D. noticed the smattering of applause and saw that an impromptu welcoming committee was waiting for them.

"Welcome to the twenty-first century!" Helen exclaimed, rushing forward to enfold P.D. in a hug. "My lands, you two look like you've been through the wars."

Behind Helen, Syd reached out to shake Elam's hand, and Elam's brothers yanked him close for hugs and exuberant slaps on the back.

"Did you win, Elam?" Barry demanded, good-naturedly succumbing to a hair ruffling from his older brother.

"I don't know, Barry. There's still one more day of the contest."

P.D. regarded the fairgrounds teaming with people. Fairy lights had been strung over the bandstand a few yards away and a country-western group was crooning a ballad. Couples wound an intricate circle around the dance floor while children dodged in and out of the bleachers. The night air was rich with the smells of fried foods, cotton candy, and roasting meats, while various charities offered handmade goods or arcade games to raise money for community causes.

A contest official strode forward, glancing at his watch and noting a time on his clipboard. Then he extended the familiar yellow envelope.

The sight of it was enough to make a lump settle into the pit of P.D.'s stomach.

"Congratulations to you both," the man said. "And thanks again for your help in taking care of Jennifer Tompkins. Latest word from the hospital is that she's resting comfortably, but they're keeping her overnight. She's pretty dehydrated and the head wound is looking a little more serious than first supposed. It's a lucky thing that you found her when you did. You were one of the last groups to check off that particular challenge. If not for you, it could have been hours before she got the help she needed." He touched his hat and backed away. "We'll see you two tomorrow."

With that, he turned to disappear into the crowd again.

"What's next?" P.D. asked.

Elam ripped open one side of the envelope and pulled the contents free. But this time, rather than a typed piece of paper, there was a heavy vellum announcement and two hotel key cards.

"What the hell?"

P.D. leaned close to see that the announcement was an invitation to the Cattle Barons' Ball and Awards Banquet at the Serenity Resort. Rather than another full day of events, their last challenge would be the costume contest. In the meantime, the resort was giving the finishing contestants complimentary rooms to rest and recover from their efforts.

"Holy cow!" P.D. breathed. The Serenity Resort was a *chi-chi-pooh-pooh*, five-hundred-dollar-a-night resort, which had recently opened several miles up Liberty Canyon. P.D. had always wanted a peek inside one of their little guest houses.

But Elam was distracted by their challenge. "A costume contest," he said in disbelief. "That's it? We don't have to . . . I don't know . . . weave our own cloth on a loom or something?" He checked the back of the invitation just to be sure.

"Happily, no." Helen grinned. "Your costumes are ready to go. The banquet isn't until seven tomorrow night, so I'll bring both of your outfits to your rooms around four or five."

Elam grimaced. "It's going to take two hours to put on a pair of pants and a string tie?"

Helen patted his cheek. "Honey, if that's all you want to wear, be my guest."

P.D. was still trying to wrap her weary mind around the information bombarding her. "But . . . what are we supposed to do? Walk to the hotel? Ride?"

Bodey squeezed her arm. "P.D., you're done with all that," he said gently. "There's nothing left to do but show up at the dance."

"But the keys are for . . . sleeping? That's it?"

"Well, you and Elam could—"

Before Bodey could finish whatever he'd been about to say, Elam abruptly turned, and somehow, his elbow hit Bodey square in the gut.

"Sorry, Bode. Didn't know you were so close."

This time it was Jace's turn to snicker.

"Come tomorrow, you'll be glad you have a room on-site," Helen said. "Believe me, getting to the Awards Banquet *en regalia* isn't that easy in your average vehicle. Most of the attendees to the Awards Ceremony are already booked into the Resort. The place is sold out, despite being pricey." Her eyes twinkled. "Syd and I are staying in the Safari Bungalow." Leaning close to P.D., she murmured, "I'm planning on bagging a tiger tonight."

P.D. snorted, then smothered her laughter when Elam glanced her way.

Helen hugged her again, then rose up on tiptoe to kiss Elam on the cheek. "You two go have a good night's sleep. You've earned it. Syd and I will gather up your gear and your weapons and Jace can take them back to the Big House. You two enjoy the rest of the evening."

With great relief, P.D. removed her holsters and handed them to Syd. Having the heavy weight lifted away offered an immediate sense of relief.

Bodey reached to enfold P.D. in a hug as well. "Just so you know, the contractor and his men put up Sheetrock yesterday. Things are proceeding ahead of schedule. They're hoping to start painting the first of next week, but they want you to take a look at things first. He said he'll meet you at Vern's at eight Monday morning. Let him know if that's too early."

He slapped Elam on the back. "Everything at your place, on the other hand, is supposedly done. Jace and I gathered a fresh change of clothes, your dainties, and your shaving gear, and put them in a bag in the back of your truck. P.D., Helen couldn't get into your house. Said it was *locked*." His brows rose to his hairline. "But Jace, being the little safecracker that he is"—Jace rolled his eyes—"managed to get in through one of the windows. He unlocked the front door, since Helen refused to climb in through the window for some reason. Anyway, she put together some things for you as well. So there's no reason for you both not to enjoy the free rooms and the endless supply of hot water." He threw Elam his keys. "The Ram's parked over by the sale barns."

"Can we go get an elephant ear now?" Barry asked, his tone indicating that he'd been about as patient as he planned on being and he was ready for one of the supersized fried scones.

"Sure, let's go." Jace touched his hat with a finger. "'Night, you two. Good work."

They'd gone only a few steps when Barry turned, still walking backward. "Bodey, come on!"

"The master has spoken. Great job, you two. We'll see you tomorrow for the results." He jogged ahead to catch up to Barry, but turned at the last minute to shout, "Make sure you're *extra purty*, Elam! You'll need it with that ugly mug of yours!"

Elam opened his mouth to retort, caught P.D.'s gaze, and changed his mind.

"Go ahead," she urged.

"I probably shouldn't. There are innocent ears around."

One of her brows arched. "Like who's?"

"Barry's."

P.D. laughed.

"You wanna stick around?" Elam said, gesturing to the crowd.

"Actually?" She thought about it only a moment. "No."

He pocketed the invitation and the hotel keys and draped an arm around her shoulders. "Shall we?"

They began ambling away from the crowd toward the parking area.

"Do you want to drop by Vern's?"

Vern's.

Only days ago, her entire world had revolved around Vern's. She'd lived and sometimes slept there. She couldn't remember the last time she'd taken a day off, let alone a vacation. Six days a week, fourteen hours a day. Even after she'd trained her staff and her manager to work independently of her, she poured all her time and energy into her business. It was even her sole reason for joining the Games. She'd been intent on winning that prize money so that Vern's could recover and return in better shape than ever.

But somehow, in the last few days, things had changed. She'd begun to realize that, although nurturing her restaurant was satisfying, it couldn't be her only sense of fulfillment. She had lots of good, loyal employees. Maybe it was time she started letting them take over now and again.

"No, I'll wait until Monday." And since her answer was surprising to her as well as to Elam, she added, "It's dark and who knows if there's any lighting installed. Plus . . ." She grimaced. "We've been living so long in the nineteenth century, I'm finding it hard to return to the real world."

He squeezed her shoulder to show he understood. "As long as that doesn't apply to our transportation, because I'm not walking to Serenity."

Elam tapped the button on his key fob and the truck lights flashed, showing them where it had been backed into a space. After opening the driver's door, Elam helped P.D. slide inside. Then, after a glance in the bed, he climbed in behind her.

"Somehow, I think Helen did a better job of packing for you than my brothers did for me."

P.D. yawned. "It's not like you need a whole lot. Men are spoiled that way."

"We are, huh?" he asked as he started the truck.

P.D. didn't think she'd ever heard a more wonderful sound than the low throb of the engine. And when cool, air-conditioned air blew onto her cheeks, she sighed in delight. "I take it back. I really, really like the twenty-first century. All I need now is a couple of days in a hot tub and a week of sleep."

"Amen to that," Elam said with a kiss to the top of her head.

IT was dark by the time Elam pulled into the resort's parking lot. Muted lighting led toward the main offices, which were located in a Victorian house complete with elaborate gingerbread. Paths bordered with garden lights led the way to other small Victorian-inspired buildings which had been given names such as "The Bunkhouse" and "The Garden Cottage." Checking the keys that he and P.D. had been given, he noted that he was in "The Bachelor's Quarters" and she was in "The Briar House." The two buildings were within sight of each other, but not nearly as close as he would have liked them to be.

Matter of fact, he wouldn't have minded sharing a room with P.D.—and he might even have done some sweet-talking to make it happen. But after so long away from the creature comforts, he was sure his clothes could stand up by themselves. He needed a shower, a shave . . .

And more condoms.

Of course, he didn't want to admit that fact to P.D. Once he'd cleaned and changed, he could make a trip into town. Then, after he'd returned, he'd see how things progressed from there.

Damn. He just wasn't smooth about these things. Bodey would have announced to his woman *du jour* that he needed to stop to pick up a couple of cases of condoms on the way. Then he would have invited himself into her room and made sure that they took a shower together. After that, he wouldn't see a need for a change of clothes in a very long time.

But Elam . . . it wasn't that he was out of practice with the finer points of single life; it was that he'd never been good at them in the first place. His mother had once said that Elam had an old soul, and he supposed she was right. He'd always been a one-woman man. Hell, he'd fallen in love with Annabel in kindergarten, and she'd been the only woman he'd ever pursued.

Until now.

He felt a tug near his heart at the thought of Annabel, but only a tug. Barely a week ago, the thought of her could bring him to his knees. But he'd since discovered that what he'd had with Annabel didn't diminish what he was experiencing with P.D. It was just . . . different. And yet . . . the same.

Which scared the shit out of him. Was he rushing headlong into something with P.D. simply because it felt good and he was tired of being alone? Shouldn't he hit the dating scene like Bodey rather than focusing on one single woman? If he was going to have a relationship with P.D., shouldn't he know for sure that he was emotionally ready for such a step?

Following the signposts, Elam wound past the main building to the parking spaces in front of the Briar House. The building was a cute Tudor-style bungalow complete with a cottage garden and a cement statue of Brer Rabbit. P.D.'s rooms were located in the back.

Elam put the truck in park and idled there for several minutes. Damnit. It shouldn't be this much hard work, figuring out what to do next. They'd just spent several days alone together, and he hadn't had a second thought about any of his interactions with P.D. But there had been something idyllic about their time together, like being marooned and fighting for common survival. By returning to the realm of responsibilities . . .

Shit, shit, *shit*.

P.D. lay against him, her lashes thick against her cheeks as she slept. She was worn out, poor thing. She'd given each of the challenges all her energy. He wouldn't be surprised if she'd learned a thing or two about herself. And about him. Hell, he'd learned more than he ever would have thought possible about her. She was kind and funny—and as much as she might want to deny it, there was a streak of romanticism running through her core. Even more than that, he knew that her upbringing had left her searching for a place to sink her roots. And her parents' indifference hurt her more than she would ever admit. She wanted a home—something that she'd found in Bliss to some extent. But he also sensed that, more than a place, she was searching for what he'd had with Annabel. A connection—a sense of *belonging* to a person, of needing someone who needed her.

And he couldn't promise her that. Not after all he'd been through. He didn't know if he could ever commit to a woman again, not when he knew the utter devastation that loving someone could bring if Fate or fickleness snatched her away.

Hell, what a mess.

As if sensing his own inner turmoil, P.D. stirred, then blinked. Seeing the bungalow in front of them, she wiped her eyes and yawned. "Is this it?"

"Yeah."

Elam opened the door and slid out, leaving the engine running. Grabbing P.D.'s suitcase, he followed her to the door, slipping the key from his pocket.

P.D.'s gaze flicked to the truck, to the lights that spotlighted them in the darkness.

Elam slid the key into the lock, waited for the light to blink green, then held the door open for her until she'd stepped inside. Then, staying firmly outside, he said, "Sweet dreams, P.D. I'll see you a little later."

She blinked and regarded him with confusion, but finally nodded and murmured, "You, too, Elam."

He leaned forward, planting an awkward kiss on her cheek, then quickly backed away, knowing what he really wanted was to haul her into his arms, push his way inside, and lock the door behind them.

"See you soon, then."

Quickly turning his back to her, he strode to the truck, climbed inside, slammed the door, and eased out of the parking space. All without looking back.

But even as he drove toward his own hotel room, he wanted more than anything to go back the way he'd come and drown in P.D.'s embrace. Even an hour's separation seemed too much. So he'd take the fastest shower on record, make a trip into town . . .

And invite himself into the Briar House.

NINETEEN

———•◦•———

P.D. stared blankly at the door as it slid shut. The lock hit
home with a muffled *snick*.

What happened?

For days, she and Elam had been inseparable—and no,
she didn't mean they'd lived in each other's pockets. There
had been an emotional synchronicity between them. And the
chemistry, the passion . . .

They could have set the valley on fire with the heat of their
glances, let alone the desire that flared between them at the
slightest touch.

And yet . . . he'd left her at the doorstep with a grand-
fatherly kiss and a "sweet dreams" as if she were . . . what?

A child?

Her hands balled into fists and she stomped into the bathroom, stripping out of her Victorian attire with such force that
one of the straps on her chemise tore. Where once she'd thought
it would be a great adventure to dress up like a pioneer bride,
now she was intimately acquainted with the not-so-idealic realities of the role. Her clothes were ripped and filthy—and she
doubted that even a modern-day washer could ever get them

clean. Burrs and thistles had tangled into the lacy flounces of her petticoats, and her corset, even when unhooked, held the phantom shape of her body.

Twisting the knobs to the shower, she stripped out of the rest of her clothing and stepped under its pounding spray. As the heat seeped into her sore muscles, she grimaced as rivulets of grime ran down the drain. Beneath the rush of water, she became aware of every ache, every scratch, every throbbing muscle.

But all of that was nothing compared to the emotions that took her by storm as she scrubbed her hair and her face, then scoured her body with the provided body gel and scratchy hotel washcloth. Her inner turmoil began with a familiar haunting sense of abandonment and confusion. Then, she was pummeled with memories of the fire at Vern's, the competition, and her own burgeoning attachment to Elam. All too soon, the events of the past week seemed to grip her chest, squeezing the breath from her, making her body shudder in reaction, until the warmth of tears plunged down her cheeks, mingling with the cool water from her shower.

Impatiently, she dashed the moisture away, twisting off the taps.

Damn, damn, damn. She never cried. Never. Ever. But since she'd met Elam, her emotions were all out of whack. Everything she felt was stronger—laughter, sorrow, and yes, anger. Damn that man! He'd led her to the door of her hotel as if she were a stranger or . . . or a little sister. If she'd done something to offend him, he should have told her to her face, not, not . . .

Kissed her on the cheek like a little girl.

Filled with righteous indignation, she stormed into the main room and threw her suitcase on the bed. A small portion of her acknowledged that she was overreacting. Maybe Elam was too tired to deal with her right now—or he wanted some time alone. But the man could have explained the situation. Things between them were tenuous enough without her having to guess his thoughts. Maybe that had been his modus operandi with Annabel, but it sure as hell wasn't the way P.D. worked.

Unzipping her bag only far enough to reach inside, she grabbed the cotton nightgown Helen had folded on top and dragged it over her head. Then, snatching her key from where she'd left it on the bathroom counter, she dodged outside.

Thankfully, there was no one else walking along the paths— not that it would have stopped her if there had been. She was going to drag her answers from Elam, one way or another. Because right now, she was fighting her own inner demons, the ones who were whispering to her that less than a week of knowing Elam Taggart had been long enough for him to discover that she wasn't the type of woman who could keep his attention for long.

Her hair hung down her back, dampening her nightgown and making her conscious of the fact that it was her only covering. She quickened her step, thankful that there weren't any other hotel guests in sight. As soon as she spied Elam's truck, she cut across the grass. A sign bolted to the side of the quaint clapboard building read, BACHELOR'S QUARTERS. How fitting.

Another angry tear coursed down her cheek and she swiped it away.

Stop it! No man was worth tears. Anger, yes. But not tears.

Lifting her hand, P.D. prayed she was about to pound on the right door. But the muted sound of a shower and a muddy pair of boots sitting on the stoop confirmed her suspicions.

Bam, bam, bam!

Her knuckles stung from the strength of her knocks. Too late, she realized she should have planned what to say. Because when the door wrenched open and Elam stood on the other side, clutching a towel to his waist, water running in rivulets down the body she was just beginning to learn by touch . . . she immediately fell into an old familiar web of desire and need and . . . and . . .

She shouldn't have forced this confrontation. Not because of what Elam must be thinking as he saw her standing like a wet, bedraggled kitten on his doorstep. But because her own feelings for this man had become blindingly clear to P.D. In an instant, she realized how deeply she'd begun to care for him.

Dear God, she was falling in love with him, with Elam Taggart, Bliss's own Desperado.

A man who would never love anyone but his first wife.

She took a step backward. Then another.

But before she could turn and run back to her own room,

Elam yanked her inside and slammed the door. Then, somehow, her arms were around his neck and he was hauling her against his body. Her legs locked behind his back as his towel fell to the floor and he slammed her against the wall. And yes, he was blazingly aroused and fighting with the hem of her nightgown, his lips slanting against hers. There was no finesse, no tentative overtures. It was pure, unadulterated need, and his blatant hunger touched hers like a match to dynamite.

When he discovered that the nightgown was all she wore, he ripped his lips free and swore. "I didn't . . . I don't . . . I . . . shit!" He carried her to the bed, dropping her onto the bed, then whirled, searching until he found his bag. "Look. I need to go into town—"

"What?" P.D. was sure she'd heard him wrong. Damnit, how could one man send her from despair to ecstasy to utter bewilderment?

She stared at him, her mouth agape. But before she could speak, Elam returned to frame her face with his hands. "I'm out of condoms, damnit. I just came into my room long enough to take a shower. I was going to throw on my clothes and run into town. Then . . ." He grinned. "I was going to come back and wake you up."

Relief surged through her. "Why didn't you say that?"

He must have suddenly understood what had caused her to storm over to his bungalow like Carrie Nation in search of demon rum.

"Shit. You thought that I . . . that I didn't . . ." He kissed her again, more slowly this time, then groaned. "What you do to me . . . All I have to do is touch you and I come unglued. I was afraid that if I let you tempt me inside, I wouldn't be able to think straight, let alone stop." His lopsided smile was rueful and filled with heat. "You have that effect on me."

Those words, more than anything else, had the power to reassure her that Elam's ardor hadn't eased now that they'd returned to the reality of modern living.

"So talk to me next time, okay? I can't read your mind."

His lips hovered over hers. "It's a good thing you can't, or you'd know that I spend most of my time thinking about you"—he pressed a kiss to her cheek—"and me"—her jaw—"doing this"—her neck. Then he found her mouth with another searing kiss. One that he only allowed to develop for a minute before pulling back.

He stood, searching the room.

"I'll go with you. Into town," P.D. offered, then suddenly frowned. "Shoot. I left my clothes in my bungalow."

He reached to stroke her cheek with his thumb, obviously not trusting himself to do any more. "Just . . . stay here, okay? Relax. Rest. I'll be back. Twenty minutes, tops."

She nodded.

"Offer up a prayer that Bodey packed clean jeans and a decent shirt."

He moved to the foot of the bed, where he finally found his bag. Throwing it on the mattress, he unzipped the top. Then, to P.D.'s amazement, he started to laugh.

Wondering what on earth had caused this abrupt about-face, she leaned over to look in the case. She'd expected to see Elam's clothes stuffed in a haphazard jumble the way Bodey was prone to packing for his competitions. But as she glanced inside, she had no idea if Bodey had packed any clothes at all because the duffel was stuffed to the brim with condom packages.

Her own laughter joined Elam's—and she vowed to bake a batch of Bodey's favorite rum raisin cookies and deliver them to his doorstep. But not tonight. Tonight, she had other plans.

"Remind me to thank him," P.D. said, grabbing one of the packets from the top. Then she pushed the bag onto the floor, where it tipped over, leaving a cascade of rainbow-colored squares spilling out over the carpet.

"Don't you dare," Elam growled, allowing her to pull him onto the bed. "It will only encourage him."

"Oh, I dare," she whispered as his body pressed her into the marshmallow softness of the featherbed. "I definitely dare."

THEY made love off and on throughout the night, interspersing their bouts of passion with a hearty meal from room service and long soaks in the jetted tub. Tired as she was, P.D. battled her weariness, hoarding each kiss, each caress until, finally, neither of them could keep their eyes open and, in a tangle of limbs, they fell asleep.

Late-morning sun was slanting through the slats of the blinds when P.D. fought her way to consciousness again, her body rousing her with a curious mixture of pain and pleasure. She would have willingly drifted off again if it weren't for the featherlight kiss pressed to her shoulder.

"Morning, sleepyhead."

She twisted to peer out of lashes that were heavy as lead. But she was rewarded for her efforts. Elam. Dear sweet heaven above. Did anyone have a right to look that good in the morning? His hair was tousled and stubble etched the planes of his jaw. And his eyes . . .

They were filled with an inner light that grew with each passing day.

Groaning, P.D. realized that she must look a wreck. She hadn't braided her hair the night before so it fell in a riot of curls. She was scratched and scraped, blistered and bruised— and heaven help the person who told her she was going to have to hike anywhere anytime soon.

Squeezing her eyes shut, she buried her face in the pillow, but not before she realized that Elam was fully dressed in jeans and a button-down shirt.

"Why are you up so early?" she mumbled.

"It's past noon."

She groaned again.

"Here. This might help." The bed dipped.

Even through the fluff of the pillow, P.D. smelled coffee. Heavenly, heavenly coffee.

Chancing a quick look, she saw that Elam had stretched out beside her, propping his back against the headboard with pillows. In his hand, he held a huge foam cup.

The sight alone was enough to make her sit up. She eagerly reached for the beverage, blowing at it before taking her first sip. A sound of pure bliss seeped from her throat.

"Where have you been?" she croaked.

"I borrowed your key and retrieved some clothes for you." He gestured to a pile on a nearby chair. "I figured you wouldn't want to make the trip back to your room in nothing but your nightgown."

No kidding. Especially since they'd ripped it in their eagerness to make love sometime in the middle of the night.

"Thanks." With each sip, she was becoming a little more coherent.

"I also got us some breakfast." He reached for a sack on the bedside table and P.D. immediately recognized the colorful logo.

"You've been to the Cake Dump," she said reverently, referring to Evertson's Sweet Shop. Situated across the street from the local high school, the bakery had been affectionately nicknamed by the kids, and unfortunately for the Evertsons, the moniker had stuck.

"I didn't know what you'd like, so I got a little bit of everything."

He opened the bag for her perusal. Inside were two glazed twists, a pair of bagels, a cellophane sack of donut holes, and two huge hot rolls.

P.D. immediately grabbed one of the hot rolls. Twice the size of a normal dinner roll, the bread was still warm and the generous pat of butter that had been thrust through the upper crust into the softness beneath had already melted and been absorbed.

"I've got gravy, too, if you want it." Elam gestured to another Styrofoam container on the nightstand.

"Brown or white?"

"Brown."

Her eyes nearly rolled back into her head in delight and she moaned her approval. Heaven. This was heaven. Elam, hot rolls, coffee, and gravy. Life couldn't get much better than this.

Again, Elam laughed. "I see you're easy to please first thing in the morning." He took her coffee, setting it on the table, then grabbed the gravy and another hot roll for himself. Soon, the two of them were sitting cross legged, dipping hunks of bread into the rich brown gravy—a treat that P.D. had never even heard of before moving to Bliss.

"We've got several hours until Helen shows up. Do you want to go to Vern's?"

P.D. thought about it for a moment, then shook her head. "There's nothing I can do until I meet with the contractor, so there's not much point."

Her answer seemed to surprise Elam as much as it did her, so she tried to explain. "For a long time now, Vern's has consumed me. Every minute of every day was spent worrying about how to make it better. But by stepping away for a few days, I'm beginning to see that I was starting to burn out. I was going through the motions, but I wasn't really . . . emotionally and mentally present." She frowned, remembering the incident with the line cook who'd stolen steaks from her freezer. Normally, the missing meat would have hit her radar long before it had. "Does that make any sense?"

Elam's features grew still and thoughtful. "Yeah. Yeah, it makes perfect sense."

"So I've decided that I've got to reexamine all of my employees' work history and train a couple of them to take over part of the day. That way, I can have a personal life as well."

Her words hung in the air, providing the perfect opportunity for Elam to reassure her that he'd love to be a part of that "personal life." But he didn't take the bait.

"You don't trust Bart with that?"

She ignored the twinge of hurt at Elam's apparent obliviousness to her concerns, focusing on his question instead. Normally, Bart would be the natural choice to take over Vern's in her absence. But there'd been such a weird vibe between them since Bart had seen Elam kissing her in the parking lot. She didn't know if she wanted to deal with the man's bruised ego.

P.D. tossed the rest of her roll into the sack, no longer hungry, wishing she'd steered the conversation in another direction. All this talk about Vern's was making her realize that her time alone with Elam was becoming more limited. All too soon, the real world would intrude, if it hadn't already.

Elam set the gravy aside. "Hey, I didn't mean to bring back all your worries. You're right. We've both been too caught up in our heads lately. I let the construction of my new house become my main focus. Hopefully, now that it's pretty much done, I can concentrate on the ranch, my brothers." He caressed her cheek. "As well as other things . . ." He leaned forward to kiss her. "Other people."

He grabbed the back of his shirt, pulling it over his head and revealing that killer chest and rock-hard abs that P.D. couldn't seem to stop exploring.

"So let's enjoy all this as long as it lasts."

Then, he was drawing her into his arms and P.D. no longer had the power to think of anything but ridding him of his remaining clothing. Just as it had so many times already, passion erupted between them like wildfire, until she couldn't touch Elam enough, couldn't hold him tightly enough.

Only when he plunged inside her was she given some relief from her hunger for this man. She gripped him tightly through her release, her fingernails digging into his shoulders. And when he threw his head back with his own shuddering climax, she watched him, desperately absorbing each minute emotion that crossed his features until he finally collapsed on top of her. Then, cradling him against her breast, she slipped her fingers into his hair, toying with the silken strands, absorbing the knocking wildness of his heart with her own flesh.

SO let's enjoy all this as long as it lasts.

Much later, after Elam had fallen asleep beside her, the words reverberated in her head.

As long as it lasts.

P.D. supposed that she'd finally been given the answer that she'd sought. Where she had briefly allowed herself to think of happily-ever-afters, Elam had already begun to prepare himself for the moment that their relationship would end.

She closed her eyes, rolling away from the warmth of his body and burying her face in her arm to keep Elam from seeing even an echo of the devastation that rocked through her body. Yes, she'd warned herself of such an eventuality. From the very beginning, she'd told herself that she would end up being Elam's transition relationship. The woman who convinced him that his heart could make room for someone new. And she'd known that a return to the "real world" and the responsibilities it held could prove the tipping point. She'd even convinced herself that she could handle whatever Elam was willing to give.

But what she hadn't realized was just how much it would hurt when he alluded to a time when he would move on.

Again, she was rocked with a flood of doubt and misapprehension. What was she doing here? In Elam's bed and Elam's life? Why couldn't she be content with the fact that she'd found a home here in Bliss?

An overwhelming ache bloomed in her chest, threatening to cut off her breathing altogether. She focused on getting air into her system, on fighting back the misery that threatened to consume her. Biting her lip, she forced the emotions away until, finally, enough of the pain had subsided for her to slide from the bed.

The movement roused Elam, just as she'd feared it would.

"You're not leaving yet, are you?" he asked sleepily.

"Yeah." She swallowed, forcing away the tightness of her throat when her voice emerged husky and thick. Hopefully, Elam would attribute it to her exhaustion. "Helen will be here soon and I need to shower and start working on my hair."

"Mmm."

He didn't open his eyes and P.D. couldn't help herself. For several long minutes, she drank in the sight of him sprawled on his stomach, a sheet barely covering his hips. Even now, she wanted to touch him, to let her fingers roam the planes and valleys of his body until she knew them by heart. She wanted to thrust her fingers into the silky softness of his hair and let the stubble on his chin rasp her palms.

He looked so different from the man she'd met only a week ago. He'd lost the haunted look to his eyes and the rigid posture that had conveyed he was waiting for the next blow life would throw at him. He was . . . at peace with himself.

P.D. supposed that if there was any comfort to be had from their relationship, it was that she'd been the one to help him get to that place.

* * *

WHEN Helen arrived at her room, carrying her magic carpet bag and towing her sewing machine and supplies in a special set of wheeled cases, P.D. pasted a happy smile on her face and did her best to field her gentle prying. It was easy to see that, in Helen's mind, her matchmaking efforts were a success and wedding bells were forecast for the near future.

P.D. didn't have the heart to tell her the truth. P.D. wasn't even sure what she intended to do herself. So she pretended to take an interest in the preparations for the Cattle Barons' Ball and the awards announcements that would follow.

"I think you're ready. Have a look."

P.D. blinked, wrenched from her thoughts.

Through most of the dressing process, Helen had insisted that P.D. keep her back to the mirror so that P.D. would be surprised by the overall effect. Layer by layer, she'd been adorned in Victorian finery—a silk chemise and pair of pantalets, ivory thigh-high hose and lacy garters, and cream-colored ivory high-button shoes. This was followed by an embroidered corset cinched so tight that P.D. discovered immediately why women of wealth in the nineteenth century needed a ladies' maid to help them dress—and why her shoes had been put on before the rest of her costume. She couldn't have bent over to adjust her hose, let alone put on her shoes.

Over her hoop, Helen had dropped a flounced petticoat dripping with lace, then a full skirt made of ivory organdy embroidered with swirling soutache and ruffles made of silk habatoi. Last, she'd helped P.D. slip her arms into a matching off-the-shoulder boned bodice.

Turning, P.D. crossed the room to the full-length mirror that had been attached to the back of the closet doors, and she gasped.

"Helen, it's beautiful."

"You're beautiful, honey. The dress is merely the frame." She carefully pinned P.D.'s contestant number to the spray of silk millinery flowers at her waist.

P.D. stared wistfully at her expression, realizing that she looked every inch the pioneer bride. Her hair had been arranged into an upsweep with intricate braids and ringlets that dropped over one shoulder. A clip made of lace, pearls, and a feather had been pinned over one ear. Against the ivory of her gown, her skin appeared creamy and smooth—aided by the powder Helen had used to disguise the remains of her sunburn.

"The sisters are looking especially fine," Helen remarked, referring to the way the corset had pushed her breasts up against the low, lace-bedecked berthe of her bodice. And her waist, sheesh! It looked tiny and delicate compared to the fullness of her skirts.

"I thought my dress and corset were supposed to be black and red?"

Helen's eyes twinkled. "They were smoke damaged in the fire, and much as I tried, I couldn't get them clean. So I changed my mind about the whole ensemble at the last minute and used the other pieces as your pattern so that we wouldn't need to worry about alterations."

P.D. fingered one of the silky ruffles. "You did all of this in four days?"

"And I had a grand time doing it. Nothing better than a marathon of sci-fi movies and costume creation. Some people do heroin, I do fabric."

P.D. turned and enfolded her friend in a hug. "Thank you so much."

Helen's embrace was tight and scented with lavender. "My pleasure, sweetie."

As if on cue, there was a knock at the door.

"There's Elam," Helen said. She hurried to the bed to retrieve a lacy shawl, a pair of elbow-length gloves, and an ivory fan made of ostrich feathers. "The judges for the costume contest will be hidden in the crowd watching you throughout the evening, so keep your back straight and your movements slow and genteel."

"As if I had a choice in this corset," P.D. muttered.

As soon as P.D. had tugged the gloves up to her elbows, Helen opened the door.

Dear heaven above, how was she going to survive the evening?

Elam stood resplendent in tailored trousers and a frock coat with a black jacquard vest embroidered in gold and ivory. A crisp white shirt with an intricately tied cravat emphasized his tan and the blunt angles of his jaw, and a gambler's hat finished the outfit.

But what held and kept P.D.'s attention was the way Elam was looking at her. His eyes suddenly blazed with passion . . . and more, so much more. If she didn't know better, she might have thought that he was beginning to fall in love with her a little bit, too.

With some effort, he wrenched his gaze from P.D. and sent a flicking glance toward Helen.

"Do I have to wear the hat?"

"Yes!" P.D. and Helen said in unison.

He sighed, but when he looked back at P.D. again, it was clear he didn't mind.

"Shall we?" he asked, holding out his arm.

P.D. moved toward him in a rustle of organdy and lace.

"You two have fun tonight, you hear? But don't do anything to mess up your outfits. I expect both of you to win," Helen called out as they slipped from the room.

P.D. felt as if she and Elam had entered another dimension as they strolled down the walkway through the period-inspired hotel bungalows. And she must not have been the only person to think so, because when they maneuvered around a young woman and a little girl, P.D. heard the child whisper excitedly, "Look, Mom, there's another princess!"

In the distance, they could see the carriage house, where the banquet would take place. Huge doors had been flung open to the courtyard, where dancing had already begun. Tea lights flickered from mason jars that were hung from the tree branches, and fairy lights had been strung to the arbors, making the whole space look as if it were illuminated by lightning bugs. P.D. waved when she saw that Manny's band had been hired for the gig.

"It's so beautiful," P.D. breathed.

Elam stopped her, framing her face in hands sheathed in white cotton gloves.

"You're beautiful," he insisted. He bent to kiss her, softly, sweetly—and she would have automatically melted into his embrace if it weren't for the fullness of her skirts. "You make my heart beat faster every time I see you."

The sentiment was so achingly romantic that P.D. could scarcely breathe. But Elam didn't seem to require a response because he slipped her hand around his arm and led her forward.

"Let's dance."

Never, in her wildest imaginings, had P.D. thought that Bliss's Desperado would dance—with anyone, anywhere. But she found it even harder to believe that he was dancing with her. The moment he drew her into his arms, she melted against him like a stick of butter in the sun, regardless of the fullness of her skirts. Soon, with a bittersweet country-western tune floating into the air from the band in the corner, she found her head on Elam's shoulder and his arm around her waist, his other hand laced intimately with her own.

For a while, they rocked together, hardly moving. And for a few minutes, P.D. could believe that this was real, that she'd finally found a man who wanted more from her than compassion or friendship. Closing her eyes, she could convince herself that this was the place where she belonged, her true home. In Elam's arms.

Maybe there was a chance for them after all.

The music segued into a faster song, forcing P.D. to draw back.

"Should we go get something to eat?" Elam asked.

She nodded, even though food was the last thing on her mind.

Inside the carriage house, a buffet line had been set up along each of the walls, with dozens of smaller round tables in the middle for eating. P.D. preceded Elam through the line, her appetite returning when she saw prime rib, rolled chicken with asparagus, shrimp, and glazed ham. There were grilled vegetables, new potatoes in cream, and three kinds of salads. Once they moved to a table, there were homemade rolls and corn muffins heaped in a basket, along with gravy boats filled with exotic sauces.

It wasn't until they reached the table and P.D. set her plate down that she realized she had a problem on her hands.

"What's the matter?" Elam asked, holding out her chair.

P.D. looked around for anyone who looked like a judge

before saying, "How am I supposed to sit down in a chair with this contraption on?" She gestured to her hoop skirt.

"That one lady in the Games got hers into a camp chair."

P.D. rolled her eyes. "And it took her twenty minutes to wrestle with her skirts enough to do it. And I don't have just a chair to contend with, I've got to get my skirts under that table."

Elam leaned close. "I've got an idea." He pulled the chair out a little farther. "Go ahead. Sit down."

With Elam firmly holding her chair so that the yardage wouldn't push it over, she managed to lift her skirts ever so slightly so that the hoop would collapse enough for her to sit. Then, she was left with the conundrum of how to scoot forward so that she wasn't a foot away from the table. But just when she opened her mouth to tell Elam to push on her chair, he moved away and pulled his own chair even with hers. After taking his seat, he pulled the table into place over her lap.

"Nicely done," Helen said cheerfully. "Mind if we join you?"

She and Syd took their places and the men adjusted the table again so that Helen's lap was covered as well.

"And who says chivalry is dead," Helen commented gleefully.

Within minutes, Bodey and his date joined them, then Jace and Barry, who was wearing a scowl along with his Sunday jacket, crisp snap-front shirt, and string tie.

"What's wrong, Barry?" Elam asked when his youngest brother took his seat.

"Jace wouldn't let me wear my coonskin hat."

Bodey's lips twitched, but he covered his amusement with a napkin.

"Where is it?" Elam asked.

Barry sat slouched in his chair, ignoring his food.

"He's got it stuffed in the back of his waistband where he thinks I can't see it," Jace said. "I keep telling him that Davy Crockett would not have worn his hat to dinner."

"I don't see why not," Barry mumbled. "It'd keep his hair out of his eyes."

"Davy wanted to make sure the tail of his hat didn't drag in the gravy. That's why he'd put it on as soon as dinner was done," P.D. offered.

At that thought, Barry perked up. "So I can put it on after I eat?"

Elam looked at Jace, who rolled his eyes. "Sure. Then you can ask P.D. to dance. Davy always wore his hat when he danced."

Barry looked hopefully at P.D. and she saw a trace of Elam in his features as well as little-boy hopefulness. Not for the first time, she wondered what he would have been like if the accident hadn't trapped him into perpetual youth.

She smiled tenderly. "I'd love to dance with a gentleman who has the finest hat in the county."

As Barry began to eat as quickly as he could, P.D. felt an ache in the center of her chest. This is what it would be like to be part of a real family, one with siblings who shared mutual goals and genuine affection for one another. Yes, sacrifices were made, but they were always made for the right reasons.

"Hey, Barry, I got you something," Elam said.

"Is it a present?" Barry breathed, as if saying the words might jinx them.

"Yep."

Barry scowled at Jace. "You said he wouldn't be able to bring me a present 'cause there wouldn't be any stores."

Jace shrugged. "I stand corrected."

Barry's scowl morphed into a confused frown. "You're not standing up."

"Then I sit corrected," Jace offered smoothly.

Elam reached into one of the vest pockets and withdrew a smooth round rock.

Barry blinked, clearly disappointed. "A rock? We got rocks on the ranch, Elam."

"Not like that one." Elam pointed to his offering, which was oddly round and smooth. "That's a geode."

"A jode?"

"A geode. Take that home and very carefully whack it with a hammer—Jace or Bodey can help you. There should be a surprise inside."

"Like an egg?"

"Kind of. But this rock will have sparkly crystals inside."

"You're sure?" Barry asked doubtfully.

"Pretty sure. But you won't know until you crack it open."

Barry rapped it against the table experimentally, his nose wrinkling in thought when it didn't split as easily as an egg. But he carefully put it in his pocket, then returned to his food.

After a few minutes, Elam said, "Barry, I was wondering if you'd like to come spend a few days with me up at the cabin." Elam looked up from the roll he was spreading with butter and sweet strawberry jam. "I'm going to need some help this week getting all of my stuff unpacked and moving in the furniture. How about a sleepover?"

Barry's eyes grew huge and a forkful of chicken hung suspended in front of his mouth. "Really? You want me to do that?"

"Sure. We haven't been seeing enough of each other lately."

"C-can I come tonight?" Barry asked.

"I don't know how late this thing will run, so why don't I pick you up bright and early tomorrow? We'll go to the Corner for breakfast then maybe head over to Logan to look at some new beds. If you're going to spend time at my house, we might as well set up a place for you in the cabin. You can have your own room."

Barry's smile could have lit the ballroom. "That'd be good, Elam, really, *really* good!"

"It's a deal, then."

Barry quickly shoved the last of his food into his mouth and bounded to his feet. Dragging the furry raccoon hat from beneath his dress shirt, he tugged it over his head then rounded the table, stopping by P.D.'s seat and bowing deeply. "May I have this dance?"

Obligingly, the others moved the table so that P.D. could stand, and she followed Barry outside onto the dance floor.

She couldn't account for the way that Elam's actions had touched her. She clearly remembered when Barry had asked Elam to bring home a present. P.D. hadn't given it another thought, but Elam must have been looking for something special from the very beginning. Then, in telling Barry that they needed to go hunting for a bed . . . Elam had made it clear he wanted his little brother to feel welcome in his home.

Drat it all, she didn't think she could grow to care for this man any more than she already did, but he'd surprised her yet again.

"P.D., did you hear? I'm going to get a new bed in Elam's house."

She squeezed his hand. "I heard, Barry. Isn't that wonderful?"

"I've been missin' Elam a lot lately. But the other day, he took me to the Corner, an' now he wants me to come to his new house."

"And you'll have your own room there."

"Are you going to help us move?"

P.D. hesitated. There was nothing she would rather do, but she also found herself reading between the lines of Barry's remarks. It had been a long time since he and Elam had connected. Maybe he would like some "alone" time with Elam more.

"I'll think it over, Barry. It sounds like fun."

"We could get you a bed, too. Then you could come on a sleepover with us."

And there was nothing she would rather do.

What would it be like to be a part of a family like this? To know that, simply through accident of birth, you had a group of people who gave you unconditional love and support. True, the Taggarts had experienced a lot of tragedy, but they'd pulled through it to become stronger than ever.

"P.D.?" Barry asked, not quite meeting her eyes. "Please say you'll come to the sleepover."

"Wouldn't you rather spend time alone with Elam?"

"Yeah, sure. But . . ."

"But what, Barry?"

"But he's a boy and . . ."

"And what, Barry?" she prompted, confused by the sudden twist in thought.

Barry bit his lip, but finally said, "When I was little, I had a sister, too."

P.D.'s heart lurched. Sometimes she forgot that in the same accident where Barry had been injured, his parents and twin sister, Emily, had been killed.

"I miss having a sister." Barry blinked up at her. "Could you be my sister? Just for pretend?"

P.D. suddenly realized that there were ramifications to her relationship with Elam that she had never considered before. Although she'd been welcome at the Taggart home and had interacted with Barry on numerous occasions, she had always been there as a "friend." How confusing would it be if P.D. suddenly appeared at Elam's house for "sleepovers" then disappeared again, only to return to "friend" status.

She squeezed Barry's hand. "Tell you what, Barry. I'm going to have to think about whether or not we should pretend that I'm your sister. It might be a little confusing for Bodey and Jace. And, well, then they'd want to be my brothers, too, probably."

Barry's eyes widened. Clearly, he didn't want to lose his exclusive claim to P.D.

"While I'm thinking, though, I think you could call me your buddy. A buddy is more than a friend. A buddy is the person you would choose to have as your brother or sister if you could."

Barry suddenly grinned. "Oh-kay!"

They danced for a few more minutes—or rocked rather. P.D. moved from side to side in her voluminous skirts while Barry tried out some of the moves he'd seen on television. But within a few minutes, the frown reappeared between Barry's brows.

"What is it, Barry?"

"Do you have a hammer in your purse?"

She did her best to keep the amusement from her expression. "Sorry. I don't think Helen thought to pack one in my bag."

"Would Elam have one?"

Heavens, all they needed was for Barry to search through Elam's suitcase.

"No. I'm pretty sure he didn't think to bring his tools—and the truck he brought doesn't have a tool box in the back."

Barry worried his lip with his teeth. "I want to see what's inside my rock. Elam says there's a 'prise inside."

P.D. thought for a minute then said, "Maybe you could find a bigger rock somewhere and try hitting it with that."

Too late, she realized that she probably should have waited until the song was over, because Barry dropped her hands. "I'll ask!" Then he bolted toward the carriage house.

"Barry!"

He barely paused.

"Tell them I'll be back in a little while."

"'Kay!" He waved to show he'd heard.

Suddenly, he veered off the path toward one of the ornate mounds of flowers situated around the perimeter. She saw Barry bend, then straighten again, struggling to carry a hefty boulder.

"That should do the trick, Barry," P.D. murmured to herself as he staggered into the carriage house.

As she watched him disappear inside, his tall, gangly body at odds with his mind's childlike innocence, she felt a frisson of gooseflesh. She'd grown to love Barry over the past few months. Despite what she'd told him, she already regarded him as the closest thing to a little brother that she'd ever had. And she wouldn't do anything to hurt him. Which meant that she needed to think things through very carefully. She wanted to pursue her relationship with Elam, but the two of them were going to have to work out the best way to do that.

P.D. slowly moved to the side of the dance floor, feeling a wave of exhaustion wash over her. For days now, she'd demanded more of herself physically than she'd done in years. Even the mental strain of deciphering clues and mapping out strategies had been taxing. She'd eaten whatever had been available and slept the bare minimum to keep going. Now that the contest was all but over, her strength was draining away like air out of a leaky balloon.

Suddenly, she became aware of every battered inch of her body. Her shoes rubbed in all the wrong places, the bruise on her back throbbed, and what little food she'd eaten sat in her stomach like a lump. Even worse, her corset felt far too constrictive, making it impossible to drag a full breath into her lungs.

Geez. Was that why the heroines in her beloved historicals were always fainting? Because they had someone like Helen gleefully yanking on their corset strings so they could fit into their clothes?

P.D. pressed a hand to her aching ribs and searched the shadows. Despite the fact that she'd hardly danced, her heart was beating quickly and she couldn't seem to catch her breath.

Her gaze automatically surveyed the crowd. She wasn't sure when the costume judges were supposed to observe them, but surely she could go somewhere on the outskirts and gulp some air into her lungs.

ELAM and his brothers jumped when Barry dropped a jagged rock onto the table.

"Can we open my present now? P.D. said we could hit it with this."

Elam's gaze bounced from the rock, to his little brother, to the room beyond.

"Where's P.D.?"

"Outside. She said she'd be here in a minute."

Unaccountably, Elam felt a prickling of unease. The competition might be in its last stages—and P.D. might be surrounded by people—but after everything that had happened . . .

"I'll just go get her," he said, pushing to his feet.

Bodey stopped him with a hand on his arm. "You're the 'jode' expert. You help Barry; I'll get P.D."

Elam wanted to argue, but since Barry was eagerly watching him, he motioned for his little brother to follow him. "We'd better do this outside or the hotel people might have a coronary," he said. "You take the geode, I'll bring the bigger rock." He pointed to a side door where there weren't as many people. "We'll go out there."

Barry scooped up his rock and hop-skipped toward the door, the tail of his coonskin cap bouncing behind him.

Elam grunted as he hefted the boulder Barry had chosen. Clearly, it would do the job as well as a hammer.

Jace joined him, his ambling strides eating up the distance.

"You look good, Elam," he said as they wound through the tables.

Elam's brows rose. "What? You thought I couldn't handle the competition?"

"No. I knew you'd be in your element."

When he didn't continue, Elam prompted, "But . . ."

"But I didn't know if you were ready for . . . spending that much time alone with a woman who wasn't Annabel."

Trust Jace to lay it all on the line. Anyone else would tap dance around their concerns. But Jace, who was a man of few words, tended to make every conversation count.

"She's a keeper," Jace said after a beat of silence. "So don't screw this up."

Bam! Had he just been schooled by Jace of all people?

But before he could respond, Barry stopped at the sidewalk on the other side of the door. He was bouncing up and down in excitement. "Do it, Elam. Crack it open!"

"We need to wait for P.D."

As if summoned, Bodey appeared. "I couldn't find her. Helen went to see if she's in the ladies' room."

Knowing that Barry was about to explode, Elam motioned for him to put his rock on the ground. "Stand back."

Crouching beside the geode, Elam experimentally tapped it with the heavy rock without much effect.

"It didn't work, Elam."

"That was just a practice shot, Barry."

"Give it all you got, Elam!"

This time, Elam allowed the rock to fall on it full force and they were rewarded with a sharp *crack*. When he lifted the boulder out of the way, Barry's geode lay on the ground in two halves. Inside the gray, nondescript outer stone was a glittering inner landscape of jagged crystals in shades of violet, lavender, and white.

"Wow!" Barry said reverently, kneeling to pick up the two halves. "How did you know this was in here, Elam?"

"I was about your age when Dad showed me what to look for. He told me that people were about the same as this rock. They might look hard or plain on the outside, but inside, there's always something wonderful."

Barry held the halves, one in each hand, then extended one of them toward Elam. "You need this half to help you 'member. 'Cause for a while, you've been kind of scary on the outside.

But now you're my brother again." He jumped to his feet and said, "I'm going to go show Syd."

Then, he was gone, leaving Elam shaken to the core.

It seemed that the last few days he was getting a healthy dose of tough love—first with P.D., who'd let him know he needed to communicate more, then Jace, and now Barry.

When he looked up, he found Bodey with his mouth open, clearly ready to add his two cents.

"Shut up," Elam said with a warning finger. "I get it already. I've been a bastard lately and I'm working my way out of it, okay? Yes, this whole arrangement with P.D. has been the catalyst, so thank you, Bodey, for breaking your ankle and setting us up. But from here on out, I'm going to go about things my own way. And no, I don't plan on doing anything to screw things up," he added, directing that comment to Jace. "Thankfully, I'm not so stupid that I don't know how great she is and how much she's grown to mean to me. So back off a little bit and let us get to know each other, okay?"

Bodey grinned openly while Jace's lips twitched in silent satisfaction.

"Why don't you two clean up this mess while I go find P.D. so we can dance again?" Elam deftly suggested, slapping the geode into Bodey's hand. "Keep this for me, so I can hold my girl."

P.D. followed the path that wound away from the carriage house. There, she found a spot where a small bridge spanned a fish pond full of exotically colored koi. Resting her hands on the railing, she closed her eyes and counted *one, two, three* . . . hoping that her quick, shallow breaths would help to ease the aches and pains that threatened to take root and spoil her evening. But with the tightness of the boning, her heart continued to flutter against the stricture of her corset as if it were a bird throwing itself against a pane of glass.

"P.D.!"

For a flashing instant, she thought it was Elam who had come to find her. But when she turned, she found Eddie Bascom, one of her former employees.

P.D. stared at him uncomprehendingly. It seemed as if a lifetime had passed since she'd become aware of a serious shortage of beef in the freezer. Had it only been a week or two since her manager, Bart Crowley, had proved it was Eddie who'd been stealing the meat, and P.D. had fired the young man?

"P.D., I didn't do it, I swear."

She lifted a hand to rub at the headache forming between her eyes.

"Eddie, we've been through all—"

"Why won't you listen to me?" he shouted, his hands balled into fists. "Damnit, I need that job!"

"Is that why you took a tire iron to my Dumpster?"

He swore and visibly tried to calm himself. "That was a mistake. I—I was angry and . . ."

Eddie's hands were still tight with rage and P.D. edged to the side so that she wouldn't be pinned with her back to the railing.

"Look, I just found out my girlfriend was pregnant. I need that job so we can move in together and start saving for the baby and—"

"And you decided stealing was the best answer?"

"No! You're twisting things around."

"I'm not twisting anything, Eddie, and I'm not going to talk to you about this. Your job has already been given to another person."

"Damnit!" he shouted so loudly that P.D. jumped. "It's not fair! You've got to hear my side of things!"

"No." She began to back off the bridge. "I've already made my decision, and unless you want me to press charges, you'll leave me alone from now on. And I'd better not see you anywhere near Vern's either."

Before Eddie could respond, she picked up her skirts and ran back toward the carriage house. Her heart was pounding now, and she could feel herself shaking from the confrontation. More than anything, she wanted to escape the Games—this party, these clothes—and return home to jeans and T-shirts, cupboards stocked with real food, and a familiar bed. She wanted her life to become normal again. Even if she wasn't quite sure what "normal" had ever been.

She was just reaching the warm glow of the dance floor when she saw Elam stepping out of the carriage house. He was scouring the couples circling the polished boards when the band segued from a rousing swing number to a slower ballad. And to her horror, P.D. recognized the opening words.

Annabel, oh, Annabel. What I'd give for one more day . . .

No, please, no. After everything that had happened between her and Elam, she didn't want him to be reminded of Annabel. Not now. Not when he'd pushed his grief to the side.

She tried to move toward him, but there seemed to be hundreds of people in the way. With the onset of a slower song, more dancers were joining the floor and the area had grown crowded. Turning the opposite way, P.D. tried to skirt the dance floor altogether. That way, she could circle back around to the carriage house.

She took a side path around a decorative clump of bushes. But just as she was out of sight of the dance floor, from the corner of her eye, she saw a figure trying to head her off. P.D. had only a moment to realize that he was striding purposefully toward her, his eyes narrowed, his arm raising. There was the glint of moonlight on the barrel of a revolver. She heard the explosion, saw the flash of muzzle fire.

Then her legs buckled and she fell hard, blackness swamping her.

TWENTY

———•—•———

ELAM saw the flash of P.D.'s skirts as she tried to get through the crowd—saw her dodge around a mound of pine trees and clumps of flowering bushes—and he knew immediately what she'd assumed. Only a week ago, the same song had brought him to his knees, drowning him in a tidal wave of memories. But this time, he'd barely noticed what the band had been playing. He'd been too busy looking for P.D.

If he'd learned anything since meeting P.D., it was that he had the strength to come to terms with the death of his wife. Although the past would always be with him—and his love for Annabel would be a part of it—he'd discovered that the heart was a powerful organ, one capable of stretching and redefining its capacity for giving. He would always love Annabel. His romance with P.D. didn't diminish what he'd had with his wife; it merely added a new dimension to his present capacity for loving.

The feelings he had for P.D. were different.

And the same.

Weaving between the other couples, Elam headed in her direction, wanting to reassure her. But in that instant, when he heard the shot and saw her fall—then watched a figure fleeing into the darkness—Elam's whole world collapsed around him.

"No. No, no, no!" he shouted, racing to P.D. Turning her over, he was horrified to see a gaping wound in her side. Blood was pouring from the spot, soaking into the fabric of her dress.

Laying her down, Elam stripped off his frock coat and wadded it into a ball, pressing it tightly against the injury.

"I need some help here!" he shouted. "Someone call 911!"

Attracted by the gunshot and his calls, several people ran toward him. A woman in a bustle and cape pulled a cell phone from her reticule and began dialing. More and more people were rushing out of the carriage house, the wind carrying snatches of conversation Elam's way.

"Has she been shot?"

"What the hell!"

"Who would do such a thing?"

Elam raised one bloodied hand to point to the trees. "He ran off that way."

Several men dodged in that direction.

Thankfully, Elam saw Jace break loose from the onlookers and race toward him.

"What happened?" he asked.

"Someone shot her."

Jace offered a blazing epithet. "Who?"

"I don't know. I couldn't see who it was in the dark."

P.D. was growing pale, her lashes dusky shadows against her cheek.

"An ambulance is on its way," the woman in the bustle gasped as she approached. "I've told them to send the police as well."

"Good." Jace gestured to the main building of the hotel. "Can you see if they can get us some blankets and extra pillows? We need to get her feet up."

The woman nodded, running to do as she'd been asked.

"Oh, my Lord!"

Elam looked up to see Helen breaking through the crowd. When he saw her panicked expression, his heart turned over in his chest. Her shock, more than anything, conveyed the seriousness of P.D.'s condition.

It took an eternity before the distant sirens could be heard bouncing off the canyon walls. And where time had at first been so slow, it now adopted the speed of light as the EMTs cut P.D. out of her restrictive clothing, fastened her to a gurney, then sped off into the night.

Leaving Elam standing alone and dazed, feeling as if they'd whisked away his only chance at happiness.

He felt Bodey grasp his shoulder.

"Jace went with them?"

Elam managed to nod. "He . . . uh . . . he could do more for her than I could."

"Where are the keys to your truck? We need to follow them."

But Elam couldn't move. He could only stare down at his hands.

So much blood.

P.D.'s blood.

Bodey shook him. Hard.

"Elam?"

Images flashed through Elam's head. A missile exploding in a ball of light and sound. His buddies writhing on the ground. His wife pale and small in her casket.

God.

God.

"Elam!"

He finally became aware of Bodey holding him by the shoulders, staring at him, a muscle working in his jaw. "She's going to be all right, you hear me?"

But she wasn't all right. She was badly hurt. Bleeding.

Realization hit him like a lightning bolt. All week, he'd been so sure that he could never fully commit to another woman, that he'd been willing to throw away a good portion of the here and now. He'd held himself back. Not physically, but emotionally. He'd been willing to show P.D. how much she turned him on, but just as she'd accused, he hadn't fully conveyed to her how he *felt*. He'd never admitted how her smile warmed him from the inside out, how her unabashed desire made him seem all but invincible . . .

How she'd brought him back to life again and shown him he could still care deeply for a woman.

In a blinding flash, Elam realized that lightning *could* strike a person twice. Sure, he'd only known P.D. a short time. But even in that short time, he knew that his feelings for Prairie Dawn weren't superficial—and they weren't a product of the Games. He wanted to get to know this woman, really know her. He wanted to spend time with her, learn what made her laugh, what made her cry. He wanted to wallow in the brilliance of her smile and explore the wild abandon of her lovemaking. He wanted more time with her—as much as she was willing to give him. He wanted . . .

P.D.

And she needed to know that.

Hell, with what little she'd told him about her childhood, she probably needed the words more than anything.

Spurred into action, he backed away from Bodey, heading toward his room. "I'll drive to the hospital in my truck and meet up with P.D. But I need you to stop by my house and do a few things for me. Please. It's important."

Bodey's brows creased in confusion, but he quickly followed. "Sure. What do you need?"

ELAM paced the confines of the emergency waiting room like a caged mountain lion. The walls were closing in on him—and more than anything, he wanted to burst out of the beige waiting room into the beige hall beyond and tear aside every beige curtain until he found which one hid P.D. from his sight.

Within minutes of arriving, he'd discovered that since he was not a relative or a spouse, no one would tell him anything. He'd tried to explain that P.D. had no family nearby—that they were in a relationship with each other. But that didn't seem to sway the hawkeyed nurse who stood guard at the main desk. A huge red sign on the wall behind her proclaimed, NO ADMITTANCE WITHOUT PROPER AUTHORIZATION.

The outside door burst open and Bodey stormed in. "Any word?"

Elam shook his head. Belatedly, he realized that he was still wearing his bloodstained period attire. No wonder the nurse thought he was a crackpot.

"Where's Barry?"

"Helen and Syd volunteered to take him to the Big House and keep him entertained until one of us can get back. He's pretty upset. He keeps saying something about buddies being like sisters and he has to have at least one. I can't make heads or tails out of what he means."

"What about the shooter?"

"They caught him," Bodey said baldly. "Just after you left. Hells bells, you'll never believe this. It turned out it was Bart Crowley, P.D.'s manager."

Elam stared at his brother, stunned. "What? Are you sure?"

Bodey nodded. "Apparently, he's been stealing supplies from P.D. for months now, and when she figured out something hinkey was going on, he managed to pin the deed on Eddie Bascom. But Eddie wasn't about to take his lumps and move on. So Bart decided to cover his tracks. He paid a couple of teenagers to set fire to the restaurant, figuring that way, it would be his word against Eddie's—and Eddie has already had some run-ins with the law. But the fire was stopped before it could get out of hand. Then, knowing how much P.D. needed the prize money, he bribed one of the groups into stealing your horse. When that didn't work, the man lost his freaking mind and started trailing the two of you. He's already admitted to pushing P.D. down that hill. And the rock that hit Jennifer Tompkins was his doing, too. She was dressed like P.D. and he didn't realize it was Jennifer until after she'd collapsed."

Elam felt a searing rage rise from the pit of his stomach. "So why'd he shoot her?"

"Near as I can tell, Eddie Bascom tried to talk to P.D. at the party. Bart was afraid that Eddie had been able to spill the beans, so he got desperate and shot her."

"He'd better be behind bars," Elam growled.

Bodey grasped his arm. "They took him away in cuffs. Sheriff Hamblin is likely to lock him up and throw away the key." Bodey gestured toward the emergency room. "So why aren't they out here giving us an update?"

Elam shook his head. "They won't tell any of us anything because we're not related and that nurse over there wouldn't give me the time of day, let alone allow me inside."

Bodey's eyes darkened with determination. "Let me try."

Elam felt a spark of hope. "Do you know her?"

"Not yet," Bodey said, flashing the stern-faced blonde a hundred-watt smile as he strolled toward her. Elam watched in amazement as he leaned his forearms on the counter and bent toward her.

Bodey could charm the birds out of the trees and into his skillet if he had a mind to do it. And Elam had evidence of his brother's supernatural powers when the blonde regarded him suspiciously at first, then began to smile, leaning in toward him like a glacier melting beneath the sun. Soon the two of them were murmuring and laughing. Then Bodey leaned close, whispered something next to her ear and jerked a thumb toward Elam.

The nurse flicked a glance his way, then said, "Let me see what I can do."

Waving her badge in front of the security lock, she slipped into the emergency bays. A few seconds later, she returned and crooked a finger in Elam's direction.

Like a little boy being allowed access into the forbidden faculty room, Elam hurried to follow her. She led him down a series of exam beds divided by beige striped curtains until she reached one close to the end.

"Miss Raines? You have a visitor."

Elam stepped from behind the curtain. His heart sank to his toes when he found P.D.—a woman who had always been so full of life and purpose—looking small and vulnerable in a too-large hospital gown. She was incredibly pale, dark shadows hovering under her eyes. A nearly empty blood bag and an accompanying IV bag dripped fluid in one arm, while a blood pressure cuff wrapped around the other. A cannula under her nose hissed softly in the silence. But Elam pushed his misgivings away, focusing on the most important issue at hand.

P.D. was alive.

"Hey," Elam said softly, his voice tight and husky with all of the emotions that roiled inside him. More than anything, he wanted to haul her into his arms just to feel the warmth of her body next to his, but he settled instead on lacing his fingers with hers.

"Hi."

"How are you feeling?"

She grimaced. "I've felt better." Her chin wobbled. "And my beautiful dress is ruined."

A doctor stepped into her cubicle and said, "Better a dress than your liver."

Elam shot him a concerned look, relaxing only when the man shook his head. "No harm done to that. The bullet creased her here." The doctor pointed to his side. "We've cleaned her up, given her intravenous pain medication and antibiotics, and a whopping thirty-two stitches." He peered at Elam disapprovingly as if the gunshot were all his fault, then continued, "Thankfully, none of her vital organs were hit, but she'd lost a lot of blood by the time she got here, so we topped off her tank." His gaze bounced to P.D., becoming much warmer. "So, as much as we'd love to have you remain in our gracious accommodations"—his eyes twinkled—"I'm kicking you out."

He ripped a paper from his pad, handing it to P.D. "This is a prescription for some oral meds as well. The nurse will print out the written instructions for you to take home." He pointed a finger at P.D. "I want you off your feet as much as possible for at least a day or two. You're also extremely dehydrated—which wasn't too surprising to me after I heard you were part of the Games." He glanced at Elam. "See she has plenty to drink. I want to see her again in my office in town on Thursday." He handed Elam a business card. "Call first thing in the morning and have the nurse make an appointment."

And with that, he sailed from the room again, leaving the curtain fluttering in his wake.

Knowing they probably had only a few minutes before the nurse reappeared, Elam bent to kiss P.D. on the forehead.

"How are you. Really?"

"I . . ."

She was going to lie—he could see her trying to formulate a sunny answer. But then, she said in a soft whisper, "I don't know."

The fact that she trusted him enough to tell him the truth made him realize how far they'd already come as a couple. She was willing to be honest with her emotions and he needed to do the same for her.

"Hurts like the devil?"

He was rewarded with a rueful smile.

"Yeah."

Elam took a deep breath. There was so much he wanted to say—he *needed* to say—but he couldn't seem to corral his thoughts into a logical path, so he kissed her instead, knowing that he would never tire of feeling her lips against his.

"You scared the hell out of me," Elam whispered as he drew back. His voice shook, betraying a portion of the emotions that swirled in his gut. He cleared his throat, then began again. "I'd appreciate it if you'd avoid getting shot in the future."

She tried to smile. "I'll do my best."

But he saw the betraying wobble to her chin and realized she was probably still hovering close to shock. No doubt, she was pissed at herself for not being able to rein in her seesawing emotions.

"Hey, Elam. Are you here to take P.D. home?"

Elam straightened to see one of Bodey's old girlfriends striding into the cubicle.

"Yeah. I'll be taking care of her."

P.D. tried to object, but he took the prescription from her fingers and tucked it into his pocket.

"Here's her instructions and an envelope with enough pills to tide you over until the pharmacy is open in the morning." The woman handed the items to Elam, then turned to P.D. "Go ahead and stay in the hospital gown. We've got you all nice and clean, so there's no sense putting you back in your stained clothes. Just have Bodey drop it off later in the week if you want."

It was clear that the woman hoped Bodey himself would make the delivery.

P.D. nodded.

The woman efficiently removed P.D.'s cannula, the IV line, and the blood pressure cuff. Then she announced in a too-happy voice, "I'll get you a wheelchair and you can head home."

Again, they were left in silence. Elam's pulse thudded in his ears, urging him to say something—*anything*. But he couldn't seem to find the words.

Luckily, the nurse returned at that moment with a cheerful, "Here we are!"

P.D. grimaced, sweeping back the covers and trying to gingerly move to the side of the bed. But Elam slipped his arms underneath her knees and gently transferred her to the chair in a single motion.

"Are you parked out back?" the nurse asked.

"Yeah."

They made their way past the emergency bays and into the waiting room. Bodey immediately stood.

"How are you, doll face?" he asked, rushing toward her.

P.D.'s smile was weak. "I've been better."

"I bet. Let me know if there's anything you need, okay?"

Elam dug the prescription out of his pocket. "Can you get this filled in the morning?"

Bodey glanced at it and nodded. "Sure."

"I'm going to take her home."

Bodey's smile was slow and filled with meaning. "That sounds like a good idea. I'll head back to the hotel and gather your things. I'll bring them by in the morning after I get her meds."

"Thanks, Bodey." Elam handed Bodey the hotel key cards, then almost held out his hand, but at the last minute, he pulled his brother close for a back-slapping hug. "Thanks for everything."

Bodey pounded Elam's back with equal force. "Take care of her, Elam. Then try to get some sleep yourself."

With a nod, Elam hurried to bring the truck to the curb.

P.D. welcomed the darkness that surrounded Elam's truck as he drove out of the hospital parking lot. He'd folded up his Carhartt jacket as a makeshift pillow and covered her with a utility blanket to keep her warm, even though the air outside was warm. She'd stretched out, using as much of the seat as possible so that she wouldn't pull at her bandages.

She was suddenly exhausted—physically, emotionally, spiritually—and that weariness played havoc with her mood. One minute she was calm; the next, she hovered on the verge of tears.

Elam reached over to take her hand. "It's natural," he said quietly.

"What?"

"You've been shot, P.D. Your body is still processing the shock, so your emotions will be out of whack. Feel free to cry or shout or mutter cuss words if it will make you feel better."

A laugh pushed involuntarily through the tightness of her throat. But then she grew serious. "Have you been shot?"

He nodded. "And once they had me back on base, I cried like a baby, punched out a wall, then cursed a blue streak all in the space of a minute and a half."

P.D. shot him a disbelieving look, but she felt the tension in her shoulders ease, realizing that she didn't need to be on her guard. And oh, how sweet was that? To be so accepted by another person that she didn't need to censor her emotions.

Resting her head against the window, she concentrated on breathing in and out. Despite the pain pills, her side throbbed in time with her pulse. But she knew she wouldn't fall asleep anytime soon. Her thoughts were whirling too violently for that.

"Did they find Eddie?"

"Eddie?"

"Eddie Bascom. Isn't he the one who shot me?"

Elam's features were limned by the light from the dashboard. He shook his head. "It was Bart Crowley."

"What?"

"He confessed that he's been stealing supplies from you for months—then he blamed it all on Eddie."

"So Eddie was telling me the truth," P.D. breathed, ashamed that she hadn't given him more of a chance to explain.

"There's more. Bart started to panic when he realized Eddie wasn't going to slink away with his tail between his legs. So he offered some money and booze to a pair of kids if they'd torch Vern's, not knowing that you'd be there."

"If I hadn't been in the office that night . . ."

"Vern's might have burned to the ground."

She shuddered. It could have burned to the ground with her in it as well.

"There's more," Elam said tentatively.

"Was he watching my house?"

That question made Elam pause. A muscle worked in his jaw. "I don't know about that yet, but he worried that once Vern's was back in business, you'd be examining the books more carefully."

"I took them home with me the night after the fire. He must have discovered that they were gone."

"He bribed that other group to steal our horse."

Her jaw dropped.

"And he's the one who pushed you down the hill."

"That son of a bitch."

"And he dropped that rock on Jennifer Tompkins."

"What?" P.D. touched a hand to her temple, sure that she'd begun to hallucinate. The information she was receiving was so at odds with the man she'd thought that Bart Crowley had been—staid, dependable. A friend.

"He thought it was you. She was wearing clothes similar to yours, had her hair in a braid . . ."

A chill raced through her.

"That could have been me. I could have been the one with my head gashed open."

"You say that like it's worse than being shot."

He had a point there.

Elam reached over to take her hand. "You scared the life out of me tonight, P.D. I thought I'd lost you."

Her stomach flip-flopped crazily at the raw emotion in his voice—but she didn't know how to respond. She glanced out of the window instead, watching the moonlit fields flashing past them. It took several moments for her to realize that Elam had passed the turnoff to her house.

"Where are we going?"

"I'm taking you home." He paused, squeezing her hand. "To the cabin."

She remembered hearing that the contractors had finished working there. And although she was curious to see what had been done, right now she just wanted to burrow beneath the covers of her own bed.

Elam must have read her thoughts because he said, "I don't want to take you back to your bungalow until the sheriff can do a walk-through. With everything else that Bart has reportedly tried, I don't want to chance that he's done something to your house."

When she became alarmed, he hurriedly assured her, "It's just a precaution, P.D. Helen and Bodey said your house was locked up tight, remember?"

She nodded, glad that Elam had insisted on installing the hardware on her doors before the Games had begun.

"Besides, if you're up to it, I've got something I'd like to talk to you about," Elam added hesitantly.

He looked so serious that P.D. immediately feared what he had to say.

Please, please don't let it be the infamous "Let's Be Friends" speech.

She opened her mouth to stall him, but quickly closed it again. No. She wasn't going to borrow trouble before it came. She'd told herself from the beginning that she would take whatever Elam was willing to give her—and now she had to trust in her own judgment.

Nodding, she closed her eyes. The pain medication was giving the whole evening an "otherworldly" air, so she kept them tightly shut—even when she knew they'd turned into Taggart Hollow, when they'd begun the ascent up the hill, when he pulled to a halt near the back steps.

"Wait here. I'm going unlock the door and turn on the lights."

She nodded, finally blinking until her gaze focused on the shadowy shape of the cabin. Several windows lit up with a golden glow, then the light above the door flashed on. P.D. watched as Elam hurried back to her with purposeful strides. For the first time, she noticed that his vest was stained with blood—her blood. Poor Helen. She'd gone to so much work to make their costumes so beautiful and historically accurate. P.D. doubted that any of them could ever be worn again.

Elam opened the passenger door. Again, when she tried

to sit up, he gently gathered her in his arms and carried her up the steps of the newly finished deck. P.D. had only enough time to absorb the ornate wrought-iron railings that had been installed, and the gleaming BBQ grill and patio furniture that had been set up in the far corner.

As he moved inside, P.D. had a glimpse of the kitchen's shiny maple cabinets and granite countertops before he crossed into a shadowy hall. His feet made no sound on the thick carpet as he climbed a set of circular stairs and traversed another short hall. Then, stepping through a set of double doors, he went into a huge bedroom.

P.D. made a soft "Oh!" of delight when she saw the oversized antique four-poster bed, bureaus, and nightstands. Opposite the sleeping area was a sitting room with slipcovered chairs and an overstuffed sofa. Beyond that was a wall of windows that looked out over Taggart Hollow and the glittering lights of Bliss. As Elam settled her onto the couch and draped a fuzzy blanket on her lap, P.D. realized that the color scheme Elam had chosen was a mirror to that in her own home—a soothing mix of whites and off-whites interspersed with splashes of color.

Elam saw the direction of her gaze and turned in a small circle. A satisfied smile spread over his lips. "They did a great job, didn't they?"

She nodded. "It's beautiful."

"Bodey stopped by to stock the fridge, crack open the windows, and make sure there were sheets on the bed." Elam seemed suddenly unsure of himself. "I hope that you don't mind staying here, in the master bedroom. The other rooms still need furniture, and I was warned some of them had fresh paint and . . ."

He broke off, running a hand nervously through his hair before gripping the back of his neck. He appeared to mull something over in his mind before coming to a decision.

"You said . . . you wanted to talk to me," P.D. offered slowly, giving him a verbal nudge.

"Yeah, I . . ." He laughed softly to himself and straightened, shoving his hands into his pockets, rocking back on his heels. "I don't know why the hell this is so difficult. I mean . . . it's not as if . . ."

P.D. was gripping her hands so tightly, her knuckles gleamed white. "I know what you want to say," she whispered. "The Games were . . . intense . . . and things are bound to change now that we've returned to the real world—"

"No," he interrupted forcefully. "That's just it . . ." He sank onto the floor in front of her, framing her face with his hands. "P.D., this past week has been . . . *incredible*."

Not exactly the response she had expected.

"But it doesn't matter to me that the Games are over or that real life is about to reassert itself."

Oh-kay . . . And where was he heading with that statement?

"I don't need more time to know what I want." He grazed her lower lip with his thumb. "I want . . . you. I want to spend time with you. I want to take you dancing and horseback riding. I want to show you what I do on the ranch and have you show me what you do at Vern's. I want to know everything about you—your favorite foods, your favorite color, your favorite movie. I want you to feel like my home is yours and I hope you'll let me do the same."

He smiled, a slow, sweet smile that tugged at her heartstrings. "Most of all, I want you to consider the fact that what we have together is . . . beautiful. And I want to see where it will take us. Because as crazy as this sounds"—his voice dropped to a whisper—"I think I might be falling in love with you."

P.D. waited, sure that she hadn't heard him correctly and that his next few words would contain a "But . . ." When he didn't supply one, she gave him one of her own.

"But at the hotel, you said we should enjoy . . . *this* . . . as long as it lasts." She waved a hand in a vague gesture between them.

Elam frowned, then reached to caress her cheek with his thumb. "Is that why you were so anxious to leave?"

She didn't answer, but the moisture that flooded her lashes must have been more than eloquent.

He leaned forward to brush her lips with his. "I meant the *hotel stay*, P.D. I didn't mean us."

Elam drew back and the expression on his face was so gentle . . . so *adoring*, she couldn't believe that it was directed toward her.

"What about Barry?"

Elam's brow creased.

"Elam, tonight he was talking about Emily and asking me to be his sister and I don't want to confuse him or—"

Elam laughed. "That's what he was trying to explain to Bodey." He stroked her cheek with his thumb, whispering, "But don't you see? You're already his sister. You bring him food and footie pajamas and you care that he's healthy and happy. Despite his injuries, Barry's a bright kid. Besides, a wise woman told me that it's best to explain your feelings. So we'll be honest with him." He leaned closer, his words against her lips. "We'll tell him that we care about each other, but relationships are best if you give them a little time."

Time.

This man was willing to give her something that had proven to be so elusive to her in the past. Time.

P.D. leaned forward, kissing him softly, sweetly, absorbing the enormity of having a man who wanted more than anything else in the world to spend *time* with her.

Elam Taggart, a man who'd been to hell and back.

A man who wanted *her*, Prairie Dawn Raines.

Looking deep into his eyes—eyes that were fierce with passion, possessiveness, and joy—she shoved away years of insecurity, loneliness, and regret and threw caution to the wind, baldly stating, "I think I'm falling in love with you, too, Elam Taggart."

She tugged him onto the sofa next to her and he gently drew her onto his lap. "Ah, sweetheart . . . I was a dead man walking until you burst into my life like a ray of sunshine."

He drew back, his eyes intense, willing her to believe him. "I loved Annabel. I'll never lie about that. But what you have to believe is that what I feel for you is just as intense, just as all-consuming"—his voice grew husky with the depth of his emotions—"just as magical. It's the same . . . but different."

Tears sprang to P.D.'s eyes, but this time, she didn't bother to fight them back. Instead, she reveled in the emotion she saw shining from Elam's eyes. The heat from that gaze sank deep into her heart, seeping into that tiny corner she'd never allowed anyone to touch. Burying her forehead in Elam's shoulder, she realized that she didn't have to hide from her fears anymore. Elam accepted her as who she was, scars and all.

"You are so beautiful," Elam whispered against her hair. And for the first time in her life, she felt beautiful.

Special.

Loved.

Elam was quiet for a moment, then he said carefully, "There's just one thing I need you to know, P.D."

She waited, sensing his unease. "I've been kind of out of things the last year or two at the ranch. It's time I stepped up and started pulling my weight again. With the ranch, my brothers . . . and especially Barry."

She stopped him with a finger on his lips. "I don't mind. In fact, it makes me feel a little less guilty about the time I'll need to spend at Vern's."

Elam laced their fingers together. "We're a pretty good fit, aren't we?"

She nodded. "We're a very good fit."

The phone in Elam's pocket rang and he swore, reaching to throw it onto the seat beside him. But when P.D. saw Bodey's name on the caller I.D., she said, "You'd better answer it."

"He can call back—"

"Just answer it."

Reluctantly, Elam unlocked his phone and held it to his ear. "This had better be good."

P.D. could hear the indistinct cadence of Bodey's voice, but not the words.

Then, Elam relaxed beneath her, leaning back against the cushions and bringing her with him so that she lay across his chest.

"Yeah, I'll tell her. See you tomorrow, Bodey."

He ended the call—and this time, he hit the power button so that no one else could disturb them.

P.D. patiently waited for him to tell her what Bodey had said. But when he began laughing, she tipped her head up to see him better.

"What's up?"

"Bodey wanted to pass on some news."

"Mmm?" She began tracing idle circles around the studs of his shirt.

"We won."

P.D. frowned. "We won what?"

"We won the Wild West Games."

It took a moment for the full meaning behind the words to sink into her brain, and when they did, she pushed herself upright.

"You're kidding."

"Nope. Evidently, our costumes were judged when we were wrangling over how to get your skirts to fit under our table. The scores for our outfits pushed us to the top." He grinned at her. "They'll be bringing the check for ten thousand dollars by tomorrow."

She stared at him a moment longer, then laughed and said, "We won." Then louder and more excitedly, "We *won*!"

Her arms wrapped around his neck and she began peppering kisses all over his face. But when he held her still to capture her lips, she whispered, "We have to tell Helen."

"She already knows. She was there when the contest people called." He kissed her softly, then drew back to murmur, "We'll sink the whole ten thousand into Vern's."

"But—"

He stopped her objections with another kiss.

"But, Elam, you—"

"You'll need the money to hurry the repairs along." He began interspersing his speech with kisses that grew longer and more passionate. "Because . . ."

Kiss.

"I'm dying to get more of your cooking . . ."

Kiss.

"As well as more of this . . ."

Kiss.

"And this . . ."

Melting into the embrace of her wild Desperado, Prairie Dawn Raines was more than happy to oblige.

AUTHOR'S NOTE

Those who know me will recognize that Bliss, Utah, bears a striking resemblance to my own hometown in northern Utah. I came to this valley as a newlywed and a "city girl." Now I'm a country girl through and through, and I couldn't imagine living anywhere else.

The Single Action Shooting Society, also known as SASS, is a real organization. For several years, I shot with the group under the moniker "Twisted Sister." I've been told the rather "ribald" scenarios I've presented during the costume contests have helped me win more than a few times.

I was introduced to SASS by the real Helen and Syd, who are only marginally fictionalized in the book. Helen is a master costumer and seamstress, and Syd, the love of her life, keeps me well supplied with reloaded ammunition. Thanks to both of you! If you happen to attend a SASS competition, look for "Queen Helen" and "Syd Shaleen" and say hello. They'll either be shooting stages or selling Helen's hand-sewn items from their tent. If you have a minute, check out my website, where Helen has graciously given me permission to include her recipe for Dutch Oven Cherry Chocolate Cake, and Syd, who really did help to put the space shuttle into orbit, will include the ATK/Thiokol scientists' diagram of the perfect arrangement of charcoal briquettes. If you've ever had their cooking, you'll agree they are masters at their craft.

The little secluded cabin located in a hidden valley is also real. Thank you, Tom and Cindy, for the invitations to your Fourth of July celebrations. Visiting your cabin is like dropping out of civilization into an idyllic piece of the past for a few hours. I can't think of a better way to celebrate our nation's beginnings. Don't be surprised if your getaway reappears in more of the Taggart Brothers' novels.

If you'd like more information about my crazy life as a writer, teacher, mother, or the wife of a farmer/cattleman, you can visit my website, lisabinghamauthor.com or my Facebook page, lisabinghamauthor/facebook.com or join me on Twitter @lbinghamauthor.

W ATERBOARDING.
      Caning.
The Rack.

Bronte Cupacek tightened her fingers around the steering
wheel and swore to heaven that when the government of the
United States outlawed cruel and unusual punishment, there
should have been special provisions made for mothers locked
in minivans for the duration of a cross-country trip. Especially
if said minivan contained two adolescent siblings who'd been
at each other's throats twenty minutes into the journey.

What had she been thinking?

But then, she hadn't been thinking at all, had she? On that
first, chilly April morning, she'd been so consumed with guilt,
panic—and yes, a healthy dose of fear—that she hadn't bothered
to consider the ramifications of her actions. With the haste of a
thief leaving the scene of a crime, Bronte had awakened her two
daughters at the crack of dawn, helped them cram their belongings into all the suitcases they possessed, and then stuffed everything into the "Mom Mobile." Less than forty minutes after
their frantic preparations had begun, she maneuvered away from

the Brownstone she'd shared with her husband for sixteen years, and began the long drive west.

Bronte hadn't even looked as Boston was swallowed up in her rearview mirror. She drove in a daze, the black highway an endless ebony ribbon stitched down the middle with yellow thread. For the sake of her girls, she pretended that she'd been planning this spontaneous adventure for months. They visited Gettysburg, Mount Rushmore, and highway markers commemorating countless historical sites—all much to Kari's dismay. At fifteen-going-on-thirty, she considered history of any kind "lame" and Bronte's choices in entertainment "lamer." Lily was less inclined to complain, which worried Bronte even more. With each tick of the odometer, she retreated into mute, self-imposed exile—to the point where Bronte would have suffered any personal indignity for a hint of a smile.

By the time they'd reached the Great Divide, Bronte had given up telling her girls they were "on vacation." Clearly, she'd been no better hiding the need to flee than she'd been at disguising the bruise on her cheekbone. Day by day, it faded from an alarming shade of plum to the sickly yellow of an overripe banana. She'd tried to conceal the injury with layers of foundation, but at bedtime when she rubbed the makeup away, she would catch her daughters surreptitiously studying the telltale mark. But they didn't ask what had happened. Somehow, they must have known that to acknowledge something was wrong would pry the lid off Bronte's tenuous emotional control.

She supposed it was that need—that *obsession*—to finally put this journey behind her that caused her to pull off the road and stare blankly at the sign proclaiming:

BLISS, UTAH—POPULATION 9672
(Sign donated by Bryson Willis—Eagle Scout Project 2014)

The world still had Boy Scouts?

"Why are you stopping?" Kari demanded. She glowered at Bronte from the passenger seat, radiating the pent-up vitriol of a teenager who'd been forced to leave her friends two months before the end of the school year. "Let's just get to

Grandma Great's house. The sooner we get there, the sooner we can go home."

Bronte had heard that same demand at least once an hour for the last *bazillion* miles, and it took every ounce of will she possessed to bite back her own caustic reply. Little did her daughter know, but Bronte had serious doubts about ever returning to their "life" in Boston.

Phillip had seen to that.

There was a stirring from the rear of the van. Like a groundhog cautiously emerging from its burrow, Lily raised her head over the edge of the seat and blinked in confusion.

"Is this Great-Grammy's?"

Kari rounded on her sister before Lily had the time to rub the sleep from her eyes.

"What do you think, genius? That Grandma Great lives on the side of the road?"

"Enough," Bronte barked automatically. The fact that Kari rarely got along with her younger sister had only been acerbated by hours of travel. The teenager was like a chicken, pick, pick, picking at her more sensitive sibling until both Lily and Bronte were raw.

"If you can't be nice, keep your opinions to yourself, Kari."

How many times had Bronte said *that* in the last hour . . . week . . . lifetime?

Kari rolled her eyes and huffed theatrically. She was barely fifteen and already filled with rage and defiance. Bronte had to get a grip on their relationship before Kari discovered the truth about her father or . . .

Don't think about that now. Not yet. Later. Once you're at Annie's, you can take all the time you want to decide what to do. Away from Phillip's influence.

She nearly laughed aloud. Yes, she was away from her husband's influence—thousands of miles away. But he could have been sitting in the seat beside Bronte for her inability to forget him. His ghost had accompanied her every step of the way—and her phone was filled with unretrieved messages, texts, and emails that she should have erased the moment they appeared.

Should have erased.

But hadn't.

Because there'd been a time when she had loved him so much that a handful of kind words from him had felt as intimate as a caress.

But that had been a long time ago.

A million years and two thousand miles ago.

Ultimately, the state of her marriage had become a case of "fight or flight." This time, she'd chosen "flight." And after coming so far, she didn't have the strength to confront her own actions, let alone those of her daughter. But soon. They were almost at her grandmother's farmhouse. Once there, she could burrow into the peaceful solitude of this tiny western town and begin to piece together the torn remnants of her lifelong dreams.

"Are you going to drive anytime soon?" Kari inquired, her tone dripping with sarcasm. "Or are you waiting for a sign from God?"

Closing her eyes, Bronte counted to ten before responding.

"I haven't been here since I was seventeen, Kari. I need a minute to get my bearings."

Kari huffed again, fiddling with the button to the automatic window, making it go up, down, up, down. The noise of the motor approximated an impatient whine.

"I thought that's why we bought a map at the last gas station," she grumbled under her breath. "If you'd get a GPS like everyone else . . ."

Please let me get through the next few miles without resorting to violence, Bronte thought to herself as she put the car in gear, waited for a rattletrap farm truck laden with bags of seed to pass, then eased into the narrow lane.

As they drove through Bliss proper, Bronte grew uneasy. Over the years, she'd imagined the area would remain like a time capsule, unchanged and completely familiar. Either her memories were faulty, or urban sprawl had begun to encroach on this rural community. To her dismay, she could see that some of the mom-and-pop establishments had given way to newer, sleeker buildings bearing franchise names and automated signs.

For the first time, Bronte felt a twinge of uneasiness. She'd tried to contact Annie, without success. What if they'd come for nothing? What if Annie couldn't offer Bronte the haven she had hoped to find?

Instantly, Bronte rejected that thought. Grandma was the one constant in the world. A beacon of love that made no demands. That's why, when Bronte felt as if she'd drown in her own silent anguish, she'd gravitated instinctively to the spot where she'd been happiest. A place where she wouldn't have to present a chipper façade to the world to hide the fact that everything she'd once held dear had long since crumbled to dust.

"Well?"

Bronte had stopped at a red light—probably the only one in town. In her efforts to orient herself, she'd missed the change to green. There wasn't another soul in sight, but trust Kari to pound home her irritation at the minute delay.

"It's this way," she murmured—more to reassure herself than her children.

Turning right, she prayed that she'd chosen the correct side road. Victorian farmhouses and bungalows from the thirties were crowded by newer, turreted McMansions that looked alien in such a rural setting. But as she wound her way along the old highway, she began to pick out landmarks that were familiar to her: the train trestle that spanned the creek; the boxlike outline of pine trees surrounding the pioneer cemetery; the old mill which had apparently been converted into a bed-and-breakfast.

"It's not far now," she reassured her children.

"I hope so," Lily admitted, her eyes wide as she studied the passing scenery.

Ashamed, Bronte realized that she shouldn't have let so much time elapse before coming to Utah. But Phillip had insisted that any place without a Starbucks or a subway wasn't worth visiting. So Bronte had kept the peace and instead arranged for Grandma Annie to visit them occasionally. The visits had become more sporadic and her children had been denied so much because of Bronte's cowardice. They'd never ridden a horse or hiked up a mountainside to drink from an icy artesian spring. But this summer, they would have a chance.

"I have to go to the bathroom," Lily whispered. "Will Grandma Great let me use her bathroom?"

"No, she'll make you pee in a bush, stupid."

"Kari!"

Raindrops splatted against the windshield. Leaning forward, Bronte eyed the flickers of lightning with concern. They were almost there. They should be able to outrun the storm.

Lily stirred restlessly in her seat. "How much farther?"

"Less than a mile."

Intermittent drops continued to strike the glass, leaving perfect circles in the dust, but Bronte hesitated in turning on the wipers. The blades—much like her tires—should have been replaced months ago. If she turned them on now, the rain and dirt collected on her car would muddle together in a streaky mess, and she needed to see the towering willow tree that marked the end of the lane . . .

There!

For the first time in years, Bronte felt a flutter of joy and hope. They were here. They were finally here!

Slowing the car, she turned into a narrow gravel road. The tires crunched over the weathered ruts, the noise bringing a sense of excitement that edged out the weariness and pain.

A strip of winter-matted grass grew up the middle of the rutted track, and puddles gathered in the potholes. On either side of the lane, fence posts had been linked together with strands of barbed wire. The fields beyond were just as she'd remembered, loamy carpets of brown sprigged with chartreuse shoots of sprouting grain. As they drew closer to the house, the fences gave way to dozens of lilac bushes that had grown so closely together that they formed an impenetrable hedge. To Bronte's delight, she saw that grape-like nubs had begun to appear amid the leaves. Any day now, they would explode into a fragrant wall of purple and pink and the air would grow rich with the scent of the blossoms and the drone of bees.

"Look!" she exclaimed to her children. "Annie's lilacs will

be in bloom soon." She cracked the window, allowing the heady fragrance of rain and soil to fill the car.

Lily eagerly pressed her face against the glass, but Kari remained stony and silent. Nevertheless, Bronte sensed an expectancy in her daughter's posture that hadn't been there before.

"Where's the house?" Lily breathed.

"Past the next bend."

As Bronte eased around the corner, a part of her was a child again. She expected to see Annie waiting on the stoop wearing a cotton dress cinched tight by an all-encompassing apron. Bronte could almost smell the yeastiness of freshly baked bread that clung to the house and taste the moist carrot cookies that were pulled from the oven the moment she and her siblings arrived. As soon as Bronte ran up the front steps, she would be enveloped in her grandmother's warm, bosomy embrace. She would breathe deeply of Annie's unique scent—face powder, lilies of the valley, and Nilla Wafers, which Annie stowed in her apron pockets for when she needed a "boost."

Bronte was so enveloped in the memories that it took Kari's sharp inhalation and Lily's plaintive, "Oh!" to pierce the fantasy.

Easing to a stop, Bronte peered more closely through the rain-streaked windshield. As her eyes focused on the weathered farmhouse, a mewl of disappointment escaped her lips.

If not for the porch light and a dim glow emitted from the garret window, Bronte would have thought the house had been abandoned. Weeds choked the once beautiful flowerbeds and the lawn was burned and nearly nonexistent. The sagging wraparound porch was missing half a dozen balusters and the front steps were rickety and threatening to collapse.

The outbuildings had suffered a similar fate. Bronte remembered the chicken coop, barn, and garden being painted a pristine white. When she'd seen them last, they'd been perched on an immaculate lawn edged by tufts of peonies and iris. But if any of those perennials had survived, they would have to fight their way through thigh-high weeds and thistles.

"I thought you said this place was *nice*."

Kari's tone made it clear that she thought Bronte teetered on the verge of senility.

Bronte didn't bother to comment. What could she say? Her memories weren't so gilded by age and distance that she could have mistaken this . . . this . . . *mess* for the idyll she'd enjoyed each summer.

Reluctantly, she eased the car closer to the main house. Rain began to fall in earnest now, but even the moisture collecting on her windshield couldn't hide the utter neglect.

"Are you sure Grandma Great lives here?" Lily whispered.

"Of course she lives here," Kari snapped. "But Mom didn't bother to tell us what a *dump* it is."

Rain pattered against the roof of the car, the rhythm growing frantic as the downpour increased. Conceding to the inevitable, Bronte switched on the wipers, waiting vainly for the streaks of grime to be swept away—as if by cleaning the windshield she might find the condition of Annie's house had been a trick of light and shadow.

If anything, the view was more depressing.

A part of her wanted to throw the car in gear and leave. Bronte didn't want to consider that her fondest memories could be tarnished by this current reality. But she honestly couldn't go any farther. She'd pinned her hopes and her endurance on reaching Annie's house. Now that she was here, she didn't have energy left to alter her plans.

Needing to validate her decision, Bronte turned off the car. For long moments, the drumming on the roof and the ticking of the cooling engine underscored the silence.

Then she said, "Stay here."

There were no arguments as Bronte grasped the map from the dashboard. Holding it over her head, she threw open the driver's door and darted into the rain. Avoiding the damaged step, she hurried to the relative shelter of the porch and pressed the doorbell.

As she waited for her grandmother to appear, Bronte could feel her children's gazes lock in her direction. Once again, she realized that she should have waited until she'd been able to reach her grandmother. If Grandma Annie had known they were coming . . .

What?

What would she have done?

Weeded the flowerbeds? Thrown a coat of paint onto the house?

Why hadn't it occurred to Bronte that she and Grandma Annie had aged at the same rate? In her mind's eye Annie had remained the same vivacious woman she'd been when Bronte had seen her last. She must have slowed down in the past few years. Obviously, the maintenance of the property had become too much for her.

Dear God, what if she weren't up to an impromptu visit?

Bronte's gut suddenly crawled with new worries. *Damn, damn, damn.* She'd been desperate to get her children away from the trouble brewing at home. Bronte had thought that if she had time alone with her girls, she could mend the brittleness that had invaded their relationships. Then, when the opportunity arose, she could explain that the move from Boston was permanent.

As well as the separation from their father.

"Ring it again!" Kari shouted from inside the car.

Foregoing the doorbell, Bronte opened the screen and pounded with the knocker. Annie could have grown hard of hearing. She had to be . . . what? Eighty-five? Eighty-six?

Why hadn't Bronte kept in touch more? Why hadn't she pushed aside Phillip's overwhelming demands and reached out to her grandmother? Instead, Bronte had grown so ashamed of her situation and her inability to make it better, that she'd limited her contact to cheery phone calls and the "too, too perfect" letters tucked into family Christmas cards.

The grumble of a distant engine drew her attention. Allowing the screen to close with a resounding bang, she wiped the moisture from her face as a pair of headlights sliced through the gathering gloom.

For a moment, she was exposed in the beams as a pickup rolled from behind the barn and headed toward the lane. At the last minute, the driver must have seen her, because the path of the truck altered, veering toward Bronte and her children.

A growl of thunder vied with the sound of the engine as the vehicle jounced to a stop. It was a big truck, purely utilitarian, with a stretch cab and jacked-up wheels with shiny rims unlike anything Bronte had ever seen in Boston. The window to the passenger side slid down and a man leaned closer so that she could see his shape like an indigo cutout against the pouring rain. Much like the truck, he was built for hard work with broad shoulders and powerful arms.

"Do you need some help?"

His voice was deep enough to carry over the drumming of the rain and something about its timbre caused her to shiver.

Using the map as her makeshift umbrella, Bronte ran closer. "Yes, I'm looking for Annie Ellis. I can't get an answer at the door. Do you know if she's expected back anytime soon?"

The stranger in the truck removed a battered straw cowboy hat, revealing coffee-colored hair tousled by rain and sweat and eyes that were a pale blue gray. A faint line dissected his forehead—whiter above, a deep bronzed tan below, conveying that he spent most of his time in the sun. He had features that could have been carved with an ax, too sharp and blunt to be considered handsome, but intriguing, nonetheless.

"Exactly who are you?" he asked bluntly.

Normally, she would have bristled at such a tone, but she was tired—emotionally and physically. All she wanted was a hot cup of tea and sleep. Deep, uninterrupted sleep.

"My name is Bronte Cupacek. Annie is my grandmother."

The man's gaze flicked to the van, the Massachusetts license plates, and the children who were pressed up against the windows watching them intently.

"Ah. The Boston contingent."

Something about his flat tone rankled, but before Bronte could decipher his mood, he delivered the final blow to an otherwise devastating few months.

"Your grandmother fell down the stairs yesterday afternoon. She's in a local hospital."

Discover Romance

berkleyjoveauthors.com

See what's coming up next from your favorite romance authors and explore all the latest Berkley, Jove, and Sensation selections.

See what's new

~

Find author appearances

~

Win fantastic prizes

~

Get reading recommendations

~

Chat with authors and other fans

~

Read interviews with authors you love

M1G0610